Violation and Repair in the English Novel

Steven Cohan

Violation and Repair in the English Novel

The Paradigm of Experience from Richardson to Woolf

WAYNE STATE UNIVERSITY PRESS   DETROIT, 1986

Copyright © 1986 by Wayne State University Press,
Detroit, Michigan 48202. All rights reserved. No part
of this book may be reproduced without formal
permission.

Library of Congress Cataloging-in-Publication Data

Cohan, Steven.
   Violation and repair in the English novel.
   Includes index.
   1. English fiction—History and criticism.
2. Experience in literature. 3. Innocence (Psychology) in literature.
4. Self in literature. 5. Sex in literature. I. Title.
PR830.E98C6   1986   823'.009   86-1297
ISBN 0-8143-1794-4

For my parents and my sister

Contents

Acknowledgments ix

1.
The Paradigm of Experience   *1*

2.
Clarissa: "I will wrap myself up in mine own innocence"   *47*

3.
The Waverley Novels: "Am I then a parricide?"   *75*

4.
Bleak House and *Great Expectations*: "Guilty and yet innocent"   *101*

5.
The Mill on the Floss and *Middlemarch*: "An intimate penetration"   *131*

6.
Realism as Modernism: "Why must they grow up and lose it all?"   *171*

Conclusion: Violation as Repair   *223*

Notes   *227*

Index   *239*

Acknowledgments

One may normally think of writing as a singular activity, but what I have discovered during the course of this book's composition is just the opposite. Many people are inscribed in the following pages, more than I can easily acknowledge in the space of just two pages. A few people, however, deserve specific mention, so I want to take this opportunity to thank them.

To begin with, I studied under three people whose teaching I continue to value and whose intellectual presence I still sense in whatever I write: Carey Wall, Alexander Welsh, and Max Novak. Furthermore, many of my fellow students in graduate school helped me to begin clarifying my ideas about the novel years before this book first took shape in my mind; among them, Ina Rae Hark and Ina Ferris have been special friends—and of special help to this book, too, because of our numerous conversations about fiction over the past ten years. I have also been fortunate to have colleagues at Syracuse University who are eager to listen, to talk, to argue, and, above all else, to offer good advice: in no particular order, Richard Fallis, Stephen Melville, Donald Morton, Mas'ud Zavarzadeh, and, not the least, Judith Weissman, who has allowed me to include in this book a section on *Great Expectations* which draws on an article we wrote together several years ago. That essay, I now see in retrospect, was the impetus for this book's argument.

Acknowledgments

By the same token, I owe a debt to many of my students, whose unfailing enthusiasm kept me going during the long and frustrating process of composition. I am referring to my students in the Scott course I taught at UCSD in 1975 and to those in my various undergraduate novel courses at Syracuse, namely Sharon Steiff; Roger Hoffman, Kelly Shipley, and Krys Kornilowicz; Chris Iwanicki, of course, and Sherry Fairchok; René Pastolove, Susan Howard, and Rose Riband; and to those in the novel theory seminar of Spring 1984, including Eric Chandler, Ray Fallon, Glenn Petry, Andrea Bien, Robert Daly, Johanna Gelb, and Daphne Moon.

Speaking more practically, the assistance of several people during the composition of this book helped immeasurably to ease the burden of writing and revision: my research assistant John Delaney, and my typists Jean Rice, Julie Rigall, and Marilyn Bergett. The writing of this book was funded by grants from several sources at Syracuse University: the Office of Graduate Affairs and Research, the Senate Research Committee, and the English Department. For this assistance I wish to thank Paul Theiner, Arthur Hoffman, Gershon Vincow, and Volker Weiss. In addition, early versions of Chapters 2 and 4 appeared, in quite different form, in *ELH, Literature and Psychology*, and *American Imago*, and I thank the editors of these journals for allowing me to include that material in this book. I also want to express my gratitude to Kathryn Wildfong, my editor at Wayne State University Press, for the meticulous care with which she read the manuscript of this book to prepare it for publication.

Finally and most importantly, I owe a debt to my friends and colleagues Linda Shires, Felicity Nussbaum, and Jean Howard, whose insightful criticism of my manuscript helped me make the finished book better than it would otherwise have been.

1
The Paradigm of Experience

In the "Proteus" chapter of *Ulysses* Stephen Dedalus walks along Sandymount shore, where he examines the "signatures of all things I am here to read."[1] Throughout this excursion Stephen's interior monologue reveals the extraordinary degree to which his mind simultaneously records, stimulates, invents, and distorts his sense of reality. As he walks on the beach, referring to the phenomenal world around him only to establish the temporal and spatial dimensions of his consciousness, Stephen's footsteps echo Don Quixote's. Though highly intellectualized in its content and abstruse in its narration, Stephen's monologue is in fact no more than a quixotic daydream, and it is not that far removed in spirit from the more standard type of wishful daydreams of characters in other novels. Pip, for example, who sits for hours visualizing Estella's face in the fire of Joe's forge, is much the same type of daydreamer as Stephen. Neither Pip nor Stephen can easily disentangle his sense of reality from the pressures and pleasures of his imagination. Stephen does not actually visit his Aunt Sara, although he imagines the visit as if it does take place, just as Pip scripts his Great Expectations to make them serve his desire to be loved by Estella.

Admittedly, there are important differences between Pip and Stephen, but in his own way each reminds us how often novels engage their characters in the quixotic task of distinguishing illusion from reality. While it is true that we can find many daydreamers in other literatures—Raskolnikov, say, or Emma Bovary, or Gatsby—the quixote building castles (or faces, or visits) in the air has always been of special importance to the English novel. Think of how many English novels lead their characters down Quixote's path towards disillusionment and sobriety, interpreting this movement from innocence to maturity as a progressive journey, the self's necessary education in reality.[2] Although the English novel developed the innocently deluded quixotic figure into one of its most popular conventions for eccentric characterization (Parson Adams, the Shandy brothers, and Pickwick come quickly to mind), novels like *Clarissa, Pride and Prejudice, Waverley, Middlemarch,* and even *Women in Love* and *To the Lighthouse* are much more typical of the way English fiction mainstreamed the quixotic example to produce characters who struggle for selfhood in a world that assaults and yet encourages their egoism, and whose experience leads them to growth and knowledge, to comprehension of and integration with the world beyond the self.

Critics have described this pattern in a variety of ways, calling it the assertion of reality over illusion, of experience over innocence, of realism over romance.[3] They all agree that the classic English novels force their characters to learn, as Pip says at the very start of *Great Expectations,* "the identity of things."[4] Pip accomplishes this task by mastering a hard lesson, that reality is antagonistic to his desire. George Levine calls this realism's process of "disenchantment," which sacrifices innocence in order to harmonize "the relation between the dreaming self and the indifferent other."[5] While Levine by and large treats this pattern as a characteristic of nineteenth-century realism, I think it is safe to say that an imaginative effort to breach that opposition between "the dreaming self and the indifferent other" marks the recurring psychological adventure of the English novel as a continuous tradition.

One of my purposes in this book is to chart the many intricacies of this story. To begin, let me point again to the similarity between Pip and Stephen. True, Pip learns to correct

The Paradigm of Experience

his blinding egoism whereas Stephen, defiantly, does not; but while each character may be drawn in different shades, the colors are taken from the same palette. As a child Pip discovers a world that seems determined to subdue him physically and psychologically. In the churchyard Magwitch violently shakes him upside down; later Mrs. Joe treats him as a criminal when he returns home. As an adult Pip submits to the authority of this external world because as a child he learned, among other things, that it can harm his body and contest his identity. By contrast, in *Ulysses* and, especially, in *A Portrait of the Artist as a Young Man*, Stephen encounters a world much like Pip's, but he responds by internalizing it in an effort to make that reality an extension of his imagination. In the *Portrait* he thinks of it as "the contemplation of an inner world of individual words mirrored perfectly in a lucid supple periodic prose."[6] Still, no matter how hard Stephen tries to absorb that outer phenomenal world (of bird-like girls and dogs and gypsies on the beach) into the ken of his mental life, he always remains separate from it, to the point that he too becomes "disenchanted," estranged from his own body as well as his country, family, and religion.

The figure of Stephen, in this regard, is merely that of Pip turned inside out. Pip comes to respect the authority of the world beyond his own "small" and "shiver[ing]" self,[7] and this movement redresses his initial alienation. Stephen, on the other hand, rejects the small, shivering world around him and becomes increasingly alienated and discontented as a result. Despite the way each character's experience inverts the other's, however, both Pip and Stephen feel a profound sense of guilt; they share a similar lost innocence in realizing, as children, their separation from the surrounding world. This realization determines the shape and texture of their experience as characters, for it provides the standard by which they fashion a self out of their experience and define their awareness of what exists apart from the self.

To be sure, the construction of experience as a journey into selfhood finds its fullest, most straightforward expression in a bildungsroman like *Great Expectations* or Joyce's *Portrait*.[8] But this pattern also informs the whole of the English novel because of the genre's longstanding imaginative preoccupation with the relative status of innocence and maturity. This preoccupation is not too surprising, given the social and moral values which the ideas of innocence and maturity traditionally represent, and given the way the two work together to organize time—a character's plotted life—into psychological space—a fictional consciousness. As Alan Friedman points out, "innocence" and "maturity" are conventions which mark out the progressive directions of a fictional experience. "The relative innocence of central characters," Friedman explains, "is a truism; what is perhaps only barely less obvious is that 'innocence' is a function of the organization of events, and may therefore serve as a very useful source for a theory of the dynamism—the motivation—of narrative form."[9] For a fictional experience to support this burden of meaning, it must reflect *consequence*, which the novel establishes, first by placing events within a structure that organizes them in time as a *movement* from one state of consciousness (innocence) to another (maturity), and then by processing that movement through a value system to direct it as a *progressive* movement.

All the same, because it interprets experience through an imperative to mature, this typical construction is not simply a convenient framing device for organizing events in time to form a plot and create characters. The equations of innocence with illusion (and, by extension, with isolation) and of maturity with reality (and, by extension, with socialization) are cultural assumptions of value that are highly charged, with all the positive weight placed on a character's achievement of maturity. The novel repeatedly declares that innocence *must* be challenged by reality if characters are to move forward in time and reap the benefits of their experience. Pip is once again exemplary. For all his errors in judgment and perception, he does learn to identify things correctly; and while his effort may cost him his "enchantment" it nonetheless allows him, finally, to hold more accurate and reasonable, if not great, expectations about his life. In his case, the necessary condition for his maturity is the recognition of the important claims which reality—whether understood as his childhood past, as his culture, or, in Levine's phrase, as "the indifferent other"—makes upon his innocent, dreaming self. Furthermore—and this is one of the points I want to emphasize

The Paradigm of Experience

and, later, to reexamine—although Pip's recognition results in a painful loss of innocence, because lost innocence is equated with maturity, and maturity with self-knowledge, we seem meant to appreciate his disenchantment as more of a gain than a loss. We have only to recall the adult (and undomesticated) Stephen's painful alienation from reality to get the message: once learned, the teachings of experience, however hard, cannot be easily contested; nor, common sense would seem to say, should they be.

If in recognizing this commonplace about the novel I may seem to be implying as well an appreciation of realism without calling into question its conservative value system or its privileged status as a synonym for "the novel," then I want to make clear that this is not actually the case. I am, it is true, interested in the conventions that characterize realism, the sorts of narratives they produce, and the sets of assumptions about the nature, complexity and shape of experience which at times authorize and at other times undermine those conventions. In this respect, my objective is to rework the map of realism by extending its borders to include some new territory. I want to show that the familiar realistic construction of experience is not in fact limited to so-called realistic novels. In advancing this claim, I do not mean to ignore the fact that "realism" still retains its traditional historical meaning as a term distinguishing some novels (George Eliot's, say) from others (Virginia Woolf's). Rather, I am proposing that terms such as "realist" and "modernist" describe particular arrangements of a fundamentally similar type of novelistic construction.

I have therefore begun by evoking the most familiar convention by which the novel constructs experience—namely, realism's rite of passage out of innocence and illusion—in order to begin isolating the paradigm underlying the genre's operation. What I am calling the paradigm of experience in the English novel is the genre's repeated demonstration that innocence must be challenged by reality if characters are to achieve selfhood. Granted, at face value this may sound like still another description of realism; but I want to reexamine this familiar operation precisely to show that, notwithstanding all its outward claims (that reality is superior to illusion, for instance, or that maturity compensates for the loss of

Chapter 1

innocence), the English novel, even in its most realistic treatments of experience, is in fact much more ambivalent towards its conservative value system and much more resistant to its progressive momentum than it seems on the surface.

The paradigm of experience in the novel, I am arguing, is a dialectical operation. While outwardly it works to stabilize the self by structuring experience as a process of maturation, the novel also instigates, through the turbulence and disruption it envisions as the way out of innocence, the very dread of maturation which its construction of experience seems intended to mitigate in the first place. Therefore the loss of innocence, rather than the acquiring of maturity, is the fundamental issue raised by the genre's construction of experience. To be sure, the positive value of maturity for the novel results from the way it exposes innocence as a state of blindness and confusion. The innocent self rushes headlong into its errors of judgment because it fails to perceive the other accurately *as* something other, as a reality fundamentally different from and thus indifferent to desire. In this light innocence is a liability, a flawed vision of reality—in short, the dangerous work of illusion and immaturity. Nonetheless, the confusion of self and other implies a coherent vision of another sort, that of an original unity of self and other so harmonious that reality easily accommodates desire. Once maturity is understood not as the product of growth but as the absence of innocence, its achievement appears much more disturbing. Working to transform that harmonious state of similarity into a discordant state of difference, maturity irrevocably alters the self's unity with the other; more importantly, this alteration violates the self's original integrity as a self.

That the novel treats the notions of both innocence and maturity with equal ambivalence begins to explain what is so provocative about its paradigmatic construction of experience: a consciousness of lost innocence—of imperfection and corruption and, hence, of guilt—frequently underlies the accomplishment of maturity. While the novel shows that innocence is dangerous in its self-enclosure and so looks ahead to maturity, at the same time it also looks backward to innocence. By the same token, while the novel confirms that maturity is beneficial because of the heightened awareness that comes with the achievement of selfhood, it also discovers that maturity is a state of lost innocence and, therefore, a consciousness of guilt. In other words, rather than working merely to confirm the authority of maturity and the "real," the novel constructs experience as a response to the problematic status of innocence: that is, innocence is at once desirable and repulsive. What complicates the novel's construction of experience, to give it energy as a dialectical operation, is a regressive momentum (the longing for innocence) which resists its progressive momentum (the imperative to mature) in some manner. This resistance to the novel's forward momentum colors its construction of experience with a feeling of dread, an anxiety about living experience—in more specific terms, a fear that maturity requires the loss of self because it is a violation of innocence. The conventions by which the novel constructs experience as some kind of rite of passage thus originate in response to this anxiety, and they underlie the genre's effort to imagine maturity repairing that original violation.

I can describe this dialectical operation with more precision by looking at it in terms of the dynamic interaction of romance and realism, a dynamic which I think characterizes the novel as a genre and determines its paradigmatic construction of experience. Because of the genre's proclaimed commitment to realism, most critics tend to consider the novel as a form alien to the sensibilities and drives of romance. In some respects this type of thinking seems unassailable. Throughout the eighteenth and nineteenth centuries English novelists repeatedly made a concerted effort to identify the novel generically as a realistic document by declaring it to be the antithesis of romance. Ian Watt calls this preoccupation the genre's "formal realism." Its conventions of individualized characters, narrations modeled on non-fictional forms of discourse (autobiography, letters, history, and the like), and the accumulation of materialistic, psychological, and sociological detail all aim to create the illusion of being "a full and authentic report of experience" as lived outside of books.[10] Another approach recognizes the origin of the novel's realism in Cervantes's parodic subversion of romance as a means of establishing textual authenticity. As Harry Levin observes, "a true novel imitates critically, not conventionally; hence it becomes a parody of other novels, an exception to prove the rule that fiction is untrue."[11] By projecting such a critical stance towards other fictions, the romance and its exploitation of desire in particular, the devices of realism aim to make the text itself represent, paradoxically, "the world beyond words" which characters experience in their collision with reality.[12] So George Levine points out that textual self-consciousness becomes a crucial, if disturbing, convention of realism, one which always threatens to undermine the text's claim of representing a reality outside its own language. Still a third view of the novel's realism discounts its source in parody and its textual self-consciousness to define it instead as the achievement of a homogeneous intelligibility, and then looks (in appreciation or mistrust) to the supposed transparency through which that consensus is confirmed by a centered, self-effacing discourse.[13]

While I do not disagree with these descriptions of realism, they do not account for the novel's imaginative range, especially as far as realism is concerned, nor can realism—or the novel itself, for that matter—be so easily disentangled from the romance form it tries to reject. For it would be more accurate, I think, to say that the novel defines itself, in Bakhtin's term, as a "dialogic" engagement of romance and realism,[14] and that it derives the source of its imaginative energy as a genre by casting this "dialogue" in the form of an "interrogation" of one mode by the other. This is why the novel is a dialectical operation; and it is in this context that I want to examine in some detail the discussions of realism by two critics in particular: Patrick Brantlinger and Leo Bersani. Both understand the novel as an inherently realistic document; at times they even use the terms "novel" and "realism" interchangeably. Brantlinger defines realism (or the novel) as the antithesis of romance in its psychological structure and moral value system. Bersani defines it as a structure which expels desire with the purpose of confirming the stability and coherence of personality. Though each critic is often reductive in his approach to realism, I have found their work useful because what they say helps to underscore the dialectical motivation of the novel's paradigmatic construction of experience.

The Paradigm of Experience

Brantlinger equates the novel with realism to start with because he reads the entire genre in terms of realism's confirmation of the reality beyond the self: "Although it would be too simple to say that the romance form is subjective and the novel form objective, the first fundamental of realism is the assumption of the existence of a physical realm external to self."[15] He then goes on to describe romance and realism in terms of their radically different psychic landscapes, aligning the former with the fragmentation of unconscious desire and the latter with the integration of egocentric development. "The romance form," he explains, "always shadows forth a regressive journey inward and backward, through childhood states of mind, threatening the dissolution of the adult ego, while the novel form resists and punishes such dissolution, and also invokes the higher principles of socialization and adult moral growth" (p. 21). In its regressive movement, romance "implies wish-fulfillment, and is bound up with dreams and illusions" (p. 15), so it invokes primal "childhood" emotions to dissolve "the adult ego" into a landscape of desire by returning self to the primacy of the unconscious; there reality ceases to exist as something "other," separate and distinct from the self. The novel, Brantlinger claims, asserts just the opposite by journeying outward and forward in an ego-dominated landscape. "Realistic novels are shaped by struggles for rational self-awareness in ways impossible in dreams, even though these struggles may be weak or may fail; but romances reject the rational and tend to imitate dreams" (p. 17).

Most useful in Brantlinger's schematic outline of romance and realism is the language he uses to distinguish one from the other. The landscapes he describes record the two opposing psychic states which characterize experience in the novel even in its most realistic phase: primitive unconsciousness, which dissolves the difference between the self and its world, and its radical opposite, the adult ego, which achieves its stability and coherence by establishing differences between the self and its world. To be sure, Brantlinger appreciates the psychological insights of a "romance" like *Wuthering Heights* (and even wonders, at one point, if the realism of a novel like *Middlemarch* might not be a defense against

Chapter 1

the unconscious), but a remark he makes early in his essay is revealing: "On a rudimentary level, realism functions like psychoanalysis, unmasking the infantile and irrational bases of illusion in its characters" (p. 16). From this analogy it seems clear that Brantlinger's scheme of romance and the novel as two radically different literary landscapes follows traditional psychoanalytic thinking. This view assigns infantile unconsciousness and adult consciousness to separate compartments of the psyche and then, by analogy, locates them each in a radically different type of fiction, with one (romance) giving way to wish fulfillment and encouraging symbolic readings to rationalize its "unreal" content and the other (realism or the novel) more wisely respecting the "truths" of the reality principle so that it is full of sense to start with.[16]

Leo Bersani conceives of realism in a similar light. But even though he more or less agrees with the polarity outlined by Brantlinger, Bersani wants to cut against the grain of conventional psychoanalytic and literary thought regarding the value of a stable, integrated, and mature self. In his book he examines works such as *Wuthering Heights* which challenge what realism has taught us to understand about "the self as a fundamentally intelligible structure unaffected by a history of fragmented, discontinuous desires."[17] While Bersani does not define realism specifically in terms antithetical to romance, he does ask us to understand it in a framework much like the one Brantlinger proposes: as an attempt to restrain or "expel" expressions of desire. "Realistic fiction," he observes, "admits heroes of desire in order to submit them to ceremonies of expulsion" (p. 67). Desire is dangerous to realism because in collapsing the difference between self and reality, or everything that is other than the self, it also collapses structures of meaning. "Personality and perhaps even gender," Bersani continues, "provide fragile identities which desire easily disrupts. Desire makes being problematic; the notion of a coherent and unified self is threatened by the discontinuous, logically incompatible images of a desiring imagination" (p. 84). For this reason, "desire is a threat to the form of realistic fiction. Desire can subvert social order; it can also disrupt novelistic order" (p. 66). In other words, desire undermines the epistemological,

The Paradigm of Experience

cultural, aesthetic, and psychological premises of realism, so it is no wonder that it stimulates, as it were, alien and subversive imaginative energies. And just as it does for Brantlinger, realism's opposition to the desiring imagination becomes for Bersani synonymous with the energies of the novel genre as a whole, so that although Bersani directs his attack specifically against realism, his target is actually the novel's repressive ideology of psychological coherence, "a commitment to a *psychological* integrity or intelligibility which has been a constant in Western culture" (p. 57).

While Bersani's approach to desire is convincing, it nonetheless oversimplifies realism in three ways. First of all, though no one could deny that realistic novels do in fact take pains to create intelligible characters, Bersani pretty much discounts their efforts to document maturity as a rite of passage marked by difficulty *and* desire. Second, he makes exclusive to realism a preoccupation with personality—the self's coherence as an "intelligible structure"—and with "significant design"—the organization of experience into a similarly intelligible pattern—when surely these concerns apply to the novel as a genre, perhaps even more so to modernist works than to realistic ones. And third, he fails to appreciate the self-reflexiveness of realism, its own mistrust of "significant design" as a distortion of reality by desire.[18]

For all his oversimplification of realism, however, what is most intriguing in Bersani's discussion is that his explanation of desire actually reveals the degree to which realism—and the novel as a continuous tradition—depends upon the desiring self that it seemingly rejects. To begin with, Bersani establishes a polarity between realism's structured (or conscious) expressions of desire, which work through repression and sublimation to uphold the integrity of a single continuous personality, and the fragmentation and discontinuity of unstructured (or unconscious) desire, which overwhelms the constraints of personality to break down the difference between self and other. As Bersani explains it, desire is "fragmented," "discontinuous," "aggressive," and "violent," so it seems to be synonymous with unconscious instinct: unstructured desire, the bête noire of realism, is regressive infantile desire. But, Bersani goes on to explain, even this state of

Chapter 1

"pure" desire is inconceivable without some structure and resistance, since "desire depends on the withdrawal of satisfaction" for its stimulation as desire (p. 13). Put more precisely, desire is a state of friction. It relies on the tension it generates between conscious and unconscious, adult and infantile, perceptions of reality. This friction overwhelms consciousness because desire anticipates a return to the "harmony" or "oneness" of self and other experienced in the unconscious prior to the formation of a discrete and separate personality. At the same time, since desire ceases to be desire once its object is obtained, it thrives on resistance. The friction generated by desire therefore defines consciousness, too, by working to distinguish the self from the other to underlie a perception of reality, of all that is *not* the work of desire.

Bersani thus calls attention to the role of desire in the process of distinguishing self and other, and in doing that he indirectly reveals how realism is more problematic than he appreciates. For example, when discussing *Women in Love* he explains:

> To desire is to experience a lack or an absence; and the sign of desire is movement (actual physical movement or the mental movements of thought and fantasy). We move in order to remove the lack, to make something absent present. Such movement is also the sign of individual life. It indicates a sense of a particular existence, that is, a sense of the self as not being all reality. To begin to live psychically as an individual is to recognize, in desire, the existence of realities distinct from the self. Desires provide a kind of negative of one's individuality: they implicitly define the self by explicitly defining what it lacks. Thus individual life is inseparable from desire and movement. (p. 181)

Because what Bersani says about desire here would make perfect sense of Dorothea Brooke's epiphany in chapter 80 of *Middlemarch*, it seems to contradict his simpler claim that realism is an outright expulsion of the desiring self. If realism requires, as Levine argues, "a continuing alertness to the secret lust of the spirit to impose itself on the world,"[19] then it also formulates a landscape of desire for its characters in order to establish their "sense of the self as not being all reality." This goal is indeed evident in the novels of Scott, Dickens, and Eliot (as well as in those of Lawrence and Woolf), where the dialectic of reality and desire is an unavoidable

The Paradigm of Experience

consequence of their realism. Bersani himself explains that a reality which opposes the self ends up stimulating its desire all the more; and he even clarifies this matter by appealing to a perspective that does not seem all that different from Eliot's realism: "this awareness" (of the world existing beyond the self's perception of it), he says—now about *Wuthering Heights*—"is the necessary condition for imagination and for desire: without a sense of the realities beyond us, we would be incapable of experiencing the lack without which desire is inconceivable" (p. 207).

Clearly, Bersani's explanation of desire implicitly demonstrates that realism stimulates desire by working to contain it, just as romance, the voice of desire, stimulates realism. Every realist novel carries within its narrative its own romantic opposite. This dialectic quite vividly informs the construction of experience in *Waverley* and *Bleak House*. In reaction to the "dangerous" desire embodied by its characters, each novel locates them in a realistic landscape that respects their psychological coherence by projecting their desire onto other characters. As a consequence, that realistic landscape is overcast by desire, which at times obscures the psychological integrity of one character to place him (or her) in the service of another character's desire (in *Bleak House*, furthermore, desire cannot always be explained by the psychological history of any one figure). While Scott's and Dickens's conscious mixture of modes perhaps accounts for the interaction of romance and realism in their novels, what can one say about *Middlemarch*, which similarly projects a landscape of desire for its characters? As I will explain in chapter 5, the climax of *Middlemarch* achieves its purpose of teaching Dorothea, Will, Lydgate, and Rosamond the difference between one self and another in order to lead them to an empathetic understanding of the other; and it does so, strangely—though fittingly—enough, through the startling effect of "fusing" their personalities. Although *Middlemarch, Bleak House*, and *Waverley* each equate desire with egoism, since their constructions of experience register the voices of desire in an effort to make them speak sense, they allow those voices to resonate through and disturb their narratives. To borrow a phrase from Terry Eagleton, the result in each of these examples is that "the novel is not quite identical with itself."[20]

Chapter 1

I have reopened the question of realism's relation to romance because I think that we will gain a critically useful understanding of the novel if we do not respect that traditional line of separation between them—even when novels may seem to respect that line themselves. To be sure, one could argue that Brantlinger and Bersani arrive at their "purer" version of realism simply by taking the novel at its own word. After all, don't all those quixotic daydreamers give ample warning to heed their example and *not* confuse the novel with the romance? Furthermore, since realistic novels like *Waverley* and *Bleak House* and, most of all, *Middlemarch* do uphold the rational, do expel desire, do confirm the intelligibility of personality—why shouldn't we read them straightforwardly on their own terms, as realism pure and simple?

In support of my method of approach, I can turn to Meredith Skura's recent discussion of psychoanalytic criticism. Skura's project is to show the critical usefulness of a psychoanalytic model, not for the purpose of analyzing an author or her characters as case studies, but for revealing how both infantile unconsciousness and adult consciousness are modes of representing reality. Like Bersani, Skura recognizes that each represents the world in a radically different way; but, she explains, their meaning as representations arises from their *interaction*. Making use of the French and American reinterpretation of Freud, Skura refutes the assumption that we must draw clear and uncrossable lines between the regressive expressions of primitive desire in literature, which require a symbolic reading, and those progressive demonstrations of a structured adult self, which ask to be taken at face value. She argues just the opposite: "in literature, as opposed to case history or fantasy, we are never sure which reading to choose. The literary text should be placed in the space between literal and symbolic reading."[21]

To begin with, Skura points out that most critics misunderstand the unconscious, underestimating and simplifying its relation to "adult reality." For one thing, the unconscious is usually equated with wish fulfillment or regression, the suspension or rejection of the reality principle. Wish fulfillment, however, is actually a misrepresentation of unconscious mental activity. A daydream, for example, necessarily translates unformed primitive

The Paradigm of Experience

fantasy into an adult vocabulary in order to formulate desire as a "wish." "The daydream is a polished and rationalized final product, not only because it already takes account of adult reality and includes defenses as well as wishes, but also because it is organized enough to distinguish between wish and defense, in the first place, and between self and resisting reality." Unlike wishes, primitive fantasies collapse that distinction. Indeed, they are "primitive" because they derive "from the earliest stages of life, when wish fulfillment could not be separated from a whole way of seeing the world; and that way differs radically from any adult view" (p. 77).

In a similar vein, if a daydream makes us think of the unconscious in terms of wish fulfillment, then a night dream encourages us to equate it with regression. The commonplace assumption about a dream is that its regressive fantasy replaces an adult wish with an infantile desire, or that it relocates the wish in a censored memory. In either case, the dream plots a rather clear course for its interpretation. The actual dream process, however, is much more complicated. In a regressive fantasy the unconscious actually overlays an infantile representation of reality—"a relapse into seeing things as we did before we ever separated self from world" (p. 87)—upon an adult representation. But this does not mean that the dream suspends that adult construction of reality or ignores it altogether. "This reversion is not a denial of reality but a return to a mode of thinking in which wish, fear, and other subjective, emotionally tinged views have not been distinguished from reality" (p. 138). Nor does this mode of pluralist thinking distinguish among fantasies; instead it multiplies fantasy, arranging "a whole network of associations, thoughts, and images related to each other and represented in the dream in the strangest, most diverse ways" (p. 147). Even then, this primitive mode of thinking is just one of the dream's methods of representation, since the dream also invokes the vocabulary of adult life—in the dream narrative and, later, in its telling. The dream, in other words, establishes a site where adult and infantile modes of "thinking" collide and interact. As a result, the dream continually shifts between adult and infantile modes of representation, as well as between various fantasies. The shifting is what causes the

Chapter 1

dream to appear confusing in its surface narrative. More to the point, the shifting requires that the dream's "reader" use a variety of interpretive skills.

With this established, Skura goes on to argue her main point: even though the unconscious makes no distinctions between "person, place, or time," it is not consequently alien to (or alienated from) the structured adult consciousness which recognizes the world in terms of "discrete events and separate individuals" (p.77) "The fantasy does not replace adult experience," Skura explains, "but instead brings the intensities of childhood experience to bear on current adult life. It adds depth by evoking the unconscious remnants of infantile experience, without substituting that experience for an adult one" (pp. 73-74). Something similar, she concludes, happens in works of literature, where "the fantasy is never present nakedly but is seen in the light of sophisticated, adult ways of thinking; *and it is the interplay between surface sophistication and primitive fantasy that matters* (my emphasis; p. 274).

Keeping in mind the conventional psychological meanings attributed by critics like Brantlinger to romance (i.e., the expression of "primitive fantasy") and realism (i.e., the expression of "surface sophistication"), I think Skura's argument is especially appropriate to the novel. The novel uses conventions of romance as well as realism (if only to invoke one set of conventions to discount the other) and brings them together to create a narrative texture much like the one Skura describes in the night dream. In other words, the novel's dialectical engagement of romance and realism does not work to embed a regressive fantasy beneath its surface; rather, this dialectic overlays the novel's representation of conscious reality with an evocation of unconscious desire, requiring different modes of reading at the same time. The kind of interaction I am talking about, for instance, is what makes the climax of a "realistic" novel like *Middlemarch* so powerful. This does not, I must repeat, mean reducing Eliot's novel to an infantile content. What is at issue is the way her narrative is suddenly not quite identical with itself—which is to say that it registers "the interplay between surface sophistication and primitive fantasy" in its representation of experience,

The Paradigm of Experience

opening a space between symbolic and strictly literal meanings so that both are pertinent in the way each informs the other. Realism in general tries to disguise this aspect of its own construction as an imaginative (rather than rational) engagement with the energies of primitive unconsciousness; but then romance similarly tries to disguise its engagement with sophisticated consciousness by imagining (without rationalizing) a fantastic world.

As a result of this interplay between romance and realism we can, when analyzing the novel and its construction of experience, usefully distinguish between the "primitive" vocabulary of one and the "sophisticated" vocabulary of the other without having to split the genre in two. On the contrary, if we appreciate their interaction we can account for the novel's operation as a genre: how, in the first place, it processes the volatile and infantile energy of romance ("the regressive journey inward and backward") through the stabilizing and adult value system of realism ("the higher principles of socialization and adult moral growth"), and in the second, how it can do that and yet not suppress the former entirely. This procedure, furthermore, makes sense of the novel in the light of its history as a predominantly realistic narrative. In casting a suspicious eye back to its own origin in romance, realism inevitably built into the genre the very regressive energy it meant to subvert. Since realism is just one motion in the novel's operation as a genre, the claims of the desiring imagination must be recognized as well, no matter how strongly they are resisted by realism's aggressive push forward.

Out of this particular dynamic, the forward momentum of realism competing with the backward momentum of romance, the novel establishes its paradigm of experience. In its barest form, the story goes something like this: The novel constructs experience as a journey into selfhood to record the transformation of an immature self into a mature one. To motivate this journey, the novel demonstrates that because the innocent self does not distinguish between desire and reality, it fails to see the world in terms of difference and therefore falls victim to illusion-making; the mature self, on the other hand, corrects such blindness. Experience is therefore constructed to educate characters in the important distinction between the desiring self and the indifferent other. Viewing this education as a dynamic operation, the novel imagines the self as a kind of seed, a "pip" blossoming or wilting under the impact of reality, and it does so in order to project an impression of organic continuity over an experience of potential discontinuity. This familiar organic metaphor of growth thus works to obscure the fact that maturity is also a sign of discontinuity: maturity can effect so radical an alteration of the innocent self that it seems like a violation. In other words, contrary to the original premise that living in reality is superior to living in illusion, experience may actually reveal that the mature self is so new and different that it now bears no relationship to the old.

Because maturity is different from innocence, to the innocent self maturation is a dreadful process of alienation and loss, of becoming something other than itself. This fear that maturity is tantamount to self-loss accounts for the specific shapes which the other assumes as it contests the self's innocence. Most commonly, the other appears as the other sex, whose violence and aggression depict maturation as a dreadful achievement indeed, one alien to the self's sense of its own innocence. Appearing in this shape, the other dislocates desire from the self (the violence and aggression enacted by the alien other sex underscoring by comparison the innocence of the self), only to end up relocating it there (confirming the self's maturation by forcing it to identify with the other's alien sexuality). At other times the other takes the more benevolent shape of the parent, to heighten its attractiveness (in offering security, warmth, and unity) and its dreadful alien nature (in exacerbating the adult's difference, mystery, and power over the child). When it confronts the other in this form, the self must similarly come to terms with what it desires and dreads: its own transformation into an adult. In either of these two shapes, the other anticipates the end result of maturation—adulthood—so it forces the self to identify with what it considers to be alien to its own nature; and this surprising identification is potentially horrifying because it prevents the self from retaining any measure of innocence.

When viewed from this perspective experience seems a violation of selfhood. Although the novel's progressive energy works to

The Paradigm of Experience

minimize this disturbing implication of violation, the self's dread of being violated cannot be easily discounted. It complicates the linear construction of experience by instigating a regressive momentum (the resistance to maturity because of its threat of violation) which counterpoints the progressive momentum (the sacrifice of childlike innocence in the interest of maturation). To mitigate this fear of violation, the novel then invests the loss of innocence with the virtue of insight in order to envision maturity repairing that necessary violation of innocence.

In proposing this model, I do not mean to reduce all novels to so schematic a content or to an identical structure. As I shall be showing in later chapters, the narrative logic of *Clarissa*, say, has special generic affinities with that of *Middlemarch* or *To the Lighthouse*, but it also diverges from them in crucial ways to make each seem quite different. Speaking practically, isolating a paradigm of experience for the novel will be of critical use only if it serves to highlight variation as well as similarity. My purpose in calling attention to a paradigmatic operation in the novel is to examine the way individual narratives orchestrate experience out of a rhythm of what I am calling "violation and repair." Throughout my discussion I will be concerned with the degree to which a given novel directs experience to result in violation or repair, for that direction helps to account for the novel's particular construction of experience. By way of final preparation for such a discussion, then, in the rest of this chapter I will look at the genre's paradigmatic rhythm of violation and repair in more concrete detail than I have yet done. And to provide an illuminating field for this examination, I want to turn to a pair of novels which I think well represent the English novel's paradigmatic construction of experience: the conservative example of *Pride and Prejudice*, which everyone agrees typifies the genre, and the radical one of *Wuthering Heights*, which almost everyone agrees, though for different reasons, does not.

Pride and Prejudice might seem a surprising first choice for a convincing illustration of my argument: feelings of "violation" and "dread" do not readily come to mind when one thinks of Jane Austen's novel, nor would one think to describe Elizabeth

Chapter 1

Bennet's experience as a violation leading to repair. This is, in fact, why I want to begin with Austen's novel. Because it places so much confidence in Elizabeth's ability to adjust her private vision to the world beyond her self, *Pride and Prejudice* is an appropriately quiet example of the novel's paradigmatic construction of experience.

Elizabeth Bennet needs correction, first of all, because she assumes she can scrutinize the people around her. Some, like her mother or Lady Catherine or Mr. Collins, she can see for what they are, but others prove to be much more duplicitous and complicated than she has anticipated. She misinterprets Darcy's motives, not to say Wickham's and Charlotte's, until she acquires his point of view by reading his letter. Then his character emerges from the shadows to which Wickham's recedes, and the revision of their relationship momentarily shakes the very foundations of her faith in her self. Inevitably she reaches a conclusion similar to the one Pip reaches when his Great Expectations tumble into a heap of deluded dreams: "Til this moment, I never knew myself."[22]

A turning point like Elizabeth's appears frequently in the English novel. Repeatedly we find moments of crisis leading characters to the realization that the self's private vision cannot be trusted. Elizabeth's journey from illusion to reality, like Pip's, follows the novelistic convention of exposing a character to the world beyond self in order to lead her from a private and immature vision to a public and mature one. Since this convention assumes that reality educates a character by puncturing her innocence to expose her self-deception, it convincingly equates her change with growth, with gains, not loss, with wholeness, not disintegration. Everything that happens in *Pride and Prejudice* therefore pivots around that crucial moment when Elizabeth comes to realize that she has never known her self. The value of her experience lies in its impact on the self, and her education in reality can be achieved only when Darcy challenges her confidence in what she sees, understands, and feels. To be sure, his letter drives a wedge between Elizabeth as she was and Elizabeth as she now is, but the momentum of growth informing her experience is strong enough to maintain a sense of continuity. When Elizabeth looks backward to see her self for the first time, she is in effect

The Paradigm of Experience

re-viewing her self to envision it continuously. Yet this conventional procedure also carries with it a potential for registering psychic discontinuity in its very orchestration of change, of growth emerging out of crisis.

Elizabeth's achievement of maturity, first of all, is representative of the genre's typical forward momentum, and it can be summarized in this simple fashion:

Starting Point	*Midpoint*	*Endpoint*
illusion	illusion vs. reality	reality
E despises D and finds W attractive	D courts E without her realizing it	E sees D and W correctly and falls in love with D
action initiated	action complicated	action resolved
sexual immaturity	emerging sexuality	sexual maturity
childhood	adolescence	adulthood

At this basic level of construction, *Pride and Prejudice* charts Elizabeth's experience as a rite of passage from immaturity to maturity; its conventional linear organization of experience into a plotted dramatic form implies a developing psychological organization for her character. Most novels, *Pride and Prejudice* included, do not reduce their plots or their characters to such a schematic organization, nor do they record an actual biological growth. Strictly speaking, only a bildungsroman invents a protagonist who moves in time from childhood to adolescence to adulthood. Obviously, *Pride and Prejudice* is no such novel. Elizabeth's experience, though so crucial to the emergence of her mature self, is of proportionately short duration. Too, at the book's start she has a bearing and insight that few readers would be inclined to call "adolescent," let alone "childish." Yet while it might seem to distort the literal duration of Austen's narrative, the analogy I have drawn in the fifth step nevertheless holds as a way of marking off the relative stages of Elizabeth's development to show the progressive weight each succeeding stage has to bear.

In contrast to the finished self envisioned by the book's end, Elizabeth's initial consciousness seems very childlike indeed. Living in a culture preoccupied with the business of getting married, she is, curiously enough, the least marriage-minded of all the major characters. Like Emma Woodhouse, Elizabeth still considers herself her father's daughter, an observer of the rituals of courtship, not a participant in them. This position certainly has its advantages, for her "quickness of observation" alerts her to "the follies and nonsense of others" (p. 9); however, since hers is initially "a judgment too unassailed by any attention to herself" (p. 9), it works to her disadvantage as well, encouraging her overconfidence as a "studier of character" (p.29) once Darcy and Wickham assail her judgment by paying her attention. Elizabeth assumes her discernment is objective, and yet procedes to misread the two men, because she does not take her own sexuality seriously. Her innocent understanding of her self at this point prevents her from recognizing the sexual vanity which motivates her relations with Wickham and Darcy by causing her to be "pleased with the preference of one, and offended by the neglect of the other" (p. 144). It never occurs to her that Darcy could have any motive other than his disapprobation (p. 35), even though her blindness regarding him is made all the more evident by the fact that both Charlotte Lucas and Caroline Bingley immediately notice and correctly interpret the reason for his interest.

Elizabeth's agitated relations with Darcy initiate her movement out of innocence. By prompting Elizabeth to confront the reason for her naïveté as a reader of complex people, herself included, Darcy's letter forces her to confront her own sexuality as well; and this double exposure disturbs the complacency with which she has previously identified her self exclusively in terms of her family. For this reason Darcy's presence unsettles her; he reminds her of a frame of reference outside her family, thereby forcing her to enlarge the standard against which she defines her self. He makes her face the consequences of what she has already noticed about the impropriety of her family's behavior, for example, just as she also teaches him what she discovers: that she and Jane should be judged independently of their family. And since Darcy's courtship leads her outside the protective domain of her family to seek a more independent social and personal identity as lover and wife, it is significant that he initially proposes to her not at Netherfield or Longbourn but at Hunsford, away from her native home, and that he begins to woo her all over again at

The Paradigm of Experience

Pemberley, the point from which she later dates her newly discovered love for him (p. 258). Finally, Elizabeth's marriage to Darcy, a "union that must have been to the advantage of both" (p. 214), completes her maturation in every respect. This new identity confirms her corrected vision, her sexual fulfillment, and her liberation from her family, who now depend on her and Darcy for happiness and instruction. Put simply, by the end of the novel Elizabeth has come to define her self in terms of the other: another gender (the male), another house (Pemberley), another family (the Darcys), but also, I want to add, another self as well: "Til this moment, I never knew myself."

When I called *Pride and Prejudice* a conservative example of the genre, I did so because in the long run Elizabeth does not seem to experience much discontinuity of self. She does not build a new self so much as recognize her myopia. In the short run, however, the impact of seeing her self for the first time does generate at least a momentary sensation of discontinuity. Reading Darcy's letter, she quickly falls into a state of extreme agitation and disbelief. Competing emotions flood her consciousness. "In this perturbed state of mind," she rehearses every emotion she seems capable of feeling, though "her feelings as she read were scarcely to be defined." At first she reacts with "amazement," "astonishment," "apprehension," "even horror": Darcy's letter cannot possibly be just in its accusations, so she is angry. Then, as she ponders the contents of his letter, she feels ashamed and humiliated: "blind, partial, prejudiced, absurd" does her behavior now seem in retrospect. This is not the same confident woman who teased Darcy at the Netherfield ball or laughed at him with Charlotte behind his back; and yet, surely, it is: she has just never before seen her self in all its "prepossession and ignorance." Still later she feels "compassion," "gratitude," and "respect" for Darcy, establishing the basis for loving him (pp. 140-47).

As she reads his letter and engages in the self-reflection that follows, Elizabeth is severely shaken by what she discovers about the complex self that has all the while lain unexposed to her scrutiny. Though her confidence and pride are challenged, the forward momentum generated by her crisis gives her the strength to recover, the intelligence to accept this newly found wisdom and, most importantly, the assurance that there has in fact been a stable self existing all along. It is, in the end, a matter of seeing that "original" self with clear, rational, adult eyes, just as it has been from the start a question of seeing Darcy and Wickham as they really are, not as they appear.

For this reason Elizabeth's competing feelings about Darcy and Wickham are of no little consequence to her experience of maturation. Her inclination to find one man agreeable is inseparable from her determination "to hate" the other (p. 63), a motive formed when Darcy insulted her to Bingley in her hearing. So when Elizabeth thinks that "attention, forbearance, patience with Darcy, was injury to Wickham" (p. 62), she might just as well be thinking that attention, forbearance, patience with Wickham is injury to Darcy, a fitting enough repayment for his insult. Wickham's attention singles her out among the women, so it is ample compensation for Darcy's seeming disinterest in her. "He is," she admits about Wickham, "beyond all comparison, the most agreeable man I ever saw" (p. 100). Not surprisingly, the attentions of this "agreeable man" have no trouble sparking Elizabeth's vanity. Although she defends Wickham's account of Darcy's dishonorable behavior by explaining, "there was truth in his looks" (p. 60), one cannot help wondering if she is not equating truth with his *good* looks, since she is obviously drawn to Wickham's manner and flattered by his attentions and confidences, despite their impropriety (a fact she does not appreciate until after reading Darcy's letter). Consequently, it is her sexual attraction to Wickham that leads her to court illusion; so while she later blames her errors on vanity, not passion, it is significant that she invokes the adage of love's blindness to account for the way pride and prejudice have obstructed her vision: "Had I been in love, I could not have been more wretchedly blind" (p. 144). Although Elizabeth may not be "in love" with Wickham, she is certainly not immune to his sexual charm.

Austen underlines Elizabeth's initial sexual attraction to Wickham in a passage which contrasts the romantic notion of love to her own novel's more realistic and mature—and unconventional—view:

The Paradigm of Experience

> If gratitude and esteem are good foundations of affection, Elizabeth's change of sentiment will be neither improbable nor faulty. But if otherwise, if the regard springing from such sources is unreasonable or unnatural, in comparison of what is so often described as arising on a first interview with its object, and even before two words have been exchanged, nothing can be said in her defense, except that she had given somewhat of a trial to the latter method, in her partiality for Wickham, and that its ill-success might perhaps authorise her to seek the other less interesting mode of attachment. (pp. 190-91)

This passage has always struck an odd chord whenever I read it because it seems so unnecessary. Surely Elizabeth needs no justification for forming this "less interesting mode of attachment" to Darcy. Wickham gives love at first sight a bad name, at least in this novel. To love him, Elizabeth must keep reminding herself (when prodded to do so by her Aunt Gardiner), is to love recklessly. He has neither money nor prospects, nor does he bother to restrain his own desire, as his elopement with Lydia confirms to the discontent of both. Yet it is important that Wickham, not Darcy, is the man who first awakens Elizabeth's sexual desire. For Wickham makes her aware of the object of desire—the male—as an unfamiliar and indifferent other, one which resists her intelligence and exploits her innocence. Furthermore, he shows her how desire can easily—not to say dangerously—manipulate the appearances that constitute the self's construction of reality. As a result, Wickham creates a disparity between reason and desire which Darcy helps Elizabeth to reconcile by showing her the way toward a more mature and public—and certainly more rational—expression of desire, namely, "gratitude and esteem" along with "affection." Darcy, the gentleman who loves her ardently and faithfully, and Wickham, the rake who does not, define the progressive range of her emotional development: one man determines her feelings for the other. She cannot appreciate Darcy while she is infatuated with Wickham; and when she falls in love with Darcy, she outgrows Wickham.

What is interesting about Elizabeth's "change of sentiment," moreover, is not that she chooses the tamer, more socialized form

Chapter 1

of desire in Darcy, but that this other "mode of attachment" helps her to identify the origin of desire in her self. This is why her moment of insight requires an excursion backwards, when Darcy's letter prompts her to re-view her experience, before she can begin to move forward. The pressure Darcy puts on Elizabeth to re-view her self accounts for his disturbing effect upon her. Darcy makes Elizabeth realize that the unfamiliar other which she must reckon with before clearly seeing her self is not Darcy, exactly, or Wickham, so much as it is her own emerging sexuality. This realization is at first deeply disturbing—generating her emotional disorder in the midpoint of the narrative—because it locates the unfamiliar other inside Elizabeth to make "self" seem like something new and startling. The novel then authorizes this location by equating it with maturation; in doing that, the novel also authorizes the value of maturity over innocence. Once innocence is exposed as the product of "unreasonable or unnatural" illusion, it is dislocated from the self, and this process reveals the degree to which Elizabeth's immature self was never all that "innocent" to begin with. The cause of Elizabeth's feeling of discontinuity—her sexuality—therefore turns out to be the source of her continuity as well.

The frame in which I have cast Elizabeth's development is not uncommon to the English novel. The impact of emerging sexuality, so central to plots revolving around love and marriage, vividly serves to reveal the future adult self's potential, its emotional range and need for independence. The journey to maturity leaves behind any last vestiges of childhood innocence, whether we see this happening literally, as in a bildungsroman, or more implicitly, as in Elizabeth's sexual awakening. The child may be father to the man, as Wordsworth said, she may be mother to the woman, but the English novel insists that the adult self must learn to disavow its parentage of childhood innocence. Yet most English novels do not accept so radical a change for the self as benignly as *Pride and Prejudice* imagines it. To say this, however, is not to accept Austen's novel as a generic norm so much as to appreciate that her narrative gives subdued expression to the genre's premise: construct experience to challenge the self, to demand the loss of innocence, to effect a transformation. Although the novel's

The Paradigm of Experience

paradigmatic construction of experience informs the self's transformation with the implication of progress, as in Elizabeth's case, quite often that alteration of the self begets a longing for lost innocence, a despair over the innocent self which experience had to violate in order to expose it to reality. Then the potential for crisis is greater than it is in *Pride and Prejudice*, instigating a more forceful regressive movement to resist the progressive linear momentum, and this dialectic makes the self's passage into maturity a tumultuous journey.

Wuthering Heights provides a case in point. Though it initially seems to oppose the calm, ameliorating vision of *Pride and Prejudice*, in the two-part structure by which it delineates the self in crisis *Wuthering Heights* is no less representative of the genre's construction of experience. Admittedly, most of its readers have tended to see *Wuthering Heights* as a rather exotic or mutant—or at least a very different—strain of the novel form.[23] The world Emily Brontë imagines for her characters is passionate, violent, self-absorbed, offering a stark contrast to Jane Austen's type of fictive world. If for Elizabeth, as Austen reports, "self, though it would intrude, could not engross her" (p. 190), for Cathy Earnshaw, in contrast, self does intrude; it deeply engrosses her because she feels that the world outside her self is alien to it. At the same time she finds this world attractive, and since this attraction, in turn, seems to take her out of her self, she understands it as a violation of her self. In this light, her experience is the opposite of Elizabeth's. Yet in many ways Cathy's fear of self-loss, rather than Elizabeth's achievement of selfhood, is more representative of the genre's paradigmatic construction of experience as a contest between innocence and maturity. In *Pride and Prejudice* the outcome of this contest has already been decided before the opening lines. This is why the progressive energy of Elizabeth's experience can surround—and quite literally contain—her disturbing, regressive moment of self-revision. *Wuthering Heights*, on the other hand, gives its progressive and regressive energies equal weight, so that the contest between innocence and experience is genuinely a contest.

Not everyone will agree with my placement of *Wuthering Heights* at the center of the genre. As I have said, the anxiety which

Chapter 1

this novel orchestrates as the emotional content of its narrative is a far cry from the more sanguine temperament of *Pride and Prejudice*, and for many this difference makes *Wuthering Heights* seem alien to the generic spirit represented by Austen's fiction. According to Bersani's reading, for instance, *Wuthering Heights* dissolves self into an alien otherness in order to explode "the myth of personality" so central to realist novels like *Pride and Prejudice*. Bersani sees Brontë's novel building from a "confusion about the nature and the boundaries of the self" to reach a point where characters seem actually to be "without personality," since they lack "the psychological continuities which make personality possible." These characters, all sliding into and reflecting each other, no longer possess "that coherent, unified, describable self which is a premise of most Western literature" (pp. 201, 214).

Wuthering Heights certainly does approach this disturbing vision of selflessness through Cathy Earnshaw. But because Cathy desperately wants a coherent self, the novel originates in a sense of dread that her psychic disintegration actually means the death of the self, not its liberation. What Cathy discovers is that maturity generates so radical a transformation of her self—by demanding involvement in a world alien to her innocence—that loss of innocence also means the loss of self. The antithesis of everything the genre works to resolve in its forward movement towards maturity and reality, this anxiety defines the emotional content of Brontë's narrative. The first half of the novel envisions experience as a violation of the self, and the second half then works to repair that violation through Cathy's daughter, to show that lost innocence is not tantamount to the self's death.

There are several reasons why Cathy Earnshaw's loss of innocence is more problematic and disturbing than Elizabeth Bennet's. To begin with, at the start of *Wuthering Heights* Lockwood introduces us to two radically different incarnations of Cathy Earnshaw: the spirited, rebellious child who wrote the make-shift diary which he reads while at the Heights, and the ghostly spirit wandering the earth as an outcast. Nelly Dean's narration then tries to make sense of Lockwood's unsettling vision of Cathy by grounding it in her biography. To be sure, Nelly's impatience with Cathy's passionate temperament prevents her

The Paradigm of Experience

from fully explaining the ghostly apparition or its cry of despair. As far as Nelly is concerned, Cathy's maturation only amounts to a superficial change, since Cathy remains a spoiled child at heart, "a haughty, headstrong creature" who "beat Hareton, or any child, at a good passionate fit of crying."[24] Even when an adult, Cathy is too preoccupied with her own emotions to realize that Nelly does not like or respect her. Rather, in her self-absorption Cathy assumes that "though everybody hated and despised each other, they could not avoid loving me" (p. 104).

Nelly's characterization of Cathy is significant in ways she does not recognize. Far from being proof of her spoiled nature, Cathy's belief that she motivates the lives around her exposes her innocence; she imagines a wholeness of being, a self outside of time and indistinguishable from the other. Her maturation, however, places her in time, increasing her awareness of the opposition between self and other; as a result, she projects her innocent self onto Heathcliff to keep from losing it altogether. As Cathy sees it, Heathcliff stands outside of time, and thus readily personifies childhood, for two reasons. First, he is indifferent to the physical and cultural constraints which are responsible for the disturbing changes in identity that she herself experiences once she reaches puberty. And second, more than anyone else, Heathcliff cannot avoid loving her, as he confesses several times over; she even manipulates circumstances in order to force him to demonstrate the extent to which he willingly allows his love for her to efface his own selfhood. When she exclaims, "he's more myself than I am" (p. 72), or "Nelly, I *am* Heathcliff" (p.74), she considers their love to be intense enough to ignore the passage of time. But while Cathy's love for Heathcliff allows her to imagine being unified with the other, she does not exist outside of time, so their mutual identification is more disruptive in its impact than she realizes. If she *is* Heathcliff, then "Cathy Earnshaw" is the force conspiring against innocence. Put another way, by handing over her innocent self to him for safe-keeping, she is, in effect, disclaiming her origin in innocence. However much she believes that their souls "are the same" (p. 72), her identification with Heathcliff implies that she has already lost her self. As she says, Heathcliff is truer to the innocence of "Cathy Earnshaw" than she is.

Chapter 1

Cathy's fear that she has somehow lost her self in the process of maturing becomes quite clear when, on the night of Heathcliff's elopement with Isabella, she remembers her childhood in a feverish dream or trance. Though a familiar passage, it is worth quoting at length because it vividly articulates her dread that maturation has resulted in an irreparable violation of her selfhood:

> I thought as I lay there with my head against that table leg, and my eyes dimly discerning the grey square of the window, that I was enclosed in the oak-panelled bed at home; and my heart ached with some great grief which, just waking, I could not recollect. I pondered, and worried myself to discover what it could be; and most strangely, the whole last seven years of my life grew a blank! I did not recall that they had been at all. I was a child; my father was just buried, and my misery arose from the separation that Hindley had ordered between me and Heathcliff. I was laid alone, for the first time, and, rousing from the dismal doze after a night of weeping, I lifted my hand to push the panels aside: it struck the table top! I swept it along the carpet, and then memory burst in—my late anguish was swallowed in a paroxysm of despair. I cannot say why I felt so wildly wretched—it must have been temporary derangement, for there is scarcely a cause. But, supposing at twelve years old, I had been wrenched from the Heights, and every early association, and my all and all, as Heathcliff was at that time, and been converted at a stroke into Mrs. Linton, the lady of Thrushcross Grange, and the wife of a stranger; an exile, and outcast, thenceforth, from what had been my world. You may fancy a glimpse of the abyss where I grovelled . . . Oh, I'm burning! I wish I were out of doors—I wish I were a girl again, half savage, and hardy, and free, and laughing at injuries, not maddening under them! Why am I so changed? why does my blood rush into a hell of tumult at a few words? I'm sure I should be myself were I once among the heather on those hills. Open the window again wide, fasten it open! . . . (p. 107)

Cathy's confusion in this passage raises several fundamental questions about her origin in childhood innocence. First of all, this dreamy vision layers time so that Cathy is at once child and adult. With "the whole last seven years" of her life erased, she returns to childhood, which, surprisingly, causes her heart to ache because of "some great grief." The reason for her grief is not immediately clear; it takes her a moment before she can "discover what it could

The Paradigm of Experience

be." The most obvious explanation is that she is reliving the end of her childhood: Hindley, the tyrannical replacement for her loving father, who "was just buried," orders her "separation" from her "all in all," Heathcliff, because they have reached puberty. As the result of this separation Cathy ceases to be "half savage, and hardy, and free," and thus loses her self along with her childhood innocence. What remains most real to her about her childhood, then, is not its unity but the division that ends it. She dwells upon that moment of separation from Heathcliff which defines her self in opposition to the other as an "exile, and outcast"—as an adolescent.

The conjunction of the past and present in this dream expresses the discontinuity Cathy feels as an adult and does not remember experiencing as a child; nonetheless the dream's simultaneous layering of time may imply just the opposite. For this dream both expresses and contests Cathy's sense of the difference between her child and adult selves. The agent of disruption throughout is, as she says, "memory"—her memories of being a child at the Heights, of losing her father, of being separated from Heathcliff, of becoming "Mrs. Linton." These memories rob Cathy of her innocence because they locate her self in time to establish her sequential progression from child to adolescent to adult. This is why the dream's layering of the past over the present, which at first seems to reverse Cathy's maturation by returning to her childhood, finally forces her to confront the reality of her adult life. When she imagines herself in her bedroom "at home," "home" carries with it both its childhood and adult referents. At first finding herself in the "oak-panelled bed" of her bedroom at the Heights, she pushes the panels aside only to discover that she is in her bedroom at the Grange. It is at this point that "memory" bursts in upon her consciousness, and the "paroxysm of despair" she feels as she realizes her present situation succeeds her "late anguish" at being forcibly separated from Heathcliff. She now experiences a traumatic separation from her childhood self more disturbing than her separation from Heathcliff. The reason for her "despair" becomes evident as she tries to explain why she feels "so wildly wretched" upon waking up at the Grange. Since those missing seven years account for her identity as an adult, their unexpected absence makes her maturation too abrupt to be explicable. Indeed, rereading this passage, one cannot help noticing that the "great grief" causing her heart to ache is not so much the result of her separation from Heathcliff as it is an expression of her strange feeling "that the whole last seven years of my life grew a blank!" Lacking any memory of those years, Cathy can only understand her maturation as a sudden transformation, being "wrenched from the Heights," as she puts it, and then "converted at a stroke into Mrs. Linton, the Lady of Thrushcross Grange, and the wife of a stranger." Elizabeth Bennet may never have seen her self before reading Darcy's letter, but Cathy looks back on her past through this dream and finds that at some point she has lost her self entirely.

What has happened during those crucial seven years to make Cathy feel "so changed" that, as "Mrs. Linton," she is no longer her self? Her disrupting rite of passage out of childhood begins for her in earnest when she and Heathcliff unexpectedly come upon the socialized world of Thrushcross Grange. Although she wants to remain the wild child untouched by the fine dress and ribboned hair, this world draws her to it with its vision of authority and freedom, of civilization and refinement. Cathy associates these qualities with adults, so she finds that world attractive and wants to enter it—if for no other reason than to escape Hindley's brutal domination. Heathcliff, too, finds that world enticing, and probably for the same reason Cathy does: it is a world without parents.[25] "We should have thought ourselves in heaven!" he exclaims to Nelly (p. 47). Yet as he describes this scene, "heaven" does not seem much like the epitome of adulthood—not Nelly Dean's picture of maturity, at any rate: Edgar and Isabella Linton are fussing and crying, each is pulling the leg of their dog, and there are no parents around to supervise their play, or to reprimand them and give orders, or to inhibit the selfishness and violence on display. This scene confirms a child's impression of adult freedom and power, but it challenges Cathy's sense of self all the same. Her first visit to the Grange results in a change of her physical appearance; she returns to the Heights transformed from a ragamuffin to a genteel young lady, a correlative to the change

The Paradigm of Experience

her body is undergoing at the same time. This transformation places her childhood relationship with Heathcliff in an unfavorable light. Since her attraction to the Grange world causes her to be disloyal to Heathcliff—and, by her own admission, to her original self—she feels guilty about accepting the values of that world and clings instead to the belief that she is its victim.

Her guilt is expressed in another one of her dreams, which she describes to Nelly as the source of her conviction that she is wrong to marry Edgar. In this dream Cathy goes to heaven, only to discover that "heaven did not seem to be my home; and I broke my heart with weeping to come back to earth; and the angels were so angry that they flung me out, into the middle of the heath on the top of Wuthering Heights; where I woke sobbing for joy" (p. 72). Awakening from this dream, she feels relieved at having escaped "heaven"—and, clearly, she has this sense of relief in mind years later when she exclaims to Nelly, in the long passage cited above, "I'm sure I would be myself were I once more among the heather on those hills." The point of this early dream, though, is that it does not prove true; far from being expelled from the Grange, Cathy becomes its mistress. Her sense of relief at escaping "heaven" in her dream, however, tells her that she does not belong at the Grange. This warning not only allows her to deny her own willingness to enter that world and to discount the pleasure she expects to find there; it actually consoles her for the guilt she feels in having succumbed to that world's irresistible promise of adulthood.

Cathy's two dreams indicate that her maturation widens the distance between the Heights and the Grange only because she projects opposing values onto them, values which her imagination cannot easily reconcile without taking change into account. Thus her decision to marry Edgar is motivated partly by her recognition that she must help Heathcliff to escape the brutal tyranny of her brother, and partly by her assumption that, being the emotional center of both men's lives, she can easily join the world of the Heights, which for her embodies her childhood as personified in Heathcliff, with the world of the Grange, which for her embodies her newly acquired maturity as personified in Edgar. But the opposing values she attributes to each world mean that there is no

Chapter 1

room for Heathcliff in her relations with Edgar, and vice versa. No matter how hard she tries to arrange her life to be both child and adult, loving Heathcliff and married to Edgar, Cathy always seems on the verge of disintegration, especially whenever she comes into contact with Heathcliff. He convinces her that she has betrayed him by marrying Edgar; more importantly, given the language she uses to describe her deep passion for Heathcliff, she cannot help seeing this betrayal as a betrayal of her self as well.

With her unrealistic ideas of both childhood and adulthood, Cathy internalizes the betrayal of her innocence because she cannot deny that she *has* changed. Thus her two dreams focus upon her determination to keep her childhood self intact, just as they work to disguise her own complicity in leaving childhood behind her. When she dreams her way back to childhood during her illness, that dream expresses her sense of guilt and yet conceals its cause, for it erases the seven years of her adolescence and marriage and, one realizes in retrospect, the trauma for her of pregnancy. The fact of the pregnancy, along with the suppression of any reference to it in the novel until the birth of her daughter, is significant. It confirms what that dream tries to deny, that her body has been responsible for the radical alteration of her self. Because puberty, sexuality, and pregnancy are drastic bodily changes, Cathy willingly gives her body up to death, as this dream anticipates, because unencumbered by that agent of radical change she expects to regain her lost innocence. As she exclaims to Edgar, "What you touch at present, you may have; but my soul will be on that hilltop before you lay hands on me again" (p. 109). Her death, that is to say, will liberate what she considers her "true" self (her "soul," which belongs to Heathcliff) from the body given in marriage to Edgar; death will return her to "the heather on those hills," where she can be her original self once again.

Death, however, confirms Cathy's fear that maturity is an irreversible transformation. Death may return her to the hilltop but it does not repair her loss. To relocate her self, as she wants to do, somewhere in that hilltop area between the Heights and the Grange is actually to fall into the abyss she imagines in her dream. All along, this has been the implication of the competition between

The Paradigm of Experience

her own body's progressive drive to maturity and her imagination's regressive longing for childhood. Consequently, her ghost is still displaced, still in exile from the Heights and, most importantly, still not her self. The ghost that speaks to Lockwood at the opening of the book identifies herself as "Catherine Linton," not "Catherine Earnshaw" (p. 30). Death intensifies the horror Cathy feels at having lost not only her childhood innocence but also her original self. She *has* been altered by her maturity, so she cannot undo her past as she could in her dream.

The ghost's revelation should not be taken lightly. Lockwood calls our attention to it by wondering why, in his dreamy vision of this ghost, he should have unconsciously remembered the name "Linton" when he has read "Earnshaw" more often in Cathy's makeshift diary. This opening section of the novel, which reaches its climax in the vision of Cathy's lost self, establishes the importance of names to her sense of self in another context, too. Before her ghost appears to plead for reentry into Wuthering Heights, Lockwood reads what she has scrawled on the window ledge years before, her name "repeated in all kinds of characters, large and small—*Catherine Earnshaw*, here and there varied to *Catherine Heathcliff*, and then again to *Catherine Linton*" (p. 25). When she wrote these variations of her name, the adolescent Cathy was obviously daydreaming about marrying first Heathcliff, then Edgar. It is as if she were trying on different names to find the best identity for her self. The three names repeated and varied in large letters and small also reveal her unwillingness to choose one identity over the other. She would like to be all three Catherines, suggesting the fragmentation caused by her inability to accept the consequences of maturity. Then the plaintive cry of her ghost sounds to make us realize even before we learn her story that she did in fact make a choice in the end, no matter how she deplored or denied it, and it was an inevitable choice, epitomized by the name of her married adult self: Catherine Linton. Despite her efforts to equivocate and to divide her self, Cathy *has* matured. Her adult identity cannot be retracted even in death, since it still excludes her from the world of her childhood—the Heights—and still prevents her from regaining her original childhood identity—Catherine Earnshaw.

Chapter 1

The order of these names, too, records the process by which Cathy's loss of self comes about through a reversal of the forward movement typified by *Pride and Prejudice*. To Cathy's mind her experience leads her from wholeness to fragmentation. Using these three names we can chart her experience of self-loss like this:

Catherine Earnshaw	*Catherine Heathcliff*	*Catherine Linton*
complete self	fragmented self	lost self
childhood/sexual immaturity	adolescence/emerging sexuality	adulthood/sexual maturity
reality	reality vs. illusion	illusion

As Cathy remembers childhood it was a time of security and wholeness, when her self was most real to her because it was indistinguishable from the other; but from the perspective of an adult consciousness this unity turns out to be an illusion. Indeed, one is hard put to find her sense of childhood innocence realized at any point in her life. Though she later comes to see her childhood innocence symbolized in Heathcliff, his sudden appearance at the Heights when they are children actually begins to complicate her childhood. For one thing, Heathcliff's figure questions the innocence of childhood by showing the violence and brutality in the child's self-indulgent nature.[26] His joining the family, furthermore, disrupts the unity of Cathy's childhood self, since he challenges her domination of her father and since he makes her aware of his otherness: he is an invader of the family circle. At first Cathy minimizes this challenge by identifying with it. As she comes to love Heathcliff she links her self inextricably to his and arrests her idealization of him in time. But Heathcliff himself does not remain unchanged, so he further intensifies Cathy's awareness of the changes wrought in her by adolescence. Since adolescence separates them, he, not Edgar, triggers the crisis of her sexual awakening and helps her to see it not as a promise of expansion and fulfillment, but as the beginning of the disintegration of her self. Sexual awakening radically alters the temperament of their relationship; they are no longer carefree children roaming the heath and daydreaming at Penistone Crag or sharing the same bed. Heathcliff loves her sexually now, as his jealousy of Edgar shows, though their passion remains unconsummated. Having

The Paradigm of Experience

been educated in the values of the Grange world, Cathy accepts Hindley's degradation of Heathcliff as an impediment to their ever marrying, thus insuring the further frustration of their passion. Then, with her marriage to Edgar and Heathcliff's return, as "Catherine Linton" Cathy finds herself on the edge of that wide gulf she has created between her adult self and Heathcliff's. To make matters worse, he "possesses" her true self, and she seems unable to bridge the distance between them in order to retrieve it from him. "Catherine Linton" is but the shadow of her original self; in adulthood she already feels like a ghost. So to Cathy each stage of her growth, represented in the chart by her different names, seems disconnected from the others. As "Catherine Earnshaw" she feels most whole and real, whereas with Heathcliff or Edgar she feels incomplete, as if each man has usurped her true self, leaving her with nothing more than an illusion of being. Experiencing the man's otherness overwhelms her with a sense of violation; he seems to obliterate her. No wonder that she feels she has lost her self somewhere on the heath and is horrified to realize that she will never recover it, no matter how hard she tries.

These three names are no less of a clue to the book's second part, which addresses Cathy's anxiety by redirecting the regressive energy of her experience to envision the more familiar progressive movement of the self's journey towards maturity. Reading those names on the window ledge in reverse order, we can also see a record of the process by which the second Cathy eventually reaches her maturity with Hareton Earnshaw, regaining through their marriage her mother's maiden name as if to gain, as well, the complete self her mother envisioned in childhood. Here, with the names on the window ledge reversed, we now see the familiar paradigmatic movement:

Catherine Linton	*Catherine Heathcliff*	*Catherine Earnshaw*
innocent self	fragmented self	complete self
childhood/sexual immaturity	adolescence/emerging sexuality	adulthood/sexual maturity
illusion (the two worlds separated)	illusion vs. reality (the two worlds in conflict)	reality (the two worlds joined)

Chapter 1

In this respect the second half of the novel, which pivots around Heathcliff's entrapment of Cathy Linton at the Heights, corrects the sense of imbalance and disorder generated by the first half. The second Cathy succeeds in uniting the two worlds her mother saw in opposition. Through the unknowning agency of Heathcliff, who now changes from lover to ogre, this Cathy breaks away from the restrictions of her father. Edgar has unhealthily tried to preserve her childhood innocence by keeping her in the garden sanctuary of the Grange, ignorant of the world beyond, meaning Heathcliff and the Heights. Yet at the same time this Cathy can see the sadism in Heathcliff because she does not associate him with the idyllic longings of a remembered childhood, as her mother did. Whereas the first Cathy projects her innocent self onto "an unreclaimed creature, without refinement, without cultivation; an arid wilderness of furze and whinstone . . . a fierce, pitiless, wolfish man" (pp. 89-90), the second Cathy loves and marries a sniveling, weak-willed boy, more child than she, who exposes the inadequacies and limitations of childhood innocence. And where the first Cathy wanted both Edgar Linton and Heathcliff, her daughter ironically satisfies this wish in her marriage to a despicable boy who carries the names of both men. This marriage shows why the second Cathy must be exposed to the violent, passionate world of the Heights if she is to acquire an integrated adult self. Like her mother, Cathy Linton must be seduced into leaving the secure but incomplete world of her childhood in order to confront an unknown, seemingly alien world, one which brings out maturing needs that she has never before confronted. Her love for Linton, a travesty of adult feelings, indicates the danger of idealizing childhood—this child husband is unbearable and demanding, all self-indulgence—so Cathy becomes more conscious of her own childish naïveté while imprisoned at the Heights.

Because this Cathy can see the Grange and the Heights for what they are, not as projections of divisions within her self, she sustains a sense of psychic continuity that her mother could not. Her adolescence is thus an easier rite of passage. By regaining her mother's name, moreover, the second Cathy symbolically recovers the identity that the first Cathy felt she had lost. As a result, experiencing the other seems less frightening and overwhelming; the second Cathy comes to appreciate the man who at first seems most strange and alien to her, most different: Hareton. Once they marry, her home as a child—the Grange—will become her home as an adult, and her union with Hareton embodies the harmonious integration of the forces that her mother assumed were in fierce opposition. This marriage, like the Darcys', stands for an acceptance of adult reality: an acceptance of maturity and change; of instinct and sexuality; of reconciliation and compromise; of self and the other. In contrast to the mother's, the daughter's experience relieves the anxiety that the loss of innocence amounts to a loss of self too.

The growth measured by the two Cathys works out of a fear about the impact of maturity: the anxiety that experience produces a new self so radically different from the old that it is an alien self, achieved only by a betrayal of the old. I had this anxiety of self-loss in mind when I said earlier that *Wuthering Heights* in some ways is more representative of the English novel than is *Pride and Prejudice*. True, the genre typically achieves its conservative, stabilizing vision of the self's maturity much in the way Austen's novel does: by investing the reality beyond self with moral and social weight, and by directing the self towards that "beneficial" reality in a forward trajectory motion. The construction of experience in *Pride and Prejudice* works to deny credibility to Cathy Earnshaw's fear that maturity necessarily violates her innocence by rupturing her original feeling of unity with the other. Instead, the forward momentum of maturation belittles this fear: the altered self is actually a better version of the original, as Elizabeth happily learns. Viewed from its ending, *Wuthering Heights* works similarly. While this novel certainly recognizes Cathy's anguish, and respects it (a point I will return to in a moment), it also redirects her dreadful impression of maturation as a violation of self by leading a second Cathy to an enlightened—and less tumultuous—acceptance of maturity. The daughter in no way relieves the mother's anguish, but the doubling of their names does encourage us to see each Cathy as a variation of the same "self." As a result, *Wuthering Heights* records the devastating impact of experience upon one Cathy, but then moves beyond her to show another

Chapter 1

Cathy surviving the same trial. With Cathy Linton the novel tempers the anxiety generated by Cathy Earnshaw so that it can imagine maturity in a less threatening light than it originally does.

All the same, the second part of *Wuthering Heights* is problematic, to say the least, because it calls the first part into question, radically altering the value it initially places on Heathcliff's towering figure and arguing for a more sobering and "mature" perspective from which to evaluate the first Cathy's self-division. When viewed from this perspective, Cathy's dilemma may seem like a symptom of arrested development, an expression of "infantile" anger at realizing the difference between self and other, the difference which marks the beginning of an adult consciousness. Brantlinger, for example, goes so far as to claim that "*Wuthering Heights* has the quality of a temper tantrum rendered into poetry" (p. 22), just as Bersani argues that "the emotional register of the novel is that of hysterical children" (p. 203). I find it hard to disagree when I think about the novel as a whole (although I would hastily go on to add that the negative connotations of such descriptions are too strong and too patronizing of Cathy's dread) because it is difficult *not* to read the emotional content of the first part as a "regressive" display of "self-indulgence." The novel's valorization of an adult perception of reality, one based on the separation of self and other, is authorized by the second Cathy's marriage to Hareton and its location in the novel's conclusion.

Yet the conclusion is not entirely straightforward, since the novel also ends with its celebrated evocation of Cathy's ghost reunited with Heathcliff's. Therefore, readers who respond to the intense energies of the novel's first part in a highly positive light—who see Heathcliff's disruptive personality as a corrective to the restraints of civilization, for example—have to dismiss the impact and artistry of the second part because it seems to tame Heathcliff's romantic energies considerably to revalue them in the light of realism. "It's as if Emily Brontë were telling the same story twice," Bersani observes, "and eliminating its originality the second time" (p. 222). The famous and highly romanticized 1939 film version solved this "problem" simply by omitting the second part of the novel altogether. Criticism of *Wuthering Heights* has

The Paradigm of Experience

done much the same thing in its lack of interest in the second Cathy's importance as a counterweight to her mother's figure. Thomas Moser, for one, in an influential psychoanalytic reading of the novel as an expression of repressed instinct and desire, largely discounts the second part as a failure of nerve on Brontë's part, a concession to the reading public's taste for conventional domestic fiction.[27] Similarly, in their ingenious and provocative revisionist reading of the novel, Sandra M. Gilbert and Susan Gubar interpret it as a "parodic anti-Miltonic myth" of the Fall, in which a patriarchal culture conspires against woman by making the "Original Mother" (Cathy Earnshaw) illegitimate as an origin, in order "to exorcise the rebelliously Satanic, irrational, and 'female' representatives of nature."[28] I am not in disagreement with either reading, just as I am not entirely contesting Bersani's. Rather, my point is that such interpretations of *Wuthering Heights* can make their case only by emphasizing one side of the book's many dialectic tensions (nature vs. culture, romance vs. realism, isolation vs. community, the Heights vs. the Grange, consciousness vs. unconsciousness, age vs. youth, etc.) over the other, whereas Brontë's novel insists upon acknowledging the claims of each side in order to call attention to their interaction.

Admittedly, my own reading of *Wuthering Heights* may seem to privilege its second part as a controlling perspective for the first; but I am also not forgetting that Cathy Earnshaw focuses the emotional content of *both* parts so that we continually feel the dialectical tensions generated by her character. Cathy's anxiety, in other words, provides *Wuthering Heights* with its powerful emotional center; and the disruptive, regressive energy of this center, an intensified version of Elizabeth Bennet's moment of self-revision, accounts for the need to contain it through the progressive momentum by which the genre typically fashions experience as a journey into selfhood. In its double orchestration of progressive and regressive energies, *Wuthering Heights* therefore seems "eccentric" or "subversive," but only when placed next to the hierarchical arrangement of a novel like *Pride and Prejudice*. Then Brontë's novel truly seems not identical with itself, consisting as it does of two different novels—one written as romance, the other as

Chapter 1

realism—fighting each other's resolution. In this tension, however, *Wuthering Heights* only reflects the genre's dialectical operation. Although, as *Pride and Prejudice* shows, the genre constructs experience with the intention of leading characters towards health and insight, *Wuthering Heights* reveals that what motivates this direction in the first place is the need to contest the self's innocence by exposing it to an alien reality. So in voicing Cathy Earnshaw's anxiety that the loss of innocence is tantamount to a loss of self, *Wuthering Heights* is speaking for the entire genre. Built into the structural logic and value system of the genre's typical forward momentum, even in *Pride and Prejudice*, one can find reason enough to imagine Cathy's sense of dread. Experience as the genre repeatedly constructs it does seem to conspire against the innocence of the self; in short, the genre initially shows the innocent self to be the product of illusion and immaturity in order to justify the violation of its innocence and then to repair that violation by pushing the self forward in the direction of reality and maturation.

In the following chapters I will explore this paradigmatic operation in a series of novels ranging from *Clarissa* to *To the Lighthouse*. Before I bring this chapter to a close, however, one final point remains to be discussed. So far I have used as examples novels with female characters, concentrating on their sexual initiation to elicit the genre's paradigm of experience, which I am calling a pattern of violation and repair. This approach may therefore seem to imply that what will be analyzed in this book is in fact the genre's paradigm of a *heroine's* experience. And to be sure, there is some truth to this, since I will be looking at additional novels which focus on female characters. I am, moreover, well aware of the sexual connotations in my choice of a title. "Violation and repair" describe the perimeters of what Nancy Miller calls a "heroine's text." This is a novel which concentrates on a female protagonist and uses her seduction as "the determining event in the private history of a female self." According to Miller, the heroine's text revolves around a female character's sexual initiation—her fall from a culturally defined notion of innocence (virginity)—to uphold "a social contract that reads 'woman' as vulnerability." This type of fiction, Miller goes

The Paradigm of Experience

on to explain, originated in England with Defoe's *Moll Flanders* and Richardson's *Pamela* as well as his *Clarissa*, and it accounts for "one of the great traditions of the novel," namely, its fascination with a woman's sexual difference in an effort to construct her "otherness as sameness," either by imagining her tragic displacement and violation at the hands of the male world (Clarissa) or by allowing for her comic replacement and integration into that world (Moll and Pamela).[29]

In this light, my discussion of *Pride and Prejudice* and *Wuthering Heights* can be seen as extending the heroine's text and its perimeters of violation and repair into nineteenth-century fiction. But I am also going further, by assuming that the heroine's text belongs to the larger context of the genre as a whole, for I see the heroine's experience of violation and repair as an exemplar of the hero's. In saying that, however, I must also point out the obvious and significant difference between a heroine's violation and a hero's. No female character can say to a hero what Angel Clare says to Tess once he learns of her sexual history: "You were one person; now you are another."[30] The sexual initiation of a heroine—effected in a novel by marriage or by seduction or rape—is an undeniably powerful image of a transformation of the self through the agency of an indifferent other. One simply cannot think of an image quite as graphic or drastic in its implication of alteration for male characters: their names do not change with marriage, nor does their loss of virginity force upon them a radically different cultural identity. Whereas Cathy Earnshaw's self-division is epitomized by the changes in her name (recall her scribbling on the window ledge), Heathcliff's single name implies a totality and continuity of self which seems resistant to change, much to Cathy's envy.

Nonetheless, even though female characters like Cathy offer some of the most revealing, not to say disturbing, examples of violation and repair in the English novel, a similar pattern does underlie the genre's concern with the innocence of its male characters. If the heroine's text understands her fall from innocence in adult sexual terms (seduction or marriage), the hero's text imagines his fall in terms of unconscious oedipal desire, a pattern I will look at in detail when I turn to the Family

Chapter 1

Romance frame of the Waverley novels. But even this explanation will not tell the whole story. Many of the novels I will examine orchestrate their plots of violation and repair around both male and female characters, so that we cannot read her loss of innocence without considering his as well. Granted, the female other may not wield the same cultural power as her male counterpart, but as Heathcliff and Edgar discover of Cathy, she can seem just as alien, impenetrable, and indifferent to the male psyche as the male other seems to a female psyche. Indeed, the pressure to imagine female innocence results in the male's sense of violation: her loss mirrors his.

To paraphrase a famous line from *Women in Love*, every act of violation requires an aggressor as well as a victim. Lawrence's fiction dramatizes the battle between male and female as a contest over the sanctity of each other's selfhood, and a similar type of dynamic informs novels like *Clarissa, Bleak House,* and *Middlemarch*. Each of these novels constructs experience around a volatile sexual confrontation which exposes the inherent similarity of the male's and female's violation. The loss of innocence for each occurs through the discovery of an alien other sex, whose difference excites desire and resists it, just as it defines an adult consciousness by drawing a line between the self and the reality outside it. And, as those novels show, this realization of difference is as potentially horrifying for the male as it is for the female. Consequently, even though the hero's culture does not imagine his sexual consciousness as the corrupting physical displacement of innocence, his physical "invulnerability" cannot prevent him from experiencing his maturation as a violation of selfhood as profoundly disturbing in its impact upon him as it is upon a heroine.

The following chapters are organized and focused to bring out the continuity through which the English novel constructs experience, for heroes and heroines alike, in terms of this paradigm of violation and repair. Chapter 2 will consider three major eighteenth-century novels as orchestrations of this paradigm: *Clarissa, Tom Jones,* and *Tristram Shandy*. Though each of these novels voices and, in its own way, attempts to resolve the genre's insistence on lost innocence, I will concentrate on *Clarissa* and its two female characters because the construction of their

The Paradigm of Experience

experience as a contest between self and other most potently reveals the dialectical opposition of violation and repair in the genre. In Chapter 3, by contrast, I will turn from Richardson's heroines to the heroes of three Waverley novels—*Waverley, Old Mortality*, and *Rob Roy*—to demonstrate how Scott's fiction uses the familiar conventions of realism to manage the threat to innocence which makes experience so disruptive in its impact upon Richardson's characters. The Waverley novels superimpose a landscape of history upon the more confused, disturbing, and guilt-ridden landscape of oedipal desire, thereby containing the regressive energies of romance within a progressively directed realist pattern. I will pursue this line of approach further in Chapter 4, when I look at two Dickens novels—*Bleak House* and *Great Expectations*—to examine the central motivating force behind the construction of experience there, namely, Esther's and Pip's disturbing sensation that they are at once guilty and innocent. Like Richardson's and Scott's, Dickens's novels register the shocking reverberations sounded by the genre's insistence that the self must lose its innocence as the prelude to maturity. *Bleak House* projects the guilt which results onto the fictional world at large, while *Great Expectations* internalizes it within the protagonist Pip. His self-discovery clarifies and thus resolves the disturbing equation of victimized child and sexual adult that is more implicit, and thus much more highly problematic, in *Bleak House*.

In the next three chapters, then, I will examine constructions of experience which register competing progressive and regressive movements, and which organize experience around the anxiety generated when the genre's imperative to mature is envisioned as a necessary loss of innocence. In these chapters, too, I will show how each of the various novels under discussion strains, through its own construction of experience, to reenvision that initial violation as an act of repair. As a point of contrast, in Chapter 5 I will move on to George Eliot's *The Mill on the Floss* and *Middlemarch*. Although the former novel catches the same tensions of those other books, the latter novel seems to argue that no redress for a lost innocence is necessary, or even desirable. Controlled by a narrative voice which seems to espouse the virtue of achieving maturity as ordered by the paradigm in its most realistic coloration, *Middlemarch* insists upon a rigorous, if painful, disillusionment of the self in order to effect a full recognition of the other. But while this procedure seems not to equate maturity with any sort of violation, the novel's construction of experience is more complicated—and more in line with the other novels I will be discussing—than it appears on the surface, as a close analysis of the novel's climactic scenes will reveal.

Finally, in Chapter 6 I will look at several novels that delineate the genre's transition from realism to modernism—*Tess of the d'Urbervilles, Lord Jim, Women in Love* and, at greater length, *To the Lighthouse*. My concern here is to point out the similar origin of these novels in the genre's paradigm, and thus to account for their differences in the light of this continuity. Put most simply, whereas realistic fiction constructs experience by imposing the paradigm's progressive movement over its regressive energy, modernist fiction reverses that hierarchical arrangement, intensifying a longing for an innocence which it envisions as a primal memory of the self's original unity with the other. In one way or another, the novels I will examine in this chapter each push to extreme the regressive momentum of the paradigm. In doing so they valorize innocence yet also underscore its problematic attraction, revealing how a complete fusion of self and other—the innocence they strive to envision—actually results in the death of the self.

As this brief prospectus makes clear, I am especially interested in the ambivalence with which novels are built out of the genre's paradigm of experience, so throughout my discussion I will be remembering, if only implicitly, the particular example of *Wuthering Heights*, which insists that both violation and repair describe the impact of experience on the self. With this in mind it is more than fitting, when starting my examination of the English novel in earnest, that I turn to *Clarissa*. There the emblem of experience is the act of rape, an act which Richardson's narrative imagines in terms of a violation so profoundly shocking in its impact upon Clarissa that is seems to elude all possibility of repair in this life.

2
Clarissa

"I will wrap myself up in mine own innocence"

Since one of my points of concern in this book is to examine the English novel's continuity from realism to modernism in the light of its paradigm of violation and repair, Richardson's *Clarissa* is the obvious novel with which to begin. No other eighteenth-century novel raises so great a hue and cry over its heroine's violation, or strives so hard to imagine her repair, or makes her innocence so provocative that it can be attractive and disturbing at the same time, or predicts the complications in the paradigmatic operation of nineteenth-century fiction. *Clarissa* follows the paradigm in its insistence that repair cannot be imagined without some form of actual violation; it extends this premise throughout its long narrative by intensifying Clarissa's dread that the violation of her body is a violation of her self, and it then resolves this dread, at least as far as Clarissa is concerned, by imagining the restoration of her innocence in death. This narrative movement, which leads Clarissa out of innocence only to return her there, works in a manner similar to that in *Wuthering Heights*. However, because it has, in fact, *two* heroines, *Clarissa* also anticipates *Pride and Prejudice*. Set in counterpoint, Clarissa and Anna Howe direct the narrative so that it is simultaneously progressive and regressive in its momentum. Clarissa's sense of violation casts her maturation in terms similar

Chapter 2

to Cathy Earnshaw's feeling of self-loss, just as her death redirects what could otherwise be a progressive achievement of self-knowledge; at the same time, Anna's voice, as sane and socialized as Elizabeth Bennet's, rechannels the regressive energy generated by Clarissa's character as a progressive expression of maturity.

In order to begin identifying the tensions which motivate this double construction of experience, before examining *Clarissa* in detail it will be useful to place its preoccupation with lost innocence alongside some of the other major novels of its period which share that concern. The two novels which come immediately to mind in this context are Defoe's *Moll Flanders* and Richardson's own *Pamela*. Although *Moll Flanders* similarly orchestrates its narrative around a heroine's loss of innocence, we could not find a character more unlike Clarissa than Moll, who blithely takes her loss of innocence in stride. After being seduced by her first lover and then married off to his brother, Moll soon realizes that her tarnished virtue can be easily repaired by a skillful rearrangement of outward circumstances; this lesson, in turn, teaches her that innocence is a liability, perhaps even a falsehood, so her loss of innocence is hardly a violation. Richardson's *Pamela*, on the other hand, would seem to offer a more useful illustration of the paradigm, if only as a sort of rehearsal for *Clarissa*. But Pamela is simply the antithesis of Moll. For all B.'s efforts to corrupt Pamela's virtue in a fashion similar to Moll's first lover, her innocence proves unassailable; therefore, it is never an issue so much as the unvarying condition of Pamela's characterization. Seeming at first to examine the merits of her virtue, in the end the construction of experience in *Pamela* exempts her innocence from the kind of close scrutiny Clarissa's receives.

In their different responses to innocence, *Moll Flanders* and *Pamela* each offer incomplete versions of the paradigm: the former novel refutes the value of innocence, the latter novel refutes the threat of corruption, so each in its own way obscures the paradigmatic axis of violation and repair. Much the same can be said of Fielding's *Tom Jones* and Sterne's *Tristram Shandy*. Although both *Tom Jones* and *Tristram Shandy* follow the paradigm in a manner resembling *Clarissa*, neither novel shows the strain with which *Clarissa* at once reinforces and challenges the value of innocence. *Tom Jones*, in effect, imagines experience as repair, *Tristram Shandy* imagines it as violation, whereas *Clarissa* strains to imagine it as both violation and repair.

To be sure, *Tom Jones* would seem to be more straightforward in its application of the paradigm than *Clarissa*, and a less disturbing treatment of experience at that. Fielding makes much of the paradigmatic contest between illusion and reality, just as he patterns his narrative on the conceit of the self's journey. But here the self's experience of reality ends up respecting its own inherent innocence. Tom does not become reality's victim, though it seems, in delightfully comic fashion, that this may well be the case up until the time he is saved from execution. Immediately before then, incest is added to injury, so to speak, once Partridge has let slip to Tom the true identity of Mrs. Waters. When Mrs. Waters finally explains who Tom's parents really were, however, she reveals his origins to the world, proclaiming his innocence—of murder and incest—as well as his gentry status. With Tom exculpated of these charges, society sees him as a different person, Allworthy's heir instead of Jenny Jones's bastard, a young man whose inherent stature and innocence, whose moral and social worth, like his good looks and generous temper, all receive quick validation in the eyes of others. As Squire Western exclaims to Tom, "All past must be forgotten. I could not intend any Affront to thee, because, as *Allworthy* here knows, nay dost know it thyself, I took thee for another Person; and where a Body means no Harm, what signifies a hasty Word or two?"[1]

Despite the effort at generosity, Western's reasoning seems rather hypocritical and self-serving. Tom has in fact been waylaid by many "a hasty Word or two." But the discomfort behind Western's apology also serves as an index to the self's experience in this novel. Western cannot tolerate the thought that he has encountered different shadings of Tom's character: Tom as bastard, as comrade, as poacher, as murderer, as heir. Instead, the squire thinks each impression reflects a different "person," corresponding to the different responses in himself. Learning the identity of another self requires him to sift through the various impressions to arrive at the genuine one. With this accomplished,

Chapter 2

"All past must be forgotten," and Tom is welcomed back with open arms to the garden world of his origins.

One of the ironies of literary history is that so many generations of nineteenth-century readers found *Tom Jones* morally disturbing; actually this novel insists on human innocence as a fundamental truth of human experience. Being a satiric novelist Fielding exposes human imperfection, of course, but he restores in Somersetshire a world which reassures us that the transition from child to adult does not incur anguish. Maturity does not require the loss of innocence as the self is originally made to fear. Adults are merely large children, children little adults, so maturity is neither frightening nor disturbing in the growth it instigates. While Tom must learn through experience to temper his sexual drives, else he will not win Sophia, his adult personality, like his antagonist Blifil's, was already formed in childhood and obvious even then to anyone perspicuous enough to take notice.

That the past can be forgotten or erased once the right "person" is acknowledged in the eyes of the other minimizes almost beyond recognition the kinds of traumas Fielding exploits throughout his novel. Adolescence, with its disturbing psychosexual alteration of the self, does not complicate Tom's journey from childhood to adulthood, even though the book's plot seems to suggest otherwise. The complications that beset his fortunes suggest that Tom undergoes some kind of oedipal rite of passage from childhood to normal adult sexuality, for the two worst crimes he is accused of committing are parricide and incest: desiring his supposed father's death and sleeping with his mother. When the facts emerge to expose the reality behind misleading appearances, however, they undo this oedipal pattern, erasing it from Tom's past. He becomes "another Person," as Western says, yet he has been that very person all along. This son was wrongly expelled from home, and the parental figures welcome him back at novel's end with open arms and a revised will. According to this resolution, the novel's highly orchestrated plot is always taking Tom backwards to his childhood world after first removing it of its blemishes, namely, Blifil and his coterie of sexual hypocrites. Fielding therefore teases us with glimpses of the disruption that makes the passage to adulthood a bumpy journey, when he is actually reassuring us that in the final reckoning the journey's effect is negligible as far as the self's innocence is concerned. In this novel, sexuality, the body's announcement of childhood's end and the sign of the adult's fallen state, is an appetite, not a disturbing complex of guilt, desire, and egoism as it is in *Clarissa*.

Few English novelists share Fielding's sane, generous viewpoint about human sexuality. This is not the occasion to explain why, though we can assume that it is related to the English novel's strong ties, established with Richardson and solidified in the nineteenth century, to the Protestant middle-class culture which is the genre's subject and audience.[2] For the most part the English novel, in the light of its paradigmatic construction of experience, strives to retrieve Fielding's faith in innocence without having to sacrifice the paradigm's value system to do so. In other words, again and again the English novel reminds us that the self cannot sustain its innocence or avoid the other without sacrificing something essential, namely, its imperfect humanity. That in our humanity we are not innocent is the sobering underside of the paradigm's imperative to mature, and the reason for the tension between regressive and progressive energies in the genre's construction of experience. Through the paradigm the novel rehearses the loss of innocence and the anguish it occasions, as if the genre must continually reaffirm the basic premise behind its faith in the reality of otherness as the compensation for the self's inevitable loss of innocence.

That the loss of innocence cannot be repaired as easily as *Tom Jones* would have it is particularly evident in *Tristram Shandy*. Both novels look backward to childhood to authorize it as the source of sense-making norms. But whereas *Tom Jones* socializes the garden world of the father to insure that Tom's maturity be understood as an act of repair, *Tristram Shandy* finds in that very idyllic world a continual source of imaginative rupture and sexual impotence. The disasters that beset Walter and Uncle Toby prefigure Tristram's own traumatic experience as an adult: his isolation, his impotence, his incurable disease. His conception turns out to have been the first of many lasting bruises his fragile self must endure as it moves through time. Not the least of these bruises is shown in Walter's correct understanding, absurdly put as it is, that his son is born without benefit of the charms—the proper conception, the proper nose, the proper name—that can potentially ward off the damaging impact of reality. In the seemingly innocent, guileless world of Shandy Hall every day brings about a painful reminder to the characters of their violation by a reality hostile to the self's imaginative longing for the kind of world Fielding creates in *Tom Jones*.

Tristram's famous conception, more a miss than a hit as far as both Walter and his wife are concerned, encapsulates what adult experience means to the self in this novel. The frustration and pain of experience originate in the male's anxiety about his sexuality.[3] In terms of the paradigm, this world is fixated upon memories of childhood, so the energy of the maturing self cannot easily move forward to meet the other. Just the opposite is true of *Tom Jones*. Fielding sees no barriers obstructing the passageway between childhood and adulthood; he can imagine sexuality as a relatively harmless human appetite, perverted only when the hunger is repressed or concealed. No harm to the self occurs because of its sexuality. Tom survives his promiscuity with little guilt or damage, and though Sophia remains chaste until marriage to insure her culture's "proper" idea of womanhood, she too has an appetite, succumbing to Tom's charms before he desires her. Sterne, on the other hand, frustrates his characters' sexuality again and again to remind them of their traumatized existence. Experience in this novel wounds the self by challenging its comforting prepubescent memories of masculine comraderie and robust play. Without the hobby-horse, the self feels only frustration, unable to turn back, unable to move ahead, stuck in the middle of an incompleted action or sentence. The regressive momentum of the hobby-horse allows the self to form a protective seal over the phallic wound, but also directs it away from otherness, especially when the other takes the form of woman, as it does for Uncle Toby. His courtship of the Widow Wadman comically expresses his inability to function as a sexual adult male. Once he learns of the Widow's reason for asking to see where he was wounded, Toby makes a hasty retreat to Shandy Hall. Earlier, his brother has complained to his wife that if he marries the Widow Toby will unfortunately lose a certain freedom, which Walter pictures in characteristically absurd fashion. Toby, he explains, will "never . . . be able to lie *diagonally* in his bed again as long as he lives."[4] This is a great loss indeed, for Sterne's joke here, like all the phallic jokes in the novel, sounds a note too threatening in its reverberations for the male psyche to take lightly.

In *Tristram Shandy* desire traumatizes the male, since eros teases him with the promise of a penetration that cannot be completed because impotence and castration are ever-present threats, however comic or absurd their manifestations. Walter's own relations with his wife, for instance, obviate desire. His sexual penetration of her body is perfunctory and infrequent at best and, more importantly to him, he can never penetrate her mind to make her aware of his separateness as a self. The polarization of men and women in this novel, exacerbated by the pervasive—if comic—situations exposing the male's impotence, transforms that other sex into an alien other, one that resists the reassuring systems with which the hobby-horse satisfies the self's need to imagine its own innocence as an objective reality. The impotence of the characters underscores their isolation which, in turn, both exposes their frustration and tries to relieve it by sealing off the other altogether. Lying diagonally in bed is to sleep safely alone, whereas sleeping with the other sex violates the self's hermetic existence, forcing it to confront what it desperately wants to avoid: recognition of its wounded, impotent condition.

Even worse, because it is imagined throughout the novel as a continual wounding, experience in *Tristram Shandy* turns out to be a process of dying. So as composer of his own narrative the adult Tristram rides his hobby-horse back into the past, recreating in the pages of his text a memory, often of secondhand origin, evoking the childhood world he has lost. As a result, his narration "is digressive, and it is progressive too,—and at the same time."[5] The closer Tristram approaches death, the further backwards in time he travels, until he comes to the story of Uncle Toby's courtship of the Widow Wadman, which predates his birth. The innocence of childhood is an illusion Tristram would like to believe in as a reality. Yet his words, no less than his wounds, remind him that innocence is a lost state, achieved for his imagination only through memory and writing. But even then the very act of composition, which juxtaposes narrative time and writing time, story and discourse, exposes the breach between experience and memory to make him more conscious of loss as the inescapable norm of human existence. By contrast, Walter and Uncle Toby can survive more happily because they have each other as implicit ties to their childhood and because they have their hobby-horses to blunt consciousness by serving as a buffer between self and the traumatizing impact of reality. Tristram himself has lost the comfort of Shandy Hall and its playground—his father and uncle are both long dead—and writing, his own hobby-horse, merely aggravates his sense of impotence, forcing him to confront in any incompleted sentence, in every multivalent word, a self whose coherence is disrupted continually by its experience as either actor or writer.

Thus for Tristram, in stark contrast to Tom Jones, the identification of his origin promises continuity only by virtue of its having enacted the very first moment of violation—his being taken from the womb at birth—to instigate a sequence of successive violations unaffected by any kind of repair. In this respect Tristram's narration moves forward and backward, forward to tell his life story, backward to seek a moment that preexists his origin as the wounded, dying child of misfortune. Unhappily, however, even when he reestablishes his point of origin by narrating his conception, he cannot break that rhythm of violation; he can only find an earlier and quite similar point of origin. Tristram tries to imagine at least a moment of childhood innocence—if not at birth, then at conception—only to see actual experience erasing it so completely that no traces of its presence remain except in the imagination. While the imagination allows the self to construct the illusion of repair through the hobby-horse, it only exacerbates the impact of actual experience, because the hobby-horse (war games, philosophy, or writing) is just a competing illusory system located entirely in the self and thus indifferent to or irreconcilable with the other.

I have raised, as a prelude to looking at *Clarissa*, Fielding's and Sterne's constructions of experience around the desire for innocence because the anxiety about human sexuality and lost innocence in *Tristram Shandy* and *Tom Jones* gives a comic force to a similar dread of experience voiced by the characters in *Clarissa*, where sexuality also breaks down the self's hermetic existence once desire leads it to seek out the other. In all three novels sexuality epitomizes a special province of adulthood, that area of human life from which the child is excluded. Not surprisingly, as the paradigm moves characters from immaturity to maturity, their dread of becoming an adult hinges upon their apprehensions about sexuality as an experience opposed to their sense of being innocent. Since *Clarissa* pushes this apprehension to the point of hysteria, it is especially revealing of the tensions within the paradigm. Lovelace's violation of Clarissa's body forces her to discover her own sexuality, which she tries to deny because her culture has made her equate the self's purity with the body's. When envisioned at this extreme, not as a natural process but as the consequence of a rape, Clarissa's transformation into an adult woman seems an especially sudden act of violation, to both her body and her self. Yet her body is as much to blame in that it has been leading her out of childhood all along. The only way to arrest that movement is to ease the self out of the body altogether: hence Clarissa's death asserts her innocence, in effect arguing that her will did not suffer the same violation her body did.

No doubt the easiest way to describe the central experiential tension in *Clarissa* is to see Richardson's heroine willfully defying forces (family, society, lover) that would deny her economic, political, and emotional freedom. Most critics read the novel from this perspective, emphasizing, quite rightly, her stubbornness and independence rather than her virtue or her prudence.[6] "Upon my word," she writes to Anna, "I am sometimes tempted to think that we may make the world allow for us and respect us as we please, if we can but be sturdy in our wills, and set out accordingly."[7] Her self-assertion, when she opts for imprisonment and censure rather than marriage to "odious" Solmes, demonstrates to all who would read her letters the strength of her "sturdy" will, and it sets the narrative's paradigmatic construction into motion, by positioning Clarissa against the other—Lovelace, her family, her culture in general—as if the violation of her self were demanded as a consequence of her willful assertiveness.

Chapter 2

When Clarissa refuses Solmes on the grounds of "personal dislike," she in effect assumes that her family will acknowledge the integrity of her feelings. But the Harlowes, surprised by her resistance to their will, claim they have never seen "so mixed a character" as hers (1:272), presaging what Clarissa herself will later come to realize about Lovelace. Her predicament arises, then, because her feelings surprise her as much as they do her family. From the very first page her character is "mixed" in so far as she wants to remain within her family as their daughter and yet have Lovelace too; so for the first four hundred pages of the novel she will not choose one over the other. In attempting to appease the family she equivocally offers not to marry without their consent; to Lovelace she promises not to marry if she does not wed him.

Equivocation leads to rupture, however, not to containment, for her inability to choose reflects her self-division. Having fled the family, her later imprisonment in Mrs. Sinclair's house becomes, as Anna Howe puts it to her, "a trial between *you* and *yourself*."

> And what is the result of all I have written, but this? Either marry, my dear, or get from them all, and from him too.
> You intend the latter, you'll say, as soon as you have opportunity. That, as above hinted, I hope quickly to furnish you with: and then comes on a trial between *you* and *yourself*.
> These are the very fellows that we women do not *naturally* hate. We don't always know what is, and what is not, in our power to do. When some principal point we have had long in view becomes so critical, that we must of necessity choose or refuse, then perhaps we look about us; are affrighted at the wild and uncertain prospect before us; and after a few struggles and heartaches, reject the untried new; draw in our horns, and resolve to *snail* on, as we did before, in a track we are acquainted with. (2:318)

In her response to Anna's letter, Clarissa claims that she intends not to "*snail* on," but to discover instead what is in her power to do. "The trial," she writes back to Anna, "which you imagine will be so difficult to me, will not, I conceive, be upon getting from him, when the means to effect my escape are lent me; but how I shall behave when got from him; and if, like the Israelites of old, I shall be so weak as to wish to return to my Egyptian bondage" (2:345).

Clarissa

By "bondage" Clarissa means having to submit not only to the will of another but to her own desire as well. Defying her family and her culture by demanding the freedom to choose a husband, she opts for the uncertainties ("the untried new") that accompany freedom. In this she is very courageous—and very determined to find her own way in spite of the nets thrown before her path by Lovelace. But for all her claims of independence, of embracing "the untried new," Clarissa never forgets that she is James Harlowe's daughter. In running away with Lovelace to St. Albans, she is responding not to his seductive pressure, as he supposes, but to the tyranny of her family. During the first volume of the novel, her negotiations with the family, the imprisonment they impose upon her, the future they choose for her—these are always foremost in her thoughts. Then, once with Lovelace, Clarissa transfers the fear and anger previously directed against her family to the figure of her lover, coloring her rebellion with its sexual overtone. The force threatening to constrict her is no longer her family, whose motives she can understand and whom in the past she has been able to control, but Lovelace, who seems "wild and uncertain" and who forces Clarissa to collide with the "untried new," the alien otherness of a virile male sexuality which, given the asexual men in her family, she has never before confronted or expected; and that sexuality is exciting.

Another reason for Lovelace's volatile effect on Clarissa is that he forces her to internalize her experience, exacerbating her own sense of guilt for finding him attractive; that is the bondage with which he threatens her, as Anna and Clarissa both intuit. He embodies the alien otherness within her self—her own emerging sexuality—which repels her all the while it compels her, just as he does. Consequently, when Clarissa does strike out at "the untried new," she turns her "gaudy eye inward" and discovers "more *secret* pride and vanity than I could have thought had lain in my unexamined heart" (1:419-20). She confesses to Anna that she has now learned the necessity of subduing those passions arising from personal vanity and concludes that they both must "look into ourselves, and fear" (2:236). By these passions Clarissa means her sexual impulses, explaining why a man like Lovelace is not "naturally" hated and why Clarissa herself might not want to leave her "bondage." Clarissa miscomprehends such impulses and thinks them dangerous because she has no vocabulary for articulating them. She has mistrusted herself, she confesses to Anna, "having [had] no reason to apprehend danger from headstrong and disgraceful impulses" (2:262). Without a vocabulary to understand sexuality, those feelings are kept locked within the shadowy recesses of the "unexamined heart" and thought to be strange. "The man," one way Clarissa and Anna refer to Lovelace in their letters, takes on his powerful connotation of mysterious yet compelling sexual energy because the two women have no other way of suggesting their attraction (or "bondage") to him. Part of Clarissa therefore wants to remain the dutiful daughter because it is a less uncomfortable and more secure identity, whose familiarity does not openly confront "the headstrong and disgraceful impulses" that make sexual demands on an adult woman and yet are given neither expression nor recognition by any of the social roles available to a woman of her age and position.

Clarissa, then, quite clearly suspends its heroine in the moment of transition from daughter to woman, from sexual innocence to sexual maturity, and the narrative keeps her there for most of its duration, to prevent her from moving backward to a full state of innocence and to resist moving her forward to a full state of maturity. Because of this stalemate, *Clarissa* propels the maturing self into the kind of abyss Cathy Earnshaw discovers through her dreams. For Clarissa, too, family, friends, community—the sources of security for the child and later for the adult—fearfully, unexpectedly, even maliciously, it seems, betray the self by condemning it as a rebel for responding to the pressures of maturity. Much like *Wuthering Heights*, Richardson's novel originates in the anxiety that maturity, meaning here independence and individuation, subverts the self along with the social order. This explains the pervasive language of self-division and self-loss in Clarissa's letters, and the disturbing atmosphere of imprisonment and enclosure that beclouds her world.

In this regard, though she is seventeen when the novel opens and he in his twenties, emotionally speaking Clarissa and Lovelace are still adolescents. They center their lives around their turbulent emotions, writing letters and analyzing their feelings with a characteristically adolescent urgency. Being adolescents, Clarissa and Lovelace luxuriate in their sense of "the untried new," meaning the liberation they feel as emerging adults, yet they fear that society understands their maturation as a defiance of its authority. So while Lovelace goes to one extreme by advertising his rebellion, and Clarissa to the other by denying it, both use their letters to explore their sense of guilt and to rationalize it. While Clarissa and Lovelace want to mature, to achieve the kind of power and authority adults exert over them, they are scared to death—Clarissa literally so—of maturity. The adults in the novel, being foolish (like Lord M.), or greedy (like James), or impotent (like Mr. Harlowe and the uncles), confirm their dread rather than alleviate it. Like Cathy Earnshaw, Clarissa and Lovelace fear that maturity means not the complete and satisfying fulfillment of self but its social domination or moral condemnation.

As a consequence, despite all the apparatus of communication (and for all Lovelace's sexual bravado in the face of women), Clarissa and Lovelace remain frightened of actual communication. They stubbornly rely on confidants of the same sex and encourage their adolescent dread of each other's sexuality to avoid a more mature and complicated form of communication: that between adult men and women. Their letters, written to the moment, inform this fear with its oppressive sense of urgency.[8] The letters force the characters to experience the moment in all its incompletion by keeping them in a state of desire rather than fulfillment and by directing their attention always to the self. For the problem at hand when they write—"should I run away with Lovelace?" or "should I rape Clarissa?"—has yet to be realized at the moment of composition. The letters therefore place the characters in the midst of experience as process, rather than at the beginning or at the end. Clarissa seems to recognize this when she gives Anna the following explanation of why she writes:

> And indeed, my dear, I know not how to *forbear* writing. I have now no other employment or diversion. And I must write on, although I were not to send it to anybody. You have often heard me own the advantages I have found from writing down every thing of moment that befalls me; and of all I *think*, and of all I *do*,

Chapter 2

that may be of future use to me; for besides that this helps to form one to a style, and opens and expands the ductile mind; every one will find that many a good thought evaporates in thinking; many a good resolution goes off, driven out of memory perhaps by some other not so good. But when I set down what I *will* do, or what I *have* done, on this or that occasion, the resolution or action is before me either to be adhered to, withdrawn, or amended; and I have entered into *compact* with myself, as I may say, having given it under my own hand to *improve*, rather than to go *backward*, as I live longer. (2:128)

With these remarks in mind we can understand why Richardson keeps to his snail's pace throughout the novel. Clarissa and Lovelace, both want to stall the action as a means of advancing desire, to move backward *and* forward to preserve the self from the change that could end desire. While they rehearse the various alternatives available to them in their various predicaments, they control the suspended moment of choice; they retain the power to direct the closure of their experience because they can imagine closure taking so many different forms, none of which impinges upon their lives so long as it has not yet been actually experienced. In other words, they can project a variety of possible endings for a given situation to avoid a single determinate ending that may confirm their helplessness in the face of experience. This explains why marriage is so great a concern throughout this long novel: postponement of the end of maturation—marriage, with its disturbing sexual implication of lost innocence—epitomizes the self's desire for immunity from change. As Lovelace complains to Belford, his contest with Clarissa over marriage actually presses the issue "whether I am to have her in *my own way*, or in *hers*" (3:92).

Clarissa wants Lovelace to court her according to punctilio, even though Anna warns her that once she leaves her family, matters of form in their relationship will no longer be relevant. Despite her friend's repeated advice to marry Lovelace as soon as possible, Clarissa hesitates to name a day whenever he does propose, explaining that she does not wish to seem "as ready to accept his offer as if I were afraid *he never would repeat it*" (2:181). Such a demure response on her part seems inappropriate, for when Clarissa gives this reason Lovelace has just proposed for the fourth time. Why does Clarissa keep him at bay when marriage would seem to best suit her interests? This question is the crux of the novel. She and Anna agree that only during courtship can the female have any degree of power over the male. As Anna observes, the difficulty of the entire marriage business, which defines their lives as women in their culture, occurs because they are "courted as princesses for a few weeks, in order to be treated as slaves for the rest of our lives" (1:131). After the exchange of vows, that is to say, the woman must exchange her name and identity for her husband's, conforming to his wishes and losing her own personality in the process. That is the sad story of Clarissa's mother, which Anna refers to again and again. Clarissa's reliance on punctilio, her "overniceness," intends not only to preserve her virginal dignity, but also to extend indefinitely the liberating—if transitory—period of courtship, during which, she imagines, she can be herself in all her individuality and therefore occupy her own private space.

Like Clarissa and Anna, Lovelace would also prefer not to marry because of the permanence of both the act and its symbiotic emotional bond. "And determined to marry I would be," he complains to Belford right before the rape, "were it not for this consideration, that once married, and I am married for life" (3:181). He further strives, in his dealings with Clarissa, to break free of the constraints of courtship because he feels "soberized into awe and reverence" at the very sight of her (2:400); and because, as Anna knows, he doubts Clarissa's love of him, he wants to turn the tables around, to master her in the very act of taking her.

For both Clarissa and Lovelace the wooing is more at issue than the wedding. Yet the freedom of the wooing—the power over the other sex—is at once intoxicating and dreadful. If Clarissa makes Lovelace feel unsure of himself during his courting of her, he does the same to her: thus all their physical confrontations in the novel acquire an explosive quality. In the fire scene, Lovelace may plan to rape Clarissa, but when he sees her he cannot; before the rape can finally take place, he has to drug her so that she cannot respond to him personally. In one important scene before the rape, Mrs. Sinclair's girls tease Lovelace about his inability to seduce Clarissa, so he decides "to take *some liberties*, and, as *they* were received, to take *still greater*, and lay all the faults upon her *tyranny*" (2:375). He intends to treat Clarissa as he thinks the typical woman wants to be treated and then to place all blame for what happens on her shoulders. But he forgets that she is, in his words, a soberizing siren. Once she enters the room, he hesitates and loses all self-assurance. He does love and, in his own way, respect her; ironically, *her* strength of mind intimidates *him*. She enters "with an erect mien," and he can only conclude from her seemingly inviolate and intimidating presence, "this is an angel." When he then rails out at her, "You make me inconsistent with myself" (2:375), he means that she makes him feel shy and insecure, not rakish and cocky as he wants to be in order to terrify her into submission.

In scenes such as this one, Lovelace fearfully senses that Clarissa, though remaining impenetrable to him, has instead penetrated him to make him feel "inconsistent," or as he exclaims later, "drawn five or six ways at once" (2:460). Always more aware than Lovelace, Clarissa feels just as insecure, just as exposed, just as inconsistent, and just as confused and frightened by his otherness. When she starts to leave the room to close this scene, his courage returns, and the more she struggles, he explains to Belford, the more he desires her, so much so that "I could have devoured her." Before she can leave, he does manage to kiss her hand, "with a fervour, as if I would have left my lips upon it," suggesting his desire to fuse his self with hers in an attempt at possessing, even ingesting her otherness so as to make it an extension of his self. His aggression here frightens Clarissa all the more as another glaring instance of his "encroachments" upon her. She even reports later that her hand is still red from his violent kiss. "See you not how," she complains to Anna, "from step to step, he grows upon me?" (2:376-78). He "grows" upon her as if he were a sort of infection draining her energy or a demon usurping her self, challenging her identity by making it seem unstable and unpredictable.

Lovelace's need to "devour" Clarissa as fully as he can, either physically through the kiss or the rape, or psychically through the fictions he wants her to accept as reality, stems from his own sense of helplessness in the face of her strangeness: she does not act or feel like any woman he has ever known, and he cannot resist her or understand her power over him. Clarissa similarly reads him as something strange and alien, "a perfect Proteus" (2:82). When she looks at him intently with "an eye that penetrates all things" (2:223), she does so to pierce through the barrier of disguises and lies which he constructs to protect his self. Every time she comes into contact with him, however, he seems as impenetrable to her as she seems to him.[9] She can only admonish him, "Deep! deep! deep!" (2:51). His "deep" personality, stimulating her desire to penetrate it yet repelling her effort to do so, emphasizes for her the elusive, alien reality of his male sexuality. As a consequence she feels much as he does, able to be penetrated by the other but unable to penetrate it in return. Hence, too, the rhythm of confrontation and withdrawal whenever they come into contact prior to the ultimate confrontation of self and other—the rape— and the ultimate withdrawal—her death.

Since Lovelace only confounds rather than clarifies her identity as an adult woman, Clarissa sees his "deep" personality as the source of her confusion, projecting back onto his figure the disturbance she feels within. Only by such a projection can she imagine a continuous self. But even then she feels discontinuous. When she suspects that Lovelace has engineered her flight from Harlowe Place, she interprets his "vile premeditation" as "a snare to trick me out of myself" (2:47). In her letters, Clarissa frequently calls upon this image of self-loss, of being forced or "tricked" out of her self through his actions, to describe the agitating and contradictory emotions stimulated by her own reactions to him. Ultimately, this sensation of not being her true self, aggravated by her madness after the rape (when, significantly, she writes a short poem bidding farewell to her youth), pushes her back to the privacy of her writing closet where she can zealously guard against Lovelace's snares. Painfully susceptible to invasion by his otherness, the body means nothing, the self everything. Only with this kind of division can Clarissa make her claim, as she does toward the end of the novel, that her will, if not her body, remains inviolate.

One reason the will can remain inviolate is that the self cannot be fully penetrated. But if this is the case, then neither can the self be exculpated of blame. After reporting on that encounter with Lovelace (when he felt impelled to "devour" her), Clarissa concludes her letter with the observation that "*self* here, which is at the bottom of all we do, and of all we wish, is the grand misleader" (2:379). She can never fully understand herself, let alone Lovelace, because her behavior brings out dimensions of her consciousness—such as her love for Lovelace—that undermine her identity as the exemplar of daughterly virtue. In particular, as we have seen, her attraction to Lovelace stimulates feelings which cast her self in the new light of its adult sexuality, discrediting the motives and rupturing the stability of her identity as her father's virtuous daughter.

Because the letters emphasize the self's consciousness of its experience as a self, and because Clarissa, being daughter and woman at once, is always conscious of discontinuity, even before she is actually raped she reads her experience as moments of violation. "Intrusion," "encroachment," "interruption," "insult," these are the types of words she uses from the very start of her experience to describe the impact of others upon her consciousness. Such language, of course, implies that she is passive, that she receives rather than effects action because she wants to see herself as "a person out of her own direction" (1:345), not held responsible for what ensues. But remaining steadfast in the face of challenge is itself a form of action. Indeed, for all of her assertions of timidity and passivity, Clarissa is clearly more lion than lamb, and she knows this. Quite early in the novel she realizes that her family "have all an absolute dependence upon what they suppose to be a meekness in my temper." She then adds, with much ominous understatement given the two thousand pages to come, "But in this they may be mistaken" (1:37). Later, the language of self-division in her letters to Anna reflects the contest between meekness and strength. This division, she comes to learn, has led her into Lovelace's arms. To be sure, because the retrospective angle of the novel's epistolary narration gives Clarissa ample opportunity to review her experience, she has the capacity, in keeping with the paradigm, to discover a self very much like Elizabeth Bennet's, one misled into error by "prepossession and ignorance." But Clarissa's longing for innocence works against this kind of tempered self-consciousness. Whereas Elizabeth accepts her loss of innocence with grace, Clarissa cannot. When her strength and meekness are placed in opposition—with guilt and subversion on the one hand, innocence and obedience on the other—we can see why Clarissa cannot achieve the psychic growth which experience stimulates for Elizabeth.

Thus Clarissa equivocates, postpones, stalls, fences, all in an attempt to sustain a belief in her innocence. "When I have tried every expedient," she explains to Anna about the seemingly endless negotiations she undertakes with her family over Solmes, "I shall have the less to blame myself for, if anything unhappy should fall out" (1:141). But despite the care—and stubbornness—with which she establishes her claim to innocence, her elopement undoes all of her careful preparations, forcing her to accept her loss of innocence. "I have cleared *them* of blame," she confesses afterwards in a moment of severe self-incrimination, "and taken it all upon *myself!*" (1:487). Until the rape, her desire for familial reconciliation always takes precedence over her feelings for Lovelace, much to his chagrin, because reconciliation, she imagines, will help to reverse that disturbing, even fatal acknowledgment of blame.

The regressive-progressive momentum of the novel arises, then, because while experience moves Clarissa forward to discover that self is "the grand misleader," she tries to move backward, finally to restore her innocence through death, and the sentimentality of her death gives sanction to this restoration.[10] After Lovelace follows her to Hampstead, Clarissa exclaims, "I will wrap myself up in mine own innocence" (3:75). She repeats this intention when she writes to her uncle after the rape to defend herself against rumor: "Yet I think I may defy calumny itself, and (excepting the fatal, though involuntary, step of *April* 10) wrap myself in my own innocence, and be easy" (4:106). Clarissa orchestrates her death precisely to wrap her self in innocence, using her death, one cannot help suspecting, as a return to childhood. Like Cathy Earnshaw, Clarissa would like to erase her sexual history. As Nancy Miller remarks, "Death provides Clarissa with the security that she could never have in life: infallible protection against disruptive sexuality."[11] Her coffin

Chapter 2

marks her demise as April 10, the date of her flight, of her supposed liberation and independence from family oppression; but actually, as the letter from which I quoted above makes clear, that date marks her "fatal"—if "involuntary"—fall into sexuality. By contrast, heaven, to Clarissa as to Cathy, is a place of innocence, not guilt; of childhood, not adulthood; it is a world purified of all the difficulties and anxieties encountered during her experience in the novel. When Anna sees her dear friend's corpse she makes this view of heaven all too clear: "*Thou* art happy, I doubt not. . . . O may we meet, and rejoice together, where no villainous *Lovelaces*, no hard-hearted *relations*, will ever shock our innocence, or ruffle our felicity!" (4:403). No brutal lovers or oppressive parents inhabit heaven, so there can be no "shock" to the self's innocence, only unruffled "felicity."

Death, in other words, is the perfect fusion of self and other, "perfect" because it allows for a self without change or blemish; it is the only possible repair Clarissa can imagine for her violation, since to both her and Lovelace reparation means erasure of the discontinuity wrought by change. Lovelace presses for "the ceremony which would repair all" (3:399), but Clarissa refuses. To marry him after the rape would merely blur the horror of his act of violation; it would socially condone it. So instead she courts "another lover," in Lovelace's words to Hickman, whose "name, in short, is "DEATH!" (3:493-95), and this new "courtship" eases her sense of blame without minimizing her sense of having been violated. In dying as the repentant daughter, child of both Harlowe and God, she acts, the family complains, "as if she were innocent, we all in fault" (4:53). Once dead, she even exists in their memory as she did in her youth, as the personification of innocence itself, with "not one fault remembered" (4:467). Given Clarissa's desire for innocence, "DEATH!" is an irresistible lover indeed.

Taken on these terms, Clarissa's death can be read as a stubborn, immature, self-indulgent, even cowardly reaction to her violation. She refuses to face a sordid, imperfect, and adult reality by returning to her "father's house" (4:157), by recreating the security of her childhood at the Smith's, and by preparing, with a great deal of pious morbidity, for her own funeral. Such an unsympathetic reaction to Clarissa's death, however, misses the spirit of the novel, which uses her broken heart to provoke a powerful insight about the alien nature of human experience—alien because it challenges the self's insistence on its own innocence. Hence reality seems hostile to the inner life, resistant to it; yet, paradigmatically, the inner life is also tantamount to a world of illusion, as Lovelace, the grand fiction maker, testifies. Clarissa' death is therefore the supreme fusion of self with the other; then loss becomes gain, violation becomes triumph. But the tragedy behind this divine transformation (we should not forget that Clarissa, like Richardson, reads her life as a tragedy) is that it can only be achieved somewhere beyond the human, for Clarissa cannot assert herself successfully as an adult woman within her culture; she can, finally, wield power only as a dying angel wrapped up in the shroud of her innocence. Her death therefore epitomizes the sexual repression of her world, while exalting it as a value. Death seems, in fact, to turn a psychic fear into a social norm. This is not the case, however, because of the presence in the novel of Anna Howe.

Anna's function, first of all, is to insure our sympathetic response to Richardson's protagonists. She helps us to see why Clarissa and Lovelace are so attractive and so complicated that their world fails to understand them and cannot choose between them until the rape takes place. Anna always works to validate Clarissa's feelings: her sense of injustice at her family's oppression, her attraction to Lovelace, finally her abhorrence of him. Even more importantly, however, Anna's experience normalizes Clarissa's. She even seems to be aware of this function. "The result is this," she writes at the very onset of Clarissa's trials, "that I am fitter for *this* world than you; you for the *next* than me—that's the difference" (1:43).

All the while Clarissa is being abused and imprisoned, Anna experiences more socialized and much calmer kinds of human interaction—courtship, visits, balls, holidays, gossip. Certainly, Anna's refreshingly sane voice helps to modulate the hysteria generated by the self-involvement of Richardson's protagonists. As Clarissa analyzes her own feelings and examines clues of

Chapter 2

Lovelace's "deep" personality, Anna shrewdly reads between the lines of her friend's letters, analyzing what Clarissa reports with more distance and objectivity. She counterpoints Clarissa's high-minded seriousness with her own lively, ironic pragmatism, especially when it comes to the delicate matters of relations between men and women or parents and children. "To *demand* is not to *litigate*," she warns Clarissa, who obviously pays no attention to her friend's good advice (1:255). Using this principle herself, Anna is more successful than Clarissa in resisting the authority of parent and lover. She eventually gets her way, just as she eventually scores her points against anyone who gets in her way—her mother, her fiancé Hickman, Clarissa's sister, even Lovelace.

More mature than Clarissa, Anna has no qualms about thinking she knows better than the adults who try to govern her because she thinks of herself as an adult. In particular, Anna resents the social restrictions imposed on a woman by her culture, often using her letters to complain about the enforced dependency of a woman on a parent and then a husband. She is therefore aware of the sexual politics operating behind Clarissa's dealings with her family and Lovelace, and she cannot contain her anger at the denigration of women that results. So when Anna accepts Clarissa's reasons for not prosecuting Lovelace, she still argues that rape should be a capital offense, explaining:

> To this purpose the custom in the Isle of Man is a very good one.
> "If a single woman there prosecutes a single man for a rape, the ecclesiastical judges empanel a jury; and, if this jury find him guilty, he is returned *guilty* to the temporal courts: where, if he be convicted, the deemster, or judge, delivers to the woman a rope, a sword, and a ring; and she has it in her choice to have him hanged, beheaded, or to marry him."
> One of the two former, I think, should always be her option. (3:379)

Of anyone in *Clarissa* Anna has the clearest sense of self. Unlike Clarissa, Anna does not cling to the role of daughter and is not afraid of relationships beyond the family circle; nor, as her opinion on rape shows, does she feel guilty about asserting her sense of power as a woman or about expressing her anger at the fools and tyrants who denigrate women.

Aware of a woman's precarious situation in her culture, Anna takes seriously the question of marriage, refusing to commit herself to Hickman because she knows a woman's emotional and intellectual, not to say economic, freedom is at stake in the game of courtship. Like Clarissa, she prefers to remain single for as long as she can; but whereas for Clarissa not marrying is a compromise, for Anna it is a choice, a preferred way of life. "The suiting of the tempers of two persons who are to come together is a great matter," she writes; "and yet there should be boundaries fixed between them, by consent as it were, beyond which neither should go: and each should hold the other to it; or there would probably be encroachments in both. . . . would it not surprise you if I were to advance, that the persons of discretion are generally single? Such persons are apt to consider too much, to resolve. Are not you and I complimented as such? And would either of us marry if the fellows, and our friends, would let us alone?" (1:340-41). Actually, Anna does not have to "consider too much"—or at least not as much as Clarissa does; she acts more swiftly and directly because she is more attuned to her emotions. She knows that she does not love Hickman and that Lovelace is more attractive. She quickly realizes that Clarissa loves Lovelace, and chides her friend repeatedly for not admitting it. And until the rape she is more impatient than anyone else for negotiations between Clarissa and Lovelace to be resolved, since to her it is clearly a simple matter either of marrying him or leaving him.

Because Anna does act quickly and speak her mind, Richardson has to continually place circumstances between the two friends, sometimes quite clumsily, to keep Anna from rushing to Clarissa's side and acting for her. After Clarissa writes from London that she is still not certain about Lovelace's intentions, Anna replies that were she, "a girl of spirit as I am thought to be," in Clarissa's position, she would find out just what Lovelace intends to do in no more than fifteen minutes, which is "all the time I would allow to punctilio in such a case as yours" (2:156). As the reports of Lovelace's abusive behavior increase, Anna gets angrier and loses her patience: "But upon my word, were I to have been that moment in your situation, and been so treated, I would have torn his eyes out, and left it to his own heart, when I had done, to furnish the reason for it" (2:317). But Anna also knows that the hyperbolic solutions she has in mind are not proper forms of dispute, and society—especially where a single woman is concerned—demands subtle methods. After the rape, when she finally and nervously confronts Lovelace at the assembly ball, she confesses that she "could have killed him" then and there, but she composes her anger and goes to the door of the room, snapping her fan in Lovelace's face when he tries to follow (4:21-22).

The friendship between Anna and Clarissa mitigates the pressures each faces as a woman by shielding them from the aggression of the men and parents who control their lives. As Clarissa kisses Anna's portrait to say good-bye, she murmurs, *"Sweet and ever-amiable friend—companion—sister—lover!"* (4:340), as if this relationship with the same sex can expand beyond its ordinary emotional range to compensate for the feelings abused by the other sex—namely, her brother and her lover. Several times in the novel Anna even explicitly identifies with Clarissa. "You are me," she reminds Clarissa (1:43), and she obviously shares her friend's trials and depends on the integrity of their friendship as a source of comfort in a society that conspires against a woman's integrity. Ultimately, Anna expresses their intimacy as a kind of marriage, seeing Clarissa as "the true partner of my heart" (3:517).

Somewhat less consciously, Anna also identifies with Lovelace, who zealously demonstrates the kind of social freedom she would like to have, and whom she herself would like to have married if he were more moral and she were equal to his energy. Like Lovelace, Anna enjoys using outrageous rhetoric in her letters. The idiom of her style is very much like his, though her wit relies on irony more frequently and more playfully than his. Both characters theorize about love and marriage partly to engage in diatribes against tyrannical parents or guardians, who, they each say at different times, have "no bowels." Both like to fantasize about puncturing the pretensions and security of the people they do not respect. While Clarissa worries at length about marrying

Clarissa

Solmes or being taken to the moated house of her uncle, Anna jokingly imagines what Solmes, Lovelace, and Hickman were like as little boys:

> Solmes I have imagined to be a little sordid pilfering rogue, who would purloin from everybody, and beg every boy's bread and butter from him; while, as I have heard a reptile brag, he would in a winter morning spit upon his thumbs, and spread his own with it, that he might keep it all to himself.
>
> Hickman, a great overgrown, lank-haired, chubby boy, who would be hunched and punched by everybody; and go home with a finger in his eye, and tell his mother.
>
> While Lovelace I have supposed a curl-pated villain, full of fire, fancy, and mischief; an orchard-robber, a wall-climber, a horse-rider without saddle or bridle, neck or nothing: a sturdy rogue, in short, who would kick and cuff, and do no right, and take no wrong of anybody; would get his head broken, then a plaster for it or let it heal of itself; while he went on to do more mischief, and if not to get, to deserve, broken bones. And the same dispositions have grown up with them, and distinguished them as *men*, with no very material alteration.
>
> Only, that all men are monkeys more or less, or else that you and I should have such baboons as these to choose out of, is a mortifying thing, my dear. (1:244)

Anna's saucy view of men parallels Lovelace's view of women (and both confess that their cynicism about the other sex is the result of having been disillusioned by a first lover, in Anna's case a rake). "Men must not let us see that we can make fools of them," Anna reminds Clarissa (2:103); and she herself finds it difficult to respect men like Hickman, whom she can easily ridicule and dominate.

Thus, like Clarissa, Anna is attracted to Lovelace's sexuality and yet mistrustful of it at the same time. "I really believe," she confesses, "that could Hickman have kept my attention alive after the Lovelace manner, only that he had preserved his morals, I should have married the man by this time" (2:104). Indeed, she later confesses that Hickman is a second-best choice; he does not please her eye nor divert her ear, but then he does not "*disgust* the one nor *shock* the other" as Lovelace would. Rather wistfully she assumes that at least Lovelace will always keep up Clarissa's attention—"you will always be alive with him, though perhaps more from fear than hopes"—and observes that, given their different personalities, she should have been the one to have chosen Lovelace, and Clarissa, Hickman. But she also comes to realize that Hickman, though not as exciting a lover as Lovelace, will satisfactorily do for her because while she would have given Lovelace a run for his money, "heart-ache for heart-ache," he would have been too much for her to deal with in the long run: six months would have been all she could take (2:177-78).

Lovelace senses Anna's attraction to him and even claims that she loves him, although this declaration seems more a sign of his egoism than his insight. He boasts that he is the only man who can tame her feisty spirit: smugly, self-righteously, he daydreams about engineering a gang rape of Anna, her mother, and their maid. As if she could read his thoughts—or his letters—Anna begins to dream about him in terror after she learns that he has read her letters—or her thoughts—about him (3:385). When the rape makes her aware of the brutality and violence of Lovelace's sexuality, she slowly begins to see Hickman in a more favorable light. Through Clarissa, her alter-ego, Anna learns to appreciate both the vitality and the danger of a sexual man. Clarissa's relationship with Lovelace awakens Anna's own sexuality, but in an impersonal way, since she is an observer and commentator, not a direct participant.

I have discussed Anna at length because the abridgments of *Clarissa* tend to omit her letters, thereby stifling her voice. At the same time, I do not want to exaggerate Anna's rather obvious sexual identification with Clarissa and Lovelace, except to say that both characters externalize areas of Anna's self—namely her own sexual desire—which she must fear and only vicariously confront if she is to survive in her culture. Much of the sentiment and ordeal surrounding Clarissa's death transforms her funeral into a public celebration of the end of innocence. Clarissa must die in order to intensify the appeal of innocence and to dramatize the full force of its loss. If Clarissa's violation were truly reparable, the rape would lose its sense of being a violation in the first place. But although Anna witnesses her friend's profound loss, she also survives it, so she can embody a more mature self, the kind that succeeds adolescence by making an easy transition to adult life. Thus Richardson has Anna married happily to Hickman in the conclusion: she has learned to appreciate the shared intimacy of husband and wife. As the novel's normalizing voice, then, Anna resolves Clarissa's dread of experience. She, not Clarissa, reassures us that the self *can* be socialized without losing its vitality or entirety, even if normality means accepting second-best and being more for this world than the next one.

Anna's characterization—her wit and intelligence, her recognition that the self's integrity ultimately acquires its value and power through social expression rather than isolation—prepared the way for Jane Austen's heroines. Indeed, if we can see in Clarissa a predication of Cathy Earnshaw, then in Anna we can see the makings of Elizabeth Bennet. *Pride and Prejudice* imagines the kind of world and relationships Clarissa (and Cathy Earnshaw, too, for that matter) wants but cannot realize, and this potential for stability and continuity in adult experience is glimpsed in *Clarissa* through the personality and point of view of Anna Howe. What *Pride and Prejudice* typifies, in fact, is the stabilizing pattern with which the nineteenth-century novel came to re-read Clarissa's disturbing equation of self-discovery with self-loss through Anna Howe's penetrating eyes and normalized personality. Yet even more important than Austen to nineteenth-century fiction's effort to normalize Clarissa's dread of experience is Sir Walter Scott's series of historical novels. In these we will find a narrative pattern that transforms the self's violation into a process of repair without having to resort, as *Clarissa* does, to the erasure of experience by death in order to wrap the self in innocence.

3
The Waverley Novels

"Am I then a parricide?"

In *Clarissa* experience builds simultaneously from the energies of romance (the seduction plot, Clarissa's retreat to innocence) and realism (the psychological density of the characterization, the particularized social context, Anna's normalizing voice). A similar collaboration is evident in Sir Walter Scott's Waverley novels. These books orient their narratives around a male protagonist who undergoes a familial dislocation rather like Clarissa's. In his case, however, the conflict with authority centers political tensions in a longing for reconciliation with the father. This comparison notwithstanding, we must realize to start with what is obvious about Scott's fiction: his heroes lack the richness, complexity, and vitality of Richardson's characters, for they fear self-consciousness rather than rush towards it. One's attention when reading Scott always focuses more upon plot than character. To say the least, no one has ever lauded Scott for the originality of his heroic characters. More often than not he has been criticized for creating heroes seemingly drained of the volatile energies and passions (and humor, too) which he usually gives his villains.

Although the hero often seems prissy and shallow—too much the stiff young swain—the highly complicated plotting of a Waverley novel serves to dramatize the hero's disoriented psychic

Chapter 3

life by outlining it against the objective, impersonal backdrop of history. This context allows the narrative to voice the hero's anxiety about maturation because it uses history to displace that anxiety away from its origin in the self. The paradigmatic tensions in the Waverley novels are therefore developed through the plotting of historical conflicts that seem, at first glance, to be unconcerned with, even irrelevant to, the persistent feelings of guilt which, finally, account for the impact of history upon the hero.

The Waverley novels by and large work out of a single premise: an impressionable young man confronts a particular moment of crisis in British history to learn the virtue of accepting the present and forsaking the romantic call of a past order. The paradigmatic base of the novels provides experience with a measure of continuity that is all the more crucial for the hero to appreciate since his life is played out against the turbulence of impersonal historical forces that make sense only in retrospect. History offers the hero personal as well as civic instruction in the nature of selfhood. But while history rather than desire moves him paradigmatically from illusion to reality, the hero cannot evade desire altogether, for he experiences history as a field that seemingly engulfs him with his own unconscious desires. The hero's attraction to politically subversive figures, for instance, reveals his own radical impulses, just as his ultimate rejection of those figures serves as a public disclaimer of those impulses and an acceptance of the status quo, signaling that he has finally become, as Alexander Welsh puts it, "an ideal *member* of society."[1]

Of even more importance in the novels is the way familial tensions repeatedly mirror political tensions, and vice versa. That the hero's complicity in a subversive cause coincides with his effort to define a self apart from his parent makes him dread the consequences of maturation; the coincidence forcibly, if unexpectedly, validates his apprehensions about the guilt that results from decisive, independent action. Too, since the hero's father, like his king, unhappily stands in the way of self-definition, he turns to substitute parents—pretenders to the home as well as the throne—as he experiments with different political loyalties, and hence with variations of his identity, to satisfy his desire for liberation without diminishing his passive, guiltless self-image.

The Waverley Novels

In essence, the Waverley novels translate the regressive momentum of romance into the progressive momentum of realism, all the while sustaining these two modes in an alliance so that the movements occur concurrently. On the one hand, Scott's novels argue credibly for the value system of realism, as critics like Welsh and Levine recognize. The hero defines an identity that takes stock of forces larger and more important than the self and its desires. As Welsh observes, with, I think, the Waverley novels particularly in mind, "Historical realism in the nineteenth century makes much of the crisis of identity but argues ethically that personal identity is defined by the community of which the hero is a part: hence the hero's identity will be secured by history."[2] On the other hand, the novels also evoke a more intangible, self-centered landscape of desire. History "secures" the hero's identity only after taking him on a personal journey that encourages him to explore his identity through doubles and parental surrogates in a fictional world that now calls to mind the logic of myth, folk tales, and romance.[3]

In particular, I want to argue, the Waverley novels manipulate history so as to structure experience for the hero along the lines of the psychological narrative Freud called the Family Romance.[4] The two types of landscapes evoked by these novels—that of history (realism) and that of desire (romance)—are in fact not incompatible, for Scott socializes the psychological drama enacted through the Family Romance story. With this accomplished, history can then ably serve the hero as an arena in which he, the son, liberates himself from his father's insistence that he remain a son because, as a royal subject if disloyal child, he finally remains obedient to the will of the king and the laws of the state. Only then can the paradigmatic movement be completed without incurring the anxiety and guilt that the narratives toy with in their construction. The interplay of romance and realism, in other words, allows the hero to rebel against the stifling inhibitions of authority, familial or political, without his becoming an actual criminal in the process.

To begin with, as a frame for analyzing the construction of experience in the Waverley novels, the Family Romance is particularly revealing of the tensions that motivate Scott's recurrent plots about naive young men whose maturation occurs during a historical crisis. According to Freud, the Family Romance tells a story that symbolizes "the liberation of an individual, as he grows up, from the authority of his parents."[5] Either in its primary (a child's actual daydream fantasy) or secondary (myth, folk tale, romance) manifestation, the Family Romance plays out ambivalent feelings about parental authority through the motif of illegitimacy. In the Family Romance daydream, the child starts to define himself in conscious opposition to his parents; but since this conflict troubles him with its implications of defiance, he imagines a new set of parents to create a new familial context for his identity. The Romance fantasy therefore allows him to displace the more disturbing antagonism he feels towards his actual parents. Fantasies of being illegitimate call into question a parent's right to wield authority because they make the parent's legal "ownership" of the child dubious. To obscure the child's sense of origins and secure his innocence, Family Romances cast non-familial figures—usually more powerful, exalted ones, such as kings, queens, fairy godparents, and the like—as ideal substitutes for real parents; or they idealize the real parents by making them absent and replacing them with more blatantly oppressive familial figures, such as wicked step-parents or jealous siblings. In the first situation the child is a sort of bastard who yearns for parental recognition (to suggest his desire for parental approval); in the second he is a sort of foundling who suffers under the abusive guardianship of a false parent (to suggest his distrust of parental authority). On the surface, either fantasy situation may seem tantamount to rejection or condemnation of the parent, though more often than not it is the other way around, the child giving voice to his fear of parental rejection or condemnation by turning the family relationship inside out as a defense. In fact, Freud insisted that "the child is not getting rid of his father but exalting him" through this re-creation of familial origins. "Indeed the whole effort at replacing the real father by a superior one is only an expression of the child's longing for the happy, vanished days when his father seemed to him the noblest and strongest of men and his mother the dearest and loveliest of women."[6]

Two interrelated psychological themes are evident here. First, the child blames his parents for his discovery of a reality indifferent to his desire, and he compensates for this discovery by imagining a new set of parents. Second, for the child to define his own identity—and the creation of a new familial origin is nothing more than an attempt to imagine a self independent of parentage—he must start to conceive of his psychic life apart from his parents. Not surprisingly, a confusion of guilt and desire underlies the Family Romance, as is clear in the most famous version of the story, the Oedipus myth. In the Family Romance, then, the child imaginatively compensates for his discomforting exposure not only to reality (his parents' own very human imperfections) but to his own maturing (and just as human) desires as well.

Freud explained the psychological significance of Family Romances by claiming, with reference to their ultimate oedipal tensions, that they "serve as the fulfillment of wishes and as a correction of actual life. They have two principal aims, an erotic and an ambitious one—though an erotic aim is usually concealed behind the latter too."[7] The child's maturing psyche makes him aware of desires that seem illicit because they threaten his securely determined role of child within the family. By challenging the identity of his parents while expressing his own ambitious and erotic drives, the child can then challenge the right of his parents, as personifications of authority, to oppress those drives. Furthermore, the Romance daydream defends the child against the conscious realization that he *wants* liberation from his parents. He desires to be independent, to be more than his parents' child, so he imagines himself as the child of other parents to avoid realizing what he knows unconsciously: that liberation means, finally, he can no longer be anyone's child in the sense that he has always understood childhood. Consequently, since the child's own maturing psyche disrupts his identity as a child, he projects the cause of that disruption onto his parents by obscuring their identities and by making them the disrupters of the family order. This imaginative reconstruction of his psychic life allows him to preserve faith in his own inherent innocence. Or as Marthe Robert puts it, "the subtle displacement that results" from the Family Romance substitutions of parental authority "enables the child to resolve, at least in his imagination the otherwise insoluble problem of growing up while still remaining a child."[8]

The Family Romance is arguably one source of the novel's paradigmatic construction of experience as a contest between romance and realism. In declaring of the Romance story that "it is the genre," Robert goes on to delineate two separate novelistic transformations, one centering around the Foundling or child-dreamer, and based on Don Quixote, the other centering around the Bastard or child-rebel, and based on Robinson Crusoe. "There are but two ways of writing a novel," she explains: "the way of the realistic Bastard who backs the world while fighting it head on; and the way of the Foundling who, lacking both the experience and the means to fight, avoids confrontation by flight or rejection." These two figures, she insists, the realist and the romancer, though born out of the same psychological dynamic, make for different novels. "Generally speaking each novelist is compelled nonetheless to be either for reality (when the oedipal Bastard predominates); or (when the Foundling has the upper hand) to deliberately create another world—which amounts to being against reality."[9]

I do not think the Foundling and Bastard can be so neatly distinguished as originators of two different types of novels, for that thinking ultimately leads us back to seeing romance and realism as two distinct genres. The Bastard and the Foundling are fundamentally alike in that both are abandoned children, and the similarity is important to the novel's use of the Family Romance. Clarissa, for instance, can be called a Foundling in her self-image as abused, deserted daughter, as well as in her fear of confrontation and in the creation of her own Family Romance story through her death, when she replaces her real father with God in order to reconcile self with its original, most primal parent. Yet there is unmistakably just as much of the Bastard in her too, since her world makes her a rebel because of her stubborn, audacious determination to steer her own way out of the turbulence caused whenever she acts upon her desires. Given her lamb-like submission to the will of authority and her leonine anger at its oppression, one could perhaps conclude that she is a Bastard in a Foundling's gown; but that designation would still mean that her figure draws on both. In this duality Clarissa is a conventional novelistic figure.

The resonance of the Bastard-Foundling dichotomy in the novel genre, I want to emphasize, emerges from its instability. Like romance and realism, one category is defined by its not being the other, so they must coexist in some sort of dialectic engagement to reflect the anxiety caused by an inability to fix innocence as a determinate, constant attribute of the self. It is therefore necessary, when sensing traces of the Family Romance in the novel, to appreciate the child figure's potential for being both Foundling and Bastard, like Clarissa at once naive and wise to desire, at once innocent and guilty of responsibility for her action. This is why the novel can so easily recast the child of the Family Romance as a young adult whose maturation is not yet complete. No longer an actual child, the character's adolescent personality now captures the anxiety of finding herself caught between two securely fixed identities—child and adult. The genre's paradigm of experience therefore builds upon the Family Romance, but in doing so it becomes much more than that story. The paradigm instigates its regressive movement by working backwards to retell the child's Family Romance, but since this retelling is now aligned to the child's achievements of maturity and socialization, the paradigm instigates its progressive momentum as a counterforce.

We can clearly see this procedure operating in the Waverley novels when Scott literalizes the Family Romance by involving the hero in an actual rebellion. Because the Waverley hero becomes, unwittingly or not, an accomplice in a political conspiracy against his king, the social parent, his experience can allow him to enact rebellious impulses without fully acknowledging their source in his own oedipal conflict with the father. The Waverley hero therefore is also both a Foundling and Bastard, much to his discomfort since he needs to believe in his own innocence. His education in history resolves this anxiety by teaching him to understand the concrete personification of authority (the parent) as a less threatening abstraction (the state), and it can do so only by redirecting his oedipal attention from parent to king, from son to subject. This lesson defuses the impact of his defiance of authority in either form. The hero can then achieve the kind of self-knowledge which Elizabeth Bennet gains without feeling the kind of self-loss which traumatizes Cathy Earnshaw upon her realization that she is no longer a child. Put in broader terms, history disguises the regressive energy of romance in the Waverley novels to generate in its place what we recognize as the progressive energy of realism; and yet, all along, the imaginative operation behind that realistic program is in fact the displacement activity of the Family Romance.

To explore this operation in more detail, I want to look at three of the best known and certainly most representative works in Scott's series of historical novels: *Waverley, Old Mortality*, and *Rob Roy*.[10] For the purpose of clarifying the full extent of the paradigm as it builds upon the Romance story in Scott's fiction, however, I am not going to discuss the last two novels in the order in which they were written. Instead I want to direct my discussion towards *Old Mortality*, which exemplifies Scott's most persuasive realistic construction of experience through the displacement of desire and which consequently seems the least romantic in texture of the three novels. To be sure, my argument about Scott could well be construed as a reading of the Waverley novels as informed by a reading of *Old Mortality* in particular, and in fact that has been the case. Nonetheless, I will begin with works from the series that make the displacement of desire somewhat more obvious and problematic than it is in *Old Mortality*. *Waverley*, the first in the series, is the logical novel to start with since it establishes quite explicitly the dread of parricide that is implicit in the other novels. *Rob Roy* is an unusual Waverley novel because it allows the hero to tell his own story; and while it may seem somewhat more concerned with property than with history, reflecting its narrator's own preoccupations, this version of the Family Romance further reveals the imaginative logic behind Scott's program in general, his subordination of the hero's struggle for psychic independence to the impersonal movement of history as it strives to conserve relations between a citizen and his state. With this context established, it can be more clearly shown how *Old Mortality* brings together these concerns in a realistic narrative that seems to leave behind its origin in the Family Romance.

Edward Waverley, the first of Scott's heroes and the prototype of all those to follow, is a quixotic daydreamer. Ignored by his father, spoiled by his uncle, Edward is egocentric and unsocialized, indifferent to everything around him except books, which he never even finishes, and his uncle's romantic tales of the Jacobites, which provide a content for his daydreams. Edward's initial attraction to the Jacobites occurs because the Highland world resembles his daydreams. Following the example of *Don Quixote*, Scott satirizes Edward's imagination to expose his hero's immaturity. Edward will come to see his self with greater acuity once he enters a volatile environment—the politically unstable Highlands—that first appears to make his daydreams real. With wonder and excitement he believes that he has, finally, left behind his dull, commonplace, and very English world and has "actually" entered "the land of military and romantic adventures," where, as in his daydreams, "deeds of violence should be familiar to men's minds, and currently talked of, as falling within the common order of things, and happening daily in the immediate vicinity" (pp. 148-49). True to convention, Edward therefore arrives in Scotland expecting romance but ultimately discovers instead "the end of my day-dream" (p. 313).

More to the point, Edward's quixotry brings closer to consciousness a self whose desires surprise him. From the very beginning of the novel his "wavering and unsettled habit of mind" (p. 98) has made him inattentive—at times downright oblivious—to what is going on around him, so his own indecisive and flighty character leads him to participate in "the civil crime . . . of high treason, and levying war against the king, the highest delinquency of which a subject can be guilty" (p. 250). Thus his journey from civilized England, where "every thing was done according to an equal law that protected all who were harmless and innocent" (p. 230), to the wild and lawless Highlands educates him in the importance of laws—of the social order—by revealing his own capacity for lawlessness. Once embroiled in the

Chapter 3

Jacobite cause, he is accused of treason by the English, a charge epitomizing the subversion of the very laws he believes in. Furthermore, that the state charges him with "the highest delinquency of which a subject can be guilty" suggests that treason against the social parent may not be too far removed in its psychic force from treason against an actual parent.

This implication becomes even more striking as Edward's complicity with the Jacobites intensifies. Discovering the consequences of his irresponsible behavior, he learns with a shock that his own "indolence and indecision of mind" have caused people close to him to suffer "misery and mischief" (p. 328). In this important scene, Edward is dressed, somewhat absurdly, in picturesque Highland costume, as if to enact his daydreams. But as he begins to look around the Jacobite army, he realizes the serious implications of his position and suddenly "wished to awake from what seemed at the moment a dream, strange, horrible, and unnatural." At that moment he sees his English commander, now his enemy, about to be murdered by a Jacobite. Horrified, he "felt as if he was about to see a parricide committed in his presence" (p. 331). That he imagines his guilt as an act of parricide is not accidental: later, when he learns of his father's death and uncle's imprisonment and feels responsible for their fates, he wonders once again, "am I then a parricide?—Impossible!" (p. 408). Edward can reject this "unnatural" thought by reasoning that his indifferent father, so often absent from home, could not have been mortally affected by the knowledge that his son has been accused of treason. But when he remembers that his association with the Jacobites has also put his uncle's life in jeopardy, Edward blames himself for an action, "if possible, worse than parricide" (p. 408). All of this makes clear that Edward has begun to find his own way, leaving his family behind him in order to explore his romantic sensibility through Fergus and the Jacobites. When he sees this rejection of parental figures—his actual father, his beloved uncle, his English commander—as acts of parricide, his anxiety suggests the ambivalence he feels about acting decisively on his own.

To be sure, Edward's need to rebel against parental authority is not without justification. Richard Waverley has been an

The Waverley Novels

inadequate father, ignoring his son. So, much like the child in the Family Romance, Edward responds to all the other male characters in the novel by making each a replacement for this absent father, as a way of postponing adult action on his own part. Because he does not consciously want to undermine a father's authority, he moves to other father figures—his uncle, his commander, the Baron, Fergus, and Colonel Talbot—until he finds one who will approve of his wish to act independently without making him feel guilty of parricide.

Edward finally reaches maturity by way of these father figures, so that a regressive movement (the orchestration of various child-parent relationships) underscores the more obvious progressive movement (his disenchantment and maturity). While each father represents an incomplete model of an adult identity, each nonetheless tells Edward something about the importance to him of adult power. This sort of relationship with the other male characters allows Edward to encounter alternate images of his self in the guise of the other. Edward's actual father, first of all, makes the regressive journey necessary because he has been an indifferent parent. This father, moreover, though faithful to the Whig government, lacks imagination. He respects the immediacy of a political moment but cannot inform his attitude with ideals from the past. Later, his fall from political power confirms that his view lacks historical continuity. Whereas Richard Waverley is a loyal servant to the state, Edward's uncle, like the Baron, has rebelled against the government in the past. This parent can grasp romantic ideals but not act practically. Thus once in Scotland Waverley easily forgets his father and uncle and becomes enamored of Fergus, who reaches back to the Jacobite past to act according to a set of romantic ideals that seemingly project continuity.[11] Waverley finds in Fergus an instance of an adult man who has succeeded his father and is responsible for his own actions. But Fergus's love of power corrupts his romantic loyalty to the Stuarts and emphasizes the egoism behind his subversive position.

Colonel Talbot, on the other hand, represents a more socialized example of maturity for Edward and ultimately provides the model Edward follows. Though Talbot respects the past, he knows the value of the political present. "Colonel Talbot was in every point the English soldier. His whole soul was devoted to the service of his king and country." These strong points in "the character of Colonel Talbot dawned upon Edward by degrees" (p. 360), paralleling the same slow pace with which Edward falls in love with the proper heroine, Rose, and takes her away from Fergus. Yet even with Talbot Edward feels unmerited self-recrimination. When he learns that Talbot's infant child died at birth and that Mrs. Talbot has fallen ill because her husband left her to rescue him from the Jacobites, who, in turn, have made Talbot a prisoner, Edward immediately blames himself. For all his anxieties about parricide, Edward fails to realize that he has in fact reversed this haunting fantasy, having saved the life of his most fitting father when Talbot was captured by the Jacobite army. Furthermore, when Waverley returns to Scotland he uses the passport and identity of Talbot's favorite nephew, a disguise which emphasizes the colonel's parental role and the new, more independent identity Edward has begun to create. Indeed, after inheriting his father's estate Edward sells it to Talbot, thereby acknowledging Talbot as the final replacement for his real father.

In *Waverley* the hero has enough father figures to give him the luxury of committing acts of parricide in thought but not action, so he never has to see himself consciously as a heinous criminal. His relationships with these men thus serve as the main index to his maturation because they dramatize the process of self-definition which he undergoes as his preparation for adulthood. In working out his resistance to parental figures of authority created in response to his absent father, Edward comes to accept an institutionalized figure of authority: society. Paradigmatically, his daydreaming, which encourages him to see reality as a projection of desire, brings him to consciousness so that he can learn to distinguish between desire and reality, self and other. At the same time, we can see in his education an unconscious process which leads him to respond to adults as surrogate versions of himself. Ultimately, this displacement liberates him from a reliance on *parental* models as his means of self-definition. Only then can he conceive of himself as an adult rather than as a son without having to commit parricide to effect his liberation.

The Waverley Novels

Another way that the Waverley novels rely on the Family Romance story, concentrating on the hero's disturbing equation of maturity with parricide, is through the books' concern with property. This provides a second important link between parent and society as symbols of authority for the hero. As Francis R. Hart argues, Scott seemed to realize that "his imagination was essentially topographical; that its true 'engine' was less a sense of history than a sense of *place*; that a house would serve most naturally as the symbolic focus for many of his narratives."[12] The dramatization of British history in the Waverley novels readily serves as a macrocosmic image of the family, with the conflict of rulers and subjects over the kingdom—the idea of the nation— becoming an analogy to the domestic conflict of fathers and sons over actual property. Property, the economic base of both the hero's society and his family, also raises a discomfiting relationship between a son and his father. The acquisition of property validates the son's maturation, but because property can only be possessed upon the father's death, succession implies parricide. The hero's dilemma, his precarious attraction to a politically subversive cause, therefore generates—if not directly, then indirectly—from a crisis over the rightful possession of an estate. Like so many other English novels—*Clarissa, Tom Jones, Wuthering Heights, Bleak House, Middlemarch, Howards End*—the Waverley novels continually raise the question of who in the family has the moral, not to say legal, right to property. Underlying Scott's concern in this instance is the royalist myth. Since the monarchical structure of British government sees the king as a father to his subjects, any crime against the state acquires the psychic force of parricide. In a Waverley novel this myth serves to heighten the unsettling resonance of the domestic conflict, making the son's right to inherit social status through property the central issue.

Rob Roy typifies what property means in the Waverley novels and how it provides a locus of energy for the Family Romance story. Frank Osbaldistone's bourgeois father has been disinherited in favor of his younger, more gentlemanly brother, Sir Hildebrand. This original disinheritance repeats itself in Frank's own disobedience and fear of being disowned in favor of Sir

Hildebrand's youngest son, Rashleigh. Rashleigh continually plots to make Frank appear guilty of treason and to exacerbate the estrangement between Frank and Mr. Osbaldistone. Even though Frank repeatedly professes his innocence, the charges of treason suggest the guilt he feels in having initially defied the wishes of "a kind, though not a fond father" (p. 8). Furious at his son's refusal to enter his business, Mr. Osbaldistone has warned Frank that Sir Hildebrand "has children . . . and one of them shall be my son if you cross me farther in this matter" (p. 19). Frank cannot escape his fear that one of his cousins, most likely Rashleigh, will assume the only identity he has ever known: his father's son. This hero discovers that he too may be a Bastard as well as a Foundling.

By rights Frank should not feel guilty for standing up to his father, for he is merely repeating the latter's own youthful act of self-assertion. Like his father before him, Frank wants to choose his own adult identity, in this case to be a poet, not a tradesman, a member of the gentry, not the middle class. Here in *Rob Roy*, as in the other Waverley novels, Scott remains sensitive to the rise of bourgeois power. As Nicol Jarvie realizes, credit replaces honor as the basis of this mercantile world's practical vocabulary, and in the end Frank does join his father's business, after first saving its credit. Scott nevertheless builds the plot from the contest over a more aristocratic objective, which he uses instead of business to gauge Frank's maturity. Osbaldistone Hall, which Sir Hildebrand, a younger son, inherited instead of Mr. Osbaldistone, represents the source of Frank's conflict with his father. Mr. Osbaldistone went into business precisely because he lost his property; and while a mercantile house certainly summarizes the economic power base of Frank's culture, it does not completely replace real property—a gentleman's estate—either in social or psychological value as the objective of Scott's characters. Frank, Rashleigh, Rob Roy, and Diana Vernon all feel deprived of their right to independence because they have lost their right to property. Without property they have no tangible social credit, since credit is determined by the economic power base of property.

Scott therefore transfers the novel's focus from business, which a son can participate in while his father lives, to property, which a son can possess only upon a father's—or, in this case, an uncle's—

death. This transference censors Frank's antagonism towards his father, who threatens his identity but cannot be openly fought because he is a "kind" parent. By the end of the novel, Frank instead succeeds his uncle, in whom he has little emotional investment as a parent figure. Rashleigh, moreover, who openly works to undermine both Sir Hildebrand and Mr. Osbaldistone, enacts the ambition and eros that Frank himself suppresses. Like Rashleigh, Frank wants to inherit Osbaldistone Hall as a means of validating his adulthood; and since Diana Vernon has sworn to marry the heir or enter a convent, his competition with Rashleigh for her love furthers his desire for the estate. While he has originally resisted his father's authority, Frank ultimately rescues his father from Rashleigh's selfish scheme. Next to Rashleigh's, Frank's behavior seems downright docile, submissive, and obedient, so Scott rewards Frank with what Rashleigh consciously wanted all along—Osbaldistone Hall and Diana Vernon.

But because there are so many other heirs standing in line before Frank, in order to gratify his hero's desire with the unexpected gift of Osbaldistone Hall, Scott has to exploit the novelist's legerdemain and kill off Sir Hildebrand and five of his sons in two pages. To be sure, Frank's inheritance of Osbaldistone Hall redresses the earlier wrong committed when his grandfather dispossessed his father. Yet it also emphasizes the fear of parricide implied by the severe cost of retribution: the lives of his uncle and cousins. The abruptness with which Scott eliminates most of the Osbaldistone clan creates a startling impression of Frank's psychic liberation from his family. His uncle and cousins threaten him as his father originally did because he cannot assert his right to their property, and hence to his adulthood, while they remain alive. Reality therefore seems to collaborate with desire to make Frank feel more at home than he could have imagined even in the very best of Family Romance daydreams. Frank not only defies his father's authority and satisfies his wish to find love and power in an area exclusive of his father's control; he saves his father from Rashleigh's sinister clutches as well. As a privileged oedipal son, Frank is allowed to reject his father (rather than actually kill him or see him die) and then restore him to a level of psychic power subordinate to his own.

Chapter 3

Although reality in *Rob Roy* seems to conspire with the hero's unconscious by masquerading as a landscape of desire, this does not mean the novel is merely sweeping trouble under the rug to avoid the implications of Frank's oedipal desires. Scott's fiction always remains sensitive to shifts in political and familial power because it recognizes, in Freud's words, that "the whole progress of society rests upon the opposition between successive generations."[13] This fictive world acquires its stability because of its conscious adherence to an abstract code of social behavior which denies the implication of parricide when a son succeeds his father to inherit property. Since it revolves around the inheritance of property, however, this cultural value system merely heightens the subversive elements—the impulses to commit treason and regicide, to be sexually aware and reject one's father—transforming the hero's innocent world into a terrifying, alien landscape. The hero finds himself at odds with his father but does not see this conflict as his passage to maturity. Instead, he feels overwhelmed with guilt and needs to blame someone else. In *Rob Roy*, when Diana implies to Frank that Rashleigh has betrayed her in some way, she means that Rashleigh holds over her the secret that her father is still alive, but Frank immediately assumes that Rashleigh has tried to seduce her, unintentionally expressing his own sexual attraction to her. Although it is a natural and understandable response, Frank feels guilty about desiring Diana and projects the thought onto his cousin, a fitting enough alter-ego for his sexual consciousness since Rashleigh also plots against both Frank's king and father. When Diana finally becomes available to Frank as a potential wife, she returns to the novel with a subdued, less energetic personality; accompanying her father (whom Frank at first jealously assumes is her fiancé), she is dressed as a boy to minimize the sexually mature motives for their marriage. Since Diana and Frank do not act rashly, so to speak, but consciously restrain their sexual impulses, they avoid an open confrontation with their oedipal guilt. When Rob Roy, the novel's idealized parent figure, kills Rashleigh, it is as if to show that rebellious sons always deserve—and receive—punishment when they put their subversive thoughts into deeds.

Rashleigh enacts Frank's own desire to rebel against authority, which Rob Roy, in turn, ultimately stifles by his murder of Rashleigh. This desire, in fact, urges Frank to move from the role of irresponsible son to responsible adult, from immaturity to maturity; but when articulated by Rashleigh it seems instead to epitomize egocentric and subversive behavior. The bond between hero and villain in *Rob Roy*, typical of such relationships in the Waverley novels, displaces the hero's Foundling-Bastard confusion, making him more secure in his innocence since this doubling allows him to see the Bastard part of himself as the other. Scott's hero inevitably feels guilty, taking seriously the public accusations of treason even though he has not committed such action, as if he intuits that his emotional makeup includes illicit desires. Unlike Austen's characters, Scott's hero needs, in a manner of speaking, to be a stranger to his self, and this need encourages the romantic, dream-like texture of his experience. In effect, Scott relieves his hero's anxiety, for the narrative disguises the hero's desires by displacing them onto the villain, who does act illegally, to reinforce the fear that those desires endanger the hero's social identity and must therefore be suppressed. Self and other thus become confused to make the world outside the self reflect the self's desires all the more. As Bersani explains, "In denying a desire, we condemn ourselves to finding it everywhere."[14] This is certainly true of the Waverley hero and his fascination with the villain and, when there is one, the dark heroine. Welsh makes much of this aspect of Scott's fiction when he examines the psychic bonds between the light and dark pairs of heroes and heroines. "The center of activity in the Waverley Novels," he concludes, "at most proves to be the *resistance* to romantic energies. This implies, in author and reader, a sympathy with resistance—with prudence, in fact—as well as a tribute to the force resisted."[15] That the hero and the reader find the dark characters attractive validates the importance of their subversive energies: the conservative momentum of the narrative removes these impulses as far away from the hero as possible, displacing the guilt which might otherwise radiate from the heroic point of view.

Yet, as we have seen, the hero cannot avoid his guilt, no matter how much the narrative structure of his novel may seem willing to soothe his anxiety. Even his frequent appeal to the law, which ought to respect his right to property and protect his innate innocence, instead makes him out to be a usurper of property and a heinous criminal. Since his maturation is associated with the forces of egoism and subversion, the domestic values centered upon marriage and property work to control his anxiety about maturation, normalizing it for the fictive world. By the end of the novel the hero has rescued his family's estate or honor (in *Waverley* the two are combined in the very name of the property: Waverley-Honour), thereby vindicating himself from charges of treason, disobedience, selfish desire. Likewise, whereas the hero's initial attraction to the villain is a displaced expression of his own subversive energy, his ultimate rejection of the villain serves as a public assertion of his innocence. This transformation necessarily precedes the social integration confirmed by his marriage to the heroine.

The Family Romance story of the Waverley novels therefore builds into their construction of experience an anxiety which history can relieve because it neutralizes the hero's discomfort at having to threaten his parent/king by becoming an adult. The many father substitutes and villainous doubles—all surrogate versions of the hero's self—displace his desire to commit parricide; the progressive movement of history itself then proves that the oppressive parental authority and subversive political cause belonged to a reactionary force, which had to be overthrown in order for the hero and his society to continue. In *Rob Roy*, as in *Waverley*, the circumstances of political rebellion all seem to explain the hero's guilt. Although, as we have seen, that guilt is complicated and deeply rooted, once the circumstantial evidence is accounted for and the hero exculpated of treason, his innocence is proved to the state's satisfaction. This is, finally, how history serves to vindicate the hero. In the case of Frank, who seems attracted to the Jacobite cause mainly because of his interest in Rashleigh and Diana, the end of the novel underscores the fact that this political movement has become historically inappropriate, as Diana finally realizes when she marries Frank, who is neither Catholic nor Royalist. Frank's involvement with the many Jacobite characters, furthermore, reveals his own political moderation, since his passions pale in comparison to theirs.

Finally, his adventure returns him to his father and his father's business, dispelling his oedipal anger by giving him a vocation that respects the economic power and historical vitality of his father's class.

Old Mortality takes this procedure and moves the hero one step further towards realism, for here he finds himself in a landscape less receptive to his desires. This novel shows the full extent to which the other Waverley novels implicitly turn history into a psychological field for the hero's expulsion of oedipal desire. But since this novel firmly roots the hero in an historical landscape, he cannot secure his innocence as easily as Edward and Frank seem to do. Forced into exile because of his political activism, this hero must finally confront and live with the guilt caused by his engagement with history.

With its very title redolent of lost innocence and maturation, *Old Mortality* follows Scott's program of forcing a sober yet vital self to emerge out of the hero's confrontation with history. The hero here, Henry Morton, is "one of those gifted characters, which possess a force of talent unsuspected by the owner himself" (p. 138), for he seemingly is weak, uncommitted, and reserved at the opening of the novel. Henry's joining the rebel army then brings out a latent "firmness of character" (p. 139) which he himself has not previously recognized:

> A mild, romantic, gentle-tempered youth, bred up in dependence, and stooping patiently to the control of a sordid and tyrannical relation, had suddenly, by the rod of oppression and the spur of injured feelings, been compelled to stand forth a leader of armed men, was earnestly engaged in affairs of a public nature, had friends to animate and enemies to contend with, and felt his individual fate bound up in that of a national insurrection and revolution. It seemed as if he had at once experienced a transition from the romantic dreams of youth to the labours and cares of active manhood. (pp. 265-66)

Henry joins the insurgents "for recovery of a birthright wrested from us" (p. 302), and while he means his legal birthright, which guarantees him freedom to choose his religion and protection against political harassment, he also fights to recover his psychic birthright, meaning the freedom with which to make a successful "transition" from the undeveloped potential of his "youth" to the maturation of "active manhood."

Being "a mild, romantic, gentle-tempered youth" to start with, Henry feels the stings of both royal and parental oppression. Until he takes a political stand against his government, at home he remains weak and impotent, dominated by the "sordid and tyrannical" figure of his uncle Milnwood, who begrudges him food, money, and education. Milnwood loves his nephew but treats him like a little boy, making him feel guilty whenever he tries to act for himself. Milnwood's own weak and frightened figure, in fact, promises a bleak adult future for Henry if he cannot acquire the strength with which to resist his uncle's petty domination. Yet more than his uncle's "tyranny," Henry's own fear of adult action is the cause of his timid demeanor. After hiding Burley in his uncle's barn, he goes to the house to get food and knocks on the door with "a sort of hesitating tap, which carried an acknowledgment of transgression in its very sound, and seemed rather to solicit than command attention" (p. 51). He acts as if his very presence transgresses authority; and the housekeeper, Mrs. Wilson, then scolds him for "coming hame and crying for ale, as if ye were maister and mair" (p. 52), to remind him that he is less than "maister" in this house which is not his own. With the need to prove to himself that he is a powerful and guiltless adult, Henry takes his first steps towards manhood by joining the insurgents and forming an uneasy political alliance with Burley. Significantly, when he later returns to his uncle's estate after leading the attack on Edinburgh, "Henry's knock upon the gate no longer intimated the conscious timidity of a stripling who has been out of bounds, but the confidence of a man in full possession of his own rights, and master of his own actions,—bold, free, and decided" (p. 266). Somehow his achievement of "active manhood" has required an act of rebellion on his part against both parent and state.

For Henry to mature he must first exorcise the influence of his real father, "whose memory he idolised" (p. 49), but who serves as an unrealistic parental model. Burley, in fact, senses Henry's dependence on his father's memory as a behavioral model, so he

The Waverley Novels

draws the young man more firmly into the insurrection by continually alluding to the time when he saved Silas Morton's life during the Civil War. In this respect, Burley, his father's friend and savior, also acts as a parental model for Henry; but this model serves to pervert the idealized memory of his real father. Having actually broken ties with Silas Morton during the Restoration, Burley pushes the former's heroism and politics to the extreme of self-righteous cant. Although Henry struggles against Burley and quite rightly resents the fanatic's hypocritical, self-serving appeal to "justice," he also senses how Burley embodies rebellious impulses that he himself tries to control by remaining an obedient nephew and citizen. "In some moods of my mind," he thinks, "how dangerous would be the society of such a companion!" (p. 61). Henry is drawn to Burley because his "sordid and tyrannical" uncle and the oppressive forces to which his uncle passively submits have given him no other choice; he needs to explore those "dangerous" moods. He also needs to be loyal to the idealized and more satisfying memory of his real father, which he at first mistakenly associates with his father's friend, the rebel.

Henry's "dangerous" moods, however, pitch him against his idealized parent. Because Burley's allies embrace him as "the son of the famous Silas Morton" (p. 187), they expect Henry to be like his father, repeating the latter's valiant heroism in battle. Henry remains quite sensitive to this charge: "'I have no retreat,' he said to himself. 'All shall allow—even Major Bellenden—even Edith—that in courage, at least, the rebel Morton was not inferior to his father'" (p. 261). But in order to become more than a son to other men, Henry must ultimately act on his own. Assuming responsibility for his rebellious action, he learns the necessity, not only of choosing moral and political sides, but of choosing to reject parental models as well. Henry learns that following what he considers to be the rightful path of action means, in deed, that he must betray at least one of his many fathers, which makes guiltless action impossible. After all, his "first enterprise in active life" results in an attack upon Tillietudlem, home of his beloved Edith and, more to the point, defended by her uncle, Major Bellenden, another good friend of his father's, a man "to whom he personally owed many obligations" (p. 234) and who also thinks of him as a

Chapter 3

son. Henry therefore cannot extend his options in an open-ended, daydreamy way—as Waverley can do—because they are mutually exclusive. Furthermore, he has to realize that moral independence does not necessarily follow psychic liberation. Henry may have the security of relying on several parental models, but he must face up to all the insecurity and peril of living a single life.

This lesson is underscored through the novel's sexual plot, the triangle involving Henry, Edith, and Lord Evandale. Since both their guardians forbid marriage, Henry's love for Edith intensifies his oedipal defiance of authority. To assert himself sexually he must deny the claims of his parentage, and this is, of course, difficult for him to do consciously. So if Henry sees in these older men versions of a parent which rehearse his unresolved oedipal feelings towards his real father, then in his rival Lord Evandale he finds an ideal surrogate self who begins to work out the oedipal tension in his desire for Edith. Evandale acts as a double to stimulate Henry's growth, by establishing a youthful, romantic, and sexual counterpoint to Silas Morton's aged heroic figure. Not surprisingly, Henry is somewhat in awe of Evandale. Because Evandale is respected, powerful, and rich, whereas Henry is not, Henry feels himself less deserving of Edith's love. To make matters worse, his rival is fatherless, and can therefore act with the assurance and independence that Henry himself craves.

This sexual tension is resolved through the displacement activity of the novel, which uses surrogate figures to act for Henry and history to vindicate his maturity. Burley censors Henry's oedipal desires because the fanatic's hatred of Evandale—the liberated, parentless son—allows Henry to reverse the parricide fear (just as Burley himself once saved Morton's father). This most violent and insane of Henry's fathers wants to undermine the son's success, reaffirming the son's fear of the father's authority and justifying his oedipal rebellion against both parent and state by making it an act of self-defense against a reactionary, irrational force. Burley tries to kill Evansdale three times, but Henry succeeds in frustrating only the first two attempts. Since Henry has decided not to stand between Edith and economic security, Evandale finally has to die in order to stop Henry from making himself a martyr to a romantic, anti-social and reactionary ideal.

The Waverley Novels

When Henry returns from exile, he wants Edith to think he is dead so that she can be free to marry Evandale, but he is wrong to think he does not deserve her, since history proves him to be the more proper husband.

Given Henry's oedipal conflict, the particular time period of the novel is telling, for the various generations of characters extend its scope to cover two traumatic moments in English history involving revolutions against a king—the Civil War and the Glorious Revolution. Like his father, who first rebelled against Charles I (participating in a public act of parricide) but then accepted the restoration of the monarchy in 1660, Henry remains the most historically vital of the novel's characters. The others have acted out of self-interest, blind to the historical forces that built the Scottish insurrection against the government of James II. History finally excuses Henry's very active part in the rebellion, however, because his motives for participation foresaw the coming to power of William and Mary in 1688. Ten years after the insurrection, the other characters—Burley, Claverhouse, Evandale—all find themselves surprisingly, not to say uncomfortably, on the side of the reactionary Stuart cause. The exile of James II, a "glorious" and bloodless public act of parricide that softened the trauma resulting from the Civil War and execution of Charles I, marks the end of the old royalist class and the value system that Edith's grandmother comically follows in her foolish obsession with the visit of Charles I during the first war against the Stuarts. Evandale's death therefore indicates how Henry embodies historical timeliness in his vision, his experience, his political loyalties. Evandale's death, furthermore, liberates Edith from what would be an historically inappropriate marriage and allows her to respect Henry's rise to power by marrying him. This act validates Edith and Henry as new sources of social and historical energy for the novel's fictional world.

When Henry Morton replaces Lord Evandale as Edith's fiancé, he makes final the novel's historical acceptance of the post-Jacobite world, which destroyed the worlds of each of Henry's fathers. Once that older generation has died and the new political climate been accepted as a given, Henry can, like Edward Waverley, easily finish his transition from romantic waking dreams to domestically active life. History, in this respect, has conspired with the hero's unconscious by allowing him to participate in a social version of parricide—political insurrection—to displace onto a battle field his own private oedipal drama. Thus can the novel seem so concerned with impersonal forces of political change all the while directing the hero's maturation. Unlike Edward's maturation, however, Henry's remains more obviously defined by his guilt, which history can explain but not erase. He has actually committed treason and been made to suffer for it during ten years of exile; therefore, unlike Edward or Frank, he cannot restore or idealize his childhood past through some sort of reunion with a parent. His innocence must be sacrificed, and this recognition makes *Old Mortality* a novel more committed to maturity, in ways prescient of *Great Expectations* and *Middlemarch*, than the other Waverley books. Too many people have died—most of the major characters, in fact—for Scott to ignore the heavy price Henry pays in recovering his birthright.

Seen in the context of what I have explained about the other two novels, *Old Mortality* shows most cogently how Scott builds his fictive world from the paradigm by exerting stress upon the Family Romance story to push it towards the sobering vision of realism. Experience plays upon the hero's anxiety concerning maturation, but it ends up proving in retrospect, as *Old Mortality* relates quite vividly, that the son's defiance of parental authority has actually been directed towards a conservative, historically appropriate goal all the time. With history serving as a field for the hero's anxiety about his maturation, Scott's narratives can be at once realistic and romantic in their imaginative texture, the contrivances of plotting working to fragment the hero's self into surrogates, so that history becomes, for the hero, a landscape of his desire. Yet unlike the hero's own romantic daydreams, this landscape forces him to confront his maturing psyche, to teach him the difference between parricide, an act truly "strange, horrible, and unnatural," and maturity. By making the hero's anxiety reflect an actual historical movement, moreover, Scott interprets the hero's growth as a social process, minimizing his oedipal guilt so that it appears less personal, less specific, less dreadful: no matter how much it is dreaded, maturity can never seem as awful as parricide.

Scott, then, transforms the Family Romance into a realistic narrative, but traces of that romantic origin remain visible in order to define the realistic ambitions of his novels. The hero works backward to make contact with his child-self through surrogates and to redefine his relations with parental authority as his primal act of self-definition, and this actually moves him forward because he experiences desire in the shape of the other. Since Scott does not view his hero's oedipal desire as a "normal" stage of development, he continually imagines it in its most shocking and horrific form: acts of "parricide" engineered by others. At the same time his novels focus, again and again, upon the wish to commit such an act. Therefore, in order to normalize the hero's self, the narratives displace that desire onto figures of the other, surrogates who stand in for the hero as mirrors of his psychic life. This displacement makes the historical crisis reflect a tumultuous psychic landscape, with the hero attracted to and repelled by the other at the same time. By being placed in this landscape, the hero can lose his innocence but understand his violation as a process of repair. With this pattern, Scott sets forth the conditions by which nineteenth-century fiction constructs experience according to the paradigm. In *Old Mortality* especially, we can see emerging the ambivalence towards lost innocence so characteristic of Dickens's novels, as well as the sober acceptance of maturity so characteristic of George Eliot's.

4
Bleak House and Great Expectations

"Guilty and yet innocent"

To turn from Scott to Dickens is actually to continue examining a similar dialectic engagement of romantic and realistic energies. The Waverley novels use history to displace the hero's egocentric desire in order to exculpate him from guilt. While the historical plots move the hero forward through experience to vindicate his political innocence, they simultaneously move him backward to orchestrate a Family Romance story about his oedipal desire that recounts his loss of innocence. Dickens's novels, abounding in orphaned, abandoned, or bullied children, similarly recast the Family Romance story through a forward-backward construction of experience. The Romance concerns of these novels underscore their justly famous preoccupation with the social disorder that results from living in a hostile, dehumanizing urban environment.[1] Here, too, in the streets of London rather than on the battlefields of history, a child figure encounters surrogate parents in the form of good and bad guardians. Here, too, he searches for his origin—his rightful familial place in a teeming, disorderly world—as a way of feeling at home in a universe which, to quote John Jarndyce in *Bleak House*, "makes rather an indifferent parent."[2] And here, too, a progressive movement (the process of socialization and growth) competes with a regressive movement (the persistent mystery of origins, the

Chapter 4

longing for a caring parent, the traumatic effects of childhood). This paradigmatic double movement acquires its particular force for Dickens's construction of experience because his novels, obsessed as they are with the loss of innocence, nonetheless create a world which denies the self an origin in innocence.

As in the Waverley novels, the child figure in Dickens discovers he is both an innocent Foundling and a guilty Bastard, terms which apply, quite literally, to the births of Oliver Twist and Esther Summerson, to name but two characters who come quickly to mind. For the child this discovery has profoundly disturbing implications. It means that he is as guilty as the parents who sired and abandoned him. His search for a stable familial identity, motivated by his search for innocence—for an untainted parent— leads him instead to a confrontation with his own guilt, where he finds the origin not of his innocence but of his fall, and this discovery violates the assumptions out of which he has constructed his sense of reality. So long as he sees adults as his victimizers, the child can believe in his own innocence, for he has not identified his nature with theirs. But because that innocence is an illusion, maturity occurs in a Dickens novel only when the victimized child comes to accept the other as something more than a dreaded version of the brutal or indifferent parent. Then, instead of feeling estranged from adults, he can identify with them and begin to repair his original sense of violation.

The whole point of experience for Dickens's characters, however, is that such acceptance of the other is easier said than done. To be sure, his novels command our respect for the sheer presence of an other so powerful in its gravitational pull that the self cannot help being drawn into its dehumanizing orbit. The novels achieve this effect by delineating a landscape larger, more palpable, often seemingly more real and more animated, than any single character. As J. Hillis Miller observes about Dickens, "The most striking characteristic of his novels is their multitudinousness, the proliferation within each one of a great number of characters, each different from all the others, and each living imprisoned in his own milieu and in his own idiosyncratic way of looking at the world. . . . Though each individual reaches out toward a comprehension of the city, the essential quality of the city is its transcendence of any one person's knowledge of it."[3] This description captures the phenomenal surface of the Dickens world, but the awesome imaginative power of this urban landscape lies in its intrusion upon each character's "idiosyncratic way of looking at the world," and that intrusion questions the difference between self and other.

Dickens's novels create a landscape that seems alien to and separate from the self because of its impenetrable materiality, and all the more hostile, I want to add, because it teasingly reflects the self's desire in the face of the other. Everywhere are frightening, even monstrous images of desire drawing the self towards the other with a compelling attraction. As in *Clarissa* and the Waverley novels, such mirrors of desire reflect discontinuity and difference, to make the self feel guilty for harboring frightening, monstrous wishes; and since these impulses radiate from figures alien enough in their otherness to discourage mutual identification, the self resists their accusations of guilt. To resist fully, however, as most Dickens characters try to do, is to arrest identity in an illusion of childhood innocence. Such illusions cannot be sustained without ignoring the impact of experience. Indeed, the Family Romance in Dickens's novels may seem to assuage the longing for innocence, but it actually recounts the disruption of childhood order—with its unloving parents, unstable family structures, confused identities—to indicate its more secret, disturbing meaning: the child's origin as a self in the violation of his innocence.

What I have been describing rather generally in these opening paragraphs is in fact the psychology of Pip in *Great Expectations*. In this novel Pip's character expresses the anxiety about lost innocence that informs Dickens's other novels in more diffuse, often more obscure ways. Because Pip tells his own story, *Great Expectations*, in George Levine's words, is one of those realistic narratives "that focus intensely around a single consciousness and absorb the world into that consciousness's needs."[4] *Great Expectations* is therefore at once realistic in the sheer materialism of the world Pip experiences and unreal—dreamlike and romantic—in that it all too readily accommodates his psyche to voice desires and anxieties of which he is not fully conscious. The novel is convincing in its telling social analysis and just as credible as a projection of Pip's inner life, using the external landscape of other people and events to provide the commentary that Pip himself cannot. By narrating both its social and psychic landscapes in first person, *Great Expectations* can delineate a landscape of desire that seems plausible because it has an identifiable origin in Pip's psyche. A similar fusion of reality with desire, of self with the surrounding other, creates the psychological texture of Dickens's other, larger novels; but there it is more difficult to locate a plausible point of origin in the psychological landscape. These larger, more sprawling urban landscapes serve as the projection of desire from a psyche that does not seem fully present—or, rather, from a character who never emerges as a unifying, synthesizing consciousness in the way that Pip directs and centers *Great Expectations*. *Bleak House,* for instance, constructs experience from the same anxiety about lost innocence as *Great Expectations,* yet it is, many readers agree, "a novel without a center"[5] because of its double narrative, which keeps distracting from and going beyond the scope of Esther's experience. I nonetheless want to examine *Bleak House* along the lines I have been describing because, although this novel prevents us from locating guilt in any one identifiable psyche, it still constructs a rich, complex psychological texture for experience that is not much different from the psychic landscape of *Great Expectations*.

In both novels, guilt is the most fundamental, most problematic feeling that defines a character's experience. *Bleak House* makes this fact clear because an obsessive, irrational feeling of guilt casts an unsettling shadow upon every character. I agree with the critical truism that Dickens uses this novel as "an indictment not merely of the law, but of the whole dark muddle of organized society"[6] and that he equates the rampant social disorder with contagious disease to "serve as a symbol and touchstone of reality in the novel."[7] If we read *Bleak House* entirely in this light, however, we discount much of the novel's psychological power as a construction of experience built out of the paradigmatic rhythm of violation and repair.

Not all critics, of course, do discount this aspect of *Bleak House*. But they tend to talk about the psychological texture of the novel using the materialistic vocabulary of its social themes. Miller, for instance, describes the rotting world of *Bleak House* as a disorienting one because the uncontrollable and inexplicable animation of its matter challenges human identity. He agrees with what I have been arguing about the characters' search for a stable point of origin, but he accounts for their anxiety by referring to their topsy-turvy phenomenal world: "The entire novel seeks to explain," Miller concludes, "by a retrospective reconstruction going counter to the forward movement of the novel, how the world came to be in the befogged, mud-soaked, fragmented, and decomposed state present in the initial paragraphs."[8] Similarly, Mark Spilka takes note of the pervading obsession with guilt in *Bleak House* to observe that the legal metaphor for social corruption "also extends to sexual realms, though always in connection with the social problem." He explains the sexual tension in the plot as an extension of that metaphor: "the whole novel is grounded in socio-sexual mystery—or in the sin of Lady Dedlock and Captain Hawdon, of which Esther is the illegitimate fruit. From Esther's childhood guilt through Hawdon's mysterious death to Lady Dedlock's death in the snow, the sexual crime informs the social muddle and provides it with a personal context."[9]

Both Miller and Spilka subordinate the psychological undercurrent of the novel—the disorientation and guilt repeatedly felt by the characters—to its more overt social themes, so that the characters' psychology finally serves as a human metaphor for the rotting institution of Chancery, itself that symbolic locus of the fictive world at large. In analyzing *Bleak House,* I want to pursue the implications of Miller's and Spilka's remarks by turning around their emphasis to understand Chancery, society, and the family as metaphoric indications of the novel's paradigmatic construction of experience. To seek out the phenomenological origins of fragmentation, as Miller suggests, or to understand the sexual crime as a "personal context" for the breakdown of society in general, as Spilka proposes, begs the issue of the novel's anxiety about lost innocence. The preoccupation with Lady Dedlock's sexual crime voices the realization that the origin of this novel's disorienting human world is the child's fall into adult sexuality. This fall is the cause of the world's degenerated state and the

Chapter 4

reason for the novel's "socio-sexual mystery." I will go even further to argue that *Bleak House* embeds within its fictional world not a unifying consciousness like Pip's to account for this anxiety but a primal scene of fallen sexuality which serves the same purpose. The legend of Ghost's Walk provides a specific point of origin for a "retrospective reconstruction" of the disorientation *Bleak House* imagines because it focuses in a horrifying and brutal sexual encounter the feeling of guilt that pervades the entire novel.

To begin with, in order to comprehend the disorientation and chaos that define the phenomenal world of *Bleak House,* we must reckon with the psychic confusion that Esther feels and tries to articulate. Admittedly, Esther provides only a partial center for the novel. A lot goes on around her of which she is unaware and which does not affect her directly. Nonetheless, her history is the backbone of the novel's plot, providing the solution to its mystery, and her character unifies the double movement of the novel so that her growth, which results from the disclosure of her parentage, allows us to sense movement occurring. Furthermore, Esther's personality focuses our attention on the unnamed anxiety that all the other characters feel just as strongly. Their shared guilt may suggest their shared responsibility for society's ills; but it also transcends that cause, since the remarkable thing about guilt in this novel is its separation from any identifiable causal action, as Esther herself realizes.

As a child, Esther finds herself in a position characteristic of Dickens's people, nursing an inescapable sense of being "unworthy" and "different," "set apart" by her own "fault," and frustrated by her inability to understand precisely why she is not as innocent as other children seem to be. But being "more timid and retiring" than other Dickens characters who share her feeling, Esther has not let anger and resentment dominate her personality. Instead, she hopes "to repair the fault I had been born with (of which I confusedly felt guilty and yet innocent), and would strive as I grew up to be industrious, contented and kind-hearted, and to do some good to some one, and win some love to myself if I could" (pp. 18-20).[10] Esther's desire to redeem her fallen state raises several basic questions. How can she effect repair if she cannot

Bleak House *and* Great Expectations

identify the source of the fault she wants to emend? How can one who has not done anything criminal be guilty enough to feel the need for reparation in the first place? And if she does have something to repair, how can she still consider herself innocent?

Bleak House addresses these questions. The problematic sensation of being at once guilty and innocent provides the axis from which the novel constructs experience for its characters. More precisely, *Bleak House* imagines a disordered, fragmented world for its characters because the expected alignment of criminal action and guilty thought has broken down. Not only has the world lost its physical and social coherence; it has ceased to make sense on a moral or intellectual level, too. As I've already begun to suggest, Chancery itself localizes in a social atmosphere the *Bleak House* world's traumatic reaction to adult behavior. The disturbing effects of this reaction can be felt everywhere in the novel, since all the characters feel as Esther does—at once "guilty and yet innocent."

Guilt in *Bleak House* arises from two sources—social irresponsibility and sexual corruption—which Dickens connects imaginatively even though he tries to keep them distinct in the actual narrative by means of his double plot. The former kind of guilt dominates Richard and the Jarndyce lawsuit, the latter Lady Dedlock and Esther. Chancery defaults on its social obligations, destroying Richard, Gridley, and Miss Flite in the process. Similarly, personal responsibility is absent in Richard's own attitudes about a career and in his treatment of Ada, Jarndyce, even Skimpole and Vholes. Both the institution and individuals must be blamed. Lady Dedlock's illicit relationship with Captain Hawdon, on the other hand, her unknowing desertion of Esther at birth, and her cat-and-mouse situation with Tulkinghorn suggest the impact of sexual corruption in an area seemingly irrelevant to Chancery. A third cause of guilt, child neglect, reveals how these two larger causes fuse together for the world of the novel. Mrs. Jellyby and Mr. Turveydrop ignore the needs of their children in the same way Chancery has betrayed the Wards in Jarndyce and Lady Dedlock her daughter. The novel's many parents of neglected children share a guilt, even if they do not acknowledge it, that contains features of both Chancery's guilt and Lady

Chapter 4

Dedlock's. These parents commit a social crime whose origin—the existence of the children in the first place—can be traced to an initial sexual act.

Since this guilt is as omnipresent as the fog and mud in London, characters become infected with it in much the same way Jo gives smallpox to Charley, who passes it on to Esther. Early in the novel, for example, Harold Skimpole is arrested for debt. When Richard and Esther help the man avoid his punishment by paying his debt, Esther discovers: "It was a most singular thing that the arrest was our embarrassment, and not Mr. Skimpole's. He observed us with a genial interest; but there seemed, if I may venture on such a contradiction, nothing selfish in it. He had entirely washed his hands of the difficulty, and it had become ours" (p. 70). Even after they settle this matter, Esther still thinks "that Richard and I seemed to retain this transferred impression of having been arrested since dinner, and that it was very curious altogether" (p. 73).

This "very curious" moment when Skimpole transfers his guilt to Esther and Richard is actually very typical of *Bleak House*. In this novel characters who seem to have no moral or social points of connection can suddenly and unaccountably touch each other psychically. Guilt easily transfers from one character to another, and although it does not make rational sense to them, few characters muster the presence of self to resist. After becoming involved in Hawdon's death and Tulkinghorn's investigation, Mr. Snagsby anxiously discovers that he "cannot make out what it is that he has had to do with." Snagsby feels guilty but does not know why. All he knows is that "something is wrong, somewhere; but what something, what may come of it, to whom, when, and from which unthought of and unheard of quarter, is the puzzle of his life." With this irrational and frustrating knowledge "that he is a party to some dangerous secret, without knowing what it is," Snagsby lives in terror, his "heart knocks hard at his guilty breast." Yet what has he actually done? As far as he knows, nothing. Nonetheless, "it is the fearful peculiarity of this condition that, at any hour of his daily life . . . the secret may take air and fire, explode, and blow up—" and he is powerless to understand when that will happen, let alone why (pp. 315-16).

Snagsby's guilt is important because it begins to bring to the fore of the Chancery plot the sexual guilt that makes Lady Dedlock's past a "dangerous secret." Snagsby never actually discovers this secret, but he senses its danger all the same. His wife more correctly intuits a "dangerous" connection between Lady Dedlock, Hawdon, and Jo. Partly because of her husband's puzzling behavior, mostly because of her own jealous imagination, she irrationally decides that "Jo was Mr. Snagsby's son" (p. 645). Although comically wrong, Mrs. Snagsby associates her husband's guilt with a sexual transgression and illegitimate birth, her suspicion unintentionally leading her closer than anyone else to the secret Lady Dedlock is trying to keep from Tulkinghorn's prying eyes.

Dickens treats Lady Dedlock's secret, that she loved Captain Hawdon and bore him a child who supposedly died, as if it involved the same social infection that festers in locations as disparate as filthy Tom-all-Alone's, where her dead lover lies buried, and fashionable Chesney Wold, where she has buried her past and, it seems, her feelings as well.[11] Lady Dedlock's "dangerous secret" draws characters like the Snagsbys into the whirlpool of her guilt, making them "party" to a crime "without [their] knowing what it is," just as Chancery absorbs Richard, Gridley, and Miss Flite. More than Chancery, however, that institutionalization of parental neglect and indifference, Lady Dedlock is central to the anxiety about adult experience in this novel because her figure concentrates—and finally explains—the sense of dread felt by everyone else. To be sure, Dickens keeps pushing her figure to the edges of his narrative, and the omnipresent narrator's inability to probe her character in depth makes her appear as a cipher. Yet as Esther's biography reveals, Lady Dedlock is the locus of disturbance for this world, embodying all that the self fears to confront in adult experience: sexuality, the antithesis of innocence. She is not only the mistress who betrayed her lover, but also the mother who deserted—however unintentionally—her child. This is Lady Dedlock's real secret, that a woman can actually be sexual and maternal—"guilty and yet innocent"—at the same time, although Lady Deadlock cannot reconcile these two aspects of her female personality as Esther will be able to do.

While the emotional texture of experience in *Bleak House* originates from the dread that Lady Dedlock's secret produces, Dickens carefully manipulates the machinery of his narrative to disguise its disturbing meaning. So in order to unravel this disguise we must approach Dickens's characters with the clue given to us by Esther, that characters in this novel closely adhere to each other through a psychic bond. We must recognize that through acts of displacement, or "transferred impression" as Esther calls it, the impulses of one self seem to rub off on others.

In reading *Bleak House* as a dream work, Taylor Stoehr follows this line of thinking, although he does not take his cue from Esther, to demonstrate how Dickens's narrative displaces the inherently sexual nature of the guilt which so permeates it. According to Stoehr, Hortense, the French maid, functions as a "stand-in" for Lady Dedlock, enacting the latter's wish to kill Tulkinghorn and absorbing the guilt for the wish as well. In this sense Lady Dedlock, unlike her daughter, deservedly feels "guilty and yet innocent" as Bucket stalks the house waiting for the true murderer to show her hand. Stoehr finds in the lawyer and the maid, the victim and the killer, extensions of the psyche Lady Dedlock has masked through her "freezing mood" (p. 13). To explain this composite image of Lady Dedlock, Stoehr argues that Dickens exploits her conflict with Tulkinghorn and complicity in the murder to direct our conscious attention away from the sexual importance of her secret. This displacement accounts for the double narrative: Lady Dedlock's secret is buried in one and her daughter moves in the other.[12] Nevertheless, while Dickens offers little concrete information about Lady Dedlock's affair with Hawdon, obscuring their story even though it determines so much of what happens in the novel, he does not totally suppress its sexual energy. The tension between Lady Dedlock and Tulkinghorn, their teasing contest of wills, brings to the surface of *Bleak House* the sexual nature of the woman's secret and its importance to the psychic atmosphere of the entire novel.

Dickens makes Tulkinghorn an enigmatic figure of power and fear. No character except Lady Dedlock and Hortense dares to go against him. Even the narrator cannot concretely envision more than Tulkinghorn's "usual expressionless mask—if it be a mask" (p. 147). But while the narrator does not distinguish the man from his black legal dress, "mute, close, irresponsive to any glancing light" (p. 14), Dickens does suggest what lies behind Tulkinghorn's mask. The allegorical painting on the ceiling of his room externalizes the sexuality that Tulkinghorn has repressed.[13] "Allegory, in Roman helmet and celestial linen, sprawls among balustrades and pillars, flowers, clouds, and big-legged boys, and makes the head ache—as would seem to be Allegory's object always, more or less." The "heavy" furniture, "dusty" tables, "thick and dingy" carpets, everything creates an air of repression in Tulkinghorn's chambers, intensified by the contrast to this painted bacchanal scene. "Allegory" probably does give Tulkinghorn a headache, and no wonder! Indeed, when Tulkinghorn enters his chambers, "Allegory [is] staring down at his intrusion as if it meant to swoop upon him," but not to be outdone, Tulkinghorn simply ignores the painting, "cutting it dead" (pp. 119-20).

"Allegory" does have the last laugh, however. While "for many years the persistent Roman has been pointing, with no particular meaning, from that ceiling" (p. 585), the figure eventually does acquire a meaning when it points to Tulkinghorn's body after he has been quite literally cut dead. That meaning, moreover, has been there in the painting all along. In an earlier scene the figure "of one impossible Roman upside down" points to Lady Dedlock as she makes her first secret journey to Tom-all-Alone's. At the moment she passes by the window, the figure on the ceiling "points [at her] with the arm of Samson (out of joint, and an odd one)" (p. 200). This ominous and somewhat disorienting description fittingly prepares for what follows in the next paragraph, the disclosure of Tulkinghorn's cynical thoughts about women. The allusion to Samson provides a mythical frame of reference to support Tulkinghorn's misogyny and, though he cannot appreciate it, to predict the later moment in the novel when Hortense—Lady Dedlock's double—justifies his suspicion of women by murdering him. "There are women enough in the world, Mr. Tulkinghorn thinks—too many; they are at the bottom of all that goes wrong in it, though, for the matter of that, they create business for lawyers. What would it be to see a woman going by, even though she were going secretly? They are all secret. Mr. Tulkinghorn knows that, very well" (p. 200). Because he sees every woman as a potential Delilah able to betray a man by destroying his manhood, Tulkinghorn's relentless pursuit of Lady Dedlock manifests his desire, as Clarissa would say, to encroach upon her sex. He senses the "anger, and fear, and shame" contending for expression in Lady Dedlock's outwardly composed figure, he even respects "what power this woman has to keep these raging passions down!" (p. 508). Because of her formidable strength, he wants to conquer her, to assert *his* repressive power over *hers*. Since he believes that women "are all secret," Tulkinghorn achieves his mastery over their sex by making Lady Dedlock's secret *his* secret. "It is no longer your secret," he arrogantly taunts her. "Excuse me. That is just the mistake. It is my secret, in trust for Sir Leicester and the family. If it were your secret, Lady Dedlock, we should not be here, holding this conversation" (p. 581).

With his rigid legalistic mind Tulkinghorn fails to realize the psychological implication of this transaction, that the woman's secret—her sexual guilt—is indeed the man's as well. He has no knowledge of the emotions that complicate sexual relationships; as far as he is concerned, women, like Chancery, create problems from which a lawyer can profit. While he confesses to Lady Dedlock that Sir Leicester's love provides one variable he cannot predict, he severely underestimates the impact of her reaction as well as her husband's. She does not actually murder him, but "her enemy he was, and she has often, often, often, wished him dead" (p. 666). Tulkinghorn's usurpation of Lady Dedlock's secret effectively serves as an image of the man violating a woman's secret self, which in sexual terms is her virginity, in social terms her honor (recall that Lady Dedlock's first name is Honoria). Whatever vocabulary we use to describe it, the violation dismisses

Bleak House *and* Great Expectations

the woman's integrity as an individual and drives her to desire the man's murder. When Tulkinghorn pulls away the mask, moreover, when he finds the reason for Lady Dedlock's surprising interest in Hawdon's handwriting, he discovers that the woman has already been made impure, reinforcing his fear of her and what she exposes about him.

The legend of Ghost's Walk further envelopes Lady Dedlock's secret in an aura of violent, guilt-ridden sexuality which builds into Dickens's narrative a fleeting impression of the corruption inherent to sexual experience, to explain why this novel insists that adulthood be approached with so much mistrust and apprehension. Here is the story behind the legend as recounted by Mrs. Rouncewell, the housekeeper at Chesney Wold. During the English civil war an earlier Lady Dedlock, the wife of Sir Morbury, found herself torn between her brothers' and husband's conflicting political loyalties, until her favorite brother was killed in battle by her husband's kinsman. She then avenged his death by trying to lame her husband's favorite horse. We can infer from this Lady Dedlock's actions that, out of vengeance, she wanted to castrate her husband, for the analogy in her mind between favorite brother and favorite horse bears out a simpler equation of man and horse. Like the second Lady Dedlock in her contest with Tulkinghorn, this Lady Dedlock also instigated a desperate, antagonistic contest with the other sex, who violated her body in retaliation for that initial act of aggression. When Morbury caught her in the stable, "he seized her by the wrist; and in a struggle or in a fall, or through the horse being frightened and lashing out, she was lamed in the hip, and from that hour began to pine away" (p. 84). What begins as an image of the woman emasculating the man turns into one of the angry, frightened man "lashing out" and physically wounding the woman in retaliation, as if she has allured him into degrading her body. This story of the doom hanging over Chesney Wold functions as a sort of primal scene for the novel (one narrated in fact for the virginal Rosa, the young maid whom Lady Dedlock will try to preserve from becoming contaminated by her secret), to show man and woman deadlocked in the dangerous

Chapter 4

frenzy of sexual encounter. Like either Lady Dedlock, the woman initiates the contest; like Sir Morbury or Tulkinghorn, the man brings it to a destructive conclusion.

If we can agree that Dickens's fictive universe posits a fallen world, and that his displacements of guilt and desire all work to sustain some measure of conscious belief in the self's innocence, then we can realize, too, that when he tries to see experience with a child's eyes what he witnesses in adult behavior (the legend of Ghost's Walk) horrifies him, so he continually works to temper that disturbing vision. Nowhere else in this novel do we sense so much disturbing sexual energy so openly generated as we do in the Ghost's Walk legend, though its presence is inescapable throughout. The male's fear of the sexual woman, imagined in the story behind the Ghost's Walk legend, explains the many domineering women and submissive men who populate the *Bleak House* world. Mr. Jellyby, for example, surrenders to his wife's overbearing presence, losing the power to do or say anything. The women who seek to invert the stereotype—Esther, Ada, Caddy—use their strength to compensate for and conceal the man's weakness. The men who seem to invert the stereotype redirect their sexuality towards their obsession with the law, the one area in the novel's world that totally excludes women from power (Richard, Tulkinghorn); or they repress their sexuality by renouncing marriage in order to remain strong and kind, meaning chaste (George Rouncewell, John Jarndyce and, until he proposes to Esther, Allan Woodcourt); or they displace it through acts of violence and egotism (Krook, Grandfather Smallweed, the elder Turveydrop).

Grandfather Smallweed reveals how the man's self-assertion is all bluster, a false front to conceal his impotence when confronted by a woman. Every time Mrs. Smallweed spites her husband by alluding to "a fabulous amount" of money which he keeps hidden in his chair, "guarded by his spindle legs," he responds by hurling a cushion at her. This "act of jaculation," as Dickens calls it in one of the novel's most memorable scenes, pushes Mrs. Smallweed's head against the side of her chair while it throws him back against his own chair. Smallweed's aggression transforms him into "a mere clothes-bag," undermining his violent intention in order

114

to emphasize that "the contrast between those powerful expressions and his powerless figure is suggestive of a baleful old malignant, who would be very wicked if he could" (pp. 258-62). This grotesque and comic ballet is another version of the sexual conflict dramatized by the legend of Ghost's Walk. Sir Morbury lamed his wife, but her ghostly walk centuries later predicts the moment when "the pride of this house is humbled" by another Lady Dedlock (p. 84), and the husband is powerless to do anything about it even though he loves the woman very much and wants to forgive her. In other words, the woman undermines the man's strength because she reveals the limits and baseness of his sexuality. He finds himself attracted to her, providing her with the power to hurt him; this, in turn, drives him to destroy her. The Tulkinghorn-Dedlock conflict is a displaced version of this contest, a kind of drama enacted for Sir Leicester's benefit. Indeed, it could even be argued that through his legal representative Lady Dedlock wants to kill her husband, who has trapped and stifled her sexuality in the frozen world of Chesney Wold, a world that exaggerates the guilt she feels for living a life of deceit and that ultimately forces her to reject her daughter a second time only moments after acknowledging her. At the end of the novel Lady Dedlock causes Sir Leicester's breakdown; she has, in a sense, killed him emotionally. The man appears at the start of this action as an impotent figure; then, by usurping the woman's sexual secret in an attempt to exert his power, he brings on his own destruction, though he blames her for it.

The sexual encounter between Lady Dedlock and Hawdon, the origin of both Esther's birth and the novel's pervasive sense of sin, develops even further the psychological meaning of the Ghost's Walk prediction that woman betrays man by making him love her sexually. The narrator examines Hawdon's body and thinks: "If this forlorn man could have been prophetically seen lying here, by the mother at whose breast he nestled, a little child, with eyes upraised to her loving face, and soft hand scarcely knowing how to close upon the neck to which it crept, what an impossibility the vision would have seemed! O, if, in brighter days, the now-extinguished fire within him ever burned for one woman who held him in her heart, where is she, while these ashes

Chapter 4

are above the ground!" (p. 136). Who is this "one woman who held him in her heart"? At this early point in the novel Dicken's narrator has not yet revealed even the fact of Hawdon and Lady Dedlock's relationship, so this passage merely reads as sentimental posturing, similar to the section describing Jo's death. In the light of Lady Dedlock's secret, however, the passage seems more accusative than sentimental, and its ambiguity arises from the terrifying image of adult sexuality pictured in the story explaining the legend of Ghost's Walk. The first exclamation states that Hawdon's mother, who held him at her breast, could not possibly have imagined his horrible and ignominious end, and while the second exclamation could be a development of this sentiment, it could also be read as casting blame upon Hawdon's mistress, who also "held him in her heart" at one time, for having abandoned him to die unloved and unknown as a "nobody." The woman nurses and loves, and yet loves and betrays: hence the need to keep her dual roles as mother and mistress from fusing, in order to preserve belief in childhood innocence.

The logic of this pattern keeps pointing Samson's finger of blame at Lady Dedlock, who remains caught in an impossible position. She betrays her lover or husband when she leaves him, yet corrupts him when they come into contact; she can neither remain nor leave without damaging him in some way. Since she is Esther's mother, Dickens tries to erase from Lady Dedlock this implication of blame through the decoy of Hortense, but he can do so only by obscuring Lady Dedlock's sexuality behind her characteristic pose of frozen animation. Lady Dedlock's secret thus accounts for Esther's irrational feeling that she is at once guilty and innocent. It explains the taint of illegitimacy which makes this Foundling a Bastard, while suggesting the baselessness of her guilt by revealing its social origin: that is, the unmarried status of her parents simply has no bearing upon Esther's true worth, as her actions keep demonstrating. But the taint of sin cannot be so easily erased. Lady Dedlock's secret tie to Esther also reminds us of their common sexuality as women. As a result, though Esther herself seems unaware of her sexuality, her unnamed anxiety—her consciousness of being guilty and innocent—is nonetheless expressive of her origin as Lady Dedlock's daughter and all that this parentage implies for the novel. We therefore can see this mother and daughter working together to delineate the daughter's growth as a fully integrated consciousness in much the same way that a similar mother-daughter composite works in *Wuthering Heights*.

Indeed, because Dickens takes such pains to deny Esther's sexuality, the secret tie to her very sexual mother acquires all the more force and significance. For the most part, Dickens tries to keep mother and daughter separate in our minds as different types of women. He will not even let Esther retain the allure—physical beauty—with which she could capture and emasculate a man, as her mother has done. Esther, however, cannot be so easily protected. Like Hortense, Lady Dedlock and Esther each appear before Jo with their faces covered by a veil, and while the boy recognizes the differences between them, he also intuits the similarity. "Is there *three* of 'em then?" he finally asks, after meeting the daughter (p. 383). There exists only "one" woman in the sense that Hortense reenacts Lady Dedlock's sexual crime by murdering Tulkinghorn and Esther experiences the guilt and accomplishes the reparation. Together these three characters demonstrate the woman's inherent contamination as a sexual figure and her redemption as a maternal figure. This configuration helps Dickens "protect" Lady Dedlock, who stands between the polarity of Hortense and Esther, from becoming the novel's declared villain, even though the logic of the narrative insists she is guilty, the male her innocent victim. When Bucket takes over Tulkinghorn's role in the last lap of the sexual contest, he more cruelly torments Lady Dedlock with his knowledge of her guilt even though he already suspects that Hortense is the actual murderer. Bucket's victory over Hortense thus obscures the accuracy of the Ghost's Walk prediction. As a male figure proving the woman's guilt and announcing it to the world, he exculpates the mother by revealing that Lady Dedlock at least did not murder a man. But then, interestingly enough, in order to relieve the pressure of her sexual threat he sentences her to death anyway, teasing her into making the frenzied journey to her lover's grave which results in her death.

Dickens also uses a double to preserve for Esther's father some measure of innocence. George, who worked with Hawdon and possesses a sample of his handwriting (which Tulkinghorn needs to establish the captain's sexual tie to Lady Dedlock), acts as a stand-in for Hawdon in the latter part of the novel, which accounts for George's circumstantial involvement in Tulkinghorn's murder. If Hortense poses as the female guilt figure, replacing Lady Dedlock, then George poses as the male guilt figure, replacing Hawdon to imagine the father as an innocent. George's arrest can be seen as a consequence of the woman's guilt: he cannot escape the contamination, the shame, even though he is innocent. But because George did not in fact kill Tulkinghorn, his unjust imprisonment serves to reconcile this male figure with his own loving mother, Mrs. Rouncewell. Only the actual, reassuring presence of his mother can protect George from Hawdon's fatal experience of betrayal, guilt, and destruction at the hand of the female. Hawdon has affirmed that the man is as guilty as the woman: he, too, is Esther's secret parent. Hawdon's double therefore escapes this guilt by returning to a child-like state of innocence where he will never be a parent himself because he will never have to face the adult world of sexuality. George reverses the normal psychological pattern of male development which the novel tacitly, if fearfully, acknowledges: the son's transfer of attention from the maternal to the sexual woman.

Esther herself makes that normal kind of transition regarding her own identity when she exchanges the role of housekeeper for wife. Before her marriage, she not surprisingly "felt guilty and yet innocent" because as a woman she shares the guilt of her sex while at the same time she sees herself as a sexless mother figure, repressing her physical attraction to Woodcourt and earning the love of others by adopting the submissive, self-sacrificing role of Dame Durden. Whereas her mother causes the disintegration of family life, Esther acts as an idealized feminine figure brought into the various bleak and disordered houses of the novel to solve other people's problems and to make their lives more secure. Posing as an angel of the hearth, she swoops into Mrs. Jellyby's, tidies up what she can and ministers kindness to the children in the place of their absent mother and emasculated father. Even at Bleak House, where Esther is the center of Jarndyce's synthetic family unit, she serves him as his housekeeper. Esther's power as Dame Durden does not threaten men because her sense of being unworthy prevents her from expecting any man to find her sexually attractive. Aside from his unappealing personality, the attention of Guppy, who discovers her secret tie to Lady Dedlock by noticing the similarity in their faces, bothers Esther precisely because it is sexual. Her housekeeping role quiets her apprehensions about the more intimate affairs of adult men and women, so Dame Durden projects a regressive identity, a child's Family Romance glorification of the sexless mother and, hence, Esther's immature idea of what being a good adult amounts to.

Marriage to Jarndyce would consequently be another regressive step for Esther, as the novel's plot makes clear by moving her in that direction only to unite her instead to Allan Woodcourt. As Jarndyce's wife, Esther would still see herself as the daughter-housekeeper at Bleak House. Indeed, when Jarndyce proposes, he insists that their father-daughter relationship will not change no matter what she decides. Certainly, Dickens sees Jarndyce, whom Esther at first fantasizes might be her actual father, as a more fitting guardian than either her real father, who was part of the corrupting sexual cycle, or her aunt, who helped to incite Esther's excessive guilt by reminding her that mother and daughter are each other's disgrace. For Esther, adults oppress the self. Her aunt, in particular, exaggerates the child's guilt to preserve the illusion of *her* innocence. Jarndyce is a benevolent parent, a child's idealization of the father, removed from the fallen adult world of Esther's real parents. Thus before Esther can come to terms with her own adult sexuality she needs to work through the parent-child tension that has distorted her sense of identity as far back as childhood, which she does by learning the truth about her origins. Then she can identify with her real mother to redirect the momentum of her life so that it moves forward. Dickens first suggests this happening for Esther when he has Jarndyce unexpectedly propose to her. Now her guardian responds to her as lover more than parent. Whereas previously Esther has seen her self either protected by adults (Jarndyce) or oppressed by them (her aunt), she begins to identify with their power and their sexuality. This engagement therefore marks the transition for her from innocence to maturity, with her eventual marriage to Woodcourt not so much replacing as advancing upon her daugh-

Chapter 4

terly relationship to Jarndyce to insure the virility and normality of marriage for her. The new Bleak House harmonizes male and female sexuality to redress the disorder—and sterility—of Chesney Wold and the old Bleak House as well.

In this light, Esther offers Dickens's most sincere effort to portray a complicated yet normal woman in this novel, a woman who recognizes her sexuality, however belatedly, without making it tantamount to total corruption of innocence. Ada, on the other hand, is another matter altogether. It is appropriate that she ends up without a husband at Jarndyce's Bleak House, for Ada is Esther's immature daydream self; she projects the beautiful, innocent, contented, and loved girl Esther wishes to be and, thankfully, is not. If Jarndyce is the father Esther never had, Ada is the innocent daughter Esther never was, and Esther fusses over her and even dominates her with the assured superiority of a mother. When Ada marries Richard, Esther responds like a mother who has just lost her daughter, "sobbing and crying" because she now sees her own life "so blank without her" (p. 615). Esther uses Ada much as she once used her doll, to compensate for her own inferior position as the unwanted illegitimate daughter and to acquire the power of a mother within the dynamics of personal relationships. After Esther first sees her real mother in the church, Lady Dedlock "took a graceful leave of Ada—none of me" (p. 231). Here Ada unintentionally receives the fulfillment of Esther's own yearning for maternal recognition. Later, as W. J. Harvey has pointed out, the climax of chapter 36, which dramatizes Esther's reunion with her mother, occurs not with this reunion, as might be expected, but with that between Esther and Ada. "The curious thing," Harvey observes, "is [that] the feelings aroused by the Esther-Ada relationship seem more intense—and intensely rendered—than those aroused by the Esther-Lady Dedlock encounter."[14] Yet is this really all that puzzling? After all, Esther's temporary "rejection" of Ada during her illness has inversely paralleled her own situation as Lady Dedlock's daughter. When Ada finally gets to see Esther again after their lengthy separation, Esther can experience the kind of innocently tearful and openly emotional scene that her own mother could not provide because the threat of exposure and shame hangs over their secret relationship. Esther, moreover, has inverted the situation to control it; she has decided when to reject Ada and when to take her back; she does not have this kind of power as Lady Dedlock's secret daughter.

Esther's intense feelings for Ada—her unconscious manipulation of Ada as an idealized second self, one more beautiful, more beloved, more innocent—suggests how *Bleak House* uses Ada as an alternate, less dreadful portrayal of the female's guilt. If the novel points the finger of blame at the female for the self's corruption, then Ada's idealized figure attempts to silence that accusation. She acts, in effect, as a reply to Lady Dedlock's secret about female sexuality. In placing Ada in this context I want not to belabor her obvious, if cloying, appeal to sentimentality but to build on Jo's suggestion of the three-faced image of woman, only this time arguing that Ada and Lady Dedlock embody the two extremes of the female self—one innocent, the other corrupt—between which falls Esther, who shares the feelings of each and thus presents the most human, most balanced face of the three.

When all is said and done, Ada offers an unsatisfying reply to the anxiety orchestrated by this novel because this "virgin mother" can embody innocence at the novel's close only by having her sexuality erased completely. In her relationship with Richard, all that remains of the Ghost's Walk image of sexual contest is the man striking the woman. Despite his good intentions, Richard ends up abusing Ada though she gives him no cause and remains faithful to him to the end. With this couple, in other words, Dickens simply removes the woman's initial act of betrayal and her revenge. Instead, the woman suffers an emotional blow which she does not deserve and which she rather easily overcomes when she moves with her child Richard back to Jarndyce's house. Ada's suffering, in fact, seems to increase the value of her purity, to make her seem even more innocent than before: "The sorrow that has been in her face—for it is not there now—seems to have purified even its innocent expression, and to have given it a diviner quality" (p. 769).

A dynamic picturing the innocent female and guilty male, however, is certainly as illogical as its opposite, the guilty female and innocent male. Because the novel constructs experience out of an anxiety about sexual guilt, it contradicts the credulity of Ada's innocence on every page. We cannot read *Bleak House,* or any of Dickens's other novels for that matter, without recognizing that its fictive world is grounded, irrevocably, in the loss of innocence that not only defines the adult self, but the child's too. Consequently, while Dickens often tries to preserve in his more idealized—or, as he would have us believe, more normalized—characters some measure of their childish innocence, especially when they are women, the larger contexts of his novels continually disprove their innocence, undermining the sentimentality with which he sanctifies it. As *Bleak House* shows, innocence cannot survive; his fictional world is too fraught with the guilt of living in the fallen adult world of sexual desire, the psyches of his characters too easily, as Estella says about herself and Pip in the revised ending of *Great Expectations,* "bent and broken"—and not necessarily, as she thinks, "into a better shape."[15] Thus Dickens's imagination finds its richest expression when he works with a character whom he sees simultaneously as child and adult, the kind of dual view implicit in Pip's narration, or David Copperfield's, but also the kind vividly dramatized by the curious relationship between Jenny Wren and her father Mr. Dolls in *Our Mutual Friend,* in which each is both abusive parent and suffering child. Child-adult and adult-child is each "guilty and yet innocent." The same, we must remember, can also be said of the first Lady Dedlock and Sir Morbury in the Ghost's Walk legend, and this makes the condemnation of adulthood as a corruption of innocence much harder to defend through the "diviner quality" of Ada's "innocent expression."

Put very simply, the adult's sexuality is the proof of original sin for Dickens: the child must grow up to be a sexual adult herself. As a consequence, the fallen world of adults generates an anxious feeling of dislocation for Dickens's characters because experience affirms their corruption by underscoring their guilt. They are not innocent, so they must accept that "what might have been is not what is," as Mr. Wilfer sadly observes in *Our Mutual Friend.*[16] This realization is hard to effect in practice, however, as Miss Havisham shows in *Great Expectations.* Whether child or adult, Dickens's characters all have in common an obsessive fixation, like Miss Havisham's, upon the traumatic moment of recognition that their innocence has been lost to them forever. Miss Havisham is therefore truer to the disillusioning impact of experience in Dickens's novels than is Ada, whose innocence he preserves by encircling her with an untarnishable halo. Miss Havisham feels abused by the other sex; he has destroyed her own Great Expectations of love and marriage. Significantly, however, she does not stop the clocks in Satis House to restore the illusion of her innocence. She rabidly fixes instead upon the moment when Compeyson violated her innocence, causing her heart to break.[17] While she clings to her identity as injured innocence because, like Ada's purified expression, it seems to proclaim her guiltlessness to the world, she responds by treating the other sex as brutally as she herself felt treated. Despite her denial of complicity in her own violation, she too is not above the sexual aggression engaged in by male and female alike as we saw it enacted in the Ghost's Walk legend.

This very lesson Pip must also learn before he can exorcise the spell of illusion which blinds him to the reality of otherness. *Great Expectations* directly focuses our attention upon the sexual guilt which I have shown to be at work behind the construction of experience in *Bleak House*, so this later novel, which processes experience through the clarifying voice of a single self, the narrator Pip, helps to pull together and centralize the more intricate and decentered patterns of anxiety I traced in that earlier work.

The education Pip receives in the course of his experience includes a psychological lesson in sexual roles as well as a moral discovery about his own pride and egoism.[18] He is made to confront his distorted impressions of women, whose absolute power he sees as the cause of masculine suffering, and to understand that men, too, can be powerful, just as women, too, can suffer. In effect, Pip redresses the destructive battle of men and women so vividly imaged in the legend of Ghost's Walk, learning first to respond to adults with less hostility and guilt, and then to realize that his repressed identification with Magwitch as a fellow man is not necessarily a sign of his own moral corruption, as his sister makes him believe. Like Esther and the other children of abusive or absent parents in *Bleak House,* Pip must learn that adult men and women are capable of kindness as well as violence. For him this is an especially difficult realization since, from his earliest perceptions on, the adults in his world inflict one damaging bruise after another upon his self.

Great Expectations directs Pip towards this realization with a clarity that *Bleak House* does not offer any one of its characters because the later novel builds experience from what the earlier novel only implies through Esther's history: that the child is parent to the adult for both are equally guilty. Dickens begins *Great Expectations* with the important moment when the child Pip first realizes his separateness as a self. His parents are dead, and of all his brothers Pip alone has survived. This realization frightens him: he feels inadequate to the task of surviving "the universal struggle" which has bested his brothers. His "first most vivid and broad impression of the identity of things" therefore results from his awareness of the bleak, desolate churchyard that contains what is left of his origins, and the discovery overwhelms him since it locates his self amidst an inhuman, alienating landscape of death. This graveyard is no garden of innocence by any means, yet it is Pip's playground, the lonely background which highlights his identity as a self. "The small bundle of shivers growing afraid of it all and beginning to cry," he concludes the second long paragraph of description, "was Pip" (pp. 1-2). As an adult he does not easily outgrow his belittling self-identification.

When Magwitch suddenly appears in the graveyard he shakes Pip up and down as if to make vivid what the boy fears most: his complete vulnerability and isolation in the face of the other. Pip's helplessness—before Magwitch, before his sister, before Pumblechook—makes him afraid of adults, so that he misunderstands the difference between child (self) and adult (other) as a contest of power in which the child invariably loses because of the adult's inalienable right to authority. Magwitch, however, calls this understanding into question at the very start. He is an ambiguous and provocative projection of Pip's self, at once guilty and innocent, adult and child, capable of great violence and yet victimized by lawyers and gentlemen. Consciously, Pip sees Magwitch as another adult to fear; subconsciously, he cannot help identifying his bruised and vulnerable self with Magwitch. The convict may be "[a] fearful man," but he is also "soaked in water, and smothered in mud, and lamed by stones, and cut by flints, and stung by nettles, and torn by briars." When he seizes Pip by the chin (a gesture uncannily anticipating Pumblechook's later arrogant display of power over Pip), Magwitch is shivering so badly that his "teeth chattered in his head" (p. 2). Behind this monstrous face of otherness, Magwitch is a "bundle of shivers" just like Pip. This unconscious identification with the convict frightens Pip because, while it brings out his own feelings of helplessness, it taints them with guilt, for, we will later learn, Pip is angry at feeling helpless, and he equates his anger with a violent desire for retribution and, hence, with guilt. Like his surrogate parents Magwitch and Miss Havisham, Pip wants vengeance against his oppressors.

Pip's anger is particularly directed at his sister, although his narration, as a reflection of his consciousness, continually displaces that anger onto other objects. When he returns home from the graveyard, frightened to death by Magwitch and aware that he must conspire with the convict to steal from his sister, Mrs. Joe's sharp answers to his questions reinforce his fear that he and the convict are kin: "People are put in the Hulks," she exclaims "because they murder, and because they rob, and forge, and do all sorts of bad; and they always begin by asking questions." Mrs. Joe can only assert her authority over Pip through brutal, not patient or tender, instruction. Pip's reaction, of course, is to feel "fearfully sensible of the great convenience that the Hulks were handy for me. I was clearly on my way there. I had begun by asking questions, and I was going to rob Mrs. Joe." Even before Mrs. Joe makes Pip feel this way, Joe has tried to fend off his wife's impatience by mouthing an answer to Pip's question, "What's a convict?" But the boy can only make out "the single word, 'Pip'" (pp. 13-14). Significantly, for Pip the words "convict" and "Pip" seem to be equated, confirming once more what he has just discovered in the graveyard.

When Mrs. Joe answers that an intelligent, curious child is no better than a convict, she violates Pip's sense of his own integrity—and of his innocence. Unlike Frank Osbaldistone in

Chapter 4

Rob Roy, Pip is dependent upon an unkind as well as unloving parent who intensifies the guilt caused by his secret resentment of her and his impulse to disobey her authority. Self-righteously, she enjoys advertising what it supposedly costs her to raise her little brother, and part of Pip believes her claims. As a result of such psychic assaults, Pip tends to distrust weak adults and to respect aggressive ones, assuming that all adults—save Joe, whom he sees as a fellow child—openly wish, as Pumblechook informs him with fork in cheek at the Christmas dinner, to carve up or disembowel any little "Squeaker" who happens to get in their way (p. 27).

Thus all his life, he tells us, still smarting after his first meeting with Estella, he has nursed his resentment of his sister's injustice. Yet he could never articulate his anger in order to act upon it. He could only dwell upon it "in a solitary and unprotected way," letting it remain a feeling seemingly alien to his self. His reticence to articulate his anger, let alone to act upon it, has made him, he now realizes in retrospect, like Esther, "morally timid and very sensitive" as a child (p. 66). There is certainly a good deal of comfort, not to say virtue, to be gained from feeling one is the passive victim of injustice. Because this feeling denies anger and disguises the irresistible impulse to pay the oppressor back in kind, it confirms one's sense of innocence. But that very response is also what has motivated Miss Havisham's desire for revenge, so it is clear, too, that by repressing his anger Pip has prevented himself from accepting his own emotions, which would let him see more clearly the humanity of male and female alike. He instead sees the two sexes in opposition, identifying women as figures of power (his sister, Miss Havisham, Estella), strong men as their pompous or ominous agents (Pumblechook, Jaggers), weak men as their victims (Joe, himself and, ultimately, Magwitch), and this distorted view of sexual power is his most debilitating illusion, the one which arrests his maturation in his unresolved childhood experience.

Not surprisingly, then, the secret, guilty feeling of kinship with Magwitch continues to haunt Pip unexpectedly at points throughout his life. As an adult he can never completely brush off "the prison dust" from his clothes or "exhale its air from his lungs" (p. 285) because he cannot avoid coming to terms with his own identity as an adult male. Indeed, the association of Newgate Prison with his adored Estella emphasizes just how closely Magwitch, like Estella and her guardian, is bound up with Pip's feelings of guilt about his sexuality, which was disturbing to him even as a child. Because Pip's repressed emotions keep pulling him back to his original moment of self-consciousness, his anxiety generates a regressive momentum that retards his growth, so his narration keeps looking backward as well as forward. Only with Magwitch's return does Pip finally begin to confront the self he has disguised all his life, for then he relives that formative experience to set right his buried emotional life.

Broadly speaking, this process involves three stages. First, alone in his room, Pip hears Magwitch walking up the stairs and imagines that the convict's footsteps are those of his sister's ghost. Because the authority figure whom he most fears has always been an intimidating woman—Mrs. Joe, Miss Havisham, Estella—the groundwork for his self-confrontation is laid through his discovery that this mysterious visitor is a man, not a woman. Second, when Magwitch discloses that he is the source of Pip's Great Expectations, Pip realizes how much Miss Havisham and Estella have exploited him. He is not yet fully dealing with his emotions, however, for he still experiences his anger towards Miss Havisham as guilt, recalling his earlier feeling that he was somehow responsible for the attack on his sister. A similar feeling colors his visits to Satis House once he knows the truth. His act of saving Miss Havisham from the fire is, in fact, an act of aggression against her, reminding us of Orlick's attack on Mrs. Joe, in that Pip has to wrestle the old lady to the ground and physically attack her in order to put out the fire on her dress: "we were on the ground struggling like desperate enemies" (p. 434). The desperate struggle with Miss Havisham expresses the anger towards her which Pip has always guiltily suppressed,[19] but which he must confront if he is to exorcise his dread of woman as the alien other sex. In this scene he repeats the action imaged in the legend of Ghost's Walk, where the female forces the male to brutalize her in retaliation for her attempt to emasculate him.

The third and final stage in Pip's self-confrontation occurs when Orlick tries to murder him in the sluicehouse. Now, after all

Chapter 4

those years of secret resentment, Pip finally hears his anger at his sister voiced:

> It was you as did for your shrew sister. . . . I tell you it was your doing—I tell you it was done through you . . . I come upon her from behind, as I come upon you to-night. I giv' it her! I left her for dead, and if there had been a limekiln as nigh her as there is now nigh you, she wouldn't have come to life again. But it warn't Old Orlick as did it; it was you. You was favoured, and he was bullied and beat. Old Orlick bullied and beat, eh? Now you pays for it. You done it; now you pays for it. (p. 461)

Here Orlick, obviously Pip's double, articulates the rage that Pip has always feared expressing. It is no coincidence that Pip falls in love with a woman who has been taught to feel nothing. As an ideal placed high above him in the stars, Estella, his sister in childhood at Satis House, cannot easily tempt him into the violence and anger that his real sister makes him feel. Orlick's accusation allows Pip to understand what had been an unsettling sensation when he learned of the attack on his sister: like Esther, he felt "guilty and yet innocent." Orlick therefore allows Pip to see the important difference between a desire and the deed. He may have nursed his resentment but he is not responsible for his sister's debilitation since he did not enact the thought; he only felt it. And if his guilt has made him learn anything, it is that he cannot disown his feelings, indeed he must not. Hence the surge of relief Pip feels upon his rescue from Orlick, and the intensified fidelity to Magwitch and then to Joe that follows upon this scene.

Once Pip works out his resentment towards the other sex, the adult world no longer seems threatening or mysterious, so he no longer needs his childish self-image as the bruised victim to defend against the acceptance of his own guilty behavior towards Magwitch and Joe. As a child Pip may not have deserved his sister's abusive treatment, but as an adult he must live with the complete absence of the illusions that once made him feel he could have been innocent if adults had only left him alone. His sense of loss as an adult, emphasized by the Miltonic echo in the revised ending, comes about because reality cannot restore the illusion of innocence that his maturity has dispelled. But what the disenchanted Pip can achieve is an honest acceptance of himself as an adult male. This is no small accomplishment. Pip is able to accept his loss of innocence because his experience has taught him the origin of his illusions, showing him where he himself was guilty (in rejecting Joe) and where he was not to blame (in resenting his sister). Once Pip understands his world through an adult's eyes, it becomes less terrible, less hostile, and he achieves a degree of self-knowledge which makes him superior to his oppressors.

Great Expectations constructs Pip's experience in keeping with the paradigm to show that in the very violation of his innocence in childhood the way was paved for the reparation that later comes with the knowledge achieved through maturity. The same is true of Miss Havisham. She similarly demonstrates that in suffering a violation by a reality resistant to desire one can arrive at a more compassionate understanding of the other sex. As she tells Pip, "until I saw in you a looking-glass that showed me what I once felt myself, I did not know what I had done. What have I done!" (p. 431). With Pip as her mirror and she his, they both come to appreciate the humanity of the other sex, tempering their anger and resentment at the inescapable and harrowing violation of their faith in innocence. The mantle of innocence may console Pip just as it consoles Miss Havisham, by defining the other as something *other*, as something whose corrupt, brutal, and horrific desires are absent in his own self and thus alien to his nature. But the point repeatedly made by *Great Expectations* is that Pip cannot wrap himself in innocence any more than Miss Havisham can, as the dreamlike landscape before him, with its many doubles and frequent revelations of his secret guilt, keeps reminding him.

Even though Pip tries to discount the underlying continuity of his experience in an effort to believe in his innocence, the bildungsroman frame of the novel insists upon the continuity between the child and the adult, distinguishing this child from the many other abused children in Dickens's fiction. Pip's very name, which he cannot change according to the terms of his Great Expectations, is an emblem of continuity, for it locates the origin—the seed—of his adult consciousness in his childhood experience. That his confused and disturbing sexual identity develops out of his childhood serves as an even denser marker of

Chapter 4

the inescapable continuity between child and adult. This is why Pip cannot achieve peace with himself until he recognizes the other sex as something other yet similar. Since women seem like creatures alien to his self—they violate his innocence by betraying his Great Expectations—he separates self from other, past from present, to keep his innocence intact. But the other—in either gender—repeatedly serves as a "looking-glass" of his desire and anxiety to show him the folly of that form of self-identification. To be sure, when Pip envisions the other sex as something profoundly alien to his self, his mistrust of that other projects his own dread of becoming an adult; and so long as he dreads the other sex, experience traumatizes him with the anxiety that his maturity is a process of violation. To reach maturity he must, like Miss Havisham, see his own suffering mirrored in the face of the other, as he does in the revised ending when he meets Estella again.

Admittedly, by casting Pip's maturation in the light of his repressed sexuality, I have concentrated on what he himself does not dwell upon as narrator: his dread of the other sex. Obviously, much of the anxiety about sexuality in *Great Expectations,* as in *Bleak House* and the Waverley novels, not to say *Clarissa* and *Wuthering Heights* too, is made striking because of the pronounced absence of any real physical sexual activity. Pip's "wrestling" with Miss Havisham, for example, like the legend of Ghost's Walk in *Bleak House*, images a sexual encounter but does not describe it as such literally. Pip's resentment of the female, as well as his eventual acceptance of her otherness, is rendered through physical action only in moments of non-sexual contact, like his saving of Miss Havisham or even his taking Estella's hand in the revised ending. The power of such sexually redolent actions in Dickens's fiction is that because of their symbolic power they make the other seem all the more vividly present to the self's consciousness. In *Middlemarch*, George Eliot moves the self even further in this direction, to make the other a very human, very tangible presence that must be confronted directly. If marriage is the conventional sign of repair for Anna Howe, the Waverley hero, Elizabeth Bennet, and Esther, in *Middlemarch* it marks the very moment of the self's violation, for then the other, in the form of the other sex, is unavoidably present.

5
The Mill on the Floss and *Middlemarch*

"An intimate penetration"

In its paradigmatic construction of experience, the English novel, so I have been arguing, directs character and reader alike towards a recognition that the adult self does offer something of value—insight—to compensate for the inevitable loss of innocence which defines maturity. This construction of experience responds to a dread that, in its insistence on the loss of innocence, maturity requires a violation of self. As a result, the genre constructs experience as a contest between a progressive drive towards maturity and a regressive longing for innocence. Though *Middlemarch* clearly follows the familiar convention of leading characters from illusion to reality, George Eliot's novel may seem to be the most notable exception to the generic model I have been proposing, because of the so-called "somber" determination with which it minimizes the anxiety occasioned by a dread of maturity. This novel trumpets the virtue of maturity as wisdom on all fronts so loudly that Virginia Woolf even called it, in short, "one of the few English novels written for grown-up people."[1]

Unlike *Clarissa*, say, or *Wuthering Heights*, or *Bleak House*, *Middlemarch* constructs experience to demonstrate that adulthood is not the horrific violation of an innocent self. This very premise makes it seem "grown-up" in comparison to these other novels I have examined. We hear no lament for a lost innocence when reading this book. On the contrary, the narrator of *Middlemarch* takes pains to demonstrate the necessity of acknowledging the claims of the other even when they seem most alien, most hostile, and most false to the self's desiring imagination. Nonetheless, we must also recognize that this "somber" vision does not always inform Eliot's fiction with so clear or confident a direction. *The Mill on the Floss*, for example, is especially pertinent to what I have been arguing in preceding chapters. I therefore want to approach *Middlemarch* by way of this earlier and more problematic novel because it helps to highlight the anxiety about experience which *Middlemarch* seemingly discounts through its narrative voice but actually exposes through its characters.

In an obvious contrast to *Middlemarch, The Mill on the Floss* complicates its paradigmatic forward direction by raising a dread of maturity through Maggie Tulliver's regressive longing for childhood. Maggie's character recalls patterns we have already encountered. Like Esther and Pip, Maggie unaccountably feels "guilty and yet innocent" throughout her childhood and adult life. Like Edward Waverley, she resorts to daydreams, "refashioning her little world into just what she should like it to be."[2] And like both Clarissa and Cathy Earnshaw, she longs for an end to the turmoil of her rebellious emotions, seeing her adult life as a prison rather than a liberation. Like all of these characters, Maggie fears that maturity leads her away from her family, her childhood and, hence, her better self.[3]

In response to this fear Maggie craves to be loved; love is "the strongest need in poor Maggie's nature" because to her mind it creates a bond between self and other (p. 34). But despite her "blind, unconscious yearning for something that would link together the wonderful impressions of this mysterious life, and give her soul a sense of home in it" (p. 208), Maggie cannot "link" her rich imaginative consciousness to the unimaginative people who surround her, particularly her brother Tom, so she finds herself trapped in a hostile world, torn between two impulses: defiance and submission. No matter how severely her family criticizes her and deflates her self-worth, Maggie is still drawn to them for security. When she rejects Stephen Guest and returns to St. Ogg's by herself "for the sake of being true to all the motives that sanctify our lives" (p. 419), her thoughts repeat her longing to feel at home. "Home—where her mother and brother were—Philip—Lucy—the scene of her very cares and trials—was the haven towards which her mind tended—the sanctuary where sacred relics lay—where she would be rescued from more falling" (p. 420). This haven sanctifies her life by giving her a sense of place, by letting her cling to her secure familial role as the childish scapegrace whom the family always forgave after first scolding her.

Just what would allow Maggie to feel "at home" with her world? "There is no sense of ease," the narrator explains,

> like the ease we felt in those scenes where we were born, where objects became dear to us before we had known the labour of choice, and where the outer world seemed only an extension of our own personality: we accepted and loved it as we accepted our own sense of existence and our own limbs. . . . heaven knows where that striving [after something better and better in our surroundings] might lead us, if our affections had not a trick of twining round those old inferior things—if the loves and sanctities of our life had not deep immovable roots in memory. (p. 135)

Here Eliot defines the sense of being "at home" rather literally. Familiar things found in the home—objects, furniture, people—all make us feel "at ease" because they evoke a Wordsworthian sense of continuity between the self and family, the self and place, the self and time. Familiar things, colored by memory, substantiate the illusion that "the outer world seemed only an extension of our own personality," a fiction of self-importance which calls to mind the pier glass analogy Eliot later uses in *Middlemarch* as a "parable" of her characters' egoism. There the narrator evokes the image of a scratched polished surface. The scratches, which are "events," actually go in all directions at once, but they acquire "the flattering illusion of a concentric arrangement" when illuminated by a lighted candle, "which is the egoism of any person." For the narrator this "parable" explains the behavior of Rosamond Vincy, who assumes that events revolve exclusively around her concerns, the world being no more than an extension of her personality.[4]

Chapter 5

Much the same is true of Maggie: Eliot makes us aware that the innocence of her childhood is more fiction than fact. Even as a child Maggie, like Pip, does not always feel "at home" with her family, let alone with the "outer world," no matter how hard she tries or how aggressively she loves. Her brother Tom abuses her in the name of love and duty, values close to Maggie's heart. While she is certainly more aware of her anger than Pip, Maggie nonetheless submits to Tom's harsh, unfeeling judgments because, as she tries to explain to Lucy, "I can't divide myself from my brother for life" (p. 384). Tom is all that remains of her childhood self after she grows up. Her earliest memory, she claims, "is standing with Tom by the side of the Floss, while he held my hand: everything before that is dark to me" (p. 268). She cannot divide herself from Tom without sacrificing the illusion that her childhood, at least, was a time of acceptance and love, and that Tom, the one stable reminder of the continuity of her life, makes her feel "at home" because he allows her to envision the outer world as an extension of her personality.

Although Tom's presence allows Maggie to imagine a continuity for her life, not to mention its origin in a time of childhood innocence, his importance to her is more complicated than that. Maggie attributes contradictory meanings to Tom in the act of loving him so wholeheartedly. Tom represents adulthood as well as childhood, insuring that sense of continuity; but he also serves as an agent of disruption and discontinuity, in that he personifies the authority of the other, of everything that Maggie herself is not. This is why she longs to extend her self to his through love. Bernard J. Paris observes that "Maggie strongly identifies with her father and brother, partly because she wants them to identify with her in return, and partly because through them she can vicariously experience her aggressive drives."[5] Even more precisely, in this scheme Tom is a replacement for her weak father, whom she idolizes and who never seems to criticize her, but whose authority is continually undermined by the Dodson family. Maggie therefore makes Tom into an inverted Family Romance parent, a substitute father who reminds her of reality's harsh indifference to her desire. Her father satisfies her need to be loved, but because she does not trust his unequivocal acceptance even though she desperately craves it, she directs her feelings towards her brother, further confusing desire and reality. Every time Tom criticizes her in the name of reality and brotherly love she idealizes him and their shared origin all the more.

This confusion becomes pronounced as Maggie grows older and becomes more disturbed by the barriers, which she herself helps to construct, that keep her from feeling "at home" with the outer world. Tom then acquires even more authority for her because he is so inextricably part of the memories recording the continuity of her life. As a child Maggie may daydream in order to escape the frustration and rejection she experiences, but as an adult she associates her "imaginative and passionate nature" with a childish part of her self, one she is very willing to sacrifice (p. 241). She mistakenly assumes that adulthood requires this sacrifice because Tom, her model of adult authority, has always lacked imagination and passion. Duty to the family, loyalty to the past—Maggie believes these are the primary responsibilities of adulthood, so she conforms to Tom's self-righteous morality and accepts him as an authority because their family has repeatedly validated his viewpoint and because she loves him (in many ways the latter reason is the consequence of the former). Even though she discovers aspects of his character which she despises—he is petty, insensitive, closed-minded, vindictive—she still equates these characteristics with an adult personality. "Her brother was the human being of whom she had been most afraid, from her childhood upwards: afraid with that fear which springs in us when we love one who is inexorable, unbending, unmodifiable—with a mind that we can never mould ourselves upon, and yet that we cannot endure to alienate from us" (p. 422). Tom, in other words, embodies both Maggie's desire to feel "at home" and her realization that her own "imaginative and passionate nature" makes her an alien in their "home." By reminding her that the outer world is *not* an extension of her personality, Tom convinces her that she can join his world only by sacrificing her personality.

At face value, then, Maggie's predicament seems straightforward enough. Pulled in one direction by Tom and her culture, she is driven in another direction by her self and its nature. But in fact these two competing directions lead Maggie towards the same

Chapter 5

end, the destruction of self inherent in desire. Maggie can never achieve a feeling of kinship with the other because the novel asks us to understand that desire as a contradiction in terms: if her self were to become an extension of the other it would cease to be "self." Thus the novel keeps placing attractive alternatives before Maggie only to undermine their attractiveness as alternatives. For the whole point of her experience is that what she desires is what she dreads: the otherness which exists outside her self and always threatens to overwhelm it.

Maggie herself understands this dilemma in rather conventional terms as a conflict between feeling and reason, "between the inward impulse and outward fact" (p. 241). If Tom stands for maturity in her eyes, then Philip Wakem and Stephen Guest appeal to her "imaginative and passionate nature," which she equates with immaturity. The contradictions in her life arise because that nature motivates and gives meaning to her life yet, as Tom keeps reminding her, it also leads her astray by encouraging her to act irresponsibly. Although his own moral arrogance makes his position suspect, Tom's judgment is in fact confirmed by Maggie's "nature." For one thing, "that passionate sensibility . . . belonged to her *whole* nature, and made her faults and virtues all merge in each other" (p. 350, my emphasis). This is why she can never succeed in her effort to be more like Tom without being unfaithful to her self or destroying it altogether. For another, her passion and imagination, so the narrator makes a point of telling us, expose a relentless egoism, as illustrated by "her zeal of self-mortification" following her father's bankruptcy (p. 257). Consequently, what makes Maggie's "passionate sensibility" disturbing is its underlying aggressiveness. This is the same young woman, after all, who confesses to Stephen, "I think I am quite wicked with roses—I like to gather them and smell them until they have no scent left" (p. 387). Maggie's reaction to the world around her is to overwhelm it with intense emotion; then she can bring it within the commanding orbit of her desire. What she fails to realize is that her "passionate sensibility" does not center her consciousness, as the will to power motivating her passion might seem to imply; it actually de-centers it by breaking down the difference which defines "self" in opposition to "other."

We therefore should not minimize the ambiguity with which the novel characterizes Maggie in terms of her "imaginative and passionate nature." To begin with, because Maggie's feelings for Philip and Stephen do place her in opposition to Tom, exacerbating her alienation from home and increasing her longing for it, she comes to understand her "imaginative and passionate nature" as a subversion of her identity. The circumstances surrounding her relationship to Philip do not cause so much as reinforce her willingness to push imagination and passion to the outskirts of her conscious life in order to retain her identity as Tom's sister. Philip is Tom's sworn enemy, so she can easily separate the pleasure he makes her feel when they are together from the main current of her life. However, since this relationship goes back to their childhood, Philip is not simply an occasional distraction from reality, as Maggie often sees their meetings, but a familiar component of her emotional life; furthermore, Philip's treatment of her is always an implicit criticism of Tom's failure to love her as Philip does, "devotedly, as she had always longed to be loved" (p. 333). Nonetheless, because Maggie cannot take that criticism seriously enough to break with Tom completely, all Philip offers her, finally, is a respite from her brother's unyielding authority, not a convincing alternate perspective from which to view her "imaginative and passionate nature" as anything more than the source of selfish daydreams and stolen pleasures.

Stephen, on the other hand, poses a more disturbing threat to Maggie's identity as Tom's sister because he offers her that alternate perspective. In contrast to Philip, Stephen forces Maggie to imagine her adult life as a rupture with childhood, not as an extension of it. Her desire for Stephen epitomizes an adult self whose sexuality obviously frightens her because it places her in a situation—the illicit elopement—which rejects every motive and every person she has depended upon and sanctified since childhood: Philip and Lucy as well as Tom (who is marginal to the sexual plot here). Consequently, although her desire for Stephen at first encourages her to imagine her self effortlessly connected to the other, after acting upon that desire Maggie claims she didn't do so by choice, feeling instead that she has been tricked out of herself.

Stephen has much the same effect upon Maggie that Lovelace has upon Clarissa. Indeed, Maggie's elopement with Stephen to Mudport is reminiscent of Clarissa's flight with Lovelace to St. Albans in several ways. Like Clarissa, Maggie equivocates about her responsibility for determining this action, explaining to Stephen afterwards, "I couldn't choose yesterday" (p. 415). Feeling "enveloped" in an "enchanted haze" (p. 407), Maggie also feels robbed of her will, "hardly conscious of having said or done anything decisive" (p. 410). This dreamy passivity exposes Maggie to the danger of acting upon desire: it amounts to a loss of self in the face of the other. "All yielding is attended with a less vivid consciousness than resistance," the narrator explains; "it is the partial sleep of thought; it is the submergence of our personality by another" (p. 410). By not resisting her desire, Maggie experiences a loss of consciousness, the erotically "enchanted haze" which has been hanging over her strong sense of Stephen as a "presence" throughout this section of the novel (pp. 335, 352). Only afterwards does she see the submergence of her personality by his as a violation of her better self.

Since Stephen's very sexual presence has the disturbing effect of making Maggie feel "absent" from her self, she finds something dreadful in his attractiveness. He is as "wicked" with her, so to speak, as she is herself with roses: he gathers her up and she has no self left, so how could she have "chosen" to run off with him? Maggie therefore rejects Stephen in an effort to reestablish her self by resanctifying the family as an extension of her personality. As she tries to make him understand, she must give him up because otherwise "it would send me away from all that my past has made dear and holy to me" (p. 420). She rationalizes her suffering and then glorifies it in another instance of zealous self-mortification because, ironically enough, in order to feel "at home" in the world, she can imagine her self as an extension of the other only through an act of self-denial. In refusing to stay with Stephen Maggie is merely exchanging one kind of self-denial (her sacrifice

The Mill on the Floss *and* Middlemarch

of love in the name of duty) for another (her rejection by Tom upon her return as if she had not given up Stephen).

The irony here is important to an understanding of the way *The Mill on the Floss* constructs Maggie's experience in keeping with the genre's paradigmatic rhythm of violation and repair. Indeed, as I have been analyzing it so far, *The Mill* moves Maggie past the point of repair, as her death makes evident. When viewed from this perspective Maggie's life turns out to be a perfect waste of her great talent and energy. With her "imaginative and passionate nature" arrested in childhood, the result of her upbringing is a rather morbid adult personality preoccupied with self-sacrifice, even self-destruction. But could it have been any other way? The novel records all the contradictions of a culture which does not appreciate an intelligent, emotional woman like Maggie but instead conspires against her vitality because, as Mr. Wakem remarks, "[it's] rather dangerous and unmanageable, eh?" (p. 374). Even Maggie's beloved father believes "a woman's no business wi' being so clever; it'll turn to trouble, I doubt" (p. 16). To be sure, one cannot keep from smiling at the realization that Mr. Tulliver misdirects his ambitions by placing all his hopes upon his son's rather weak shoulders, for Maggie, being more intelligent than her brother, would surely have had much less trouble advancing professionally to fulfill her father's aspirations—had she been a man. At times Maggie herself cannot restrain her anger at the cultural limitations she keeps discovering. When she finally tells Tom off in the Red Deeps, she exclaims that he can exert authority over her only "because you are a man, Tom, and have power, and can do something in the world," whereas she, a woman, cannot act but only "submit to what I acknowledge and feel to be right" (p. 304). And since Tom flaunts his moral status as their father's avenger as well as his cultural prestige in being a man, all Maggie can do is submit before his will.

Several feminist critics have pursued this theme in an attempt to locate a unifying set of values for the book, although they recognize the ambivalence which works against a fully clarified attitude towards Maggie's relationship with her brother and her culture. Gilbert and Gubar, for example, place Eliot in the tradition of women writers and find her using this novel "to analyze female enthrallment, born of women's complete dependence on men for self-definition and self-esteem."[6] Patricia Meyer Spacks argues a similar case but arrives at a different conclusion. "George Eliot's feminism recognizes the social injustice of woman's position only to declare its irrelevance to the more important matter of personal fulfillment: a bold stance." Or at least it is in theory, since Spacks goes on to explain that for Eliot the most satisfying form of personal fulfillment is actually "selflessness," which only serves to dignify "an ancient and self-comforting male argument."[7] As Nancy Miller points out, this culturally imposed value of "selflessness," rooted in Maggie's overwhelming desire to be loved, is an impoverishment of female desire. Miller questions what "personal fulfillment" actually means in this novel, and she puts the matter in terms of the way novels traditionally plot desire for feminine characters according to a masculine script. "Everywhere in *The Mill on the Floss*," she contends, "one can read a protest against the division of labor that grants men the world and women love."[8] As a result, Miller sees Eliot's novel contesting the romantic plots which—in contrast, say, to the Waverley novels and their location of the hero in history—formulate a woman's life in terms of love, thereby locating her ambitious wishes entirely within her erotic longings. Miller thus reads *The Mill* as "two" novels, one recording the cultural oppression of Maggie, one working to rewrite the values which authorize that oppression by making it seem natural. With Miller's reading in mind, Mary Jacobus analyzes this operation further, concentrating especially on Maggie's union with Tom in death. "What is striking about the novel's ending," Jacobus remarks, "is its banishing not simply of division but of sexual difference as the origin of that division. . . . we can scarcely avoid concluding that death is a high price to pay for such imaginary union . . . and that the abolition of difference marks the death of desire for Maggie." Jacobus goes on to propose that we see "an alternate version" of desire formulated by the "sameness" imagined in the ending. This second version of the novel's ending orchestrates "the thematics of female desire" in order to restore

The Mill on the Floss *and* Middlemarch

what a male culture denies to a woman, namely, "her most fundamental relationship: her relationship to herself."[9] Put more simply, Jacobus reads *The Mill* as Eliot's effort to write a genuine female consciousness for herself, which she achieves by "killing off" a masculine conception of the heroine, Maggie.

Since so much criticism of *The Mill on the Floss* has read Maggie as a projection of wish fulfillment on Eliot's part, one important consequence of Miller's and Jacobus's readings is that they help to disengage Maggie's emotional life from her author's imagination. Furthermore, they show the need for a plural reading of the novel, its ending in particular. Maggie's death raises a question which remains problematic, even in Miller's and Jacobus's readings: how easily can one draw that fine line between selflessness and self-destruction, between innocence and death? The unity Maggie seeks with Tom invariably places self in opposition to the other. While her sense of being different from him defines her self, it also intensifies her desire to be like him; therefore, given her strong personality, the fulfillment she craves, the fusion of self and other, can only come about through her death. Death restores her innocence in that it replaces difference with sameness, as Jacobus observes, but this transformation does not extend self outward to the other so much as mark the destruction of self altogether.

Maggie's embrace with Tom in death therefore turns out to be a disturbing and ironic fulfillment of her desire for unity. While it returns Maggie to her first memory, their dying embrace underscores the fact that she and Tom were never as close, never as one with each other, in life as in death. Furthermore, this embrace, which takes them back to the past of "daisied fields" (p. 456), contradicts what we are told at the end of the first volume, that Maggie and Tom (like Pip and Estella in the revised ending of *Great Expectations*) "would never more see the sunshine undimmed by remembered cares. They had entered the thorny wilderness, and the golden gates of their childhood had for ever closed behind them" (p. 171). Despite its irony, however, the novel's ending does not close upon just one meaning. From Maggies's point of view the flood sweeps away "all the later impressions of hard, cruel offence and misunderstanding" and restores her to childhood innocence, to "the deep underlying, unshakable

Chapter 5

memories of early union" (p. 453). With those golden gates of childhood swinging open to welcome her back to a time "when all the artificial vesture of our life is gone, and we are all one with each other in primitive mortal needs" (p. 453), she successfully escapes what she could not ignore as a child, "that bitter sense of the irrevocable which was almost an everyday experience of her small soul" (p. 58). Death, in other words, transforms Maggie's sense of dread into a transcendent moment of peace by erasing her history: "In the first moments Maggie felt nothing, thought of nothing, but that she had suddenly passed away from that life which she had been dreading: it was the transition of death, without its agony—and she was alone in the darkness with God" (p. 452).

Even then, since Maggie ends up being "alone in the darkness" not with God but with Tom, and since her effort to save him from the flood results in both their deaths, this ending simply piles contradiction upon contradiction. One response to this ambivalence has been to read the ending as a self-pitying romanticization of Maggie's belief in duty, linking duty to a fantasy of suffering, a glorification of self-renunciation as a moral value.[10] But this ambivalence cannot be so easily discounted as a mere evasion of the issues. Rather, the conclusion of *The Mill* envisions Maggie's life ending simultaneously in violation and repair. While the ending restores Maggie's innocence, allowing her to avoid the consequences of her elopement with Stephen and return to Tom, it also pushes those actions to their extreme consequence: the destruction of Maggie's personality. From this latter perspective the ending confirms what has been implicit throughout the novel, that Maggie's inability to leave childhood behind her projects a wish to die—to obliterate, by turning backwards, that disturbing self which has inexorably been leading her forward to maturity.

The ambiguity in this ending, which has always disturbed readers of *The Mill*, results from the novel's double momentum in its construction of experience for Maggie. On the one hand, her life is a "history" (p. 351)—a bildungsroman to be exact—which painstakingly records the formation of an adult self, "bent and broken" though it may be, out of the child, and which insists, with just as much somber determination, that the child herself was never as innocent as she imagined. On the other hand, because Maggie desires innocence, she and the narrator both view her dying embrace with Tom as a return to her first, most innocent memory, that "one supreme moment" (p. 456). The novel thus establishes a regressive momentum all the more psychologically credible since Maggie's "history" as an adolescent and an adult continually repeats the frustrated desire and unresolved conflicts that have marked her childhood. What is problematic about this ending is that it fuses these two movements so that the landscape of realism objectively recorded by the narrator-historian seems, at the same time, a landscape of romance reflecting Maggie's longing to die as the ultimate expression of her desire to be united with the other.

The conflation of these two movements is made clear through the metaphor Eliot's narrator uses to describe Maggie's life prior to her "great temptation" by Stephen. "Maggie's destiny, then, is at present hidden, and we must wait for it to reveal itself like the course of an unmapped river: we only know that the river is full and rapid, and that for all rivers there is the same final home" (p. 351). In this novel the river metaphor is highly charged, what with its foreshadowing of the elopement and the flood, as well as the frequent premonitions of Maggie's death by water. Since Maggie's life as a history is compared to the river which ends it to satisfy her desire, the two counterpointed movements each seem to generate from the same source, "the same final"—and primal— "home": death. Like Clarissa, Maggie can discover her origin in innocence, she can make her desired end truly like her imagined beginning, she can embrace that world beyond self, but only by losing her self altogether. Unlike *Clarissa*, however, *The Mill on the Floss* orchestrates its progressive and regressive movements so that they radiate, like concentric circles rippling on water, from the same primal and final source—the death of consciousness before and after life. *The Mill* therefore plunges Maggie into the same abyss as Cathy Earnshaw. Unlike Cathy, however, when Maggie falls, paradoxically, into that innocence which is the absence of lived experience, she does so with pleasure and relief. When this

Chapter 5

happens, her death makes vivid the unspoken anxiety underlying her desire, that to extend her self outward to the other means the self must cease to exist.

As Jacobus and Miller both point out, the ambiguity that results from this contrapuntal momentum is not due to confusion on Eliot's part so much as her determination to cast a double meaning, a double image of the self in its relation to the other. The narrational perspective of the novel suggests that Eliot wants us to identify with Maggie—to participate in her heroine's consciousness so that we respond to the self's experience as a violation—while seeing Maggie more or less objectively as a victim of her culture. Even though the narrative voice of *The Mill* does not clarify the final third of the novel to the satisfaction of her readers, it is clear that what Eliot wants to do with the narrator in this work predicts the important function of the narrator in *Middlemarch*. Eliot begins *The Mill* with a nostalgic and dreamy recollection of Dorlcote Mill in the present tense. This opening has the effect of collapsing time, so that the narrator both experiences and remembers the setting "as it looked one February afternoon many years ago." But since he (following convention, I will treat Eliot's narrator as a male voice, but only for the ease with which it allows me to distinguish her implied authorial hand from this voice) also shares the scene with "that little girl"—Maggie—who is "watching" too (p. 8), this perspective creates a double consciousness of time: the narrator is on the bridge where he stands observing and also in the chair where he dreamily dozes; the narrator is watching the scene and also watching Maggie become similarly hypnotized by the turning of the mill's giant wheel; the narrator is in the present remembering his past and also evoking the presence of Maggie from the past. The narrator's dream then fades into the novel itself.

Eliot is using her narrator to achieve a double perspective similar in effect to that created by the narration of *Wuthering Heights*, which takes advantage of Nelly Dean's temporal and emotional distance from the story of Heathcliff and Cathy to control but not diminish the intensity of their experience. An ideal

The Mill on the Floss *and* Middlemarch

voice, the narrator of *The Mill* is an impartial, impersonalized Nelly Dean, who observes the emotional texture of Maggie's life from the vantage point of his maturity; he is both in the landscape of her world and in his study. What Eliot says in talking about Dr. Kenn (who takes on part of the narrator's role in the latter third of the novel[11]) applies as well to her narrative voice, especially when we remember the opening chapter: "The middle-aged, who have lived through their strongest emotions, but are yet in the time when memory is still half passionate and not merely contemplative, should surely be a sort of natural priesthood . . ." (p. 381). Earlier in the novel Eliot presents an extended reverie about the impact of childhood, as viewed retrospectively, to explain why she wants us to see Maggie from a viewpoint "half passionate" and yet "contemplative":

> What could she do but sob? . . . Very trivial, perhaps, this anguish seems to weather-worn mortals who have to think of Christmas bills, dead loves, and broken friendships; but it was not less bitter to Maggie—perhaps it was even more bitter—than what we are fond of calling antithetically the real troubles of mature life. "Ah my child, you will have real troubles to fret about by-and-by," is the consolation we have almost all of us had administered to us in our childhood, and have repeated to other children since we have been grown up. We have all of us sobbed so piteously, standing with tiny bare legs above our little socks, when we lost sight of our mother or nurse in some strange place; but we can no longer recall the poignancy of that moment and weep over it, as we do over the remembered sufferings of five or ten years ago. Every one of those keen moments has left its trace, and lives in us still, but such traces have blent themselves irrecoverably with the firmer texture of our youth and manhood; and so it comes that we can look on at the troubles of our children with a smiling disbelief in the reality of their pain. Is there any one who can recover the experience of his childhood, not merely with a memory of what he did and what happened to him, of what he liked and disliked when he was in frock and trousers, but with an intimate penetration, a revived consciousness of what he felt then. . . . Surely if we could recall that early bitterness, and the dim guesses, the strangely perspectiveless conception of life that gave the bitterness its intensity, we should not pooh-pooh the griefs of our children. (pp. 59-60)

Chapter 5

Eliot's narrator is an idealized form of this "intimate penetration," the viewpoint of sympathy and compassion which directs her moral vision. For this reason "the middle-aged" are an appropriate moral authority in their "still half passionate and not merely contemplative" memory of their "strongest emotions." Their memory of strong feelings, in other words, leads them to identify with another's, to invest feeling with the power of ameliorating the breach between self and other in the manner of Eliot's omniscient narrator. The type of strong feelings he displays, moreover, is the very opposite of Maggie's, neither dangerous nor unmanageable because the effect of his objectivity is selflessness. This is made clear whenever the narrator of *The Mill on the Floss* draws on his experience to authorize both his tale and his wisdom. Confident of the continuity of past and present and of self and other, he can probe the mind of Tom, perhaps the most unsympathetic character in the novel, and empathize with him to conclude that "Tom, like every one of us, was imprisoned within the limits of his own nature, and his education had simply glided over him, leaving a slight deposit of polish: if you are inclined to be severe on his severity, remember that the responsibility of tolerance lies with those who have the wider vision" (p. 437).

This instruction to identify with Tom is a telling indication of what Eliot hopes to accomplish through her carefully constructed narrative voice; and nowhere in her fiction is "the responsibility of tolerance" more evident than in *Middlemarch*, which is narrated by and to "those who have the wider vision." Here the narrator stands back from the pier glass to watch how the candle's light creates the illusion of random scratches concentrically arranged. He can penetrate a character's self, that is to say, simply because he does perceive it as *another* self, a human specimen placed under analysis and scrutinized with a lens finely tuned by both reason and feeling. In its exploration of character *Middlemarch* is especially concerned with making emotions seem rational, uncovering the secret, unarticulated feelings that narrow the self's vision instead of widening it. This goal is made apparent, and its value reinforced, towards the end of the novel when Celia, learning that her sister plans to marry Will Ladislaw, asks "how it all came about." Surprisingly, Dorothea refuses to go into detail. "No, dear," she explains, "you would have to feel with me, else you would never know" (p. 602).

Dorothea's reply calls to mind Eliot's appreciation in *The Mill on the Floss* of "the middle aged, who have lived through their strongest passions." Feeling, Eliot says there, is a medium for knowledge. In *Middlemarch* she has Will explain to Dorothea that a poetic sensibility is "but a hand playing with finely-ordered variety on the chords of emotion—a soul in which knowledge passes instantaneously into feeling, and feeling flashes back as a new organ of knowledge" (p. 166). The purpose of the *Middlemarch* narrator is to express this intuitive "new organ of knowledge" in a public language. After all, his "intimate penetration" of Dorothea's emotional life has allowed the reader, in contrast to Celia, "to feel with" Dorothea throughout the novel. In order to project a "wider vision" than that of any individual character, the narrator must articulate this intuitive "organ of knowledge" by relying on his intellect as well as by probing the heart. To coordinate these two types of insight, emotional and rational, Eliot allows her narrator to investigate the emotional lives of her characters and yet positions him at an intellectual distance from them. Making use of his double perspective of intimacy and detachment, he can "feel" the truth while "knowing" it, dramatizing the singular emotional experience of each character while subjecting it to rigorous analysis. His special perspective thus allows the continuity of self and other to become epistemologically viable and, more to the point, imaginatively visible to the reader if not to the characters.

The perspective I have just described, however, is not without its epistemological and imaginative problems. The narrator's direct addresses to the reader encourage us to take his voice seriously as a credible *human* voice, yet his transparent language and totalizing viewpoint are humanly impossible. So which do we discount, his humanity or his authority? J. Hillis Miller, for example, assumes that the narrator and the characters share an identical human nature. To support his claim that the narrator's own metaphors are not exempt from the contradictions, "the dismaying dangers of metaphor," which Eliot's text exposes in the metaphors that serve only to entangle the characters in their desire, Miller appeals to an inherent similarity between narrator and characters: "What is true for the characters of *Middlemarch*," he argues, " . . . must also be true for the narrator."[12] But why must this also be true? The narrator repeatedly offers himself as a contrast to the characters. His narration represents a totalizing construction of reality which we can appreciate for just what it is, the product of a synthesizing perspective whose authority is confirmed by the structural juxtaposition of his wider vision and the much narrower sight-lines of the characters. In this respect, a more useful way to approach the problem of the narrator's contradictory position in the novel is D. A. Miller's. In his analysis of the narrator, Miller recognizes the "radically paradoxical" narration as a strategy working to enclose the novel with a complete, self-evident meaning which the text itself, constructed to pluralize the activity of interpretation, calls into question.[13]

Putting aside for the moment the question of the narrator's effort to stabilize meaning through language, I want to acknowledge the critical usefulness of both Millers' approaches: they de-center the narrator from the text of *Middlemarch* to place him, quite literally, in perspective. But my point is that the narrator is not an imposture so much as a posture. In his effort to objectify subjectivity he represents an idealized reader of human nature, posing, in a manner of speaking, as a model of adult consciousness in all his intelligence, experience, and compassion. He is an exemplary representation of maturity because he can appreciate desire without being misled by it himself, so his penetration of a character's psyche is at once "intimate" and "tolerant," encouraging us to forget that his double perspective of detachment and engagement may well be a contradiction in terms.

What is important about the narrator, therefore, is not the validity (or injustice) of his claim to full truth, which J. Hillis Miller and D. A. Miller both focus upon, but the activity that produces it. As an omniscient narrator he can easily see into a character's consciousness to explain the way Bulstrode, for instance, tries "to keep his intention separate from his desire" in his mistreatment of Raffles. Then, after penetrating Bulstrode's consciousness to expose the way this character distorts his perception of reality to satisfy desire, the narrator stands back to generalize and moralize, to draw connections of all sorts; thus, for all Bulstrode's self-serving hypocrisy, his motive is understandable because, like Dorothea, he "had longed for years to be better than he was." Through this kind of analysis the narrator widens his own field of vision, making it seem more impersonal and less subjective, especially when contrasted with the character he has been analyzing. The narrator's generous understanding of Bulstrode's self-centered motives, moreover, locates the self, the character's viewpoint, within the space of the other, the authorial viewpoint, so that it minimizes the dangerous imaginative activity of desire if only by demonstrating a comprehensive, sympathetic knowledge of the "strange, piteous conflict in the soul of this unhappy man" (pp. 516-17). In this way the narrator's sympathetic reading of Bulstrode's hypocrisy tames the desire that motivates it. Hence the tolerance and confidence with which the narrator can analyze this character's effort to separate "intention" from "desire" in a futile attempt to be "better," to be less self-serving than he actually is.

In order to achieve this compassionate and objective "wider vision" of the characters, everything that happens in *Middlemarch* is at once dramatized and verbalized through the narrator's mature intelligence. Because "signs are small measurable things, but interpretations are illimitable" (p. 18), the narrator establishes a straightforward line of communication with his reader to limit the potential diversity of interpretations operating behind the characters and the ambiguous signs that represent their subjective lives. If Bulstrode's "effort to condense words into a solid mental state" is countered by "the irresistible vividness [with which] the images of the events he desired" ultimately "pierced" and "spread" his thoughts (p. 516), then the narrator reverses this procedure: he pierces that "solid mental state" of a character's desire to concentrate it into "words." By turning secret, even unconscious feelings into narration, a public language, and thereby making desire speak sense, the narrator's translation of feelings into words counterpoints the characters' experience. They discover that their desires actually becloud their visions, preventing them from becoming better than they are, while the narrator overwhelms their states of feeling with his language to place them in the light of his informing "wider vision"; what is more, he then draws the reader into this perspective to confirm the stable coordination of language and reality which his narration represents.

Nonetheless, *Middlemarch* repeatedly demonstrates through the characters the degree to which their feelings are not words; more often than not their feelings even subvert the intended meaning of words because words depend on interpretation, and "interpretations are illimitable." For example, in explaining the difference between what Will and Dorothea say to each other during their incomplete, uncomfortable meetings and what they would really like to say if their deepest feelings could be made known, the narrator observes in passing that "the meaning we attach to words depends on our feeling" (p. 164). Until their emotional reconciliation at the end, language serves as the barrier to communication between Will and Dorothea. Subconsciously they send emotional signals to each other, yet they persist in imagining that the other finds something offensive in their conversations—or even in their silences. "Something was keeping their minds aloof, and each was left to conjecture what was in the other. Will . . . would have required a narrative to make him understand her present feeling" (p. 397).

That one's knowledge of another self depends upon non-verbal information makes the narrator's position as an authority even more crucial to our reading of the characters. The narrator himself admits that there are some things—important things since they are grounded in human feeling—that cannot be conveyed entirely, tangibly, rationally, or verbally: the way "business" is a "consecrated symbol" to Caleb Garth (p. 185), for example; or the way Lydgate and Rosamond talk with their eyes during courtship, "a delightful interchange . . . which is observable with some sense of flatness by a third person" (p. 198); or the way "little acts which might seem mere folly to a hard onlooker" help Mrs. Bulstrode to accept with dignity her husband's disgrace as her own (p. 550). As readers, we are placed in the position of that "third person" or "hard onlooker", and yet we do understand because the narrator, being an ideal analyst of human behavior, allows us to penetrate such emotional and singular constructions of reality.

The Mill on the Floss *and* Middlemarch

His "intimate penetration" of character tells us precisely what meaning to attach to words and looks and gestures; and in doing that, his analysis refutes the characters' own assumption that such knowledge cannot be conveyed in and of itself because it is emotional and intuited, not rational and verbalized.

In response to the fact that emotions do get in the way of communication, the narrator casts these various small dramas of obstructed communication in the light of his own "wider vision." He authorizes the interpretation we attach to words and actions and feelings. He establishes as a norm for the novel the intelligent sensibility towards which Dorothea, Will, and Lydgate strive and against which the limitations of Rosamond, Bulstrode, and Casaubon are measured but not condemned. The intellectual energy of the narrator, moreover, defends against the anxieties raised by the characters themselves; his inclusive reading of their experience turns their own exclusive readings upside down. *He* speaks in a public voice, not a private one. *He* acknowledges the value of feeling without incurring its dangers. *He* aggressively argues *his* viewpoint without being self-centered himself. All the same, since the narrator is only a model, a posture, it is important to appreciate that the characters humanize his vision just as much as he intellectualizes theirs. Whereas the narrator proposes a "wider vision" subordinating the self to the other, the characters are grounded in self and ignorant of the other; consequently, our attention shifts back and forth between his position of recognition and tolerance and their positions of mistrust and misrecognition. It is in this sense that the construction of experience in *Middlemarch* is not identical to its narration. For most of the novel the characters' experience contradicts the narrator's faith in reason and language, setting up a regressive counterforce to the progressive momentum implied by his wisdom and maturity. In other words, Eliot's construction of experience for her characters imagines another form of "intimate penetration" taking place in her novel, one which conforms more noticeably to the double meaning of the genre's paradigm of experience: not only in its insistence on the self's repair through insight, but also its recognition that violation is the necessary condition for achieving that insight to begin with.

Chapter 5

For all the narrator's "wider vision," within the fictional world of *Middlemarch* we cannot help seeing enacted vivid instances of selfish behavior—genuine, very human responses like Bulstrode's—that obfuscate one character's vision of another to show the self actively working against the kind of breadth enjoyed by the narrator. In contrast to the narrator, the characters in *Middlemarch* are all creatures of desire. "We are all of us imaginative in some form or other," the narrator observes, "for images are the brood of desire" (p. 237). From his rational perspective, the narrator means that desire begets illusion, the mental constructions of reality which rework it to satisfy desire (and which he, in turn, dismantles in his analysis). What he shows, however, is that the desiring imagination isolates the characters by coloring what they see in terms of what they feel; and because "images are the brood of desire" and not the progeny of words, the characters must either rely on the inadequate medium of language or look to other systems of signs to articulate their feelings.

Communication is therefore no easy task for Eliot's characters, despite her narrator's own dexterity with words. For desire, understood as the origin of images that have no concrete basis in reality—no basis in something outside of the imagination and its source in the self—is set against language and intensifies each character's isolation all the more. During most of the novel the characters think in secret, feel in secret, dream in secret, even plot in secret, all the time imagining the other as an alien, hostile force that betrays desire. The climax of the novel occurs through a series of volatile confrontations which not even Rosamond, the most self-centered and emotionally alienated of all the characters, can avoid. Because these confrontations break down the self's illusory images of the other to define love in terms of empathy, not fear, these scenes achieve a degree of "intimate penetration" for the characters similar to that exhibited by the narrator. Before I show how the confrontation scenes serve this purpose, however, it is first necessary to examine the barriers which the characters themselves construct to defend against being penetrated by the other, barriers which the confrontation scenes then break down.

The Mill on the Floss *and* Middlemarch

As the narrator points out, the characters cannot elude desire, as he himself can do. More to the point, he makes them seem to be victims of desire, especially when it comes to love, which draws the self towards the other as the primary object of its desire but places the imagination between them. The other is then idealized, as in the case of Dorothea and Will, or dreaded, as in the case of Lydgate and Rosamond. Either reaction makes the other seem impenetrable and reveals, in turn, a fear of being penetrated. "Marriage is so unlike everything else," Dorothea tells Rosamond. "There is something even awful in the nearness it brings" (p. 583). The "nearness" is "awful" because marriage is a form of "intimate penetration" not unlike the narrator's but certainly more dangerous and unmanageable in that it forces husband and wife to confront illusions of the other which pass for love.

The narrator addresses this problem in what is probably the most famous passage of *Middlemarch*, when he argues that "we are all of us born in moral stupidity, taking the world as an udder to feed our supreme selves." It has to be "easier," he explains, for Dorothea "to imagine how she would devote herself to Mr. Casaubon, and become wise and strong in his strength and wisdom, than to conceive with that distinctness which is no longer reflection but feeling—an idea wrought back to the directness of sense, like the solidity of objects—that he had an equivalent centre of self, whence the lights and shadows must always fall within a certain difference" (pp. 156-57). He means that if Dorothea could penetrate her husband's "centre of self" through her own feelings of unhappiness and frustration, she would see him more accurately as another self, one existing outside the perimeters of her own imaginative construction of him. Clearly, Dorothea is just beginning to learn the difference between knowing the truth of another and feeling it, and just as clearly the narrator argues that the latter kind of knowledge would close the breach between self and other by leading Dorothea to a consciousness of similarity. At this point in the novel, however, Dorothea has only an *idea* of her husband's identity, and it is an illusion, an image of him created by her desire, not "wrought back to the directness of sense," to her actual experience of him after they are married. She arrives at a fuller recognition of the other when she acknowledges her love for Will, and the value of their relationship lies in its forcing each to become more cognizant of the other's "centre of self."

The process by which Dorothea achieves her recognition of Will is much more complicated than it appears on the surface, and I will have more to say about it later. For now let me concentrate on the way the narrator directs us to see her maturation. If initially Dorothea imagines her husband as a Locke or a Milton, the projection of her daydreams, she finally comes through experience— their married life—to know him as Edward Casaubon, an insecure, repressed, paranoid man who "had hidden thoughts, perhaps perverting everything she said and did" (p. 360). Similarly, if she first sees Will as a Shelley or a Byron, she finally comes to understand him as "a living man" (p. 576) and, importantly, as a sexual man.[14] Ironically enough, the shock of mistakenly assuming that Will is Rosamond's lover leads Dorthea to perceive his "equivalent centre of self": she no longer fears him as an unobtainable and therefore "aloof" personality. Instead, when Will visits her after her "discovery," she loses consciousness of her own pain and empathizes with his: "What she was least conscious of just then was her own body: she was thinking of what was likely to be in Will's mind, and of the hard feelings that others had had about him" (p. 591). Her empathetic understanding of Will, when she loses consciousness of her own body, leads her to come to terms with his otherness, which she must do as the necessary condition for recognizing her own feelings. Although Dorothea is "afraid of her own emotion" when Will first appears in the room (p. 591), her feelings soon break down "all the obstructions which had kept her silent" (p. 594). In saying she loves him, she finally allows *him* to know what is going on in *her* mind, inviting him to penetrate her feelings, to reach her "centre of self." Thus Dorothea and Will each achieve what Maggie Tulliver dreads when she elopes with Stephen, "the submergence of our personality by another."

A similar barrier obstructs communication between Rosamond and Lydgate, whose relationship intensifies the dread of the other sex which accounts for the complications that separate and ultimately unite Dorothea and Will. Feeling the truth of another is a much more dangerous proposition for the Lydgates. To begin with, Rosamond responds to men much as Dorothea does. Both women use men as props for their illusions, and as a result both have an unrealistic impression of the other sex. Rosamond exploits her coquetry to keep men at a distance, as if fearing that intimacy is tantamount to some deep violation of her inner being. "The conditions of marriage itself" demand not only "self-suppression and tolerance" (p. 552) but also the breakdown of her illusions about the other sex. Rosamond's "terrible tenacity" (p. 427), however, reinforces her belief that "other people's states of mind" merely comprise "a material cut into shape by her own wishes" (p. 569). She spins "that gossamer web" (p. 253) over Lydgate to attract him but also to prevent him from penetrating her consciousness. As a result, her defenses isolate her from her husband to reaffirm his otherness as a male: "It seemed that she had no more identified herself with him than if they had been creatures of different species and opposing interests" (p. 436).

Rosamond's figure is especially important to the dread of the other sex in *Middlemarch* because it concentrates a fear, common in Eliot's novels, that egocentric women undermine male power and expose male authority as a fraud because they are afraid of men, an anxiety that projects, in turn, a male fear of women as the impenetrable other. Indeed, most of the men in this novel are intimidated by the women—by Dorothea and Mary Garth as well as by Rosamond. This fear, however, parallels the women's initial exaggerated respect of men. Both Dorothea and Rosamond marry assuming their husbands have the power to enrich their lives by virtue of their masculine authority. The failure of this expectation makes Rosamond, in particular, feel superior to her husband, just as it makes Casaubon feel inferior to Dorothea.

Dorothea, on the other hand, is a touchstone for the women in this novel because she wants both love *and* friendship from men. It is important that she is the means by which Lydgate comes to see women more favorably, since Rosamond takes so much explicit blame for the failure of his ideals. Originally, "Miss Brooke was not Mr. Lydgate's style of woman," being "a little too earnest"

Chapter 5

for his taste. But the narrator also warns us, somewhat slyly, that Lydgate "might possibly have experience before him which would modify his opinion as to the most excellent things in woman" (p. 69). Another contrast to Dorothea, of course, especially as it concerns his opinion of women, is Lydgate's first love, Laure, the actress who murdered her husband. Laure killed her husband not because he was brutal or because she hated him (motives Lydgate thinks he can understand) but because the man "wearied" her (p. 114). Hearing this confession, Lydgate is so shocked he believes that his illusions about women are at an end, for he now sees all women as versions of Laure. When he falls in love with Rosamond "with wonderful rapidity, in spite of experience supposed to be finished off with the drama of Laure" (p. 253), he mistakenly imagines her as the antithesis of Laure, with "just the kind of intelligence one would desire in a woman—polished, refined, docile . . ." (p. 121). Since Rosamond's will, polished and refined as it is, is anything but docile, Lydgate has merely reformulated his old illusions about women around her and is still attracted to egocentric and aggressive women (remember that Dorothea is not his "style"). Not surprisingly, he discovers that underneath Rosamond's delicate gentility lurks another Laure, plunging a knife into his soul even though she wields no actual weapon, and his initial response to the breakdown of his marriage is to see himself as the victim of his wife's "terrible tenacity." He identifies, in essence, with Laure's husband, the man he hoped, in his own youthful daydreams, to replace.

Lydgate fails to understand that he is as much to blame for initiating this aggressive contest which pits male against female to make the "nearness" of their marriage so "awful" by releasing the potential violence of both sexes:

> Lydgate sat paralysed by opposing impulses: since no reasoning he could apply to Rosamond seemed likely to conquer her assent, he wanted to smash and grind some object on which he could at least produce an impression, or else to tell her brutally that he was master, and she must obey. But he not only dreaded the effect of such extremities on their mutual life—he had a growing dread of Rosamond's quiet elusive obstinacy, which would not allow any

assertion of power to be final; and again, she had touched him in a spot of keenest feeling by implying that she had been deluded with a false vision of happiness in marrying him. (p. 483)

Of course, Rosamond cannot be entirely vindicated; but it is clear that because Lydgate dreads his own capacity for violence, he is attracted to women who themselves are quietly violent in their relations with men. In response to Rosamond's stubborn resistance, he feels surprisingly aggressive, wanting to "produce an impression" by displacing his anger, venting it physically on "some object" or verbally through "brutal" abuse. His wife makes him feel guilty—unlike the man in the Laure situation—by saying that he seduced her with "a false vision of happiness" and, more subtly, by provoking his aggression. We are led to suspect that at this level of consciousness he *wants* to see Rosamond as "his basil plant" (p. 610), who murders his soul and feeds on his intelligence, making her a projection of his own impulse to murder her.

In some respects this impulse is not without justification. Rosamond exacerbates Lydgate's suffering and his anger by refusing to acknowledge that she has hurt him deeply. When "he felt bruised and shattered," she notices "a dark line under his eyes" and turns away, ignoring his pain and blaming him for making things "a great deal worse for her" (p. 515). From both Lydgate's and Rosamond's perspectives, their marriage goes beyond the Laure pattern, which more clearly marked out the woman's guilt and the man's victimization, to approach the kind of sexual battle enacted in the legend of Ghost's Walk in *Bleak House*. Here, too, husband and wife continually bruise and shatter each other. Neither partner is innocent; both must bear part of the guilt for the breakdown of communication and for the aggression that ensues from the frustration of their original desire for each other.

In order to come to terms with the tension in their marriage, Lydgate and Rosamond both have to acknowledge their guilt. He does not realize this until he sees Dorothea with his wife. After Dorothea leaves, Lydgate finds Rosamond "meek" and "scourged." He now understands that he must accept "his

Chapter 5

narrowed lot with sad resignation" (p. 586). His complaint against Rosamond is that she has never considered his desires, never identified with him. But the chastened Rosamond is still a woman who epitomizes, now to his unhappiness, his naive fantasies about women as angels or monsters. "He had chosen this fragile creature, and had taken the burthen of her life upon his arms. He must walk as he could, carrying that burthen pitifully" (p. 586). In other words, he learns to face the consequences of his attraction to Rosamond's impenetrable otherness as a woman. He has married her perceiving the opposite of Laure; when she resists his power and asserts her own, he sees her as a kind of murderer of their peace, their love, their home, and projects his guilt onto her. But because he and Rosamond are married—legally bound to each other for life—he cannot escape the consequences of his choice. He must recognize her "centre of self" as something he can penetrate if only to understand her desire as something other than his; and he must then realize that such "intimate penetration" is not the same as aggression, even though the consequence of genuine intimacy is a de-centering of the self, the submergence of one personality by another, which is what makes marriage so "awful in the nearness it brings." The other three characters, Rosamond and Will and Dorothea, learn a similar lesson.

To be sure, none of them arrive at this realization consciously, nor does the narrator analyze it in quite the way I have begun to do; but my argument helps to account for the force of the novel's climax, when the four characters feel knowledge, as Will would say, which the narrator dramatizes but does not actually name. He cannot name it because this knowledge contests his rationalization of desire, his assumption that feeling and reason are ultimately the same, coordinated harmonically within a "centre of self." As D. A. Miller points out, on the surface these climactic scenes mean to confirm that assumption by leading the characters to a stabilizing and inclusive vision similar to the narrator's. But at the same time they make up perhaps the most turbulent and disruptive section of *Middlemarch*. Miller accounts for this contradictory effect by examining the way these scenes resist the narrator's attempt to close upon a single, self-evident meaning. According to Miller, because each character's interpretation of

The Mill on the Floss *and* Middlemarch

what happens is self-serving and different from other interpretations, these scenes actually contradict their apparent epistemological function, which is to close the narrative with a unifying disclosure that makes the meaning of what happens self-evident to everyone concerned.[15]

I want to approach this section of the novel somewhat differently, to argue that there is a logic of desire working upon these scenes which places the characters outside the narrator's perspective in a way he does not envision. While the confrontations at the end of the novel do lead the characters towards a "shared" understanding of each other, that meaning is not self-evident but relies on interpretation, so it is much more disruptive and shattering in its impact than the narrator predicts it will be in the passage I quoted about Dorothea's misrecognition of Casaubon. There the narrator says that Dorothea would recognize Casaubon for what he is if she would only see him as he exists outside her construction of him. To a large extent, the confrontation scenes work to correct the characters' myopia by forcing them to recognize the other's presence outside the self. But they also work in a different and, given the narrator's mode of thinking, unexpected way. By revealing the self in the shape of the other, these scenes break down the difference between self and other and transform the narrator's realistic landscape into a landscape of desire. What I am getting at, in other words, is something very similar to the sudden consciousness of desire which Gwendolen Harleth describes when she watches her husband drown in Eliot's *Daniel Deronda*: "I knew no way of killing him there," Gwendolen tries to explain to Daniel, "but I did, I did kill him in my thoughts. . . . I don't know how it was . . . he was struck—I know nothing—I know that I saw my wish outside me."[16]

The characters' fear of the other sex, as I have said, is the single aspect of their confused mental life which the narrator does not explicitly analyze and name in *Middlemarch*. Eliot orchestrates it through the two main romantic relationships (the two contrasting pairs of lovers predict, in fact, Lawrence's similar use of couples in *Women in Love*[17]). During the climactic section of the novel (chapters 75-83), Dorothea finally interacts with Rosamond and Lydgate. As she does so, their contact anticipates a horrific battle between men and women and then exposes that anticipation as the work of illusion through a pattern of displacement in the confrontations that actually occur. At first glance the opposite might seem to be the case. This section certainly delays the final confrontation between Will and Dorothea for as long as possible and, more importantly, it avoids one between Rosamond and Lydgate. But this section successfully resolves the fears that have been inhibiting Will and Dorothea's intimacy, just as it partly closes the wide breach that has opened up between Lydgate and Rosamond. Through Will and Dorothea, the Lydgates go through the kind of deconstruction of their fear of the other sex that Pip experiences in *Great Expectations* when he, like Miss Havisham, sees his wishes and fears outside him. Will and Dorothea force Rosamond and Lydgate to recognize the fragility of their defenses against each other; and, we will see, Rosamond in turn exposes the other couple's defenses as well.

Before the confrontations begin there are two pairs of allies—Dorothea and Lydgate, Will and Rosamond—which incongruously pair friends against lovers. In each case the friendships are temporary substitutions for the love relationships, resulting from a lack of communication between lovers. Lydgate can confess to Dorothea, but not to his wife, that he feels guilty, that he is suffering, that he now lacks confidence in his strength. Will visits Rosamond because he cannot visit Dorothea. Rosamond flirts with Will because her husband has ceased to pay attention to her desires. And Dorothea begins to crusade for Lydgate since she is prohibited from doing so for Will, who she feels has been unjustly treated first by her husband and now by her friends. Each character chooses as a replacement for the desired lover a friend of the other sex with whom a greater sense of mutual identification is possible; and each friendship defends against the necessity of being, as Lydgate says, "more open" with the lover (p. 561). Dramatically, it takes four stages of action to redress this imbalance. First, arriving at the Lydgates's house to be the doctor's advocate, Dorothea sees Will with Rosamond. Second, Will verbally attacks Rosamond. Third, Dorothea has her all-night vigil and returns the next day to speak to Rosamond alone. Fourth, after this conversation, Lydgate returns to find his wife more submissive and tolerant, and Dorothea is reunited with Will through Rosamond's interference. Psychologically, something important happens to these characters during the second and third stages which begins to revive their paralyzed relationships and which is described but not fully articulated by the narrator.

When Will verbally lacerates Rosamond after Dorothea's departure, "Rosamond . . . was almost losing the sense of her identity, and seemed to be waking into some new terrible existence. . . . What another nature felt in opposition to her own was being burnt and bitten into her consciousness" (p. 571). Besides suggesting the corrosive effect of acid, this burning and biting has unmistakable sexual overtones. Described in an evocative language which calls Lawrence to mind, the scene suggests an image of passionate sexual arousal, when Rosamond "was almost losing her sense of identity," followed by brutal penetration, when she feels the full brunt of Will's "opposition." Rosamond, like Maggie, fears desire for the reason suggested here. She uses her considerable sexual attractiveness to trap the male—Lydgate and Will alike—in a passive role as a defense against her dread that she would lose her self if she submitted to his power. Will now seems to justify her dread because he de-centers her self. He penetrates her defenses, exposing her desire to manipulate him, and then frustrates that desire to make her realize that her will to manipulate is an expression of desire. Their "nearness" in this scene is therefore "truly awful." He not only makes Rosamond painfully aware of "what another nature felt," he exposes her vulnerability and makes her conscious of "some new terrible existence": her self and his in conflict.

Will has produced the kind of brutal "impression" of his self upon Rosamond's that Lydgate has been wanting to inflict all along. In terms of the emotions he makes Rosamond experience during this scene, Will therefore enacts the role of male aggressor, standing in for Lydgate, just as he does in Rosamond's daydreams after her marriage. Will makes Rosamond conscious of her reason for having resisted her husband, for having seen him as a threat to her identity, so it is he, not Lydgate, who finally tears the

Chapter 5

gossamer web, stripping her of all defenses. Will feels impelled to "shatter Rosamond with his anger. . . . And yet—how could he tell a woman that he was ready to curse her? He was fuming under a repressive law which he was forced to acknowledge." When Rosamond sarcastically mentions his "preference" for Dorothea, however, Will's rage overcomes his exaggerated respect for women and he attacks her with "poisoned weapons": brutal, angry words. He knows he is being "cruel," but he also feels "blameless" because this woman has "spoiled the ideal treasure of his life." Dorothea has seen him as a sexual man, a discovery he fears is "an incarnate insult to her" (pp. 570-71).

When Rosamond baits Will until he voices his anger, she forces him to discover his capacity for cruelty. Will is disturbed by his anger because it is unexpected; he idealizes women and has therefore obeyed the "repressive law" of worshipful respect. In both his anger and its unexpectedness Will is like Lydgate, who also dreads acknowledging his anger at a woman, since to his mind cruelty characterizes someone like Laure or even Rosamond, not a man like himself or Laure's husband. Moreover, in the paralysis that results from this anger, we can see why Will, like Lydgate, fears more "open" and mature relationships with women. He too dreads the "awful nearness" of love because he thinks it gives him a power to hurt the woman and that, in turn, gives her a power over him. Will's fear of women has in fact been realized all along in Lydgate's marriage. Like Lydgate, Will now feels trapped by his relationship to Rosamond after his outburst, "enslaved by this helpless woman" (p. 571) because "he hated his own cruelty, and yet he dreaded to show the fullness of his relenting" (p. 588).

As for Lydgate, because he has not hurled the "poisoned weapons" himself, he can subsequently (and unknowingly) take the role of his wife's protector. Rosamond's "hysterical sobbings and cries," actually caused by Will, ironically make Lydgate assume that Dorothea has successfully communicated his feelings to his wife, "and that all this effect on her nervous system, which evidently involved some new turning towards himself, was due to the excitement of the new impressions which that visit has raised." His solution is to "soothe and tend her," and give her a drug (p. 572). He can appreciate women more, but he still lacks an under-

The Mill on the Floss *and* Middlemarch

standing of their emotions. As far as he is concerned the other sex is still another species. So in terms of the emotional orchestration of this section, Will allows us to sense, but not to witness directly, a partial transformation in Lydgate himself. Lydgate never does openly confront his wife to vent his anger, but after Dorothea's second visit he recognizes his "burthen" because he senses an emotional change in his wife, though he does not understand the cause of this change. What is important is that his resignation replaces his anger, suggesting that his previous feeling of rage has, somehow, been exorcised through the figure of Will.

Rosamond, in turn, is the agent of Will's and Dorothea's corrected perceptions of each other's sexual identity, functioning here as a substitute figure for Dorothea. Rosamond, not Dorothea, feels the impact of his sexual assault, but Dorothea, not Rosamond, emotionally resolves the anxiety that results, discovering the satisfaction of sexuality and implicitly sharing this knowledge with Rosamond. When Dorothea returns to the Lydgates' house, she allows Rosamond a means of overcoming her sense of violation by Will. Without knowing the cause, Dorothea finds Rosamond still suffering from "the first great shock that had shattered her dream-world in which she had been easily confident of herself and critical of others." Dorothea's surprising kindness, "this strange unexpected manifestation of feeling in a woman whom she had approached with a shrinking aversion and dread" (since Dorothea should, by right, be jealous of Rosamond), instead "made her soul totter all the more with a sense that she had been walking in an unknown world which had just been broken in upon her" (p. 583). As Dorothea pleads Lydgate's case, she causes Rosamond to be "taken hold of by an emotion stronger than her own . . . and then for a minute the two women clasped each other as if they had been in a shipwreck" (p. 584). Then, because of "the subduing influence of Dorothea's emotion," Rosamond pleads Will's case, "and as she went on she had gathered the sense that she was repelling Will's reproaches, which were still like a knife-wound within her" (p. 585).

Certainly, all of this makes complete sense in terms of the conscious activity of the characters. Naturally upset by Will's accusations, Rosamond makes restitution. Then, surprised and gratified by the truth, as well as moved by her deep sympathy for Rosamond's obviously troubled state of mind, Dorothea tries to calm her down, to undo the traumatic impact of the day before. She tells Rosamond to trust her husband, who "feels his life bound into one with yours, and it hurts him more than anything, that his misfortunes must hurt you" (p. 582). In addition, Dorothea is somehow healing the "knife-wound" made in Rosamond by Will. Rosamond can never resolve her fear of men on her own, because she assumes that sexual intimacy heightens her vulnerability. Consequently, whereas she initially dreads Dorothea's second appearance at her house, immaturely supposing that Dorothea has returned out of jealousy, Dorothea now teaches her about more mature "chords of emotion," encouraging Rosamond to understand that a woman can manifest strong emotions out of kindness as well as aggression.

Dorothea's emotional fervor, then, shatters Rosamond's "dream-world" just as Will's accusation has done, making "her soul totter all the more." In this respect, we can see Dorothea's kindness transforming the impact of Will's sexual aggression. After Will shatters Rosamond's identity, he stares at her in "mute rage," and she stares back with "mute misery" (p. 571). This dynamic of angry male and suffering female inverts the Laure pattern, yet both versions horribly distort sexual relationships in their simplicity. Dorothea's kindness, by contrast, her lack of jealousy, her active sympathy, help Rosamond to see the difference between an illusion of men—Will—and the reality—her husband, who is not trying to strike, not trying to fragment her self; Lydgate's life, Dorothea makes Rosamond realize, is "bound into one" with hers.

In other words, the two women come to realize that love transforms sexual relationships into acts of union with the other. The man is not an aggressor, the woman not a victim, and "binding" does not necessarily mean "wounding." This is as important for Dorothea to learn as it is for Rosamond. When Rosamond responds to Dorothea's sympathy by telling the truth about Will, she helps Dorothea to become conscious of her own feeling: Will has not meant to hurt her, just as Lydgate has not hurt Rosamond. Instead, the struggle to preserve an inviolate identity

The Mill on the Floss *and* Middlemarch

by keeping it innocent of desire has been the cause of all the obstructed communication and distorted perceptions of the other sex, making lovers out to be antagonists instead of friends. Moreover, while one woman accepts the blame for the mistaken impression of the men—Rosamond has not bothered to think about her husband's feelings, and she allowed (even wanted) Dorothea to think Will was her lover—another woman repairs the damage.

Whenever I read *Middlemarch* I find this section to be the most moving part of the entire novel. The two women come together in a moment of intimacy which will never occur again, although it will forever affect the course of their lives, their feelings, their vision. "This moment was unlike any other; she and Rosamond could never be together again with the same thrilling consciousness of yesterday within them both" (p. 583). As a result of Dorothea's unexpected visit of the day before, the two women see each other as a sexual threat and Will as a figure of sexual betrayal; their "thrilling consciousness" signals the emergence of their sexual consciousness—their awareness of the other sex and of the otherness that is their own sexuality—because each woman now perceives the other as a disturbing sexual figure, the object of Will's desire. During Dorothea's second visit, however, the two women together overcome their dread of the other sex as an alien object of desire and in doing so are reconciled to their own sexuality.

After Dorothea sees Will with Rosamond, she initially feels humiliated, angry, and indignant. Because of Will, she shares Rosamond's experience of losing identity, of waking into a terrible new existence, of walking in an unknown world; and yet this violation of her illusions exhilarates her almost to the point of sexual excitement:

> Any one looking at her might have thought that though she was paler than usual she was never animated by a more self-possessed energy. And that was really her experience. It was as if she had drunk a great draught of scorn that stimulated her beyond the susceptibility to other feelings. She had seen something so far below her belief, that her emotions rushed back from it and made an excited throng without an object. She needed something active

to turn her excitement out upon. . . . She had never felt anything like this triumphant power of indignation in the struggle of her married life, in which there had always been a quickly subduing pang; and she took it as a sign of new strength. (pp. 568-69)

Dorothea's discovery of Will with Rosamond has a two-fold impact upon her, and what happens to Dorothea creates a context for understanding what happens to Rosamond. First, Dorothea is forced, finally, to see Will "with that distinctness which is no longer reflection but feeling"; and when she sees his "equivalent centre of self"—that is, sees him in relation to another woman and thus apart from her illusion of him—she at first feels betrayed. No wonder, then, that her first reaction is to readjust her sights to the "involuntary, palpitating life" existing independently of her own desires and anxieties (p. 578), for, as we have seen in the above passage, her emotions lack an object "to turn her excitement out upon." Second, through this discovery, Dorothea is able to articulate her "silent love" for Will. The mistaken impression of Will's infidelity circumstantially reveals why it has taken so long for her to "[admit] her passion to herself" (p. 576). She fears that Will will betray her love as Casaubon did, not realizing that what she imagined she felt for her husband is not the same as what she now genuinely—and erotically—feels for Will.

In the excitement of this epiphany, Dorothea recognizes that she needs an object outside herself—a lover—upon which to focus her released emotional energy. So she must turn to Will. Thus when Rosamond takes the blame for Dorothea's mistaken impression about Will, she causes Dorothea to feel an emotion "too strong to be called joy. . . . she could only perceive that this would be joy when she had recovered her power of feeling it" (p. 585). This unconscious, uncontrollable, even unnameable feeling, which Rosamond also feels, now replaces the pain Will has previously made each woman feel. Emotionally, that is to say, the two women alleviate each other's fear of the male as a sexual invader of her consciousness. Each learns to see the joy, moral and sexual, that results from the "intimate" penetration of her consciousness by the other sex.

The Mill on the Floss *and* Middlemarch

The enlarged knowledge I have been discussing, this "wider vision" of the other, is experienced more or less subconsciously by the four characters; as they come together for dramatic purposes, the characters merge psychically, complicating and then clarifying their relationships to one another to create the kind of emotional composite I have delineated. For this reason, their contact is so volatile and intense, the atmosphere around them so charged with desire. All along their illusions about the other sex have expressed a deep fear of being exposed and made vulnerable to the other through desire. Then during these scenes their fears are unexpectedly realized through the substitution of friends for lovers. In Gwendolen Harleth's words, they see their wishes outside them—or, more precisely, respond as if they do—and what stands before them, the self's own otherness, is a shocking sight. Finally, the restoration of the suspended love relationships mitigates the dread of violation inherent in that discovery, thereby confirming what Dorothea tells Rosamond, that it is only a marriage ruined by dishonesty and infidelity which "stays with us like a murder" (p. 584).

Analyzing this section of *Middlemarch* as I have done offers us a way of articulating the emotions these confrontations generate for the characters, allowing us to understand, too, how this section forces the characters to confront the alien reality of another's self more intensely (and "intimately"), through feeling rather than intellect. Paradoxically, because of their defenses against desire, the characters can, finally, become conscious of desire only through its displacement. Certainly, given Eliot's assumptions that "images are the brood of desire" and that "strands of experience lying side by side" must be compared (p. 429), it is psychologically consistent for her characters to face their desires in a context of displacement so that all the while they are consciously engaged in one kind of action, they are subconsciously experiencing another.

More importantly, because neither couple is placed in direct opposition, the displaced confrontations help Eliot to resolve the implicit dread of violent sexual conflict—the fear that contact may well be as fatal to the self's integrity as her characters dread—to serve the interests of her narrator's tolerance and maturity. The confrontations do not make Lydgate's violence irrevocable by putting it into action, yet they allow his anger finally to be expressed by Will and resolved by Dorothea, perhaps the two least violent, least angry characters in the novel. Displaced so far from its original source, the anger motivating the violence loses its horrific and—since the violence is not realized—fantastic power to disturb the narrator's confidence in maintaining that the self's exposure to the other does not amount to a violation. The dread of the other motivating the characters can therefore be rendered more sympathetically to show their new consciousness as feeling, feeling which the narrator then translates into knowledge in the form of his rational commentary.

The climax of *Middlemarch*, then, is orchestrated so as to render the crisis in the characters' emotional lives at once subjectively and objectively. It is important to appreciate Eliot's need to imagine feeling from these two perspectives, for despite the value she places on emotion, her narration reveals that she distrusts feeling as the sole medium for experiencing the other. The narrator repeatedly intellectualizes the narrative of *Middlemarch*, itself nothing more than an imaginative structure built out of the characters' desires, because what he recounts is a story of desire fervently and persistently causing a breach between language and the reality it means to represent. Thus the narrator's intellect, the foundation of his "wider vision," makes feeling intelligible, even visible as language, just as it makes desire manageable by overwhelming it with reason. Seen through the lens of the narrator's "wider vision," each character is no more than a "small hungry shivering self" (p. 206) standing, in all its isolation and insignificance, before the commanding presence of the reality beyond self, namely, the narrator's penetrating gaze.

In this effort to minimize the character's dread of the other through its narrative voice, *Middlemarch* epitomizes the way realism constructs experience as a hierarchical arrangement of the paradigm's dialectical energies, imposing the overt progressive movement (as directed by the narrator's wisdom) over the more covert regressive movement (as directed by the character's

The Mill on the Floss *and* Middlemarch

desires). This type of construction makes *Middlemarch* a "grown-up" novel, one dependent entirely upon the safeguard of its narrative voice, which openly discounts the characters' dread of experience but cannot suppress that dread entirely. Rather, especially when placed in the light of other novels I have discussed, it is evident that *Middlemarch* can, to borrow Eliot's phrase from *The Mill on the Floss*, "pooh-pooh the griefs of our children" only by deliberately subverting the very idea of their innocence. From the narrator's perspective the characters' experience appears to repair what seems not to have been a violation in the first place, only their inevitable exposure to reality. As far as the characters are concerned, however, their experience tells another story altogether: it *is* an act of violation, and they themselves bear witness to this story during the novel's climax.

6
Realism as Modernism

"Why must they grow up and lose it all?"

By charting the continuity of the English novel through its paradigmatic construction of experience, I have at the same time documented the achievement of realism in the genre. In doing so, I have not mapped an especially unorthodox line of development for the novel. Other critics have arrived there by different routes: starting with Defoe and Fielding as well as Richardson to establish different models of realism in style and texture (Ian Watt); or marking a tradition extending from Austen and Scott to Thackeray and Trollope and then, leaving Dickens more or less on the sidelines, to Eliot, Hardy, Conrad, and Lawrence in order to document realism's concern with representing a reality beyond—and yet bound by—language (George Levine); or tracing the origins of realism in the quixotic and picaresque ancestry of the novel to argue either for the psychological basis of realistic archetypes (Marthe Robert) or for a realistic style based on Cervantic parody and irony (Harry Levin). Each of these various maps of realism coincides at points with mine. But having chosen my particular avenue of approach in order to loosen the novel's dependency on realism for its self-definition, I have placed greater stress on the romantic underside of realism's construction of experience.

Chapter 6

To sum up, my argument about the English novel's program of realism has been two-fold. First, while realism may seem, especially in its insistence upon maturity and socialization, to be synonymous with the paradigm, it would be more accurate to see it as one particular orchestration of the paradigm's rhythm of violation and repair. Realism gives the paradigm's forward movement preeminence over the backward movement; but as we have seen, instead of disappearing, that backward movement remains as a competing imaginative energy, establishing the dread which realism seeks to manage and contain. This brings me to my second point. No matter how successfully the devices of realism may seem to overcome the dread informing the paradigmatic base of the novel—the feeling that experience is a violation—realism never suppresses this anxiety entirely. While the paradigm establishes the tensions that motivate realism, it also gives texture to realism's construction of experience as a pattern moving characters backward as well as forward.

Still, because no one would deny the role of realism in promoting the paradigm's importance to the genre, one might conclude that novels such as *Great Expectations* and *Middlemarch* announce the culmination of both realism and the paradigm, and that the paradigm itself ceases to be as central to the novel's construction of experience once realism gives way to modernism. I want to argue the contrary, however. To be sure, the familiar span of nineteenth-century writers from Austen to Hardy, the arc delineating the achievement of realism, established what the "traditional" novel meant to writers like D. H. Lawrence and Virginia Woolf. In varying degrees, their novels reject the identifying features of realism—determinate characterization, linear structure, a stable authorial viewpoint—as they followed a program to innovate upon and challenge the tenets of the nineteenth-century novel.[1] Nonetheless, their novels build out of the same paradigmatic base as realism. In order to establish the extent to which the paradigm underlies the modernist novel, I will begin my discussion in this chapter by first calling attention to the paradigmatic construction of experience in *Tess of the d'Urbervilles*, *Lord Jim*, and *Women in Love*. Together, this trio of novels well illustrates the evolution of realism into modernism: modernism more or less inverts the hierarchical pattern of realism by allowing the regressive momentum to dominate, asserting, in the place of realism's call to maturity, a revaluation of innocence as a return to a primal unity of self and other. Then, in the second half of this chapter, I will examine in more detail the paradigm of experience in one modernist novel in particular, Virginia Woolf's *To the Lighthouse*. The formal apparatus of this novel may seem to signal its modernism as a break not only with realism but also with the paradigm of experience informing realism. Yet despite Woolf's rather breathtaking formal innovations, the construction of experience here is occasioned by the same anxiety over lost innocence that I have analyzed in the preceding chapters.

To begin with, a comparison of *Tess of the d'Urbervilles* and *Lord Jim* is useful in illustrating the break between Eliot's and Hardy's realism and the modernism of writers like Conrad, Lawrence, and Woolf, and for pointing out how modernism rearranges the priorities of realism. For all the obvious differences between the two novels, *Tess* and *Jim* similarly construct experience as a journey into selfhood which turns out to be fatal. The human imperfection of both Tess and Jim contests the innocence which they rely on to define themselves. Yet the loss of their innocence only intensifies their desire to regain it. With the division between self and other made unbridgeable, neither novel can imagine a means of repairing the self's violation other than death. Furthermore, in both novels the protagonist's desire for innocence competes with the narrator's recognition of corruption, and this competition instigates the double momentum of the paradigm. The regressive energy of immaturity (the innocence motivating Tess's and Jim's desire to return to an original state of unity with the other) is enclosed within a narrative voice (the experiential wisdom of Hardy's narrator and Conrad's Marlow) which respects, even insists upon, the claim of maturity's progressive energy.

There is no denying that *Tess*, in contrast to *Lord Jim*, takes to extreme the "somber" vision of *Middlemarch*. In this novel the other poses a more dire threat to the self, so while Hardy's omniscient narrator can sympathize with Tess's plight, he does not identify his vision with hers. Their lack of potential

Chapter 6

congruence, in contrast to that between narrator and characters in *Middlemarch*, makes impossible the amelioration of self typical of Eliot's realism. Hardy uses Tess to stimulate the regressive momentum of the paradigm and the narrator to insist upon the progressive momentum. The opposition that results between self (Tess's narrow vision and inarticulate voice) and other (the narrator's expansive vision and articulate voice) generates a constant state of friction: Tess's perspective stimulates a desire for innocence, which the narrator's perspective frustrates. As this double perspective indicates, innocence is an epistemological issue in Hardy's novel, a matter of understanding the self's relation to the other in terms of similarity. Whereas the narrator views Tess's loss of virginity as the sign of her being like other women, Tess accepts it as unmistakable proof of her corruption, a transgression of cultural law that implies a deviation from nature as well.

Consequently, the question of Tess's innocence—the degree to which she does or does not remain, as the novel's subtitle claims, "a pure woman faithfully presented"—becomes somewhat chimerical. Is her innocence a fact of nature or a product of culture? A state of grace or a state of mind? As far as the narrator is concerned, the answer is clear enough. "She had been made to break an accepted social law, but no law known to the environment in which she fancied herself such an anomaly." In explaining this conclusion, the narrator points out what Tess herself does not understand, that her unrelenting sense of guilt is actually no more than "a sorry and mistaken creation of Tess's fancy." She feels estranged from "the actual world" because she sees herself as "a figure of Guilt intruding into the haunts of Innocence." Naively and unrealistically, she makes "a distinction" between her guilty self and the innocence of the surrounding natural world "where there was no difference." When placed in this light Tess appears as a quixotic figure of tragic proportion, victimized by "shreds of convention" and terrified by "moral hobgoblins." She discovers a specific moral relevance in the "natural processes around her" only because "her whimsical fancy" turns the scene into "a part of her own story," a response which Hardy's narrator finds perfectly understandable, "for the world is only a psychological phenomenon, and what they [her impressions of nature's moral judgments] seemed they were."[2]

Tess's sense of guilt intensifies her consciousness of profound separation from the other in whatever shape her fancy casts it, and it also causes her to miss what the narrator sees, not signs of the marked difference between her self and the other so much as signs of the other's indifference to her self. Whereas the narrator's commentary takes pains to understand Tess as an unlucky woman overwhelmed by the impersonal forces of class, economics, and history, Tess seeks a more continuously relevant and deeply personal meaning to her experience. According to the narrator, Tess's violation by Alec merely repeats their culture's familiar history of privilege and patriarchy: the moneyed class exploiting the poor, the male exploiting the female. Tess, however, interprets the rape as a drama peculiar to her own experience and indicative of her own corruption. And who can blame her for placing her loss of virginity in such a personal context? Subjected as she is to the changing economic and social conditions of her time and culture, she lacks the distance to understand them as part of a larger historical process in the way the narrator can. To her mind the rape is neither an isolated incident nor an age-old story, but the determining factor of her adult life, the origin of her sexual awareness and, thus, the origin of her history. So long as she insists upon finding continuity between later events by reading her fall as their point of origin, she keeps exaggerating the importance of her lost innocence, intensifying all the more her desire to reclaim it, but also defining her self entirely in terms of its corruption.

Tess therefore condemns herself more severely than anyone else does in the novel, with the possible exception of Angel, who idealizes her figure as a projection (and, unconsciously, an eroticization) of his own desire for innocence. Her alienation from "the actual world"—from her culture, from nature, and, eventually, from her self—begins with her conviction that there is a crucial difference between her self and the innocence she sees made evident in nature and valorized by her culture. However, by casting a moral meaning onto the natural landscape, Tess

Chapter 6

personalizes the other: she makes it an expression of her own desire for innocence, and in doing that she collapses the difference between self and other. This confusion is what undermines her sense of identity. When she looks at the landscape around her in that scene from which I quoted a moment ago, nature seems to have appropriated her innocence and then, to add insult to injury, the landscape admonishes her for her loss. Yet the "formulae of bitter reproach" which Tess sees all around her are actually an "encompassment of her own characterization." Unfaithful to the innocence in nature, she feels she has betrayed her self as well; and this kind of thinking takes her "out of harmony with the actual world" (p. 72), to place her in the same position as Cathy Earnshaw, trapped in the precarious space between childhood innocence and adult sexuality.

Hardy's narrator puts it much more matter-of-factly: "An immeasurable social chasm was to divide our heroine's personality thereafter from that previous self of hers who stepped from her mother's door to try her fortune at Trantridge poultry-farm" (p. 63). This "chasm" cuts into Tess's consciousness more deeply than the narrator indicates. Tess internalizes that division to understand her "fall" as a transformation so abrupt and radical that it splits her self in two. She therefore later accepts Angel's condemnation without question, for he is merely voicing her own feeling of discontinuity with "that previous self of hers." "You were one person," he explains in an echo of the narrator's earlier comment, "now you are another" (p. 191). She eventually realizes the injustice of his charge, writing Angel that she is in fact "the same woman" he fell in love with—"yes, the very same!—not the one you dislike but never saw" (p. 279). But she cannot use this realization to sustain her sense of identity as "the same woman" because she cannot imagine the continuity between her adult and child selves any more than Cathy can. Angel's accusation, in fact, merely repeats what Tess herself thinks, that the woman he loves "is not my real self, but one in my image, the one I might have been" (p. 181).

Even though the narrator's commentary calls our attention to the psychological continuity of Tess's character—that she is "the same woman" before and after her journey to Trantridge—her disturbing feeling that she is two different people proves to be true. The narrator's explanation of Tess's guilt is that after the rape everywhere she looks she finds persuasive but misleading evidence that her natural progression from child to woman, abruptly brought about by an act of sexual violation, is a betrayal of her "previous" innocent self. In believing this Tess accepts the dubious and unregenerative moral authority of men and ignores her own more vital and regenerative instincts. To her mind Angel's declaration that she is "not deceitful, my wife; but not the same" confirms what she already knows in her heart (p. 194). Yet Tess tells Angel her history in the hope that his love for her will allow her to reclaim her previous self. When he then declares that it is not Tess he has been loving but "another woman in your shape" (p. 192), he denies her self coherence and continuity; and by articulating Tess's own feeling of self-division, he authorizes it for her, much as nature seemed to collaborate with her "fancy" after the rape to produce a landscape of "bitter reproach."

Angel's rejection of Tess makes her self-division irreparable because, to her mind, his condemnation is what stands between her corrupt and innocent selves. More to the point, Angel's character makes us realize that because Tess's story is indeed a history, a record of change, any effort of hers to reverse that change by restoring a "previous" self or by imagining what might have been is a futile attempt to resist history as it pushes her forward in time. When Angel returns to England intending to rectify his mistake, he is too late: Tess is indeed no longer "the very same." Sobered by his own experience in Brazil, he is at long last willing to appreciate in his wife what he could not see before, that "it was the touch of the imperfect"—in her face but also in her history—"upon the would-be perfect that gave the sweetness, because it was that which gave the humanity" (p. 127). However, when he sees Tess again, another woman, Alec's mistress, stands before him "in her shape": "his original Tess had spiritually ceased to recognize the body before him as hers—allowing it to drift, like a corpse upon the current, in a direction dissociated from its living will" (p. 314). His "original Tess" has in fact been transformed, and what is so disturbing about this new image is that it reduces her to a cipher, a mere physical shape. Lacking historical continuity (a previous self) and psychological coherence (a personality), she now displays no consciousness of her self as the "original Tess" and consequently shows no sign of possessing an identity. Like Clarissa, once Tess detaches her "living will" from "the body" that has, through its sexuality, betrayed the integrity of her previous self, she finally makes even her body into an extension of the other.

Tess's murder of Alec, which immediately follows Angel's return, is her last attempt to retrieve "that previous self of hers." By eliminating Alec she hopes to reclaim her body from him. But the murder has the opposite effect. She cannot reverse the events that have marked her life from the beginning with a "coarse pattern" (p. 63), just as, very early in the novel, she could not undo Alec's "kiss of mastery" however much she tried (p. 45). Since it now confirms, as far as her culture is concerned, her criminality as a "fallen" woman, the murder makes her life's forward momentum away from innocence irreversible. Thus when Tess and Angel finally reconcile (and, presumably, consummate their marriage) after the murder, their reunion crystallizes the extreme division of mind and body that characterized Tess when Angel saw her standing at the door. She can only be reconciled with Angel, who represents her better self, and momentarily reverse the course of her history, by excluding the other from her consciousness entirely. She herself makes this clear when she observes to Angel that she now feels safe at last because "all is trouble outside there; inside here content." The narrator concurs with her reasoning, articulating what she wants to say: "It was quite true, within was affection, union, error forgiven: outside was the inexorable" (p. 323). Outside, that is to say, is the "inexorable" other, everything that comes into contact with the body to violate the self's innocence. As in Maggie's reunion with Tom, here Tess sees her "error forgiven" only when she retreats inside her self, for then the self seems impervious to the other's impact. Her retreat "inside," in fact, is the culmination of what the novel has been painfully documenting all along: the erosion of Tess's self at the hands of the other, an attrition so complete that, with her identity fragmented and her consciousness numbed, she seems to be like a ghost even before she dies.

This vision of the self broken in half by its experience accounts for the disturbing impact of Hardy's novel. When experience is seen as a violation of this magnitude, it exceeds all possibility of repair. In this *Tess* is reminiscent of *Clarissa*, the first part of *Wuthering Heights*, and *The Mill on the Floss*. Hardy does not allow for the ameliorating ending typical of realistic novels—*Pride and Prejudice, Great Expectations, Middlemarch*—but *Tess* nonetheless follows the tenets of realism in that it mediates Tess's sense of violation through the narrator, whose perspective recognizes the other as something apart from—indifferent to—the self. His voice never achieves a point of congruence with Tess's, however, and his narration repeatedly predicts her awful end through recurring images—red on white, for instance—just as it repeatedly arranges events to conspire against her efforts to reimagine innocence. Tess cannot command her experience to orchestrate death as a return to innocence in the manner of Clarissa or Maggie, and her narrator is too wise an observer of history and culture to do so himself. As a result, the narrator's "inexorable" push forward overwhelms Tess's efforts with his ironic recognition that she is a guiltless—and thus "innocent"—victim of the other's indifference.

A similar dread of the "inexorable" other impinging upon the self to violate its innocence pervades *Lord Jim*. Although Hardy's novel is one of the traditional markers noting the end of realism in the English novel, just as Conrad's conveniently epitomizes the advent of modernism, what I want to emphasize in comparing *Lord Jim* with *Tess* is the similar tension between the experiential momentum that leads Jim away from his ideal of innocence and his attempt to redirect that unrelenting forward momentum. Put most simply, Conrad builds his narrative out of the juxtaposition of romantic (Jim's) and realistic (Marlow's) temperaments. This tension arises from the paradigm's double construction of experience, the forward moving pattern imposed upon the self by the other, the backward moving pattern created by the self in its attempt to command the other in the service of desire. The ambivalence we are made to feel towards Jim's drive to regain his innocence comes about because, in contrast to Hardy's, Conrad's novel gives each construction a similar imaginative appeal, although not, finally, equal psychological weight.

While it arranges its narrative to resist a single determinate meaning,[3] *Lord Jim* still follows the paradigmatic movement of novels like *Middlemarch* and *Tess*, which direct the self towards a confrontation with the other because, if nothing else, they are confident that the other is a discernible presence. Following the example of many a typical nineteenth-century hero, Jim builds castles in the air based on the romances he has read as a boy. His "fierce,"[4] "superb" (p. 251), and "exalted egoism" (p. 253) further lays a quixotic foundation for his innocence, which, Marlow knows, may actually be "a sort of sublimated idealised selfishness" (p. 108). Whereas until her breakdown Tess is always conscious of the other, Jim wants the other to be aware of *him*. But since he assumes that everyone knows his fatal secret, that he jumped ship, he keeps retreating from the civilization he has betrayed by pushing further into the interior, until he reaches Patusan, where his romantic daydreams become real. What Jim fails to understand is that his awareness of the "inexorable" other contesting his innocence and following him everywhere, even to Patusan, is a projection of his self. He tries to recover his lost innocence by projecting his imperfect humanity onto the other, creating a landscape of desire that forces him to recognize his own corruption in the very act of denying it.

We clearly see Jim's projecting his self onto the other in the first chapter of the novel, before Marlow intercedes as the book's central narrator. Aboard a training ship, Jim becomes caught up in a daydream, picturing himself "as unflinching as a hero in a book" (p. 5). Taken unaware when an accident occurs, he misses his chance to act heroically. Although he rationalizes his lost opportunity by arguing that this particular call to adventure was beneath his great ability, like one of Scott's heroes Jim discovers, much to his chagrin, a reality indifferent to his daydream. Whereas he can control the outcome of a daydream merely by exerting his imagination, this experience takes him by surprise and introduces variables—a sense of terror, for instance—that abruptly change his daydream's heroic script.

The accident, this collision of Jim's imagined self with a fully realized other, exposes his fallibility in the face of a "heroic" opportunity. His paralysis, however, does not lead him to greater self-knowledge but instead intensifies his desire to overwhelm the other with his imagination. "He felt angry with the brutal tumult of earth and sky for taking him unawares and checking unfairly a generous readiness for narrow escapes" (p. 6). Paradoxically, several sentences later, we are told the Jim, though angry, "could detect no trace of emotion in himself" (p. 7). This should not be too surprising when we remember that he has repressed his anger by projecting it onto the sea. In "the anger of the sea," he imagines

> a sinister violence of intention—that indefinable something which forces it upon the mind and heart of a man, that this complication of accidents or these elemental furies are coming at him with a purpose of malice, with a strength beyond control, with an unbridled cruelty that means to tear out of him his hope and his fear, the pain of his fatigue and his longing for rest: which means to smash, to destroy, to annihilate all he has seen, known, loved, enjoyed, or hated; all that is priceless and necessary—the sunshine, the memories, the future; which means to sweep the whole previous world utterly away from his sight by the simple and appalling act of taking his life. (p. 7)

Motivated by his "exalted egoism," Jim transforms the impersonal, irrational other into a hostile agent pursuing him vindictively, intent on "taking his life" by contradicting his past, "all he has seen, known, loved, enjoyed, or hated." In this light his fear of death, which paralyzes him on the training ship just as it will do later when the Patna "sinks," assumes more meaningful proportions. The other has somehow singled *him* out for violation. He has therefore made the other aware of him as the specific object of its "sinister intention," and through this projection of desire onto the other, he can begin to restore the plot of his heroic script.[5]

The episode aboard the training ship typifies Jim's effort to imagine an indifferent other and, without appreciating the contradiction, to personalize that other at the same time in order to make it an extension of his self. Jim repeatedly tries to resist the forward movement of his experience by returning to his initial moment of cowardice in an attempt to revise it. As he retreats into the interior—inside his imagination—he becomes further alienated from the other because what he sees there, repeatedly, is the mirror image of his desire. Indeed, when Marlow says that Jim is ultimately "overwhelmed by the inexplicable; he was overwhelmed by his own personality" (p. 207), the syntax equates "the inexplicable" with Jim's "personality," to suggest that they may be the same thing. Because Jim's own "inexplicable" personality, which is other than his heroic self-image, *is* the other, he can never escape his "inexplicable" corruption but sees it wherever he goes. Thus he cannot help falling victim to the manipulations of Gentleman Brown. Brown personifies that "inexplicable" corruption which Jim tries to project onto the other. Brown, that is to say, is "a sinister violence of intention" come to life. Yet whose "intention" does Brown embody? The "sinister violence" that results from Brown's appearance in Patusan occurs because Jim identifies with Brown, because he sees his own history echoed in the latter's request for a second chance. Brown is as much Jim's accomplice here as the sea was in the earlier episode; that is, Brown leads Jim to acknowledge his own corrupt humanity by recognizing his self in the other, yet this identification allows Jim to disown the "inexplicable" personality he encounters.

In short, Jim is, like Pip and Esther, paradoxically "guilty and yet innocent." Unlike them, however, he remains caught up in this contradiction to the very end of the novel. Despite all the evidence to the contrary, Jim's faith in the value of his innocence never wavers; and the novel's plot collaborates with his imagination to reinforce his faith—and to keep testing it. When Jim finds the confirmation of his daydreams in Patusan, he repeats his great mistake, his "exalted egoism" causing his disastrous misreading of Brown's intentions. This mistake, however, gives him his longed-for second chance, which he makes full use of to recover the innocence he lost aboard the training ship. All the same, in reaffirming his innocence by remaining true to his heroic ideal, Jim is also owning up to his corruption, to his responsibility in having betrayed that ideal by trusting Brown.

Does Jim's corruption therefore cancel out his innocence? This question is what draws Marlow to Jim in the courtroom. To begin with, Jim is always "inscrutable" to Marlow because his innocence belongs to childhood (he is even called a "child" several times in the novel); and in telling Jim's story, Marlow seems able to remember that innocence much as he remembers Jim, as something lost, as an absence. Though there are days, Marlow concludes, when Jim seems real, when "the reality of his existence comes to me with an immense, with an overwhelming force," there are also times when he seems just as unreal, "when he passes from my eyes like a disembodied spirit astray amongst the passions of his earth, ready to surrender himself faithfully to the claim of his own world of shades." Pushed into the shadows of reverie by Marlow's presence as narrator, Jim represents the loss of innocence in each "one of us," so he is "forgotten, unforgiven, and excessively romantic" (p. 253). Consequently, the emotional texture of Marlow's narration renders the ambivalence with which Marlow, being "one of us" too, recalls this ghost of our childish innocence and wonders at the magnitude of our loss, but also accepts its inevitability.

This is why Marlow keeps reminding us that Jim can retrieve his innocence only by disregarding reality altogether. To be sure, Jim attracts Marlow because of his naïve and quixotic ability to impress his imagination upon reality. As a result, Marlow explains, "the reality could not be half as bad, not half as anguishing, appalling, and vengeful as the created terror of his imagination" (p. 69). Among other reasons, Marlow believes that Jim is "one of us" because his innocence exposes our yearning for a reality we can command through desire. But this is a double-edged attraction. Jim's romantic temperament takes him away from Jewel, "away from a living woman to celebrate his pitiless wedding with a shadowy ideal of conduct." In other words, to achieve his dream Jim leaves behind the genuine presence of the other—"a living woman"—and enters "his own world of shades," which is actually a denial of lived reality since it dissolves the difference between self and other to fulfill his desire in death. Thus while Jim's death may glorify his innocence and justify his symbolic white clothes, all he achieves, as far as Marlow knows, is "a shadowy ideal of conduct," and all that remains, in Marlow's eyes, "is a disembodied spirit" as homeless on "his earth" (p. 253) as Cathy's ghost or Tess's spectral appearance after Angel's return from Brazil.

Lord Jim therefore counterpoints the regressive momentum instigated by Jim's "excessively romantic" desire for innocence with the progressive momentum of Marlow's realist voice, reflecting the entire narrative through the kind of double vision that characterizes the ending of *The Mill on the Floss*. The novel's progressive and regressive movements, in other words, are orchestrated concurrently. In remaining faithful to his innocence in death, Jim seeks to achieve what Cathy Earnshaw wanted, his movement towards death reversing the paradigm's forward momentum just as hers does. He moves from reality to illusion, from corruption to innocence. However, Marlow's perspective of this regressive movement reinterprets it in the light of realism, much as the second Cathy revises her mother's experience in *Wuthering Heights*. As far as Marlow can tell, Jim's death is an act of self-sacrifice in the service of an ideal which he can never realize in life. For all its value in resisting the destructive element, Marlow believes that Jim's innocence proves to be a fatal but highly seductive miscalculation of reality. The novel's ending seems to confirm Marlow's perspective only because his voice acquires a more immediate presence in the text and can therefore assert preeminence over Jim's desiring imagination, much as Eliot's narrator manages the characters' desire in *Middlemarch*.

In their different ways *Lord Jim* and *Tess of the d'Urbervilles* both voice the frustration of having to live a single life with its irrevocable history of lost innocence, and they interpret this recognition of human limitation as an act of violation. Hardy follows the forward movement of realism to envision its ultimate consequence, the self damaged by an external reality beyond the point of repair; yet in doing so, he also begins to imagine experience much as a modernist like Conrad does, as a "psychological phenomenon, for what they seemed they were." Thus the narrator of *Tess* may distinguish the other as something distinct from the self, but what he sees is of little consequence to Tess. She, like Jim, feels the impact of her inexplicable violation as if it were a sinister practical joke.[6] In contrast to Tess, Jim can trump the joker by leaving the game and escaping to his self-created reality. Unlike Tess's, his retreat to the shadowy world inside his imagination withstands the inexorable and inexplicable other because it sharpens his imaginative defenses rather than breaks them down.

Despite these different endings, in keeping with the paradigm *Tess* and *Jim* each orchestrate experience as a discordant rhythm of violation and repair. Both novels coordinate the paradigm's double movement as separate but simultaneous movements in which it is the narrator, not the character, who sees the repair emerging out of the self's violation; repair is thus an achievement of introspection like Dorothea's in *Middlemarch*, but one denied to the characters and instead made a distinct feature of the narrative text. This is, in fact, one major difference between realistic and modernist novels, and the reason why critics tend to use character as the point of demarcation between realism and modernism. As George Levine puts it, "the shift of emphasis from character is part of the whole transformation away from realism."[7] Daniel Albright explains the achievement of modernism in similar terms: whereas "realism demands that each character in a novel possesses a mind whose power and complexity seem equal to our intuition of the mind's capacity," modernism encourages "a certain loosening of the boundaries between character and character, so that all thought, emotion, perception, gesture will appear to be the reflection of a single, controlling [authorial] mind."[8]

My point is that this "transformation" does not mark a very radical departure from the paradigm of experience in earlier novels. In a manner of speaking, modernism follows the lead of a novel like *Bleak House*, which projects a landscape of desire through a narrative that subsumes the psychology of its characters, rather than a novel like *Middlemarch*, which locates desire more securely within individual characters through a narrative that insists upon sharply delineating the self from the other. In other words, whereas a realistic construction of experience insists upon the authority of the other and its denial of the innocence of the self as the stable point of reference, a modernist construction places greater emphasis upon the authority of the self and its longing for innocence. Character itself does not disappear from the modernist novel; what is effaced, as *Lord Jim* illustrates, is Eliot's type of vocal, synthesizing narrator who can confidently distinguish self from other, desire from reality, and then subordinate the characters' vision to his. By contrast, modernist novels rely on a less determinate narration to define consciousness as a fluid stream of feeling and memory transcending linear time and conflating self and other.[9]

When describing the fluidity of consciousness which modernist fiction portrays, critics often use water imagery themselves. Albright, for instance, refers to "the oceanic self" in Lawrence's novels,[10] just as James Naremore refers to the "watery world" in Woolf's.[11] These descriptions of a self totally absorbed by the other recall Freud's similar discussion in his introduction to *Civilization and its Discontents*. There he speculates about a primitive, preconscious "oceanic feeling," by which he means the "feeling of an indissoluble bond, of being one with the external world as a whole." That oneness, he goes on to explain, precedes the construction of an egocentric consciousness identified as something different from the other: "originally the ego includes everything, later it separates off an external world from itself." Freud is not necessarily insisting that the ego is constant or fixed, since "important pathological disturbances" prove the contrary, as does "being in love," for then "the boundary between ego and object threatens to melt away." Although he emphasizes the developmental process of the ego's individuation, which dissipates that "oceanic feeling," Freud's point is that "what is primitive is so commonly preserved [in the mind] alongside of the transformed version which has arisen from it."[12]

Freud's idea of a primitive oceanic feeling can help to distinguish the orchestration of the paradigm in modernism from that in realism. Modernism conceives of innocence as a primal memory, much like Cathy's or Maggie's, of having originally been united—"at home"—with the other. This is not to say that realism is indifferent to the primal significance of innocence. On the contrary, what Tess loses because of her guilt is her sense of original unity with the other. But because her guilty conscience has an inescapable cultural relevance, connoting sinful corruption of a sexual nature, the implication of moral deviation works to alienate the self from its cultural background in order to exaggerate difference. In other words, like *Clarissa, Wuthering Heights, Bleak House,* and *The Mill on the Floss, Tess* equates difference with deviation by aligning it to the myth of the fall. Although this alignment intensifies the desire for the lost unity of self and other, its mythic context makes evident the impossibility of ever satisfying that desire; thus it insists upon lost innocence as the given reality of human experience. Modernism orchestrates experience to articulate a similar competition between the longing for innocence and the recognition of human corruption, but it does so through a different cultural vocabulary: not the Garden of Eden so much as an oceanic memory, not sin so much as separation. By casting innocence in this light modernism can respond to it more benignly and nostalgically. Modernism therefore reverses the priorities of realism by allowing the regressive impetus of romance to serve as the primary energizing force behind its construction of experience. Like *Lord Jim*, the modernist novel respects the energy of romance in that its construction of experience originates in a desire to return to that remembered state of oceanic unity. When most intensely imagined this desired unity requires the death of the self as an individual consciousness. Thus like *Lord Jim* too, the modernist novel tries to counter that dominant regressive longing by recalling the assumption of realism, which insists upon the self's fallen state as a recognition of the other's difference—and indifference.

The modernist orchestration of the paradigm that I have been describing is well typified by *Women in Love*. With this novel Lawrence wanted to move beyond nineteenth-century fiction's dependence on what he called, in a celebrated phrase, "the old stable *ego* of the character."[13] *Women in Love* calls for the breaking down of civilization's unhealthy restraints in order to release the primal energy of the self so that it becomes an aspect of the other, and vice versa.[14] In this context, Freud's comment about love collapsing the boundaries between self and the object of desire is appropriate to what Lawrence's characters experience as men and women in love. Acting upon sexual desire, the self achieves "the immemorial magnificence of mystic, palpable, real otherness,"[15] first to experience the oceanic feeling—Birkin calls it "that dark river of dissolution" which underlies "the black river of corruption" (p. 164)—and then to regain the self's original innocence. Sexual experience is the means of satisfying this desire for the innocence of preconsciousness because it achieves the momentary death of "the old stable *ego*" in orgasm. In the same way, "the desire for destruction" (p. 374) motivating the death drift of Gudren and Gerald could indeed lead them to a realm of oceanic existence beyond the self in so far as "it is a desire for the reduction-process in oneself, a reducing back to the origin, a return along the Flux of Corruption, to the original rudimentary conditions of being" (p. 375).

Lawrence concentrates upon his characters' sexual experience to make graphic how the self's repair is actually inherent in its violation, its sexual penetration by and of the other. Whereas in *Clarissa* or *Bleak House* sexuality epitomizes the maturation which the self dreads because of the mystery surrounding the other sex, in *Women in Love* the rhythm of sexuality transcends its cultural connotations of debased innocence, so that the physical penetration that satisfies erotic desire returns the self to a state of oceanic unity with the other. This is one of the ways *Women in Love* inverts the hierarchical arrangement of realism, transforming the paradigm's regressive energy into a progressive momentum which leads Birkin and Ursula to a "new" reality, one that has been lost to sophisticated adult consciousness. The claims of that consciousness, which dominate a realist construction of experience, thus become the subversive element here in a reversal of the priorities which inform *Pride and Prejudice* or *Middlemarch*. The desire for innocence impels Lawrence's characters to make contact with the other sex; but while they achieve a momentary fusion, that unity cannot be sustained, so they remain in a state of desire, yearning to regain that lost oneness.

To be sure, for most of *Women in Love* the rhythm of violation and repair underlying sexual experience is not readily apparent to the characters because they approach love through consciousness. Irresistibly drawn to the other by their desire, the characters assume, as Ursula does initially, that the other sex wants her "to yield as it were her very identity" (p. 178). Such dread exposes their corruption, preventing them from regaining their innocence through the return to unconsciousness achieved in orgasm. Much like Rosamond, Gudren, for example, tries to command the other through the sheer force of her will. Dreading the obliteration of consciousness that occurs during orgasm, she instead experiences only a momentary sensation of release and then reasserts her will to become, once again, "an intense and vivid consciousness, an exhausting superconsciousness" (p. 339). This "superconsciousness" fills her with "a sense of her own negation," because she "must always demand the other to be aware of her, to be in connection with her" (p. 157). If Gudren genuinely wants "the other to be aware of her, to be in connection with her," then she must learn to be aware of the other, too. But since she understands the other as a penetrator of her body and violator of her consciousness, she represses the expansive power of desire so that it becomes a force of hostility, aggression, and, ultimately, death: she wants to master and then negate the other through sex.

The violence that characterizes Gudren and Gerald's lovemaking as a result echoes the legend of Ghost's Walk in *Bleak House*. Here too, male and female batter away at each other in an attempt to possess and master, their sexuality horrific in the aggression it unleashes. The "Moony" chapter reveals a similar dynamic operating behind Birkin's relationship with Ursula. It goes further, however, to illuminate the way out of that sexual deadlock, thereby correcting the dreadful impression of sexual experience as an act of violation. In this scene Birkin stones the moon's reflection on the water to penetrate and then break down its solid shape. But while his action seeks to effect the moon's disintegration into an oceanic oneness, he himself does not dissolve into water along with the shattered image. His inability ever to violate the moon completely, moreover, since all he can shatter is its image, intensifies the aggression and hostility with which he penetrates the water to disrupt its still surface. In this respect, he wants the moon "to yield as it were her very identity," all the while remaining aloof himself, and all the while encountering only its reflection. Each time he throws a stone, the reflected image of the moon explodes on the water's surface and loses its shape, but it quickly reforms moments later to seem whole once more: "The furthest waves of light, fleeing out, seemed to be clamouring against the shore for escape, the waves of darkness came in heavily, running under towards the centre. But at the centre, the heart of all, was still a vivid, incandescent quivering of a white moon not quite destroyed, a white body of fire writhing and striving, and not even now broken open, not yet violated. . . . it was re-asserting itself, the inviolable moon" (p. 239). Furiously, Birkin gets larger stones and throws them into the water, while Ursula watches him intently, excited by his actions, it seems, to the point of orgasm. As if she were the moon's reflection itself, she feels "dazed, her mind was all gone. She felt she had fallen to the ground and was spilled out, like water on the earth" (p. 240).

In stoning the moon's reflection, Birkin is enacting the aggression that has underlain his sexual desire, particularly during his rather volatile affair with Hermione. He thinks of woman as "the Great Mother of everything," man "as the broken-off fragment of woman," sex as "the still aching scar of his laceration" (p. 192). His desire for her compels him to penetrate her body, and his penetration is an act of retaliation against her for drawing him back to her womb, his place of origin. His aggression is thus a reaction to hers. The stoning of the moon now brings out a different, more expansive meaning of his desire to penetrate her. The imaged action in this scene—Ursula as well as the moon being violated and yet remaining "inviolable"—dramatizes an intense state of sexual activity and suggests that the death of consciousness, which momentarily occurs during orgasm, is not an annihilation of self but a prelude to its reformation, part of a continuous process of expansion and contraction, the very rhythm of sexual experience leading to orgasm. Penetrated by the male, the female loses consciousness but discovers her radiant "centre," which is "not quite destroyed . . . not even now broken open, not yet violated."

Both characters are in a sense instructed by the activity in this scene. Ursula has a premonition of what she will later learn, that contact with Birkin's otherness through sex is not an assault upon her self. His penetration of her body is more a liberation than a violation of her self, since it reveals to her, as well as to him, her inviolate "centre." Indeed, her orgasm, described in androgynous imagery, leads her to identify with his otherness as a male while retaining her separateness as a female: thus the penetration of the moon, a vaginal image, gives her the feeling of spilling to the ground like water or semen. Likewise, in watching what happens to the moon's reflection as he stones it, Birkin intuits that penetration exposes not the male's weakness, as he fears, but his strength, and his strength arises not from his phallic ability to penetrate her body, as he originally supposed in his hostility, but from his connection to her otherness, achieved through the very "writhing and striving" with which the two reach orgasm as the result of his penetration.

At this point in *Women in Love* such understanding for both characters is mostly subconscious, predicting what they will come to recognize on a more conscious level in the "Excurse" chapter when both feel reborn after making love. This earlier scene therefore concludes with the resurgence of the sexual tension between them, echoing the rhythm of expansion and contraction which the moon's reflection on the water has recorded. Ursula senses the anger with which Birkin has stoned the moon's reflection and is somewhat repulsed, and he still wants her to give her "golden light" to him (p. 241). But the rhythm of violation and repair, imagined for them through the fragmentation and reformation of the moon's reflection, has nonetheless shown them a path through which the self can meet the other "in mystic balance and integrity—like a star balanced with another star" (p. 144). In order to achieve this balance, Birkin and Ursula must each overcome their fear of the other, for only then can they realize that their immersion in "that dark river of dissolution," as evidenced when Birkin stones the moon's reflection, will not violate the self but place it in full parity with the other.

The achievement of Ursula and Birkin, in contrast to the failure of Gudren and Gerald, directs the forward momentum of experience in *Women in Love* to outline a pattern leading to insight which is not very different from that in novels with a more pronounced realistic bias. Through his love for Ursula, Birkin discovers "a strange new wakefulness. . . . He seemed to be conscious all over, all his body awake with a simple, glimmering awareness, as if he had just come awake, like a thing that is born, like a bird when it comes out of an egg, into a new universe'' (p. 303). Ursula similarly realizes "an essential new being . . . her complete self'' (p. 306), in "the oneness with Birkin, a oneness that struck deeper notes, sounding into the heart of the universe, the heart of reality, where she had never existed before'' (p. 400). Clearly, these two characters, waking with their new "awareness,'' have discovered "the heart of reality'' in a moment of insight resembling Elizabeth's in *Pride and Prejudice* or Dorothea's in *Middlemarch*. And this discovery *Women in Love* also celebrates through a marriage, fulfilling Birkin's longing for "pure unison . . . a conjunction with the other—for ever'' (p. 144).

For all this similarity, the important difference between *Women in Love* and *Pride and Prejudice* or *Middlemarch* is revealed by the language describing Ursula and Birkin's achievement. Noticeably absent here is realism's keen informing sense of disillusionment, of a myopia corrected by a penetrating jolt of reality. The key word instead is "new'': this is a "new'' reality, not one seen anew in the correcting light of the other. Indeed, the language in the very first phrase I quoted from the novel—"the immemorial magnificence of mystic, palpable, real otherness''—is emblematic of its construction of experience. With each adjective establishing a greater concreteness, the progressive movement in the syntax from "mystic'' to "palpable'' to "real'' epitomizes the progressive momentum of experience in the novel as a whole. At the same time, *Women in Love* exerts a different pressure upon the specific meanings of "real'' and "otherness,'' giving them their "mystic'' quality in order to let the romantic pole of the paradigm take sway over the realistic pole. As a result, *Women in Love* transforms the forward momentum of realism (the development of a stable, integrated self) into its own regressive movement: the destructive energy unleashed by Gerald and Gudren because of their will to master the other. Likewise, the novel transforms the backward momentum of romance (the search for the self's origin in innocence) into its own progressive movement: the creative energy generated by Ursula and Birkin as they fuse into "an essential new being.''

This scheme, however, is not as straightforward or as linear as I may have just made it seem. Because the drive to regain innocence in *Women in Love* cannot entirely master the characters' recognition of their corruption, the romance energies of the novel are, ultimately, firmly countered by those of realism. To begin with, despite Birkin's preaching, the characters cannot understand intellectually what they experience sexually (and what their intellect perverts) because desire pushes them to a level of instinct more primitive than intellect, and much more frightening. Consequently, they dread what they desire, the loss of consciousness, and believe that they can only overcome this threat through sheer mastery of the will. So while *Women in Love* constructs experience to propel its characters forward to discover "a new reality" existing prior to—innocent of—the language and thought that define consciousness as a corrupt state of difference, more often than not its characters resist this fulsome vision, keeping the claims of romance and realism continually straining against each other.

As a result, innocence finally seems to be as visible and yet as distant as the moon Birkin tries to reach by striking at its reflection on the water. This feeling of the irresistible yet elusive presence of innocence in the self is further enhanced through the novel's pervasive sexual imagery. Sexuality leads Birkin and Ursula back to an original state of innocence, which is to say that it temporarily returns the self to the telling moment prior to its consciousness of lost innocence. The inevitable resurgence of consciousness after orgasm then makes the self feel anew the loss of what it has just realized, so the self is driven by desire to regain that sensation.[16] Inspired by the continuous rhythm of violation and repair epitomized in the sexual act it designates as its emblem for experience, *Women in Love* makes the self's primal desire for innocence its motivating drive; however, since the novel recognizes that the self cannot realize that sensation of innocence for more than a moment, what endures afterwards is not innocence but the memory of innocence, which keeps the desire alive.

The competing drives of romance and realism, furthermore, cause the novel to close upon a pronounced note of separation and frustration. Birkin has failed to achieve the perfect friendship with

Gerald, and his feeling of loss beclouds his conversation with Ursula in the final scene. He refuses to believe that "two kinds of love" are, as she wants him to realize, "impossible" (p. 473). He will not be satisfied with their marriage and all it conventionally implies about the compromises necessary to sustain the "polarisation" of male and female (p. 193), much to her frustration. Yet why should she be so exasperated at Birkin's desire for more than he has? She too has yearned for "something infinitely more than love," since, as she tells Gudren, "love is too human and too little" (p. 429). While she seems to have reconciled herself to settling for love by the end of the novel, Birkin's reluctance to do so exacerbates their separation to remind them both of love's very human limitations.

Women in Love therefore does not produce a linear construction of experience out of the paradigmatic rhythm of violation and repair in the manner of *Pride and Prejudice* or *Middlemarch*, although, as we have seen, it does work out of similar tensions. In those novels a mature consciousness succeeds an immature one to define the progressive direction of experience as the losing of innocence and gaining of maturity; afterwards there is no going back. As I have been arguing, *Women in Love* responds to the call of romance by valorizing the desire to go back; to sustain this desire, the novel orchestrates experience as a continuous process of violation and repair so that there is no finality to a character's experience of either. The exhilaration Birkin and Ursula each feel in awakening to "the heart of reality," their new understanding of the self in relation to the other, has ebbed considerably by the novel's conclusion. But the frustration voiced in the final pages does not necessarily diminish the significance of the exhilaration previously experienced. Taking a cue from the novel's sexual imagery, we are meant to see the emotional texture of experience as a rhythmic series of moments of exhilaration and frustration, of desire intensified, satisfied, intensified, satisfied, and so forth. The repair inherent in sexual penetration occurs because it momentarily returns the self to a state of innocence wherein the self seems, like the moon, an "inviolable" center, having so thoroughly fused with the other as to eradicate, for the moment, a sense of difference. Violation occurs after the moment of penetration has ended, thereby intensifying the self's difference from the other and stimulating anew the desire to return to that state of innocence through sexual fusion.

Women in Love imagines the rhythm of violation and repair differently from more traditional novels in that it repeatedly shifts back and forth between the two poles of the paradigm, instead of marking out an irreversible linear direction for the characters' experience by moving progressively from one pole (romance) to the other (realism). In this effort to portray the self in a primal state of innocence, *Women in Love* inverts the hierarchical arrangement of realism but does not dispel realism's recognition of corruption and loss. The novel views the characters' innocence historically and, thus, nostalgically as an ever-present desire to return to "the original rudimentary conditions of being." *To the Lighthouse* arranges the paradigmatic rhythm of violation and repair to produce a similar emotional current, what Lily Briscoe calls "the old horror . . . to want and want and not to have."[17] Woolf's characters, no less than Lawrence's, are keenly alert to their desire for unity with the other. Unlike *Women in Love*, however, *To the Lighthouse* focuses that desire around the complex feelings stimulated by the self's attraction to "home" as its origin and source of security.

Whereas Lawrence's novel imagines the desire for primal unity through the sexual experience of its characters, Woolf's imagines this desire in terms of competing feelings of unity with and separation from the parent. *To the Lighthouse* therefore harkens back to the Family Romance story of nineteenth-century fiction, as exemplified by Scott's Waverley novels, the books which the Ramsays recall fondly in part I. In its own enactment of the Family Romance, however, *To the Lighthouse* gives it a different turn. Competing feelings of separation from the father and unity with the mother rapidly succeed each other, and this fluctuation intensifies the primal desire for an oceanic unity while heightening the anxiety which underlies that desire, namely the dread that such unity violates the self's integrity and continuity. The third part of the novel then relieves this dread by focusing upon Lily Briscoe's and James Ramsay's journeys into selfhood, which demonstrate the continuity informing the self's maturation.

To the Lighthouse thus constructs experience as a contrapuntal arrangement of the paradigm's progressive and regressive energies. The novel begins by focusing its emotional content through the presence of Mrs. Ramsay. In part I she appears both as an individualized personality—with her many petty insecurities and human failings, as well as her mystery—and as the personification of love, warmth, security. Mrs. Ramsay's maternal figure centers the novel's world and makes it radiate with the feelings of home. The alien sexuality of Mr. Ramsay's paternal figure, on the other hand, threatens that security, generating the friction behind the regressive desire for the unity of self and other which Mrs. Ramsay encourages the characters to feel. However, the end of part I does not resolve the antagonism between the Ramsays in the manner of *Middlemarch*, nor does it exacerbate it further in the manner of *Women in Love*. Rather, it simply moves beyond the tension between them by demonstrating the unity of their marriage, which transcends their differences.

The novel's second part then effects a transition from the unifying presence of Mrs. Ramsay in part I to her disunifying absence in part III. Here in part II we encounter an other truly indifferent to the self. Time overwhelms the self to the point of complete disintegration, and the death and decay recorded in this section magnify the warm appeal of Mrs. Ramsay's home all the more. Part III opens with the absence of the maternal center vividly felt by the characters, whose grief encourages them to intensify their memories of having been bound to Mrs. Ramsay. Her death confirms the pervasive sense of dread—suggested in part I and fully realized in part II—which underlies James's and Lily's passage into the imperfect adult world, a world where corruption means mortality, loss, and death, and where these meanings all cluster around the absence of the mother. With that bond between mother and child severed, Mr. Ramsay no longer seems as alien or as oppressive as he once did. In fact, he provides James and Lily with a human shelter from the impersonal other that dominated part II. Mr. Ramsay, rather than his wife, turns out to be the means of repair for James and Lily, because the successful completion of their journey into selfhood depends upon their identification with his otherness.

In order to examine the paradigmatic base of *To the Lighthouse* we must therefore recognize that this novel is in certain ways even less traditional than *Lord Jim* or *Women in Love* and yet much more so in others. To begin with, no one questions the modernism of *To the Lighthouse* when considering its formal devices for narrating consciousness. Woolf simply dispenses with much of the materialism and plotted action of realism in order to exaggerate the difference between her crafted text and the unstable world it represents in language. We are made fully aware of the "instability, ambiguity, confusion and contradiction" of her characters' world and the "coherent, unified, semantically saturated" narration that orders their world into "meanings which cannot be attributed to fictional subjects."[18] In stark contrast to Eliot's intrusive narrator in *Middlemarch*, Woolf's seems to abdicate its authority. As Erich Auerbach has put it in his classic explication of this novel's modernism: "she does not seem to bear in mind that she is the author and hence ought to know how matters stand with her characters. . . . [Consequently,] there actually seems to be no viewpoint at all outside the novel from which the people and events within it are observed, any more than there seems to be an objective reality apart from what is in the consciousness of the characters."[19] This fusion of author and characters creates a problematic narration, for it is often difficult to locate the source of a thought or feeling in either author or character. As a register of the fictive world, this authorial viewpoint orients the narrative around the characters' competing feelings of alienation and unity in order to call repeated attention to the momentary discontinuity caused by intense emotion. The peculiar texture of experience in this novel thus arises from its narration of consciousness. Taken separately, each single moment of intensely felt experience suspends the linear movement of time, concentrating previous moments of consciousness into the present so that a feeling—of alienation, say, or of unity—is perceived as a whole and unchanging vision of reality; taken together in duration, however, these single moments of consciousness record the intense, contradictory, and transient feelings of characters living in a world marked by fragmentation and instability.

To the Lighthouse renders experience through a narration that emphasizes its difference—in style, voice, subject matter—from realistic novels like *Pride and Prejudice* or *Middlemarch*. Those novels can imagine a stable self because they imagine the other as a stable backdrop for the self. Woolf's novel, in contrast, internalizes the characters' experience so that the self serves as the other's reflection and vice versa. The novel then blends these reflections of instability into the selfless emotional field of the narration. As a result, in James Naremore's words, "the whole book is the product of one voice which at times assumes the role of a given character and approximates his pattern of thought."[20] Because it can dissolve into the consciousness of the characters, this impersonal authorial voice achieves what the characters want so badly but can never realize themselves because of their humanity: a completely selfless identification with the other.

Consequently, Woolf's narration encourages the desire for unity almost to the point of making selflessness the novel's supreme value. Naremore believes that the characters' "intense desire for unity, the desire to know even one other person completely (as, for example, Lily Briscoe wants to know Mrs. Ramsay), or, in a more cosmic sense, the compulsive need to relate one's life spiritually to the vast power of nature—all these things can result in the destruction of individuality," so they actively seek immersion in what he calls the "watery world" existing beyond the self. According to Naremore, this destruction of individuality should not be understood in a negative light. On the contrary, although he recognizes the competing drives that inform Woolf's fiction, "the contest for life between the ego and the undifferentiated forces which threaten to dissolve or destroy it," Naremore reads her work as the expression of a "death wish . . . based on a view of experience which can offer consolation for the brevity of life."[21]

I read the experiential texture of *To the Lighthouse* somewhat differently, as a response to a fear of selflessness rather than a desire for it. Woolf's characters do long to escape the limitations of self in order to effect unity with the other; but that desire instills in them a paralyzing sense of dread which resists their wish for death. Because the narration encloses self and other within the shifting, fluid boundaries of consciousness, the characters repeatedly become so conscious of the self's difference from the other that they perceive the other as an alien force indifferent, even hostile to the desiring imagination. This is their moment of violation, and it makes them seek privacy. Through an act of imagining the other they recover their lost sense of the self's centrality, but only during this moment of meditation; invariably, other characters interrupt their solitary reflection, and the interaction that follows renews their awareness of a reality existing beyond the scope of imagination. The more Woolf's characters perceive the difference between self and other, the more their desire for unity is intensified, and the more they dwell upon death in their solitude. Death, as Naremore explains, is the ultimate means of overcoming the essential difference that identifies—and thus imposes limitations upon—the self as a state of consciousness defined by its separation from the other.

All the same, because they rely on consciousness to validate their existence as sentient beings. Woolf's characters are too self-centered to do more than meditate upon death. The dissolution of individuality necessary for a complete fusion of self and other, as envisioned in death, would subsume the self entirely within the other, thereby diminishing the self's imaginative power over the other. This fear of self-loss is the other side of the characters' sense of violation. Lily Briscoe, for example, experiences many moments in which she seems to transcend the limitations of her single personality. Yet this sensation only makes her question her own existence: "For there are moments when one can neither think nor feel. And if one can neither think nor feel, she thought, where is one?" (p. 288). Desiring unity with the other in order to feel "at home," and yet dreading the annihilation of self that such unity demands, Woolf's characters respond to the other's threatening presence just as Lily does, by retreating further into the privacy of consciousness. There the self can repair its violation (the extreme sensation of complete difference or similarity) through the imagination. Directed by the imagination, which internalizes momentarily for the characters what the narration externalizes for the entire novel, the shaping power of memory allows the self to feel intensely alternate moments of similarity and difference, wholeness and emptiness, unity and alienation, selflessness and selfhood, without losing the sense of continuity that is the bulwark of identity.

Woolf's narrative voice therefore does not fully invest its own selflessness as the supreme value for the characters' experience. While that voice may not advertise its synthesizing ability in the manner of Eliot's, it does imply a means of making stable and continuous, through language and form, the unstable, discontinuous fictional world it represents. For one thing, the novel is written in a uniform style, just as it delineates a similar psychology for all the characters regardless of whose consciousness anchors a particular section of narration.[22] For another, and this point I want to emphasize, the novel orchestrates a larger pattern of violation and repair from the characters' smaller moments. In themselves those moments are microcosms of the novel's experiential rhythm as a whole. Within the fictional world characters register experience as a continuous progressive-regressive momentum, at one moment moving out of the self to embrace the other, at another recoiling from the other to move more intensely back into the self. But whereas such moments seem isolated to the characters as they experience them, temporarily overwhelming their memory of previous, competing moments of vision, the book's structure insists upon the continuity between these moments by blending them together into a seamless narration moving characters and reader forward and backward in time. The novel then shapes that narration to make the forward movement dominant not through plot but through its three-part form. In this formal structure, *To the Lighthouse* conforms much more noticeably to the paradigm than either *Lord Jim* or *Women in Love*, or almost any other modernist novel that comes to mind.

The form of *To the Lighthouse* imposes upon the fictive world's continuous rhythm of violation and repair a progressive movement that directs characters forward to meet the other; at the same time, the emphasis on consciousness directs them backward into the self, where they rework experience in memory. As a result, the characters experience time as horizontal duration and as vertical introspection, a double construction of experience that is reflected in the book's form. The first part works against a forward linear movement. Since plotted action does not determine its movement, all the energy in part I seems to generate from retrospective moments of consciousness which expand vertically beneath the shallow horizontal ground of sequential time (the single day's chronological linearity). The whole of chapter I, which brings the linear movement of the first paragraph to a halt in order to reveal its vertical temporal dimension, illustrates this well. The novel's third part, however, reestablishes a linear movement for the novel, first because it has a more linearly plotted action (the trip to the lighthouse, the completion of Lily's painting), and second because here the memories of consciousness refer back to part I to close the gap between past and present, that gap widened by part II. Part III therefore implicitly shapes and directs part I, so that the competing movements of experience stand out more clearly, for both reader and characters, in retrospect.

My point about the novel's form has to do with more than the power of art to command the random sensations and events of experience into an orderly pattern, although this is one of Woolf's chief concerns as a modernist. The exaggerated difference between the crafted text and the unstable fictive world is deceptive, for the characters bridge the two. They internalize what the novel externalizes in its three-part form: the paradigmatic contest between self and other. This contest is forcibly and movingly apparent in the novel's manipulation of the Family Romance story. The first part focuses our attention upon the Ramsays as personifications, for the rest of the characters, of the other. Mr. Ramsay appears as a hostile unsympathetic parent, Mrs. Ramsay as a protective loving one. These two parent figures keep alive in the characters the regressive desire of romance, that longing to feel at home in a universe which, to turn John Jarndyce's phrase around, is a fond and sympathetic parent. The progressive thrust of the novel, fully clarified in part III, stimulates the competing energy of realism because it directs characters (James Ramsay, Lily Briscoe) towards a more accurate understanding of these parent figures.

Mr. and Mrs. Ramsay are thus central to the novel not as its protagonists but as the embodiment of what the other signifies within the fictive world. With the characters drawn most strongly to Mrs. Ramsay's sympathetic figure, her presence dominates the mood of part I, just as her absence dominates the mood of part III; her figure directs the emotions of the novel around sensations of lost innocence, meaning here the inescapable awareness of inhuman forces—the fatal erosion of time recorded in part II— that are indifferent to the self's desire to achieve an oceanic unity with the other. Throughout part I Mrs. Ramsay relieves the characters' sense of dread by striving to make them feel at home, literally in her house and, symbolically, in the universe. Part II removes this maternal safety net to emphasize the self's helplessness in the face of an indifferent, impersonal other. The characters' grief over her death in part III therefore epitomizes their overriding sense of violation by that other. At the same time, Mrs. Ramsay's physical absence in this section makes the first part seem even more emotionally rich and satisfying in retrospect, stimulating a nostalgic longing for the unattainable past; but her absence also liberates the characters from their dependence upon her so that, like Pip and Dorothea, they can now directly confront the other in the living shape of Mr. Ramsay and, in the process, achieve a mature self-consciousness. The loss of the protective mother, in other words, impels the characters to seek reconciliation with the other (the abrasive father, Mr. Ramsay) in order to effect repair for their violation, their separation from the mother. Mrs. Ramsay's death confirms the importance of memory to insure the self's continuity and to relieve its defensive need for privacy: the characters' deep love for her, which does not cease with her death, records the impact she has had upon them, demonstrating how the other becomes part of the self's consciousness without destroying it. Love therefore serves the same function in this novel that it does in *Women in Love*. But here in *To the Lighthouse* that love, expressing the desire to be united with the mother, to be sheltered under her protective wing, is even more heavily informed by the loss of innocence.

As Woolf's title suggests, the lighthouse motif shapes the flux of experience into the forward-moving pattern I have outlined. *To the Lighthouse* opens with James Ramsay's "extraordinary joy" at the prospect of making the voyage to the lighthouse. His mother's conditional encouragement—"Yes, of course, if it's fine tomorrow"—promises him "the wonder to which he had looked forward, for years and years it seemed" (p. 9). When his father announces that, on the contrary, "it won't be fine" (p. 10), James reacts by wanting to plunge a poker or an axe into his heart, a striking (and rather guiltless) oedipal wish that expresses James's begrudging acknowledgment of his father's authority: "What he said was true. It was always true" (p. 10). James's *not* going to the lighthouse exposes him to the harsh realities of an adult world where intense emotions cannot be sustained for long.

The opening scene with the Ramsays and their youngest son casts an emotional shadow on the entire novel. James sees his parents exclusively in terms of his own desire, associating his mother with the promise of its fulfillment, his father with its denial. As parental figures for practically everyone in the novel, the Ramsays embody the polar boundaries of human experience: femininity and masculinity, imagination and reason, eternity and transience, isolation and communication.[23] Mr. Ramsay's intellect is set (often antagonistically) against his wife's more sympathetic emotional sensibility. Nonetheless, each is attracted to the other in a spirit of reconciliation and compromise, and their jarring personalities are drawn in similar colors to suggest what the characters often fail to appreciate, how very much this husband and wife complement each other. For example, Mrs. Ramsay takes "the whole of the other sex under her protection" (p. 13), as if they were all her children, but so does her husband. Although at first the sight of his wife and son "fortified him and satisfied him and consecrated his [intellectual] effort," he also sees the two of them as "children . . . divinely innocent . . . and somehow entirely defenceless against a doom which he perceived. . . . They needed his protection; he gave it them" (p. 53). While

Chapter 6

Mr. Ramsay is at times abrasive and sexist, vain and intolerant, while he needs "to be assured of his genius, first of all," he also wants "to be taken within the circle of life, warmed and soothed, to have his senses restored to him, his barrenness made fertile, and all the rooms of the house made full of life . . . they must be filled with life" (p. 59). Mr. and Mrs. Ramsay each bring out the fertile part of the other through their marriage, which epitomizes the unity of self and other. Together, they *have* filled their house with life—eight lives to be precise, not to mention all the friends who make their house vibrate with an intense emotional and intellectual vitality.

Although James does not see it, their unity is revealed through their argument about the lighthouse. Mr. Ramsay refuses to encourage James's hopes because he wants his children to "be aware from childhood that life is difficult; facts uncompromising; and the passage to that fabled land where our brightest hopes are extinguished, our frail barks founder in darkness . . . needs, above all, courage, truth, and the power to endure" (p. 11). He becomes enraged at his wife's "extraordinary irrationality" because "she flew in the face of facts, made his children hope what was utterly out of the question, in effect, told lies" (p. 50). Yet at the same time he senses his wife's anger at his stubborn and intolerant behavior, appreciating her feeling: "To pursue truth with such astonishing lack of consideration for other people's feelings, to rend the thin veils of civilisation so wantonly, so brutally, was to her so horrible an outrage of human decency." As a result, he softens his previous declaration about the weather and "very humbly, at length, he said that he would step over and ask the Coastguards if she liked." After this capitulation on his part, Mrs. Ramsay responds by thinking, "there was nobody whom she reverenced as she reverenced him" (p. 51). Similarly, at the end of part I Mrs. Ramsay "triumph[s] again" by telling her husband that she loves him without having to utter the words (for all her maternal instincts, she dreads saying "what she felt"). In fact, she communicates to him through the language of their domestic quarrel. Feeling that "nothing on earth can equal this happiness," she conveys her deep love for her husband by agreeing with him about the weather: "Yes, you were right. It's going to be wet tomorrow. You won't be able to go" (pp. 185-86).

Having agreed with her husband about the weather, Mrs. Ramsay "felt angry with Charles Tansley, with her husband," but most of all "with herself" for having raised James's hopes about going to the lighthouse (p. 173). She has persisted in promising the trip, however, because she wants to protect her children from losing their "brightest hopes" too quickly. As James is taken to his dinner, she cannot help feeling "certain that he was thinking, we are not going to the Lighthouse tomorrow; and she thought, he will remember that all his life." She believes that "children never forget" their disappointments (p. 95). Her anxiety about them—"why must they grow up and lose it all?" (pp. 91, 92)—frequently breaks into her thoughts, determining the sadness with which she sees her family. Because she appreciates the worshiping love of her daughter Rose and the imaginative pleasure the girl takes in selecting jewels for her to wear every evening, Mrs. Ramsay instinctively wants to protect her daughter from growing up and losing this special feeling of innocence. She knows that one day Rose will realize "it was so inadequate, what one could give in return; and what Rose felt was quite out of proportion to anything she actually was. And Rose would grow up; and Rose would suffer, she supposed, with these deep feelings" (p. 123).

At the same time that she stands for the reassuring energy of romance, which works to arrest the more disruptive energy of realism (Mr. Ramsay), Mrs. Ramsay is fully aware of reality's inexorable movement towards death and all that it implies about mortality, loss, failure. She wants to keep her children from growing up too quickly in order to preserve for them their ability to feel, as she thinks Rose feels, an innocent love unrealistically larger than the love object itself: that is, the child's unqualified adoration of her mother. Mrs. Ramsay sincerely believes that her children, secure in their family and safe in their home, "were happier now than they would ever be again." She herself is "happiest" when carrying a baby in her arms (p. 90), because the child's life, yet to be lived, can perhaps escape "her old antagonist, life" (p. 120). This is not to make Mrs. Ramsay out to be a selfish, possessive, suffocating mother. Asking herself why children must "grow up so fast" (p. 90) or appreciating their moments of happiness is not the same as trying to retard their maturity or giving them false expectations. Rather, Mrs. Ramsay sees in her children an innocence she feels she herself has lost in her own active engagement with life:

> There it was before her—life. Life, she thought—but she did not finish her thought. She took a look at life, for she had a clear sense of it there, something real, something private, which she shared neither with her children nor with her husband. A sort of transaction went on between them, in which she was on one side, and life was on another, and she was always trying to get the better of it, as it was of her; and sometimes they parleyed (when she sat alone); there were, she remembered, great reconciliation scenes; but for the most part, oddly enough, she must admit that she felt this thing that she called life terrible, hostile, and quick to pounce on you if you gave it a chance. . . . And yet she had said to all these children, You shall go through it all. To eight people she had said relentlessly that. . . . For that reason, knowing what was before them—love and ambition and being wretched alone in dreary places—she had often the feeling, Why must they grow up and lose it all? And then she said to herself, brandishing her sword at life, Nonsense. They will be perfectly happy. And here she was, she reflected, feeling life rather sinister again. . . . (pp. 91-92)

Watching her children grow up intensifies her own sense of time rushing past her, hastening them all to their death (as part II makes emphatically clear). The phrase ringing in her mind, "Children don't forget, children don't forget," thus acquires an odd, unsettling refrain: "It will end, it will end" (p. 97).

Although she is not entirely unaware of her children's unhappy moments, as their mother Mrs. Ramsay has the power to assuage their nightmarish terrors, to serve as a protective buffer between their imaginations and the harsh truth of human life, which insists that they too will lose their childish innocence. She herself will have to confess to them that the trip to the lighthouse will not take place as promised. To soothe their disappointment she can only push that promise off into a vague future, "soon . . . the next fine day" (p. 173). But since James, seething with anger at his father, is obviously not happy, just as Cam is frightened by the skull in their bedroom later that evening, it is clear that Mrs. Ramsay idealizes both her children's innocence and her own ability to prolong it. Their emotions change as abruptly from pleasure to anxiety, from joy to sadness, as hers do. Furthermore, she well knows that she cannot protect them forever, especially since she herself will die and leave them unprotected. To be sure, perhaps she already knows she is dying; she thinks, "There was always a woman dying of cancer even here" (p. 92), and the statement is ambiguous enough in its reference to suggest that she may well be thinking of herself rather than one of the women she visits in the village. In any event, while she tells her children, "You shall go through it all," she still tries to protect their innocence, if only to retain, for herself more than anyone, a belief in innocence as a defense against her strong sense of mortality, the "doom" she and her husband both perceive.

As a result, Mrs. Ramsay's sense of "her old antagonist, life" is "something real, something private" (p. 91). The syntactic equation between "real" and "private" is important, because only in privacy does she fully acknowledge her fear of impending death, which intensifies her recognition that moments of happiness—like childhood, like life itself—end. It is therefore fitting that her anxiety about James's disappointment, which she knows will remain with him all his life, leads her into her most famous moment of privacy, when she casts off her outer self and basks in her "wedge-shaped core of darkness."

> For now she need not think about anybody. She could be herself, by herself. And that was what now she often felt the need of—to think; well, not even to think. To be silent; to be alone. All the being and the doing, expansive, glittering, vocal, evaporated; and one shrunk, with a sense of solemnity, to being oneself, a wedge-shaped core of darkness, something invisible to others. Although she continued to knit, and sat upright, it was thus that she felt herself; and this self having shed its attachments was free for the strangest adventures. . . . This core of darkness could go anywhere, for no one saw it. They could not stop it, she thought, exulting. There was freedom, there was peace, there was, most welcome of all, a summoning together, a resting on a platform of stability. Not as oneself did one find rest ever . . . but as a wedge

of darkness. Losing personality, one lost the fret, the hurry, the stir; and there rose to her lips always some exclamation of triumph over life when things came together in this peace, this rest, this eternity . . . (pp. 95-96)

Although some critics read this scene as the epitome of selflessness—Naremore sees Mrs. Ramsay embracing death as her lover[24]—the issues raised here are not so simple. What is important in this scene, as a contrast to Lily and James in particular, is that Mrs. Ramsay confronts the other and then makes it an extension of her self.

Mrs. Ramsay needs "to be herself, by herself . . . to be silent, to be alone," not to escape her self but to revitalize it. Exhausted by her maternal efforts, which leave "scarcely a shell of herself . . . for her to know herself by; all was so lavished and spent" (p. 60), she throws off the worn shell and luxuriates in a self which she can preserve from further erosion. In a moment of supreme privacy, she loosens the boundaries of her personality and feels free enough of its ordinary attachments to reach out "to inanimate things" (p. 97), in this instance the "long steady stroke" of the lighthouse, "the last of the three, which was her stroke" (p. 96). Yet at the same time, she looks inward with "her own eyes meeting her own eyes, searching as she alone could search into her mind and her heart, purifying out of existence that lie, any lie" (p. 97). By projecting her self onto the other, she makes the other an extension of her self. When she becomes one with the lighthouse beam, the light attracts her as a symbol of her own essential, purified, limitless self, so this seeming death of personality is actually a mirror of her self and its desire for unity: her eyes meet her own eyes through the medium of the other. What she sees in "the steady light" of the lighthouse beam is "the pitiless, the remorseless, which was so much her, yet so little her" (p. 99). As she watches the light "with fascination, hypnotised," she discovers as well that "she had known happiness, exquisite happiness, intense happiness" (p. 99)—so much happiness, in fact, that she can now face her old enemy, life, and feel, "It is enough! It is enough!" (p. 100). Through this vision of her self Mrs. Ramsay reconciles her consciousness of loss and limitation ("the pitiless, the remorseless") with her realization that life is still worth living even with all its pain, and justifies having told her children, "You shall go through it all." When she exclaims, "It is enough!" she means that she has had enough happiness in her time; or that this moment of intense consciousness is so overwhelming, so ecstatic, so expansive that she can no longer stand it; or that life, not death, is enough for her, and she is once again ready to confront her "old enemy" with pleasure, gratitude, even love. Thus she ends her solitude immediately after feeling "It is enough!" by reaching out to her real lover, her husband, to prevent him from walking away out of respect for her privacy.

In this scene Mrs. Ramsay quite clearly seeks to achieve a unity with the inanimate other through the dissolution of her personality. But while she believes that her expansive, invisible core of darkness cannot be perceived by another person because it is "all spreading, unfathomably deep . . . limitless," she is mistaken. There is still a self there whose solid substance—that wedge shape—can be perceived by another person; if she loses her self to "death" in this scene it is only in an imaginative moment of deep meditation on her part. Lily, for one, intuits Mrs. Ramsay's "wedge-shaped core of darkness." She paints her friend as a "triangular purple shape," feeling "the need of darkness" in her choice of color and shape (p. 81). More importantly, while Mrs. Ramsay meditates, her husband also perceives her seemingly invisible core of darkness. As her eyes meet the third stroke of light, she sees her inner inviolable self as something "stern . . . searching . . . beautiful like that light" (p. 97). At this point Mr. Ramsay passes by the window and "could not help noting, as he passed, the sternness at the heart of her beauty" (p. 98). He clearly sees the self beneath her physical shape, a self meditating on the death of its own body and personality. Feeling "saddened" and "pained" by "her remoteness" (p. 98), he can only look away "into the hedge, into its intricacy, its darkness" (p. 99). But he does not leave. Though he feels "aloof" from—even "hurt" by—his wife's "beauty," "her sadness," her unapproachable solitude, he also feels overwhelmed by a desire "to protect her," knowing at the same time, I think, that he is powerless to do so because he also senses that she is going to die: "he could do nothing to help her." Significantly, it is at this very moment that his wife ends her introspection and prevents him from leaving. She knows that he wants to protect her from her own "remoteness," so she has "given him of her own free will what she knew he would never ask"—her self (p. 100).

The strong emotional bond with her husband returns Mrs. Ramsay to a full consciousness of her self united with the other—her husband—through love, and their relationship humanizes the selfless unity she imagined a moment before with the lighthouse beam: "Often she found herself sitting and looking, sitting and looking, with her work in her hands, until she became the thing she looked at—that light, for example" (p. 97). With the lighthouse beam her self seems absorbed by the other completely, whereas with her husband she retains her self while extending it outwards, the boundaries of their selves shifting continuously, sometimes to allow the other access, sometimes to make it more difficult. Thus, as we saw with their quarrel about the trip to the lighthouse, their moments of estrangement counter moments of communication through which each reads the other's mind to become, as it were, the person, not the thing, looked at. At dinner, for example, "they looked at each other down the long table sending these questions and answers across, each knowing exactly what the other felt" (p. 144). Even more magically, earlier in the day when Mrs. Ramsay reads a fairy tale to James, an invisible part of her consciousness throbs with a "pulse [that] seemed, as he walked away, to enclose her and her husband, and to give each that solace which two different notes, one high, one low, struck together, seem to give each other as they combine" (p. 61). This particular moment of harmony does not last, of course, but then neither do moments of discord. Mrs. Ramsay quickly begins to fret about her husband's insecurity and the bill for the new greenhouse roof, blaming herself for "the inadequacy of human relationships" because she cannot sustain their unity for more than a moment (p. 62). But her self has combined with her husband's, if only for a moment, and this moment of unity is not unique. Similar ones occur throughout the day and, most importantly, one such moment closes part I: "Though she had not said a word, he knew, of course, he knew, that she loved him. He could not deny it. . . . She had not said it: yet he knew" (pp. 185-86).

Their telepathic communication allows her to unite with her husband through love without losing her self entirely, as happens, to her mind, when she communes with the inanimate other in her moment of solitude. As she looks at her husband, "smiling" with the thought that "she had triumphed again" (p. 186), her triumph is in being able to become the person she looks at; she feels close enough to him to communicate her love through a smile, or by agreeing with him about the weather, all the while retaining a sense of her separate consciousness, because she keeps the words "I love you" to herself to make this emotion hers as well as his.[25]

The love exhibited by the Ramsays is the very kind of unity Lily wants to achieve with Mrs. Ramsay, "becoming . . . inextricably the same, one with the object one adored. . . . Could loving, as people called it, make her and Mrs. Ramsay one? for it was not knowledge but unity that she desired . . . intimacy itself, which is knowledge" (p. 79). Lily, in other words, seeks the intimate non-verbal rapport with the other (as epitomized for her entirely in Mrs. Ramsay's motherly figure) which she is witness to when she sees the Ramsays together. Their love, Lily intuits, is "a love that never attempted to clutch its object" (p. 73). When Lily herself tries for such an intimate unity with the other, however, "Nothing happened. Nothing! Nothing!" (p. 79). She and Mrs. Ramsay do not become one. The paradigmatic impetus of experience in *To the Lighthouse* leads Lily towards a sense of unity with the other, not to become "one with the object one adored" so much as to make that object one with the self. What Lily fears about love is that it requires the sacrifice of her personality, her own core of darkness as externalized in her painting. Mrs. Ramsay dispels that fear in her love for her husband. Theirs is not a love that clutches its object to make the self feel violated by the other; indeed, in that their marriage is a union of opposites, their love is fully appreciative of the other. Unlike Mrs. Ramsay, however, Lily feels deeply threatened by the other, especially when it assumes the shape of Mr. Ramsay. In order to alleviate her dread that unity with the other demands a violation of her self and the privacy that defines it, and then to become one with the adored other through love as Mrs. Ramsay does with her husband, Lily— "in love with them all" (p. 37)—must identify completely the object of her love, namely *both* Ramsays. Among the other issues it raises, part III of *To the Lighthouse* recounts her accomplishment.

Lily's effort to complete her painting ten years after she has started it parallels James's struggle with his father, as Woolf's continuous juxtaposition of these two actions in part III makes emphatic. It will be instructive to look at James first, because his development follows a more straight-forward, conventional pattern. He shares his sister's antagonism towards Mr. Ramsay for having "poisoned her childhood and raised bitter storms" (p. 253). Cam, however, can also pass on to their father, "unsuspected by James, a private token of the love she felt for him" (p. 252). James resists succumbing to his affection for his father because he is more angry than his sister about their "poisoned" childhood, and more determined to remember and avenge it.

In part I James hates his father for many of the same reasons that make Lily respond to Mr. Ramsay with a similar antagonism: "But his son hated him. He hated him for coming up to them, for stopping and looking down on them; he hated him for interrupting them; he hated him for the exaltation and sublimity of his gestures; for the magnificence of his head; for his exactingness and egotism (for there he stood, commanding them to attend to him); but most of all he hated the twang and twitter of his father's emotion which, vibrating round them, disturbed the perfect simplicity and good sense of his relations with his mother" (pp. 57-58). In part III, when the trip to the lighthouse finally takes place, James retains his "old symbol of taking a knife and striking his father to the heart," only now, as "he sat staring at his father in an impotent rage," he realizes that what he wants to strike at is something larger than his father, something coming from within himself: "it was the thing that descended on him—without his knowing it perhaps: that fierce sudden black-winged harpy, with its talons and its beak all cold and hard, that struck and struck at you" (p. 273). James is struggling to confront his own sexuality. As a child he understands his sexual identity in contrast to his father's, wanting to take any phallic weapon he can lay his hands on to gash "a hole in his father's breast." Yet he sees his father himself as a phallic figure, "lean as a knife, narrow as the blade of one, grinning sarcastically," as if in assertion of a prior, more important claim upon his mother—a sexual claim (p. 10). Thus when James "[stands] stiff between her knees," his hatred of "the arid scimitar of his father" increases (p. 60). Through such phallic imagery, Woolf reveals the masculine sexuality in James's personality, which he quite naturally fears as a child when he sees it in his father but which he must acknowledge in himself to become an adult.

What therefore upsets James about Mr. Ramsay is the sexual identity they share: "there were two pairs of footprints only; his own and his father's. They alone knew each other. What then was this terror, this hatred?" (p. 275). Like Pip, James has to accept the violence and aggression, as well as the insecurity, in his own masculine nature as personified for him by his father. James distrusts his masculine side and feels alienated from it because as a child he saw his father in opposition to his mother, who defined his self exclusively as her child. His father's abrasive personality "disturbed the perfect simplicity and good sense of his relations with his mother" (p. 58). Yet James cannot escape the fact that he is his father's son. He may have hated his father's "magnificent head" (p. 57), but "with his high forehead and his fierce blue eyes, impeccably candid and pure, frowning slightly at the sight of human fraility" (p. 10), the little boy—in look and temperament—is but a childish version of his father. Now, as they approach the lighthouse, James suddenly becomes aware of his father as an old man, "extraordinarily exposed to everything," just as he himself has been "exposed" through the loss of his mother's protective "perfect simplicity" and "good sense." Since father and son are both grieving over Mrs. Ramsay's death, James can identify with Mr. Ramsay, accepting the male sensibility they share in their grief, "what was always at the back of both their minds—that loneliness which was for both of them the truth about things" (p. 301). Fittingly, James now begins talking to himself, "exactly" as his father does (p. 302), and Mr. Ramsay gives his son what the latter has desperately craved—fatherly praise—to acknowledge their bond. Like his wife, then, Mr. Ramsay communicates his love without needing to say the exact words.

Chapter 6

The trip to the lighthouse, finally completed after the aborted effort ten years before, dramatizes the process whereby James integrates one side of his personality—an imaginative, emotional, feminine side—with the other, more severe, uncompromising, masculine side. James does not lessen the importance of Mrs. Ramsay; but by acknowledging his love for his father he does cease to identify his self entirely with hers. He thus effects a synthesis of his parents' personalities through which he internalizes the union of opposites they represent—he is, after all, their progeny—to achieve an integrated adult consciousness. At almost the same moment, as Lily watches the boat sail to the lighthouse, she finally completes her painting and undergoes a similar transformation. If the voyage to the lighthouse motif measures James's growth—a literal rite of passage into adulthood—then the painting measures Lily's. Her struggle with the canvas dramatizes an inner struggle to ward off "the demons" (p. 32), her fear of everything that Mr. Ramsay represents to her.

Lily's problem with her painting is one of achieving balance, reflecting her own difficulty in integrating self with other as Mrs. Ramsay has done through marriage. Like James, Lily identifies entirely with the maternal Mrs. Ramsay and sees Mr. Ramsay as a hostile other sex threatening her with violation. He too disturbs the "perfect simplicity" and "good sense" of her relations with Mrs. Ramsay and, we shall see, of the relations between masses and colors which she is trying to organize in her painting. Lily is terrified that someone, Mr. Ramsay in particular, will violate her privacy by looking at her painting, which is an extension of her self even though its subject matter is in fact the other, Mrs. Ramsay sitting with James: "she kept a feeler on her surroundings lest some one should creep up, and suddenly she should find her picture looked at" (p. 30). Lily values her painting the way Clarissa values her body, as the symbolic core of self that can retain its integrity only so long as it remains inviolable. She even thinks of her painting as "virginal" in contrast to Mrs. Ramsay's house full of children, and this thought is both a measure of her inhibition in the face of the other and the confirmation of her bravery in putting brush to canvas: "Gathering a desperate courage she would urge her own exemption from the universal

214

law; plead for it; she liked to be alone; she liked to be herself'' (p. 77). The virginal connotation of her painting is further underscored when she finally allows William Bankes to see it. In having been seen, "it had been taken from her. This man had shared with her something profoundly intimate" (p. 83). Lily's reaction to this "loss," however, is to feel surprisingly exhilarated, because she has begun to share her "intimate" vision with another. She trusts Bankes and feels intimate with him because she sees in him a solitary personality similar to hers: "you are entirely impersonal," she thinks, cherishing his loneliness, we are told parenthetically, "without any sexual feeling" (p. 39). This remark does not mean that Lily has no sexual feelings, but that at this particular moment Bankes transcends her sexual dread of men as the alien other. In order to complete her painting, Lily has to learn to trust other men as well, especially Mr. Ramsay, whom she sees as an oppressive, tyrannical father in opposition to the benevolent, protective mother, guardian of her virginal painting, Mrs. Ramsay.

All of this is not to characterize Lily as a sexually repressed spinster, even though she self-pityingly thinks of herself as "a peevish, ill-tempered, dried-up old maid, presumably" (p. 226). For one thing, the language describing Lily's consciousness is often highly sexual in its imagery. For another, there is in Lily something larger—her own core of darkness—which gives her the potential for "subduing all her impressions as a woman to something much more general; becoming once more under the power of that vision which she had seen clearly once and must now grope for among hedges and houses and mothers and children—her picture" (p. 82). The act of painting dramatizes her ability to achieve a vision rather like Dorothea's in *Middlemarch*. The painting itself serves to organize that vision, indicating Lily's capacity to generalize her "impressions as a woman" (her childish dread of the other sex) and achieve in their place a more integrated—and integrating—personality, one able to reconcile pleasure with pain, male with female, life with death, so that she too can feel, "It is enough!"

Lily's problem with the composition of her painting therefore reflects a problem of achieving balance between her self and the other. When it comes to a painting she knows that the question is "one of the relations of masses, of lights and shadows . . . a question, she remembered, how to connect this mass on the right hand with that on the left" (pp. 82-83). Trying to convey her theory of visual unity to Bankes, she explains the problem before her. She can connect the right and left masses either "by breaking the line of the branch across so; or break[ing] the vacancy in the foreground by an object (James perhaps) so. But the danger was that by doing that the unity of the whole might be broken" (p. 83). Although at dinner Lily decides to move the tree, she does not finish the painting to her satisfaction. She thinks that even moving James, the youngest male she knows, will disrupt the unity of the whole painting. This thought voices her subconscious fear that the other sex violates the sanctity of her self by demanding sympathy, affection, security, so that, as Mrs. Ramsay feels at times, she will have nothing left for herself, "all was so lavished and spent." Woolf is not concerned with providing her characters with much of a biography; but perhaps Lily's conflict with Mr. Ramsay stems from her relationship with her own father, who has kept her from living a conventionally full life like Mrs. Ramsay's to emphasize "her own inadequacy, her insignificance, keeping house for her father off the Brompton Road" (p. 32). Mrs. Ramsay's death frees Lily to face this dread more directly.

Since her painting is working out the primal relations between mother and child as well as between father and child, Lily's difficulty in capturing what she sees beneath the apparitions of ordinary reality quite fittingly "made this passage from conception to work as dreadful as any down a dark passage for a child" (p. 32). In part III she continues to do battle with "this formidable ancient enemy of hers—this other thing, this truth, this reality, which suddenly laid hands on her, emerged stark at the back of appearances and commanded her attention" (p. 236). "This reality" Lily struggles with is still her dread of Mr. Ramsay, who challenges her vision and frustrates her effort to achieve a unified composition; she therefore cannot complete her painting until she somehow works into its composition her sense of Mr. Ramsay. "He changed everything. She could not see the colour; she could not see the lines. . . . That man, she thought, her anger rising in her, never gave; that man took" (p. 223). After she is left alone, she transfers her sense of anger and frustration onto the hedge.[26] "There was something . . . something she remembered in the relations of those lines cutting across, slicing down, and in the mass of the hedge with its green cave of blues and browns, which had stayed in her mind" (p. 234). As she paints, "she kept looking at the hedge, at the canvas" (p. 237), until she remembers the terror she felt ten years before when "suddenly Mr. Ramsay stopped dead in his pacing in front of her and some curious shock passed through her" (p. 294).

Here is what Lily remembers. In part I, before sharing "something profoundly intimate" in her self with Bankes, the two of them "stepped through the gap in the high hedge straight into Mr. Ramsay" (p. 41). Unknowingly, Lily has penetrated Mr. Ramsay's core of darkness. Trying not to recognize them, Mr. Ramsay "was determined to hold fast to something of this delicious emotion, this impure rhapsody of which he was ashamed, but in which he revelled—he turned abruptly, slammed his private door on them" (pp. 41-42). (And later, when he feels isolated by his wife's "remoteness," recall that he looks into the hedge's "intricacy, its darkness.") Lily works through her memories of Mrs. Ramsay in part III, exorcising her resentment at having been deserted by this "mother," conjuring up the woman's ghost to discover how Mrs. Ramsay has made "of the moment something permanent (as in another sphere Lily herself tried to make of the moment something permanent)" (p. 241); as she does so, her eyes keep returning to the hedge because it represents the reality beyond her self that she must acknowledge and divest of its terrors.

In part III, Lily has become one with Mrs. Ramsay through her memories, showing how the other can become part of the self's consciousness without violating its integrity as a self. But Lily cannot sustain this larger, "generalized" consciousness until she also learns to love Mr. Ramsay, whose demands for sympathy she has always found intolerable. This time, however, she begins to see herself as a woman in relation to Mr. Ramsay: "A woman, she had provoked this horror; a woman, she should have known how to deal with it. It was immensely to her discredit, sexually, to stand there dumb" (p. 228). Indeed, she thinks of herself as an old maid only because she does not know how to give sympathy to Mr. Ramsay. When she finally does capitulate, "tormented with sympathy for him" (p. 230), just as Mrs. Ramsay has done in the past, "she felt a sudden emptiness; a frustration. Her feelings had come too late; there it was ready; but he no longer needed it" (p. 231).

What Lily has discovered upon returning to the Ramsays' summer home is "a house full of unrelated passions" (p. 221). The source of unity—Mrs. Ramsay—is gone. Without her, Lily feels at once sympathetic to and frustrated by Mr. Ramsay, who is now driven by "an enormous need . . . to approach any woman, to force them, he did not care how, his need was so great, to give him what he wanted: sympathy" (p. 225). Lily telepathically satisfies his need when she remembers Mrs. Ramsay while watching the boat travel to the lighthouse. In doing so, she provides the wordless emotional current underlying Mr. Ramsay's reconciliation with his two youngest children. Emotionally, this is to say, Lily becomes a surrogate for Mrs. Ramsay. She thus achieves for herself "that razor edge of balance between two opposite forces; Mr. Ramsay and the picture; which was necessary" (p. 287).

Once Lily sees Mrs. Ramsay's ghost, "feeling the old horror come back—to want and want and not to have," she instinctively searches for Mr. Ramsay, "as if she had something she must share, yet could hardly leave her easel, so full her mind was of what she was thinking, of what she was seeing." She seeks Mr. Ramsay because now, for the first time, "she wanted him" (p. 300). Fully aware of their mutual loss, Lily no longer sees the man as the threatening other. Rather, like Pip and Miss Havisham, Lily and Mr. Ramsay share a similar consciousness of lost innocence—the absence of Mrs. Ramsay—so she can, in Eliot's words, discover her own "centre of self" by recognizing his. Consequently, as the boat reaches its destination, completing the aborted action which opened the novel, Lily feels relieved because "whatever she had wanted to give him, when he left her that morning, she had given him at last" (pp. 308-9). She triumphantly communicates to him just as Mrs. Ramsay has done in part I, wordlessly, to preserve her self while experiencing unity with the other. After this, Lily returns to her painting. The steps are now empty, the ghost of Mrs. Ramsay has disappeared, the canvas is still blurred; but she draws the line down the middle and everything coheres into a unified composition.

Who or what the line specifically represents in the painting is not made clear. What is made clear is that, in completing the painting, in unifying the right side with the left side, Lily has her "vision" (p. 310). She has given part of her self to Mr. Ramsay through love and has not felt violated as a consequence. Having linked in her own mind, as well as in the painting, the figures of Mr. Ramsay and his wife, she now realizes the power of an impersonal love like theirs, which allows her to unite her self with the world beyond without having to experience the self's dissolution, since that love does not clutch its object—as death does. It therefore does not matter where her painting will be hung afterwards, whether in an attic or a gallery. Like James, Lily has come to see the weaknesses—the common humanity—behind her distorted impression of Mr. Ramsay's abrasive, threatening, masculine strength; and with this hard-won knowledge her own emotions are no longer as terrifying or surprising, so she can relax her protective "feeler" to allow the other to penetrate her consciousness. Her vision coordinates in the painting her memory of Mrs. Ramsay from the past with her new awareness of Mr. Ramsay in the present, validating her maturity in the way that marriage does in more conventional novels.

James's rite of passage, then, provides a frame for our understanding Lily's completion of her painting as the sign of her maturation; and the achievement of both characters underscores the paradigmatic structure of *To the Lighthouse* to place this novel firmly in the tradition of the other novels I have examined in this book. However, while I want to call attention to the traditional basis of Woolf's novel, I do not want to minimize its special treatment of this conventional scheme. The progressive linear momentum of James's and Lily's maturation dominates only the latter third of the novel, and even though the third part closely parallels the first in many important details—the painting, the trip, the setting, and so forth—the two parts differ considerably in terms of the emotions each raises for the characters. The third part of the novel counterpoints the grief over Mrs. Ramsay's death against the warmth and compassion radiated by her maternal figure in part I, and this contrapuntal rhythm epitomizes the novel's response to its paradigmatic base. First the novel renders the unity and fulfillment of childhood as embodied in the mother's comforting presence, then it renders the separation and frustration of adulthood as embodied by the mother's absence. More to the point, by counterpointing these progressive and regressive energies, *To the Lighthouse* uses its formal construction of experience to underscore the continuity between childhood and adulthood.

As a result, even though Mr. Ramsay is the agency through which James and Lily reconcile the antagonism between self and other, we cannot discount the special importance of Mrs. Ramsay in this paradigmatic scheme. Her figure joins together the competing regressive and progressive energies within the novel to place them in harmonious counterpoint throughout the narrative. In her own radical changes of mood Mrs. Ramsay internalizes the contrapuntal rhythm of the novel's formal structure; in her marriage she externalizes it; and in her death she makes the other characters discover it. True, her death exemplifies the self's violation by an inanimate other whose destructive presence overwhelms human consciousness in part II. But part III ameliorates the horrific vision of selflessness recorded in that middle section to reinforce Mrs. Ramsay's acceptance of her own mortality and to fulfill her hope that memory will keep her alive even after death. "They would, she thought, going on again, however long they lived, come back to this night; this moon; this wind; this house; and to her too. It flattered her, where she was most susceptible of flattery, to think how, wound about in their hearts, however long they lived she would be woven" (p. 170). Mrs. Ramsay is right to say that children don't forget, but she fails to appreciate that their memory of violated innocence is the source of its repair in adulthood. Clearly, if the third stroke of the lighthouse beam is Mrs. Ramsay's stroke, then so too is the third part of the novel. Part III justifies her instinctive confidence in telling her children, "You shall go through it all," for it demonstrates what they do *not* lose in growing up: their sense of both mother and father, female and male, consciousness and unconsciousness, emotion and reason, innocence and maturity, all harmonically arranged within a mature self to reveal that the adult's consciousness is a continuation of the child's.

This appreciation of opposites is part of Woolf's modernist vision, and one reason for her technical break with the conventions of traditional fiction; but it also explains why she closes her novel with a conventional rite of passage. In contrast to the rites of passage in the other novels I have examined, maturation in this novel amounts to more than just the loss of innocence: it is a process of formulating the past as memory. Since memory compensates for the losses of the past by internalizing traces of what has been lost, it makes presence simultaneous with absence to confirm that the child is parent to the adult. Memory thus serves as the agency through which all of the novel's many oppositions can be harmonically orchestrated as complements of each other within the self. More to the point, with maturity resulting in the creation of memory, *To the Lighthouse* can then give full play to the genre's paradigmatic rhythm of violation and repair without having to minimize one or the other. The construction of experience in this novel therefore registers the full force of the self's consciousness of violation—its realization of lost innocence—all the while moving the self towards the repair that underlines its maturation.

Conclusion: Violation as Repair

In bringing my discussion to a close with *To the Lighthouse*, I do not mean to suggest that the paradigmatic operation of the English novel ceases with modernism. I could easily extend my discussion to bring in more recent examples that work out of the paradigm much more obviously than Woolf's novel does: Lawrence Durrell's *The Alexandria Quartet*, for instance, or John Fowles's *The Magus* or *The French Lieutenant's Woman*, or any one of Iris Murdoch's many novels. But I have chosen to end with *To the Lighthouse* because it marks a rather fitting closure to the sequence of books I have been analyzing. Lily's painting projects onto the act of aesthetic production the bildungsroman pattern that informs the realistic pole of the paradigm. Like James's rite of passage, which explicitly shows how *To the Lighthouse* follows the genre's paradigm of experience, the painting leads Lily not to a negation of self in death but to its confirmation in life. Her achievement therefore answers Mrs. Ramsay's question, "Why must they grow up and lose it all?" "The risk must be run, the mark made" (p. 235), Lily comes to learn, echoing the realization of countless numbers of characters before her, including Mrs. Ramsay herself.

My aim throughout this book has been to show how English novels repeatedly follow a paradigmatic operation instigated by

Mrs. Ramsay's type of question and resolved by Lily's type of reply. As I argued to start with, the poles serving as the boundaries for experience in the genre's paradigmatic scheme range from Cathy Earnshaw's anxiety that she has actually lost her self somewhere amidst the heather and the hills, to Elizabeth Bennet's realization that she has never known her self until she has read Darcy's letter. A novel's psychological texture as a representation of experience arises from the way it follows this scheme by charting a course for experience between these two poles. More importantly, a novel's dynamic energy as a construction of experience arises from the way it dialectically engages these two poles to stimulate a narrative tension between the regressive drive to regain innocence and the progressive drive to complete maturation. This is why I have repeatedly called attention to the double construction of experience in the novel, the forward-backward momentum reflecting the dialectical engagement of romance and realism.

The tension between desire and reality that results from this double construction helps explain why the genre's preoccupation with the loss of innocence makes its concentration on the achievement of selfhood so problematic. The drive to regain innocence expresses the self's desire to be united with the other. This desire is regressive in its attempt to reverse the historical process of maturation; it seeks a return to a time before the other asserted its presence and established the field of difference which defines the self as a separate consciousness. This regressive movement, moreover, threatens the self's ability to maintain a stable and coherent identity, calling into question the assumption that "self" *is* an identity. The paradigm then superimposes a forward moment to counter the regressive drive and its revelation of selflessness. This movement locates the self in time, delineating the loss of innocence as an irreversible condition of maturity. The paradigm's forward movement thus transforms the self's consciousness of what it loses—innocence, unity, wholeness—into insight: first, a recognition of difference, which stabilizes the self, and then an appreciation of the similarity underlying difference, which reconciles the self to the presence of the other. In short, the paradigm constructs experience as a dialectical engagement of competing drives (illusion/reality, innocence/maturity, desire/anxiety, romance/realism) in order to define what constitutes a "self" by placing it against the revealing backdrop of the other.

The linear delineation of growth informing the achievement of selfhood should therefore not mislead us into discounting the dialectic of violation and repair which motivates that achievement. To be sure, with the forward thrust of experience working to assuage the dread raised by the backward movement, the paradigm actively demonstrates that reality invades the privacy of consciousness not to violate the self's integrity, as Cathy fears, but to let a mature self emerge in full awareness of the other, as Elizabeth learns. When the forward momentum dominates, that is to say, experience educates characters in selfhood because contact with the other leads to insight, the source of the self's repair once it accepts its loss of innocence. But even then, as I have shown, the forward movement can never counter the backward movement completely. The self's turbulent passage to maturity, its adolescent sense of crisis, its fear of alteration, its dread of the alien other sex—these recurring strains disrupt and postpone the movement out of innocence by sustaining the self's yearning to return to its unaltered state. The anxiety informing the genre's paradigm of experience, the disturbing feeling that maturity transforms the self beyond recognition, cannot be easily forgotten, no matter how a novel's particular ending may try to resolve it.

Consequently, even though the paradigm's forward movement strives to arrange its rhythm of violation and repair into a linear movement, with repair succeeding violation, the imaginative and psychological power of a given novel's construction of experience is actually due to its simultaneous layering of violation over repair, repair over violation, so that one defines the other. Indeed, that violation and repair are no more than different shadings of the same experience finds its semantic proof, as *Clarissa* suggests, in the word "penetration," which means "insight" as well as "violation." This double meaning of "penetration" succinctly epitomizes the impact of experience upon characters in the novel, since the genre's paradigm organizes its various competing energies to demonstrate that the penetrated self is, at the same time, a penetrating self. Grounded in the

Conclusion

semantic ambiguity with which the word "penetration" summarizes its double movement and internal tensions, the English novel constructs experience out of the fundamental paradox that penetration is both violation and insight.

The paradigm of experience imbeds this double meaning in the genre. Although novels tend to effect closure by resolving their paradigmatic tensions, asserting one pole over the other to imagine violation *or* repair as the end of experience, before they reach this point of closure they orchestrate experience so as to bring together opposing energies and sustain them in a dialectical engagement. This engagement is, finally, what defines experience for the genre and makes it meaningful—that is, full of meanings. Through the tensions produced by its orchestration of competing, even irresolvable drives, the novel's paradigmatic base informs experience with the paradoxical double meaning of "penetration," suggesting that violation is repair. Thus the English novel as a genre repeatedly strives to imagine the opportunity for repair inherent in the violation which motivates its construction of experience. But since "penetration" may mean, as well, that repair itself is one more act of violation, the genre also strives to resolve, somehow, the anxiety generated once experience is envisioned as a process that equates repair with violation. One mark of the English novel's imaginative continuity as a genre, then, comes from its repeated effort to clarify the ambiguity that results from its paradigmatic construction of experience as both violation and repair.

*N*otes

Notes to Chapter 1

1. James Joyce, *Ulysses* (1922; New York: Random House, 1961), p. 37.
2. The influence of *Don Quixote* has been widely recognized by critics of the English novel, so to do justice to all the criticism that discusses the matter would require a book in itself. In addition to material cited below and in later chapters, some useful studies include: Edwin B. Knowles, "Cervantes and English Literature," in *Cervantes Across the Centuries*, ed. Angel Flores and M. J. Bernadete (New York: Dryden Press, 1947), pp. 267-93; Susan Staves, "Don Quixote in England," *Comparative Literature*, 24 (1972), 193-215; Robert Alter, *Partial Magic: The Novel as a Self-Conscious Genre* (Berkeley: Univ. of California Press, 1975); Harry Levin, "The Quixotic Principle: Cervantes and Other Novelists," in *The Interpretation of Narrative: Theory and Practice*, ed. Morton W. Bloomfield (Cambridge: Harvard Univ. Press, 1970), pp. 45-66; and Alexander Welsh, *Reflections on the Hero as Quixote* (Princeton: Princeton Univ. Press, 1981).
3. On the assertion of reality over illusion, see the classic essays by Lionel Trilling, "Manners, Morals, and the Novel," *Kenyon Review* (1948); rpt. in *Forms of Modern Fiction*, ed. William Van O'Connor (Bloomington: Indiana Univ. Press, 1948), pp. 144-60; and Dorothy Van Ghent, *The English Novel: Form and Function* (New York: Holt, Rinehart and Winston, 1953), pp. 9-19. Both Trilling and Van Ghent cite the quixotic model. On the novel as an assertion of experience over innocence, see Maurice Z. Shroder, "The Novel as a Genre," *Mass. Rev.* 4 (1963); rpt. in *The Theory of the Novel*, ed. Philip Stevick (New York: Free Press, 1967), pp. 13-29; and Alan Friedman, *The Turn of the Novel* (New York: Oxford Univ. Press, 1966). On realism and romance, in addition to Shroder's essay, see, of course, Northrop Frye's influential *Anatomy of Criticism* (Princeton: Princeton Univ. Press, 1957), as well as his *The Secular Scripture: A Study of the Structure of Romance* (Cambridge: Harvard Univ. Press, 1976); Patrick Brantlinger, "Romance, Novels, and Psychoanalysis," *Criticism*, 17 (1975), 15-40; and, for its discussion of the importance of parody to realism's

status as "anti-romance," Harry Levin, *The Gates of Horn: A Study of Five French Realists* (New York: Oxford Univ. Press, 1963), pp. 24-83.

4. *Great Expectations* (1860-61), ed. Louis Crompton (Indianapolis: Bobbs-Merrill, 1964), p. 1.

5. George Levine, *The Realistic Imagination: English Fiction from Frankenstein to Lady Chatterly* (Chicago: Univ. of Chicago Press, 1981), pp. 56, 156.

6. *A Portrait of the Artist as a Young Man* (1916; New York: Viking, 1964), p. 167.

7. *Great Expectations*, p. 2.

8. Shroder points out how the bildungsroman is the prototype of the novel genre, especially when viewed in terms of its quixotic origin: "The Novel as a Genre," pp. 14-16.

9. Friedman, *The Turn of the Novel*, p. 7.

10. Ian Watt, *The Rise of the Novel: Studies in Defoe, Richardson and Fielding* (Berkeley: Univ. of California Press, 1957), p. 32.

11. Levin, *The Gates of Horn*, p. 51.

12. The phrase is Levine's: *The Realistic Imagination*, p. 12.

13. For an appreciative examination of realism's achievement of consensus, see Elizabeth Deeds Ermarth, *Realism and Consensus in the English Novel* (Princeton: Princeton Univ. Press, 1983). For a critique of that achievement as the tool of ideology, see Catherine Belsey, *Critical Practice* (London: Methuen, 1980), pp. 56-84.

14. M. M. Bakhtin, *The Dialogic Imagination: Four Essays*, ed. Michael Holquist and trans. Caryl Emerson and Michael Holquist (Austin: Univ. of Texas Press, 1981).

15. Brantlinger, "Romance, Novels, and Psychoanalysis," p. 32. Further page references in this chapter will be included in my text.

16. Such a view informs Simon Lesser's influential *Fiction and the Unconscious* (Boston: Beacon Press, 1957), for example, where he explains that "fiction disguises the egotism and forbidden impulses which underlie fantasy, subjects them to the controlling influence of form" (p. 57).

17. Leo Bersani, *A Future for Astyanax: Character and Desire in Literature* (Boston: Little, Brown, 1976), p. 56. Further page references in this chapter will be included in my text.

18. I am addressing the first point throughout this book; I examine the second in my essay, "Figures Beyond the Test: A Theory of Readable Character in the Novel," *Novel*, 17 (1983), 5-27. As I've already mentioned, Levine addresses the third point in *The Realistic Imagination*.

19. Levine, *The Realistic Imagination*, p. 15.

20. Terry Eagleton, *Literary Theory: An Introduction* (Minneapolis: Univ. of Minnesota Press, 1983), p. 179.

21. Meredith Anne Skura, *The Literary Use of the Psychoanalytic Process* (New Haven: Yale Univ. Press, 1981), p. 55. Further page references in this chapter will be included in my text. In making this statement, by the way, Skura singles out Bersani as a critic who privileges a symbolic over a literal reading. I would say, however, that this is exactly what Bersani does *not* do when it comes to realistic fiction.

22. *Pride and Prejudice* (1813), ed. Donald J. Gray (New York: Norton, 1966), p. 144. Further page references will be included in my text.

23. Readers continue to argue over which category—romance or novel—best fits *Wuthering Heights*. Brantlinger, for instance, treats it as his example of the romance. It is this "generic ambiguity" which makes *Wuthering Heights* so resonant a work and, I will be arguing, so revealing of the way the novel operates as a genre. Denis Donoghue reads *Wuthering Heights* somewhat as I do, "a mixed genre, the novel under the stress of romance." In his rather brief argument about the "mixed" texture of the book he provides a summary of the critical disagreement about its "proper" genre: "Emily Brontë: On the Latitude of Interpretation," in *The Interpretation of Narrative*, pp. 124-33. Of course, not all critics who appreciate the mixture of modes in *Wuthering Heights* try to make a special case for it in the light of the novel genre as a whole. James R. Kincaid uses *Wuthering Heights* as one of his prime examples to illustrate his argument that novels are in fact rabbit/duck propositions when it comes to the question of genre: "Coherent Readers, Incoherent Texts," *Critical Inquiry*, 3 (1977), 781-802.

24. *Wuthering Heights* (1847), ed. William M. Sale, Jr., 2d ed. (New York: Norton, 1972), pp. 61, 76. Further page references will be included in my text.

25. Bersani makes this observation (*A Future for Astyanax*, p. 201).

26. Margaret Homans points out how Cathy replaces "her real [nightmarish] memories of childhood" with an "idyllic" memory to repress her recognition of Heathcliff's "diabolical cruelty" and, by implication, her own: "Repression and Sublimation of Nature in *Wuthering Heights*," *PMLA*, 93 (1978), 17-18. The significance of Homans's observation is that it reminds us not to make Cathy's own error in overly romanticizing Heathcliff or their childhood.

27. Thomas Moser, "What is the Matter with Emily Jane? Conflicting Impulses in *Wuthering Heights*," *NCF*, 17 (1962), 1-19.

28. Sandra M. Gilbert and Susan Gubar, *The Madwoman in the Attic: The Woman Writer and the Nineteenth-Century Imagination* (New Haven: Yale Univ. Press, 1979), p. 303.

29. Nancy K. Miller, *The Heroine's Text: Readings in the French and English Novel, 1722-1782* (New York: Columbia Univ. Press, 1980), pp. x-xi, 150. As I will be showing in Chapter 2, *Clarissa* actually includes both types of endings to the heroine's text, since Anna Howe's marriage counterpoints Clarissa's rape and death.

30. *Tess of the d'Urbervilles* (1891), ed. Scott Elledge, 2d ed. (New York: Norton, 1979), p. 191.

Notes to Chapter 2

1. *Tom Jones* (1749), ed. Sheridan Baker (New York: Norton, 1973), p. 746.

2. For an examination of the Puritan context of Richardson's work—especially as it creates the crisis of identity I will later be discussing—see Cynthia Griffin Wolff, *Samuel Richardson and the Eighteenth-Century Puritan Character* (Hamden: Archon Books, 1972).

3. Related to what I am saying is Patricia Meyer Spacks's survey of this fear as a theme in eighteenth-century novels in general: "Early Fiction and the Frightened Male," *Novel*, 8 (1974), 5-15.

Notes to Pages 53-65

4. *Tristram Shandy* (1759-67), ed. James Aiken Work (New York: Odyssey, 1940), p. 472.

5. *Tristram Shandy*, p. 73.

6. In addition to Cynthia Wolff's discussion, cited above, see the following readings of *Clarissa*, each responding to the novel's vivid social and psychological context: Christopher Hill, "Clarissa Harlowe and her Times," *Essays in Criticism*, 5 (1955), 315-40; Van Ghent, *The English Novel*, pp. 45-63; Alan Dugald McKillop, *The Early Masters of English Fiction* (Lawrence: Univ. of Kansas Press, 1956), pp. 64-81; Morris Golden, *Richardson's Characters* (Ann Arbor: Univ. of Michigan Press, 1963), pp. 46-71; Ian Watt, *The Rise of the Novel*, pp. 208-38; Mark Kinkead-Weekes, *Samuel Richardson: Dramatic Novelist* (Ithaca: Cornell Univ. Press, 1973), pp. 123-276; Margaret Anne Doody, *A Natural Passion: A Study of the Novels of Samuel Richardson* (Oxford: Clarendon Press, 1974); and Carol Houlihan Flynn, *Samuel Richardson: A Man of Letters* (Princeton: Princeton Univ. Press, 1982). More recently, the issue of Clarissa's placement within her world has been discussed from a feminist perspective that reads her character as the construction of her patriarchal culture: see Terry Castle, *Clarissa's Ciphers: Meaning and Disruption in Richardson's* Clarissa (Ithaca: Cornell Univ. Press, 1982), and Terry Eagleton, *The Rape of Clarissa: Writing, Sexuality and Class Struggle in Samuel Richardson* (Minneapolis: Univ. of Minnesota Press, 1982). Each of these readings of *Clarissa* draws attention to the power struggle between Clarissa and Lovelace and points out the significant difference between them in the values they represent for their world and in the way they read their experience. I certainly do not discount their difference, and I discuss it at greater length in an article which served somewhat as a rehearsal for this chapter: "*Clarissa* and the Individuation of Character," *ELH*, 43 (1976), 163-83. While not ignoring their difference, however, here I want to emphasize the inherent similarity of Clarissa and Lovelace as they respond to each other as an alien other sex.

7. *Clarissa* (1747-48; New York: Dutton, 1932), 1:22. Further page references to this, the 4-volume Everyman edition, will be included in my text.

8. From what I am saying it should be clear that, in the context of Clarissa's and Lovelace's efforts to read each other, I disagree with John Preston's view that the epistolary form of the novel poses "an existential crisis" for the characters, alienating them from lived experience by making the letters their sole reality. For his explanation see *The Created Self: The Reader's Role in Eighteenth-Century Fiction* (London: Heinemann, 1970), pp. 38-93. To be sure, the letters are subject to misreading and misrepresentation—to what Terry Castle calls "hermeneutic violence" (*Clarissa's Ciphers*, p. 71); but for the characters the letters also serve as rehearsals and reviews of experiential moments, just as they serve as accounts of the present moment while it is being experienced, since the letters are also subject to the contingency of interruption.

9. Leo Braudy notices the important pun on "penetration" at work here, its connotations both of sexuality and perception: "Penetration and Impenetrability in *Clarissa,*" *New Approaches to Eighteenth-Century Literature*, ed. Phillip Harth (New York: Columbia Univ. Press, 1974), pp. 177-206.

10. In *Reading Clarissa: The Struggles of Interpretation* (New Haven: Yale Univ. Press, 1979), William Beatty Warner deconstructs traditional interpretations of *Clarissa* to challenge their humanist assumptions about the nature of an

230

integrated self. Warner reads Clarissa's self as an artificial, even literary construction, located entirely within her own consciousness, which she then "naturalizes" so that her world, as well as Richardson's, takes it for granted as "truth." The theoretical issues raised by Warner's informed and provocative reading go beyond the scope of the present discussion. However, what should be clear is where we do agree. Whether genuine or artifice, Clarissa's self functions, in his words, to mark "the boundary between inside and outside" so that she can read "the text of her own innocence" (p. 18). Even though Warner reads the novel in terms of its own textuality, in part to give equal time to Lovelace's more fragmentary and "post-modern" sensibility, that very act of constructing a self gives rise to the strains I am talking about by granting to the novel its claim of mimetic representation. As we both argue, since the boundaries between inside and outside, or what I call "self" and "other," are never quite clear or stable, Clarissa can finally assert her innocence only by transcending them in some fashion.

11. Nancy K. Miller, *The Heroine's Text*, p. 94.

Notes to Chapter 3

1. Alexander Welsh, *The Hero of the Waverley Novels* (New Haven: Yale Univ. Press, 1963), p. 35.

2. Welsh, *Reflections on the Quixote*, p. 167.

3. For example, Lawrence J. Clipper reads *Waverley* in terms of the mythic pattern outlined by Joseph Campbell: "Edward Waverley's Night Journey," *South Atlantic Quarterly*, 73 (1974), 541-53.

4. "Family Romances" (1909), in *The Standard Edition of the Complete Psychological Works of Sigmund Freud*, ed. and trans. James Strachey, 9 (London: Hogarth, 1959), 237-41.

5. Freud, "Family Romances," p. 237.

6. Freud, "Family Romances," pp. 240-41.

7. Freud, "Family Romances," p. 238.

8. Marthe Robert, *Origins of the Novel* (1972), trans. Sacha Rabinovitch (Bloomington: Indiana Univ. Press, 1980), p. 24.

9. Robert, *Origins of the Novel*, pp. 31, 37, 39. Walter L. Reed makes a similar claim, examining the history of the novel in terms of the quixote and the picaro: *An Exemplary History of the Novel: The Quixotic versus the Picaresque* (Chicago: Univ. of Chicago Press, 1981).

10. Page references to these three novels—*Waverley* (1814), *Old Mortality* (1816), and *Rob Roy* (1817)—will be to the Everyman editions (London: Dent, 1906).

11. It is worth noting here that while Scott satirizes Edward's daydreaming to expose his hero's immaturity, the novel as a whole is more ambivalent when it comes to appreciating the imaginative attraction of romantic energy. Harry Levin believes that Scott, "at heart a romanticist . . . was less interested in exposing reality than in embellishing it" ("The Quixotic Principal," p. 59). But I think the more appropriate response is George Levine's, who concludes that "Scott's kind of fiction was thus to be somewhere between 'romance' and 'novel'" (*The Realistic Imagination*, p. 89). Levine points out further that *Waverley* does not reject romance outright, but rather leads its hero to discover that his temperament is not romantic.

Notes to Pages 87–111

12. Francis R. Hart, *Scott's Novels: The Plotting of Historical Survival* (Charlottesville: Univ. Press of Virginia, 1966), p. 86.
13. Freud, "Family Romances," p. 237.
14. Bersani, *A Future for Astyanax*, p. 6.
15. Welsh, *The Hero of the Waverley Novels*, p. 68.

Notes to Chapter 4

1. Cf. Raymond Williams, *The English Novel From Dickens to Lawrence* (New York: Oxford Univ. Press, 1970), pp. 28-59, where he talks about Dickens as the first English novelist of the city.
2. *Bleak House* (1852-53), ed. George Ford and Sylvère Monod (New York: Norton, 1977), p. 68. Further page references will be included in my text.
3. J. Hillis Miller, *Charles Dickens: The World of His Novels* (1958; rpt. Bloomington: Indiana Univ. Press, 1969), pp. xv-vi.
4. Levine, *The Realistic Imagination*, pp. 239-240.
5. Robert A. Donovan, "Structure and Idea in *Bleak House*," *ELH*, 29 (1962); rpt. in *Twentieth Century Interpretations of* Bleak House, ed. Jacob Korg (Englewood Cliffs: Prentice-Hall, 1968), p. 39.
6. Edgar Johnson, *Charles Dickens: His Tragedy and His Triumph* (1952), rev. and abr. (New York: Viking, 1977), p. 387.
7. Trevor Blount, "The Graveyard Satire of *Bleak House* in the Context of 1850," *RES*, n.s. 14 (1963), 370. Miller also examines the disease imagery as the symbol of unrestrained, unintentional contact: *Charles Dickens*, p. 209.
8. Miller, *Charles Dickens*, p. 168.
9. Mark Spilka, *Dickens and Kafka: A Mutual Interpretation* (London: Dobson, 1963), p. 206.
10. Is Esther perhaps modeled on Jane Eyre? Esther certainly does lack Jane's indignant anger and passion; but like Esther, Jane has been abused and unwanted as a child; she, too, wants to win affection and appear innocent. "I had meant to be so good," Jane confesses, much as Esther does, "and to do so much at Lowood: to make so many friends, to earn respect, and win affection." Charlotte Brontë, *Jane Eyre* (1847), ed. Richard J. Dunn (New York: Norton, 1971), p. 59.
11. Ross H. Dabney argues just the opposite of what I am saying, following what I take to be surface clues in the novel to claim, much as Spilka does, that "according to the implicit moral values of the novel, her secret is less censurable than the life she has chosen in marrying Sir Leicester." Despite the stigma of mystery surrounding Lady Dedlock's relationship with Hawdon, Dabney claims that her real crime was in having married for reasons of money and class: *Love and Property in the Novels of Dickens* (London: Chatto and Windus, 1967), p. 79.
12. Taylor Stoehr, *Dickens: The Dreamer's Stance* (Ithaca: Cornell Univ. Press, 1965), pp. 161-68.
13. Joseph I. Fradin points out that Tulkinghorn's "will to power" has its origin in his denial of a sexual life: "Will and Society in *Bleak House*," *PMLA*, 81 (1966), 95-109. A similar view of Tulkinghorn is Eugene F. Quirk's: "Tulkinghorn's Buried Life: A Study of Character in *Bleak House*," *JEGP*, 72 (1973), 526-35.

Notes to Pages 120-132

14. W. J. Harvey, *Character and the Novel* (Ithaca: Cornell Univ. Press, 1965), p. 94.

15. *Great Expectations* (1860-61), ed. Louis Crompton (Indianapolis: Bobbs-Merrill, 1964), p. 525. Further page references will be included in my text.

16. *Our Mutual Friend* (1864-65; London: Dent, 1929), p. 31.

17. Miller makes this important observation: *Charles Dickens*, pp. 255-56.

18. Many critics have already looked at Pip's growth in relation to what Dickens is doing in this novel, so to avoid repetition I am condensing and summarizing certain details in order to stress my main points. Miller discusses Pip's guilt and isolation, seeing him as the archetypal Dickensian hero (*Charles Dickens*, pp. 249-78). In addition to Stoehr (*The Dreamer's Stance*, pp. 101-37), important psychoanalytical views of Pip's guilt are: Julian Moynahan, "The Hero's Guilt: The Case of *Great Expectations*," *Essays in Criticism*, 10 (1960), 60-79; Albert D. Hutter, "Crime and Fantasy in *Great Expectations*," in *Psychoanalysis and Literary Process*, ed. Frederick Crews (Cambridge, Mass.: Winthrop Publishers, 1970), pp. 25-65; Lawrence Jay Dessner, "*Great Expectations*: 'the ghost of a man's own father,'" *PMLA*, 91 (1976), 436-49; Peter Brooks, "Repetition, Repression, and Return: *Great Expectations* and the Study of Plot," *New Literary History*, 11 (1980), 503-26; and Judith Weissman and Steven Cohan, "Dickens' *Great Expectations*: Pip's Arrested Development," *American Imago*, 38 (1981), 105-26. In my discussion of Pip, I am emphasizing certain points about his ambivalence towards women that are demonstrated with more textual detail in the last-named essay.

19. Moynahan makes this observation about the surprising violence that surrounds Pip's "heroic" attempt to rescue Miss Havisham. Even more pointed, according to Moynahan, is the fact that right before he enters the house to see her for the last time, Pip unexpectedly remembers his childish fantasy of Miss Havisham hanging from the gallows. His formerly silent resentment of the woman, no longer restrained by his expectation that she is his benefactor, is now seeking expression ("The Hero's Guilt," pp. 74-76).

Notes to Chapter 5

1. Virginia Woolf, "George Eliot," *The Common Reader: First Series* (New York: Harcourt, 1925), p. 172. Walter Allen talks about Eliot's "somber" view of human life—a conclusion I disagree with—and offers, as well, a clear summary of *Middlemarch* as it is traditionally read: *The English Novel: A Short Critical History* (New York: Dutton, 1954), pp. 268-74.

2. George Eliot, *The Mill on the Floss* (1860), ed. Gordon S. Haight (Boston: Houghton Mifflin, 1961), p. 44. Further page references will be included in my text.

3. The following critics offer lengthy analyses of Maggie's emotional turmoil and their conclusions generally agree with mine, though I am stressing a different context in which to place her character: William R. Steinhoff, "Intent and Fulfillment in the Ending of *The Mill on the Floss*," in *The Image of the Work: Essays in Criticism*, ed. Bertrand Evans, Josephine Miles, and William R. Steinhoff (Berkeley: Univ. of California Press, 1955), pp. 229-51; Bernard J. Paris, *A Psychological Approach to Fiction: Studies in Thackeray, Stendhal, George Eliot,*

Notes to Pages 134-159

Dostoevsky, and Conrad (Bloomington: Indiana Univ. Press, 1974), pp. 165-89; Laura Comer Emery, *George Eliot's Creative Conflict: The Other Side of Silence* (Berkeley: Univ. of California Press, 1976), pp. 5-54. Additionally, in her Freudian approach to Eliot, Emery also analyzes the sexual immaturity complicating the two central romantic relationships in *Middlemarch*, though once again I will be stressing a different context for explaining the significance of this complication to bring out different points about its psychological nuances.

4. George Eliot, *Middlemarch* (1871-72), ed. Gordon S. Haight, (Boston: Houghton Mifflin, 1956), p. 195. Further page references will be included in my text.

5. Paris, *A Psychological Approach to Fiction*, p. 170.

6. Gilbert and Gubar, *The Madwoman in the Attic*, p. 494.

7. Patricia Meyer Spacks, *The Female Imagination* (New York: Knopf, 1975), p. 46.

8. Nancy K. Miller, "Emphasis Added: Plots and Plausibilities in Women's Fiction," *PMLA*, 96 (1981), 47.

9. Mary Jacobus, "The Question of Language: Men of Maxims and *The Mill on the Floss*," *Critical Inquiry*, 8 (1981), 219-22.

10. There has always been a lively debate about the ending of *The Mill*, with the weight of criticism putting pressure on its wish fulfillment to argue that it is a loss of control on Eliot's part, a failure to distinguish her point of view from Maggie's. Such is the argument, by now a commonplace, of F. R. Leavis, *The Great Tradition: George Eliot, Henry James, Joseph Conrad* (1948: rpt. Harmondsworth, England: Penguin, 1967), pp. 57-58. In addition, see U. C. Knoepflmacher, *Laughter and Despair: Readings in Ten Novels of the Victorian Era* (Berkeley: Univ. of California Press, 1971), who reads the ambiguity of the ending revealing "George Eliot's acute split between romance and realism" (p. 134), and Paris, *A Psychological Approach to Fiction*, who argues that the novel dramatizes but does not correctly interpret Maggie's self-destructiveness (p. 186). I also discuss the ending of this novel as an illustration of the problematic meaning of endings in general: "Narrative Form and Death: *The Mill on the Floss* and *Mrs. Dalloway*," *Genre*, 11 (1978), 109-29.

11. Emery makes this observation, after tracing the "disappearance" of the intrusive narrator in this part of the novel: *George Eliot's Creative Conflict*, pp. 48-50.

12. J. Hillis Miller, "Optic and Semiotic in *Middlemarch*," in *The Worlds of Victorian Fiction*, ed. Jerome H. Buckley (Cambridge: Harvard Univ. Press, 1975), p. 144.

13. D. A. Miller, *Narrative and its Discontents: Problems of Closure in the Traditional Novel* (Princeton: Princeton University Press, 1981), pp. 152-71.

14. Barbara Hardy analyzes the sexual theme in *Middlemarch*, focusing on Eliot's "reticence" to explore Will's sexuality as implicitly as she does Casaubon's impotence: *The Appropriate Form: An Essay on the Novel* (London: Athlone Press, 1964), pp. 105-31. As my analysis will make clear towards the end of this chapter, I do not agree with Hardy on this point: Will's sexuality is indeed brought out, but through Rosamond more than Dorothea.

15. D. A. Miller, *Narrative and its Discontents*, pp. 175-90.

16. *Daniel Deronda* (1876), ed. Barbara Hardy (Harmondsworth, England: Penguin, 1967), pp. 760-61.

17. As far as I know, Frank Kermode was the first to draw the comparison between *Middlemarch* and Lawrence's "deep study of two marriages at the end of the world": "D. H. Lawrence and the Apocalyptic Types," in *Continuities* (New York: Random House, 1968), p. 137.

Notes to Chapter 6

1. For a full discussion of modernism as a movement see *Modernism: 1890-1930*, ed. Malcolm Bradbury and James McFarlane (Harmondsworth, England: Penguin, 1976), especially the essay by David Lodge, "The Language of Modernist Fiction: Metaphor and Metonymy," pp. 481-96. Lodge offers a clear synopsis of the modernist novel's formal program: its experimental nature occurs because of its concern with consciousness, which results in experience being rendered as an open-ended stream, so that the narrative does not depend on a straight chronological ordering or a reliable omniscient narrator, but instead seeks other means of aesthetic order and stability.

2. *Tess of the d'Urbervilles* (1891), ed. Scott Elledge, 2d ed. (New York: Norton, 1979), pp. 72-73. Further page references will be included in my text.

3. J. Hillis Miller examines the indeterminate textuality of Conrad's novel, its resistance to a definitive and single interpretation: *Fiction and Repetition: Seven English Novels* (Cambridge: Harvard Univ. Press, 1982), pp. 22-41.

4. *Lord Jim* (1900), ed. Thomas C. Moser (New York: Norton, 1968), p. 152. Further page references will be included in my text.

5. Bernard J. Paris explains Jim's character in terms somewhat similar to mine, arguing that his "anguish" is an expression of "self-hate and a despair of ever becoming his idealized self": *A Psychological Approach to Fiction*, p. 247.

6. Alexander Welsh even muses that practical jokes are inseparable from realism, beginning with Cervantes. "The vital thrust of realism," Welsh concludes, "is to define the heroism of the victim of circumstances rather than to describe the circumstances" (*Reflections on the Hero as Quixote*, p. 119).

7. Levine, *The Realistic Imagination*, p. 271.

8. Daniel Albright, *Personality and Impersonality: Lawrence, Woolf, and Mann* (Chicago: Univ. of Chicago Press, 1978), pp. 1-3.

9. Leon Edel still offers a good summary of the modernist novel's interest in consciousness and perception: *The Modern Psychological Novel* (1955; rpt. New York: Grove, n.d.). However, several recent books have been even more useful in delineating the various and subtle planes of narration characteristic of modernism's treatment of consciousness: Gérard Genette: *Narrative Discourse: An Essay in Method* (1972), trans. Jane E. Lewin (Ithaca: Cornell Univ. Press, 1980); Seymour Chatman, *Story and Discourse: Narrative Structure in Fiction and Film* (Ithaca: Cornell Univ. Press, 1978); and Dorrit Cohn, *Transparent Minds: Narrative Modes for Presenting Consciousness in Fiction* (Princeton: Princeton Univ. Press, 1978).

10. Albright, *Personality and Impersonality*, p. 25.

11. James Naremore, *The World Without a Self: Virginia Woolf and the Novel* (New Haven: Yale Univ. Press, 1973), p. 111.

12. Sigmund Freud, *Civilization and its Discontents* (1930); ed. and trans. James Strachey (New York: Norton, 1961), pp. 12-15.

13. I am referring to Lawrence's famous letter to Edward Garnett, 5 June 1914: "You mustn't look in my novel for the old stable *ego* of the character. There is another ego, according to whose action the individual is unrecognizable, and passes through, as it were, allotropic states which it needs a deeper sense than any other we've been used to exercise, to discover are states of the same single radically unchanged element. (Like as diamond and coal are the same pure single element of carbon. The ordinary novel would trace the history of the diamond—but I say, 'Diamond, what! This is carbon.' And my diamond might be coal or soot, and my theme is carbon.)" Most of this letter's text is reprinted in Mark Schorer's important essay, "*Women in Love* and Death," *Hudson Review*, 6 (Spring 1953); rpt. in *D. H. Lawrence: A Collection of Critical Essays*, ed. Mark Spilka (Englewood Cliffs: Prentice-Hall, 1963), pp. 51-52.

14. In addition to Schorer, whose essay has influenced my response to *Women in Love*, many critics have examined the novel's apocalyptic vision, its indictment of a depersonalizing mechanistic world, its call for the revitalizing breakdown of egoism through love: see, for example, F. R. Leavis, *D. H. Lawrence: Novelist* (1955; rpt. Harmondsworth, England: Penguin, 1973); Mark Spilka, *The Love Ethic of D. H. Lawrence* (Bloomington: Indiana Univ. Press, 1955); Stephen J. Miko. *Toward* Women in Love: *The Emergence of a Lawrentian Aesthetic* (New Haven: Yale Univ. Press, 1972); and T. H. Adamowski, "Being Perfect: Lawrence, Sartre, and *Women in Love*," *Critical Inquiry*, 2 (1975), 345-68. In my brief discussion of *Women in Love* I am building upon what critics have already explored at great length about the ideological and psychological ambitions of the novel in order to emphasize, more specifically, the desire for innocence (or preconsciousness) that motivates them.

15. *Women in Love* (1920; New York: Viking, 1960), p. 312. Further page references will be included in my text.

16. The dissolution of an individuated egocentric personality would seem to be attractive to Leo Bersani, but he sees *Women in Love* calling for the death of desire in that it strives to achieve "stillness" with the other, and because the sign of desire is movement as well as the absence of the object desired (*A Future for Astyanax*, p. 181). I think the metaphor of sex as Lawrence uses it in the novel actually argues against Bersani's reading because what Bersani calls "Lawrentian stillness" is only the moment of fulfillment that follows the climax of the self's penetration of (or by) the other, and that moment quite clearly remains part of the larger rhythm of sexual experience, as the "Moony" chapter illustrates, so it is transient.

17. *To the Lighthouse* (1927; New York: Harcourt, 1955), p. 300. Further page references will be included in my text.

18. John Mepham, "Figures of Desire: Narration and Fiction in *To the Lighthouse*," in *The Modern English Novel: The Reader, the Writer and the Work*, ed. Gabriel Josipovici (London: Open Books, 1976), pp. 175, 161.

19. Erich Auerbach, *Mimesis: The Representation of Reality in Western Literature* (1946), trans. Willard R. Trask (Princeton: Princeton Univ. Press, 1953), pp. 531, 534.

20. Naremore, *The World Without a Self*, p. 123

21. Naremore, *The World Without a Self*, pp. 95, 142, 143.

22. Mepham analyzes the linguistic unity of Woolf's narration to show the way even phonetic choices saturate the text with directed meaning: "Figures of

Desire," pp. 149-85 passim. Naremore also documents the novel's "carefully modulated stylistic unity" (*The World Without a Self*, p. 123).

23. Traditionally, critics tend to agree with James and Lily in part I, seeing Mrs. Ramsay as the sympathetic female principle and Mr. Ramsay as the unsympathetic male principle. A few critics reverse the sympathy with which we are to see these two characters, responding to Mrs. Ramsay as a domineering and repressive figure. See, for instance, Glenn Pedersen, "Vision in *To the Lighthouse*," *PMLA*, 73 (1958), 585-600; and Sharon Wood Proudfit, "A Key to Personal Relations in *To the Lighthouse*," *Criticism*, 13 (1971), 26-38. As Mitchell A. Leaska points out in his detailed study of this novel, the issue is much more complicated, with all the characters changing personalities, as it were, depending on where and when they are seen in the novel and by whom: *Virginia Woolf's Lighthouse: A Study in Critical Method* (New York: Columbia Univ. Press, 1970), pp. 79-80, 96-101. Yet even Leaska sees "the real Mrs. Ramsay" as "the barrier in the relationship between husband and wife, and between father and son" (p. 119). In this novel, the characters themselves project such meanings onto each other.

24. Naremore, *The World Without a Self*, pp. 141-42.

25. Mark Spilka explains Mrs. Ramsay's silence somewhat differently; and while I don't find his argument convincing, it is worth mentioning, since it is an alternate reading of the Ramsays' unity. Spilka does not discount the way they complement each other. However, he reads them in terms of Woolf's biography to make them seem like little more than fictive counterparts of Julia and Leslie Stephen. He then claims that, like Woolf's mother, Mrs. Ramsay may have had a passionate first love, so her silence here may mean "namely, that she *doesn't* love him [her husband] passionately, as Julia Duckworth loved Herbert [her first husband], and so *can't* tell him she loves him in so many words." See *Virginia Woolf's Quarrel with Grieving* (Lincoln: Univ. Nebraska Press, 1980), pp. 91-92.

26. Although he does not connect it to Mr. Ramsay's core of darkness, as I am doing, Leaska uses the hedge motif to show how recurring symbols form a pattern that helps carry the narrative forward: *Virginia Woolf's Lighthouse*, pp. 117-20.

Index

Adamowski, T. H., 236n.14
Albright, Daniel, 185, 186
Allen, Walter, 233n.1
Auerbach, Erich, 197
Alter, Robert, 227n.2
Austen, Jane, 91, 171, 172
—*Pride and Prejudice:* analyzed, 19-27; compared to *Clarissa*, 47, 48, 64, 73; compared to *Women in Love*, 192, 194; compared to *Wuthering Heights*, 28, 32, 36, 39, 41, 42; mentioned, 2, 43, 82, 179, 198, 224, 225

Bakhtin, M. M., 8
Belsey, Catherine, 228n.13
Bersani, Leo, 8, 10-13, 14, 28, 40, 41, 91, 228n.21, 229n.25, 236n.16
Bildungsroman, 21, 26, 223, 228n.8
Brantlinger, Patrick, 8, 9-10, 11, 14, 16, 40, 227n.3, 229n.23
Braudy, Leo, 230n.9
Brontë, Charlotte, *Jane Eyre*, 232n.10
Brontë, Emily, *Wuthering Heights:* analyzed, 27-42; compared to *Clarissa*, 46, 47-48, 58, 59, 65, 66, 73; compared to *Pride and Prejudice*, 28, 32, 36, 39, 41, 42; compared to *Tess of the d'Urbervilles*, 176, 179, 187; romance and realism in, 9, 10, 13, 41-42, 184, 224-25, 229nn.23, 26; mentioned, 43, 82, 87, 117, 130, 131, 132, 143, 184
Brooks, Peter, 233n.18

Castle, Terry, 230nn.6, 8
Cervantes, Miguel de, *Don Quixote*, 1, 2, 7, 80, 83, 227n.2, 228n.8, 231n.9, 235n.6
Chatman, Seymour, 235n.9
Clipper, Lawrence J., 231n.3
Cohan, Steven, 228n.18, 230n.6, 233n.18, 234n.10
Cohn, Dorrit, 235n.9
Conrad, Joseph, 171
—*Lord Jim:* analyzed, 179-84; mentioned, 46, 172, 173, 185, 186, 187, 197, 200, 235nn.3, 5

Dabney, Ross H., 232n.11
Death, 46, 187; in *Clarissa*, 47-48, 65-67; in *Lord Jim*, 184; in *The Mill on the Floss*, 139, 140-44, 234n.10; in *Tess of the d'Urbervilles*, 179; in *To the Lighthouse*, 196, 198-99, 202, 207-8, 213, 216, 220; in *Tristram Shandy*, 53, 54; in *Women in Love*, 188, 189; in *Wuthering Heights*, 35
Defoe, Daniel, 171; *Moll Flanders*, 43, 48; *Robinson Crusoe*, 80
Desire, 10-12, 15, 16, 18, 25-26, 41, 79
—displacement of, 9, 13, 185; in *Bleak House*, 108-11, 114, 115; in *Great Expectations*, 103-4, 124-25; in *Lord Jim*, 180-83; in *Middlemarch*, 159-68; in *Old Mortality*, 96; in *Rob Roy*, 89-90; in *Tess of the d'Urbervilles*, 175-76; in *Waverley*, 86; in Waverley novels, 76, 77, 82, 91, 92, 98-99, 101

Index

Desire *(cont.)*
—as loss of self: in *The Mill on the Floss*, 136, 137-38; in *Middlemarch*, 161, 164
—and narration in *Middlemarch*, 149-50, 152-53, 159-60, 169. *See also* Oedipal desire; Sexuality
Dessner, Lawrence Jay, 233n.18
Dickens, Charles, 12, 99, 101, 102, 171, 232n.1
—*Bleak House:* analyzed, 104-23; compared to *Great Expectations*, 45, 106, 122, 123-24, 126, 130; compared to *Middlemarch*, 13, 14, 131, 157, 185; compared to *Women in Love*, 44, 188, 189; mentioned, 87, 101, 102, 132, 182, 187, 233nn.10, 11, 13
—*David Copperfield*, 122
—*Great Expectations:* analyzed, 122-30; compared to *Bleak House*, 45, 104, 106, 122, 123, 124, 126, 130; compared to *The Mill on the Floss*, 132, 134, 141; compared to *To the Lighthouse*, 202, 213, 218; as example of realism, 1-5, 20, 103, 172, 179; mentioned, 98, 160, 182, 233nn.18, 19
—*Oliver Twist*, 102
—*Our Mutual Friend*, 122
—*Pickwick Papers*, 2
Donoghue, Denis, 229n.23
Doody, Margaret Anne, 230n.6
Dreams, 9, 15-16; in *Wuthering Heights*, 30-34
Durrell, Lawrence, 223

Eagleton, Terry, 13, 230n.6
Ermarth, Elizabeth Deeds, 228n.13
Edel, Leon, 235n.9
Eliot, George, 5, 12, 99, 171
—*Daniel Deronda*, 159, 167
—*Middlemarch:* analyzed, 146-69; compared to *To the Lighthouse*, 198, 202, 215; compared to *Women in Love*, 12, 44, 159, 188, 189, 192, 194, 235n.17; as example of realism, 9, 12, 13, 14, 16, 45-46, 131-32, 172, 179, 184, 185, 233n.1; mentioned, 2, 19, 87, 98, 130, 174, 180, 234n.3, 14
—*The Mill on the Floss:* analyzed, 132-47; compared to *Middlemarch*, 45, 154, 161, 169; mentioned, 178, 179, 184, 186, 187, 233-34n.3, 234n.10
Emery, Laura Comer, 234nn.3, 11

Family Romance, 79-81; in *Bleak House*, 116, 119; in Dickens's novels, 101, 103; in *The Mill on the Floss*, 134; in *Rob Roy*, 87-91; in *To the Lighthouse*, 195, 201; in *Waverley*, 85; in Waverly novels, 43-44, 77, 81-83, 87, 98-99, 101. *See also* Freud
Fielding, Henry, 51, 171
—*Joseph Andrews*, 2
—*Tom Jones:* analyzed, 48-51; mentioned, 44, 52, 54, 87
Flynn, Carol Houlihan, 230n.6
Forster, E. M., *Howards End*, 87
Fowles, John, 223
Fradin, Joseph I., 232n.13
Freud, Sigmund, 14, 90; *Civilization and Its Discontents*, 186-87; "Family Romances," 77-78. *See also* Family Romance; Unconscious
Friedman, Alan, 4, 227n.2
Frye, Northrop, 227n.3

Genette, Gérard, 235n.9
Gilbert, Sandra M., 41, 140
Golden, Morris, 230n.6
Gubar, Susan, 41, 140

Hardy, Barbara, 234n.14
Hardy, Thomas, 171, 172
—*Tess of the d'Urbervilles:* analyzed, 173-79; mentioned, 43, 46, 172, 179, 180, 184, 185, 187
Hart, Francis R., 87
Harvey, W. J., 120
Heroine's experience, 42-43, 140-41, 229n.29; compared to hero's, 43-45. *See also* Sexuality
Hill, Christopher, 230n.6
History: in *Old Mortality*, 92-93, 97, 99; in Waverley novels, 45, 75-76, 77, 82, 87, 92-93, 101
Homans, Margaret, 229n.26
Hutter, Albert D., 233n.18

Innocence, 42, 43, 44, 48, 49, 51
—as unity of self and other, 6, 46, 173, 186-87, 224; in *The Mill on the Floss*, 141-44; in *To the Lighthouse*, 195-96, 198-99, 202, 208-11; in *Women in Love*, 188, 195; in *Wuthering Heights*, 29, 39
—v. maturity, 2, 4-7, 17-18, 26-27, 44, 45, 55, 131, 173, 224-25, 227n.3; in *Bleak House*, 105-23; in *Clarissa*, 47-48, 55, 58-60, 65, 66-67, 72-73; in Dickens's novels, 102-3; in *Great Expectations*, 103, 123-30, 233n.18; in *Lord Jim*, 180-84; in *Middlemarch*, 131, 148, 149, 154-59, 169, 194; in *The Mill on the Floss*, 132-36, 137, 141-43,

240

Index

145-47; in *Old Mortality*, 93-98; in *Pride and Prejudice*, 20-23, 194; in *Tess of the d'Urbervilles*, 173-78; in *Tom Jones*, 50-51; in *Tristram Shandy*, 53-55; in *To the Lighthouse*, 195-96; 201-8; 212-21; in *Waverley*, 83-87; in Waverley novels, 76-77; in *Women in Love*, 188, 192-95; in *Wuthering Heights*, 28-40, 42, 229n.26

Jacobus, Mary, 140, 141, 144
Joyce, James: *A Portrait of the Artist as a Young Man*, 3; *Ulysses*, 1, 3, 5

Kermode, Frank, 235n.17
Kincaid, James R., 229n.23
Kinkead-Weekes, Mark, 230n.6
Knoepflmacher, U. C., 234n.10
Knowles, Edwin B., 227n.2

Lawrence, D. H., 12, 161, 171, 172, 186, 235n.17, 235-36n.13
—*Women in Love:* analyzed, 187-95; mentioned, 2, 12, 44, 46, 159, 172, 195, 197, 200, 203, 236nn.14, 16
Leaska, Mitchell A., 237nn.23, 26
Leavis, F. R., 234n.10, 236n.14
Lesser, Simon, 228n.16
Levin, Harry, 8, 171, 227n.2, 228n.3, 232n.11
Levine, George, 2, 4, 8, 12, 77, 103, 171, 185, 228n.18, 231n.11
Lodge, David, 235n.1

McKillop, Alan Dugald, 273n.6
Mepham, John, 236n.22
Miko, Stephen J., 235n.14
Miller, D. A., 148, 159
Miller, J. Hillis, 102, 105, 106, 148-49, 232n.7, 233nn.17, 18, 235n.3
Miller, Nancy K., 42, 65, 140, 141, 144
Modernism, 5, 11, 47, 179, 235nn.1, 9; compared to realism, 46, 172-73, 185-88, 197-98; of *To the Lighthouse*, 197-98, 221
Moser, Thomas, 41
Moynahan, Julian, 233nn.18, 19
Murdoch, Iris, 223

Naremore, James, 186, 198, 208, 236n.22
Narration: of *Great Expectations*, 103-4, 123, 125, 127; of *Lord Jim*, 173, 180, 183-84; of *Middlemarch*, 45, 131-32, 144, 146-54, 158-59, 168-69, 184, 185-86, 197; of *The Mill on the Floss*, 144-47; of *Tess of the d'Urbervilles*, 173-74, 175, 176, 178, 179, 184; of *To the Lighthouse*, 197-200, 236n.22; of *Wuthering Heights*, 144
Novel: dialectical structure of, 6-8, 13, 16, 27, 41-42, 45, 81, 173, 179, 185, 195, 224-26; paradigm of experience in, 6-7, 17-20, 42, 51, 80, 81, 131, 172, 223-26. *See also* Modernism; Narration; Realism

Oedipal desire, 43, 45, 79, 89, 92, 96, 99, 101. *See also* Desire; Family Romance; Sexuality

Paris, Bernard J., 134, 233nn.3, 10, 235n.5
Pedersen, Glenn, 237n.23
Preston, John, 230n.8
Proudfit, Sharon Wood, 237n.23

Quirk, Eugene F., 232n.13

Realism, 5, 7-8, 41, 42, 45, 47, 75, 77, 80, 82, 93, 179, 223, 228nn.13, 21, 235n.6; compared to modernism, 46, 172-73, 185-87, 198; and desire, 10-13; as disenchantment, 2, 4-5, 192; hierarchical arrangement of, 41, 46, 168, 173, 188, 195; interaction with romance, 7-9, 10, 13-14, 16-17, 41-42, 45, 75, 77, 80, 81, 98-99, 103, 143, 171-72, 179, 184, 187, 192-93, 194, 202, 205, 224, 227-28n.3, 229n.23, 234n.10. *See also* Novel
Reed, Walter L., 231n.9
Richardson, Samuel, 51, 171, 229n.2, 230nn.8, 10
—*Clarissa:* analyzed, 55-73; compared to *The Mill on the Floss*, 132, 138, 143; compared to other eighteenth-century novels, 43-44, 48-49, 51, 54; compared to *Pride and Prejudice*, 47-48, 64, 73; compared to *Tess of the d'Urbervilles*, 178, 179, 187; compared to *Wuthering Heights*, 46, 47-48, 58, 59, 65, 73; mentioned, 2, 19, 42, 44, 91, 80-81, 87, 103, 112, 130, 131, 188, 214, 225, 229n.29, 230nn.6, 8, 230-31n.10
—*Pamela*, 43, 49
Robert, Marthe, 79-80, 171
Romance. *See* Family Romance, Realism

Schorer, Mark, 235n.13, 236n.14
Scott, Walter, 12, 45, 73, 101, 171
—*Old Mortality:* analyzed, 93-99; mentioned, 45, 82
—*Rob Roy:* analyzed, 87-93; mentioned,

241

Index

Scott, Walter *(cont.)*
 45, 82, 98, 125-26
—*Waverley:* analyzed, 83-86; mentioned, 2, 13, 14, 45, 82, 92, 96, 98, 133, 231nn.3, 11
—Waverley novels, 44, 75-76, 81-82, 87, 91-92, 101, 102, 103, 130, 140, 181, 196
Sexuality: in *Bleak House*, 109-22, 188, 232nn.11, 13; in *Clarissa*, 57-63, 68-72; in *Great Expectations*, 123-24, 126-30, 233n.19; in *Middlemarch*, 130, 153-69, 233-34n.3, 234n.14; in *The Mill on the Floss*, 137-38, 140-41; in *Old Mortality*, 96; in *Pride and Prejudice*, 22-23, 24-26; in *Rob Roy*, 90; in *Tess of the d'Urbervilles*, 176-78, 186-87; in *To the Lighthouse*, 196, 211-20, 237n.23; in *Tristram Shandy*, 52-53; in *Women in Love*, 187-95, 236n.16; in *Wuthering Heights*, 31-32; 34-35, 36-39. *See also* Desire, Heroine's experience, Oedipal desire
Shroder, Maurice Z., 227n.3, 228n.8
Skura, Meredith Anne, 14-17, 228n.21
Spacks, Patricia Meyer, 140, 229n.2
Spilka, Mark, 105, 232n.11, 236n.14, 237n.25
Staves, Susan, 227n.2

Steinhoff, William R., 233n.3
Sterne, Laurence, *Tristram Shandy:* analyzed, 51-55; mentioned, 2, 44, 49
Stoehr, Taylor, 110, 233n.18

Thackeray, William Makepeace, 171
Trilling, Lionel, 227n.3
Trollope, Anthony, 171

Unconscious, 9-10, 12, 14-17. *See also* Desire, Family Romance, Freud

Van Ghent, Dorothy, 227n.3, 230n.6

Watt, Ian, 7, 171, 230n.6
Warner, William Beatty, 230-31n.10
Weissman, Judith, 233n.18
Welsh, Alexander, 76, 77, 91, 227n.2, 235n.6
Williams, Raymond, 232n.1
Wish fulfillment, 9-10, 14-15, 79
Wolff, Cynthia Griffin, 229n.2, 230n.6
Woolf, Virginia, 5, 12, 131, 172, 186
—*To the Lighthouse:* analyzed, 195-221; mentioned, 2, 19, 42, 46, 173, 223, 236n.22, 237nn.23, 25, 26

Steven Cohan is Associate Professor of English at Syracuse University. He has published essays on narrative theory and the British novel.

The manuscript was edited for publication by Kathryn Wildfong. The book was designed by Don Ross. The typeface for the display and text is Baskerville, based on the original design by John Baskerville in the eighteenth century. The book is printed on 55-lb. Glatfelter text paper and is bound in Joanna Mills' Linen cloth over binders' boards.

Manufactured in the United States of America.